PRAISE FOR

DEATH FUGUE

"Now a prominent novelist and a denizen of Beijing literary circles, Ms. Sheng eventually fashioned that turning point in contemporary Chinese history into a stomach-churning, exuberantly written allegory, *Death Fugue*, which recalls Aldous Huxley's *Brave New World*."

JANE PERLEZ, *THE NEW YORK TIMES*

"Sheng Keyi is one of China's upcoming star literary novelists, in part because the most powerful images in her fiction are rooted in reality."

THE WALL STREET JOURNAL

"Sheng Keyi is a bold, talented writer. Her wild, shrewish linguistic style is full of vigor and vitality."

MO YAN, WINNER OF THE NOBEL PRIZE IN LITERATURE
AND AUTHOR OF *RED SORGHUM* AND *THE REPUBLIC OF WINE*

"From Tiananmen, Sheng's novel moves into an imagined future one-party dystopia, a brave new world with Chinese characteristics that she calls Swan Valley. One thing the authorities did about it was to ban *Death Fugue* in China, but it circulates informally anyway and has been published in translation abroad. She should get an A+ for moxie, and has admirers in China among readers who can get hold of the book."

THE NEW YORK REVIEW OF BOOKS

"Anyone remotely interested in an insider's untrammeled, authoritative vision of what's going on in China will jump into this fascinating cauldron of a novel, at risk of being boiled alive."

NICHOLAS JOSE, *SYDNEY REVIEW OF BOOKS*

"A withering, absurdist allegory of the Tiananmen Square massacre of 1989 and the shadows the events have cast on a generation."

PHILIP WEN, *SYDNEY MORNING HERALD*

"Sharp talent, direct pain, constant entanglement, and struggle between artistic power and invisible extrusion are the most unique components of Sheng Keyi's contribution to Chinese literature."

YAN LIANKE, AUTHOR OF *THE YEARS, MONTHS, DAYS* AND *THE EXPLOSION CHRONICLES*

DEATH FUGUE

ALSO BY SHENG KEYI

Fields of White

Northern Girls

Wild Fruit

DEATH
FUGUE

SHENG KEYI

Translated from the Chinese by Shelly Bryant

RESTLESS BOOKS

BROOKLYN, NEW YORK

Copyright © 2012 Sheng Keyi
Translation copyright © 2014 Shelly Bryant

First published as *Sǐwáng fùgé* by Ink Books, Taiwan, 2012
First published in English as *Death Fugue* by Giramondo Publishing, Australia, 2014
Published by arrangement with Agence littéraire Astier-Pécher

First Restless Books paperback edition August 2021

Paperback ISBN: 9781632062925
Library of Congress Control Number: 2020945881

This book is supported in part by an award from the National Endowment for the Arts.

Cover design by Matthew Revert
Cover image © EmotionPhoto
Text design by Sarah Schneider

Printed in the United States of America

1 3 5 7 9 10 8 6 4 2

Restless Books, Inc.
232 3rd Street, Suite A101
Brooklyn, NY 11215

www.restlessbooks.org
publisher@restlessbooks.org

Dedicated to those born in the 1960s in China

PART ONE

1

Those who have suffered the mental strain of life's vicissitudes often end up becoming withdrawn. Their earlier zeal has died; their beliefs wander off like stray dogs. They allow the heart to grow barren, and the mind to be overrun with weeds. They experience a sort of mental arthritis, like a dull ache on a cloudy day. There is no remedy. They hurt. They endure. They distract themselves in various ways, whether by making money, or by emigrating, or by womanizing.

Yuan Mengliu fell into the last group.

He was born in the '60s, though the specific year is not known. You might say he was an unidentified person. As for the circumstances surrounding his parentage, there are many versions of the story. In the more hair-raising one, his father was an orphan who later became a soldier. One night when he was on an assignment somewhere, he had a one-night stand, sowing his seed in the virgin soil of a girl who was later hidden away in a remote snowy mountain range. She gave birth to Mengliu, then went on her merry way back to the place from where she had come. Or perhaps she had died in childbirth.

What is certain is that Yuan Mengliu's early life was like a river, with its source hidden high in the snowcapped mountains, meandering through the land of Dayang, flowing through countless provinces and cities until it finally ended up in Beiping. There his life took root and branched out into many tributaries, becoming the protagonist of many tales.

Lanky and pale, Yuan Mengliu resembled a Coca-Cola bottle in shape. His short, soft hair was gelled expertly in place, and his sideburns were meticulously trimmed. His complexion was smooth, without blemish. His scrubs were always bright white, flawless as new fallen snow, and the clothes he wore underneath them bright and fresh. When he performed surgery, he usually wore rimless glasses. It was his habit to be slow to speak. He didn't have a temper. He never made trouble, and he had no bad habits. The only drawback to his character was that he liked to play with women. Of course, he did not count this as a fault himself. He liked to say, "If men are afraid to talk about their love of women, how can the state talk about hope for the future?" One might guess that Mengliu had read Epicurus, who wrote that if a man were to give up the enjoyment of sex, he couldn't even begin to imagine what was meant by "the good life."

As a member of the silent majority, Mengliu was getting along just fine. Humanity moved along in a steady stream of disease, and Mengliu was born with gifted hands, so his use of the knife to carve out some advantage for himself was not surprising. It was whispered that he had been a poet, but the topic was taboo with him. He never mentioned poetry or acknowledged that he had once been a member of the literary group called "The Three Musketeers." His personal record did not list him as a poet. It was as clean as his scalpel, free from even the slightest fleck of blood.

Mengliu had once done something else, but he did not consider it a bad thing to have done. In order to secure a girl's favor, he had made use of the opportunity provided by surgery to kill her lover.

Of course, that wasn't quite the whole story.

It happened in the years following the Tower Incident. At that time, Yuan Mengliu wasn't quite himself, and wandered around like a lost puppy with his tail disappearing between his legs. Despite his bright new appearance, he secretly sniffed about the alleys for the scent of history. He looked forward to seeing the striptease act in which history's body would finally be exposed. His expectation in this matter was as strong as his anticipation of the first time with a new woman. He was eager to know what it would be like to bed her—her voice, her face, the excitement and tremors she would send through his own mind and body. He was convinced that, once stripped of clothing, all women would go back to their true state. The body could not lie.

He began very early on to take care of his health, monitoring his calorie intake with scientific precision. Every day he pounded a few small garlic cloves, then allowed the amino acids, enzymes, vitamins, and fiber to flow with the crude proteins in his bloodstream. As a healthy person, Mengliu did not suffer from hemorrhoids. He had no beliefs, no ulcers, no ideals, no gingivitis, and while his teeth may not have been white, they were clean, with never a hint of grain between them. He wasn't talkative, and he always drank enough water to keep his lips full and moist. He ate garlic, but he also had his own remedy to eliminate halitosis. His secret recipe eventually became the gospel his patients lived by in their attempts to avoid their own bad breath.

Yuan Mengliu could also play the *chuixun*, an egg-shaped instrument made of clay. Since childhood, the little flute had never left his side. Self-taught, he played a variety of tunes on it. In later years, he could sustain a noble, elegant melody, a sentimental tune to make girls' hearts tremble and heighten their maternal instinct. This became his fixed routine in foreplay with them.

Naturally, to feminine eyes, he was clean and charming.

On the map, the country of Dayang is shaped like a paramecium, or like the sole of a right shoe. Its capital, Beiping, is a city surrounded by a wall, which offers it both protection from external harm and the means to excrete its waste, just like the paramecium's wall. Beiping's climate is poor, its land arid. During the annual autumn storms, the city is bombarded by sand. Everywhere you look, it's a crumpled, disgraceful mess. The winters are extremely cold, the summers hot, and the air is always filled with an odd bready smell.

Beiping's main road is like a satiated python lying flat on the ground, the five-hundred-thousand-square-meter Round Square its protruding abdomen. This is the heart of the city, and one of Dayang's main tourist attractions. Some years after the Tower Incident, Round Square became home to the statue of a peace monument, a naked goddess with eyes as clear as diamonds, holding a torch in her outstretched hand. A red laser beam broke the night's black canopy, broadcasting propaganda slogans, weather forecasts, and news of current events. Occasionally a poem might even appear there, giving instant fame to the poet who penned the verse.

Sadly, there was no beauty in the language of Beiping, and its writing was ugly. For instance, the words "Long Live Democracy" were inscribed "WlOrj ldlNOr!" The words looked like tadpoles, and the pronunciation was equally awkward, as if you had a mouthful of soup rolling about your tongue that was so hot it caused your jaw to cramp. You had to make full use of your facial muscles to speak the language. Even your nostrils needed to be flexible in order to achieve the heavy nasal quality. It made you sound like an asthmatic she-donkey.

Yuan Mengliu liked calligraphy, and he collected books to use for practice. He always practiced on the eve of a major operation. He liked to write calligraphy in order to maintain a cool disposition—heart, eyes, and hand always in perfect sync. His ten fingers were as alert as a watch dog. His senses of hearing and smell, along with everything else about him, responded quickly and deftly, allowing him to cut open a belly and remove a tumor or an appendix with skilled strokes. He knew exactly where to start and just what to do next. Each finger applied just the right pressure. He was accurate, and rarely made a mistake.

"The scalpel is more effective than drugs. Not many medicines are known to humans and few doctors really comprehend their uses, just as the truth only lies in the hands of a few," Mengliu said to the interns. They were often confused.

At that time, many men in their thirties and forties remained unmarried. Mengliu was clearly aware that, in his case, the problem lay with himself. When he encountered a girl who was not too boring, had both brains and breasts, with a tiny waist and rounded hips, smooth legs, slender arms, agreeable both in and out of bed, in public and in private . . . he just couldn't do what was required to bring it all to fruition. It was not that he was committed to a life of solitude. The problem lay simply in a thought.

He believed that Qizi was still alive.

2

One summer, when Mengliu was in his midforties, temperatures reached a high of fifty degrees Celsius. The sun scorched the pale-skinned, and the streets were covered with dead insects looking like popped corn.

The streets of Beiping were wide and mighty, the river similarly open and indifferent. Anyone standing in the center might feel a slight space-time disorientation. Round Square was like a living room kept squeaky clean under its meticulous master's care. The flat ground had a yellowish luster, created by the trampling of feet. Low-rise buildings stood guard at a distance around the square, surrounding it like a reef.

In those days, setting out from the square and walking east on Beiping Street, when you came to the museum on the left, there was Liuli Street, one of the more authentic old lanes. Both sides were lined with vintage stores full of aged items, windows filled with blue-and-white porcelain, busts, old swords, rusty daggers, bronze ware . . . In an enchanting moment, you could feel the ghosts and spirits floating in the streets, whispering their secrets. Sometimes you might come across someone wearing an aged, jaded expression mingled with the arrogance of youth, and looking rather lost. Their bodies were covered with a certain demonic light that did not invite close contact.

Liuli Street was originally the site of a famous old Catholic church that had been destroyed during the Tower Incident. It was said that one of the faithful had hanged himself inside. The legend was that he had suffered from deep depression. Because it had not been set aside for protection as a heritage building, the church was soon uprooted and demolished. A tall commercial building was constructed on the site of the church, and the whole area converted into a pedestrian mall. In these modern times, the glory of the old street can only be seen in the archives.

Walking to the end of Liuli Street, you enter an area surrounded by relief sculptures fashioned in a mythic style. Beyond a stand of old trees, an imposing stone plaque displays an inscription reading "National Youth Administration for Elite Wisdom" in the tadpole-shaped squiggles of the Beiping language. The administration building's gate, constructed of Spanish granite in a classical style, stands next to two old pines that have been stripped bare by the scampering squirrels. The Spanish-style building is covered with gray roof tiles that extend out over long arcades. It is full of an air of mystery and a sense of history. The nature walks and the variety of entertainment facilities make the area feel like a resort. More widely known than the administration building is the attached amphitheater surrounded by a wall decorated with frescoes on religious themes. There is a corridor on either side of the wall around the amphitheater, extending to the grass. People call it the double-tracked wall. Originally the birthplace of an important school of thought, it has since become commercialized, filled with so many posters advertising random products that the wall has virtually disappeared. This seems to suggest that people no longer feel the need for such places, that all sorts of ideas and philosophies have simply become part of the daily lives of today's citizens.

The Wisdom Bureau, as the National Youth Administration for Elite Wisdom was popularly known before the Tower Incident, had over 50,000 employees, arranged in departments with many branches and sub-branches. The nation's intelligentsia numbered over 10,000, with a large number of elite members. The Bureau was extensive, with sub-departments for literature, physics, philosophy, music, medicine, and dozens of other professional branches. This intellectual institution might look idle from the outside, but the atmosphere inside resembled that of a battlefield.

At that time Mengliu, having just been assigned to the Literature Department, rented an old house with a few other people his age. The landlord, a skinny old man who wore a skullcap year-round, was fond of young people. He respected learning, and as long as you were a member of the Wisdom Bureau, he would offer cheap rental. In the volatile environment of the time, when resources were scarce, people held high expectations for the young elites. At the end of the day, everyone was willing to take care of these young people and to protect them.

The house was very old with green walls and timber latticed windows. Quiet and low-key, it had once served as quarters for government dignitaries. It offered the advantages of being clean, quiet, and conveniently located. Mengliu's flat, situated on the west side of the building, was playfully dubbed the West Wing. With an area of about twenty square meters, it was not very spacious. It was just large enough for eating, sleeping, and studying in, with a small space for a sitting area. Of course, Mengliu had no need for the latter.

The potted rose bush on the windowsill was part of the original furnishings. It had never bloomed. At one time during the Tower Incident, when it was especially droopy, one of his female visitors provoked it into a show of life. It budded and eventually dropped, and only bloomed a few times after that.

The acacia tree in the yard was centuries old and covered with a dark, rough bark. Its branches climbed over the gray tiled roof. In summer its leaves turned yellow and produced a lot of worms. They dangled there, bodies a bright transparent green, like pieces of amber or smooth jade. They climbed along the fine silk they spat out of themselves, swaying in the wind. A black train of feces ran along the ground, releasing a pungent odor. Having traveled through the digestive system of the worms, the feces smelled fresh and thick. Their fragrance was mesmerizing.

Mengliu did not like to shave, and he often sat writing poetry all night long with his hair disheveled. He was at an age when the mere sight of a girl aroused him. He banded together with two other vibrant young poets, Hei Chun and Bai Qiu, whose names meant "Black Spring" and "White Autumn," and the trio became known as "The Three Musketeers."

When he had nothing else to do, Mengliu sat under the acacia tree playing the chuixun.

One day Mengliu awoke feeling that there was something strange in the air. The central heating seemed to have gone off. It was surprisingly cold. He glanced out of the window and saw birds in the acacia tree, all of them tight-lipped and looking about vigilantly.

With a yelp, he got out of bed and dressed, listening to the news coming from the radio next door.

" . . . Reports have come in this morning of excitement around Round Square, where a tower made of excrement was found in the early hours, drawing massive crowds to see the spectacle . . . For now, it has not been determined whether the excrement came from an earthly creature. The police rushed to the scene to protect the tower and maintain order . . . Experts are on their way to Round Square . . . If the small group of hostile elements in the capital take this opportunity to make trouble, they will be detained and severely punished!"

The announcer's words were clipped, as if he had a mouth full of bullets. His tone was threatening, especially when he got to the phrase "They will be detained and severely punished!" It was like he had fired into the air, spitting all the bullets out. There was a burst of static, followed by the sound of explosions coming over the radio.

Mengliu had a bad feeling. He washed hastily, using his hand to wipe the traces of water from his mustache, and hurried out the door.

The wind outside was biting cold. He had forgotten his scarf. All he could do was wrap his arms tightly about himself, put his head down, and walk into the wind in the direction of the Wisdom Bureau.

The leaden sky watched indifferently, like a solitary pair of eyes. A crow voiced an assassin's cry as it shot out of a bush and into the sky. The chill offered the promise of snow.

He found that every place he passed through was in a state of upheaval. People were talking about the strange pile of feces. Their interest had already escalated to panic level. Heated comments had begun to appear on the double-tracked wall, criticizing the government's incompetence, saying its response to the excrement situation had been too slow and that it had taken too long to reach a conclusion in its discussions concerning the tower. It would be more efficient to invite the experts to eat the pile of shit.

When Mengliu saw that, he felt like laughing. Everyone was making a big fuss over nothing. It was just a pile of shit. Surely it did not portend the descent of some strange beast, intent on gobbling up Beiping. What was the fuss all about? Of course, he knew that people had been looking for a reason to vent their anger. For the past few years, everything had been in a mess. Times were hard; all over the country the rich were buying up villas while the poor could barely keep clothes on their backs. Pests had been gnawing at the fabric of society, and there were holes everywhere.

Mengliu was a bit bored now. He thought he might go to the Green Flower and grab a drink and a bite to eat. That should prove to be more interesting.

Despite his longing for a little warm Chinese wine and some fried peanuts, he found himself mysteriously wandering into Round Square instead.

The crowd in the square was beyond imagining. Some had lingered there for a long time, and in front of the newcomers their expressions filled with the pride of those in the know.

Mengliu, listening to them talking about the feces, got a general impression of it—that it was a dark brown lump smelling of buckwheat, soft in texture, and standing nine stories high. Its bottom layer was fifty meters in diameter. Its structure was like that of a layered cake, narrowing to a relatively artistic spire at the top.

Mengliu found that the masses that had gathered in the square could be divided into three factions. The first had no sense of crisis; their interest lay in the question of what sort of sphincter would have been capable of forming such a masterpiece. The second was not interested in taking sides and adopted a more neutral position as they waited to hear what those with some scatological expertise might conclude about the matter. The third group was for reform, having endured their meaningless lives for long enough. Anchorless, they held nothing dear. Their only hope was to catch a little fish out of the troubled waters through which they waded.

In a state of disbelief over the size of Beiping's population, Mengliu plunged right into the fray and became just another sheep in the mob. The rams, goats, ewes, and lambs crowded together. They rubbed and brushed against one another, bleating the gossip from one mouth to the next. The agitation encompassed everyone—office workers and menial laborers, tourists, and loiterers. They wore their expressions like masks, firmly buckled in place. Numb, expectant, worried, nervous, excited, or eager, they wiggled their bloated bodies as their noses turned red, and white smoke emerged from their mouths in the cold air. In times of excitement, even hands that are normally caged inside billowing sleeves will be let loose to the air. The people, huddled together as if waiting to witness some astronomical wonder, warmed the chilly streets.

Mengliu could not squeeze his way into the heavily guarded area, where armed police were surrounded by a group of high school students, who in turn were surrounded by a group of kindergarten children. They had formed a three-layered human wall with their uniformed bodies. Water had been sprayed on the ground and, having frozen over, it now let off a luminescent glow. The air was heavy with fog and the sun seemed to be wrapped in a cocoon, emitting only a little gray-white light.

Mengliu, pushing his way through the crowd, broke out in a sweat. Before he was able to get a good look at the famous tower of shit, he had to turn back. When he got home, he was feverish, and he felt ill.

That evening, the television news went to great lengths reporting the incident, clearly advancing the theory that the tower was made of gorilla excrement, while at the same time criticizing rumors of aliens and biological monsters. Together with sound bites, experts were seen donning their white gloves and inspecting the feces. Their wrinkled brows showed their respect for their subject and underscored the serious academic nature of their work, leaving no room for doubt concerning the rigor with which their research was being conducted. The next morning's newspapers printed essentially the same content, with nearly identical headlines appearing throughout the nation. But the majority of the people did not believe that it was gorilla excrement. Some even burned newspapers in the street as a sign of protest against the media's failings and called for the government to be more transparent in relation to the fecal matter.

Of course, the government could not easily modify its own conclusions about the Tower Incident. The media stood in a united front, offering an objective view of the event. When some papers went so far as to raise questions, their editors were immediately relieved of office for "dereliction of duty," and the reporters were likewise sacked. This provoked the public's "sense of justice," making the people all the more certain that things were not as simple as they seemed. The feelings of resentment grew, and it did not take long for some people to take to the streets in protest. The crowd got steadily bigger; the protest gained momentum.

People gathered at the site where the pile of shit had appeared. Naturally, it had been removed long ago. The ground had been carefully scrubbed clean. All evidence of it had disappeared, so finding out the truth was virtually impossible. No one could tear down the testimony of the so-called experts. They all knew of the shit's existence, and many had witnessed the oddity firsthand. But every one of them remained silent, without exception.

The news that aliens had come spread like wildfire. Then, some reported that they had seen a UFO in the sky and described it in concrete terms. Some claimed they had run into huge, strange creatures at night. As soon as evening fell, people locked their doors, no longer daring to walk on the streets after dark.

Because of the emergence of the excrement, life was no longer calm for the citizens of Beiping.

Postings on the double-tracked wall offered a detailed analysis of the Tower Incident and mentioned several news reports. They pointed out a few holes in the arguments of the experts who claimed to know that the pile of excrement had come from a gorilla just by looking at it. In fact, they said, the research was very sloppy. They called for the most authoritative experts and the most scientific testing to be employed in addressing the mystery, saying that only DNA analysis of the fecal matter would be convincing.

One of the famous writers in the "monster theory" camp wrote: "Recklessly, they first came up with conclusions to deceive the public. It's a trick for maintaining stability. The truth is in the hands of a small minority. If we go on like this, there will come a day when even the sun above us will be covered up by them."

Mengliu thought the claims of the "monster man" were exaggerated. It was just a pile of shit. It was nothing to get so worked up about. But still, he had to admit it was a well-written essay, worthy to be counted among those of the talents at the Wisdom Bureau. As he casually read through the posters, he suddenly came across poems Hei Chun and Bai Qiu had composed about the feces. They were written with a lot of passion. He was so excited that he fell into a fit of coughing.

Still suffering from his cold, Mengliu broke out into a high fever again. He didn't want to go to the hospital. He thought hospitals were places for making healthy people sick and sick people die. Some who had been admitted for nothing more than a cold had their appendices removed by mistake; someone with an inflamed gallbladder had ended up having his liver removed. This was no joke. Mengliu did not trust hospitals. He had his own remedies. He rinsed his throat, drank plenty of water, and got plenty of sleep. After a couple of days, the fever broke and he felt fine.

When he emerged from his quarantine, he walked on weak legs into the courtyard of his building. There, he heard the radio reports of the experts, still talking about the problem of the feces. They said that ignorant people had been incited into rallying at Round Square, and they were destroying the public peace. It was producing a very negative impression. They hoped that these people would quickly disperse and go home to their families, keep house, and cook for their children. The program's host similarly persuaded the young people to disband and go home—preferably in time for dinner.

Mengliu felt weightless. He was nearly blown over by the wind. After the coughing, he felt hungry. He needed to get something to fill his belly. He made his way to his landlord's shop and got two cups of warmed milk and some bean cakes. As he chatted with the landlord, it was not long before the subject of the feces came up. With the air whistling through the gap where he had a missing tooth, the landlord talked about the lively proceedings at Round Square.

"Most of the people at the Wisdom Bureau will head over there today," he said. "You are all intellectuals. We common folk are too uncultured. We don't know anything, but we trust you fellows. Whatever you say, that's how it is."

Mengliu was a little taken aback. A collective action by the Wisdom Bureau was no small thing. He finished his milk, swallowed another bean cake, and went to wave down a trishaw to take him to Round Square.

But before the vehicle could even get out of Liuli Street, it was blocked by a crowd. He had no choice but to get down and walk.

At the intersection of Liuli and Beiping Streets, he saw a mighty procession. The crowd was in uniform, in white T-shirts and with red bandanas tied around their heads. They held up placards and waved banners.

"We Want a Meeting"

"Capture the Aliens"

"DNA Testing for Stool Samples"

"Live in Truth"

The onlookers shouted warm welcomes from both sides of the street. They raised their voices in a chorus, singing the newly composed "Tower Song." There were some individuals who had always been shy and reserved, but now suddenly they produced placards from inside their clothing, as if by magic. They slipped into the crowd and raised their signs. After a few moments their faces lit up with a burst of energy.

The branches of the trees beside the street were bare, making the birds' nests there uncomfortably conspicuous. The sky was gray, and it was becoming difficult to see in the failing light.

By the time Mengliu realized that he was caught in the swaggering ranks, it was like waking up in a flood of consternation. He did not know how he came to be standing near the banner at the head of the procession. This was completely out of character for him. He was normally very cautious.

In the chaos, as Mengliu tried to find a way out, several people in blue caps squeezed their way toward him. One with a sharp face and pinched mouth said to him, "We workers came especially to express our solidarity with you. You people at the Wisdom Bureau are the best."

Hearing this, Mengliu was filled with pride. He raised his hand high up in the air, causing the banner above him to tilt.

When he did take note of the banner, he found that the other end was held by a girl with closely cropped hair, an oval face, and fair skin. Her almond-shaped eyes were dark and gentle.

He felt as if his heart stopped beating in that instant.

Just then, the short-haired girl raised her head and turned a furtive glance his way. His heart came to life again, beating double time. He felt he was a cicada emerging from its cocoon. A ray of sunlight fell on him, making him feel warm all over and full of the joy of life. Stimulated by this joy, he raised his own voice in unison with those shouting slogans. His voice was like a stone thrown by a child, skipping across a lake, and he felt ashamed at the thinness of it. His heart boomed in his chest, and he raised his voice even louder. Perhaps a new measure of courage had been injected into him, for somehow his voice came out mellow and resonant. He gained confidence in his own cries. He pretended not to bother about the short-haired girl, exaggerating the measure of his passion and the grace in his performance. He knew she was beside him, delicate and quiet as a bird perched on a branch.

The short-haired girl seemed to be withstanding a head-on invasion as she faced the storm. Her lips were shut tightly, and she remained silent.

Suddenly, a group came out of nowhere to break up the procession. After a moment of confusion, Mengliu found himself crammed into an unmarked bus. The windows were sealed shut, and everything was dark.

———————

Half an hour later, a light came on in the bus.

When his eyes had adjusted to the light, Mengliu found that the bus was full of people. More importantly, the short-haired girl was standing next to him. Her pale face made her look like a sleepwalker.

It was a rickety old bus. He deliberately turned away from the girl for a few seconds, then turned back to adjust the angle so that he could make an even bolder observation without being noticed.

She had pretty lips, full and red. The smiling mouth rested beneath a perky, slightly freckled nose. She looked down, her gaze following the bridge of her nose and landing at Mengliu's feet.

The sense of joy once again consumed Mengliu's heart. He turned a little, gaining a more direct line of sight, and continued to stare.

She was probably not much more than a meter and a half tall. She had withdrawn into herself, didn't even look up. Her glossy black hair smelled of shampoo. Or perhaps the fragrance came from her body, her fair white skin, the unique expression she wore.

As the bus rattled along, the distance between them changed, altering his perspective of her. Now she was facing him, her expression blank as a wall. She stared at the fourth button on his windbreaker as if examining its texture.

He looked her over. The more he inspected her, the closer he felt to her. The longer he stared, the more he felt he had known her forever.

When the bus had bumped along for more than an hour, making several turns along the way, it finally came to a stop. Several brawny, aggressive fellows suddenly leapt up. They separated the bus's occupants into groups and led them away to different places.

The dimly lit basement was damp and cold, with a single bulb hanging from the middle of the ceiling, its bamboo shade covered with dust. The concrete walls were uneven, and the mud-yellow floor was dirty. The shoddy tiles were broken in places and crunched underfoot as they walked. The room was furnished with a single desk and two long, narrow wooden benches. The air was bad, filled with a nauseating mixture of cooking fumes and sewage.

Mengliu and the short-haired girl were brought into the room with a young man from the construction department named Quanmu, a farmer from outside of Beiping, and also a high school student.

Before long, two men and a woman came in. It was not clear what their vocation was. Their faces were a blur, though they all looked vaguely similar. They carried with them an air of experience, street-wise people who had seen it all. A group of freckles gathered at the tip of the woman's nose. She sat down, spread her notebook out on the table and uncapped her pen. The first of the two men sat down too, and propped his feet up on the desk, while the other rested his buttocks against its edge. All three pairs of eyes made their way over the group of people who had been brought in.

"Relax. We're just here to chat," the first man said, his face rigid.

"Come on, we have the right to choose not to talk." The room was as icy as a freezer. Quanmu, seemingly quite familiar with the routine, turned and looked at his comrades. His face was bruised.

In the strange atmosphere, Mengliu wondered whether he had unwittingly gotten himself mixed up with Triads.

"What were you all doing playing in the streets? Don't you know it seriously obstructs traffic and disrupts public peace?" the first man said, ignoring everyone else. "Tell me. Just tell me all about it and you can go home."

"It was all about that pile of crap," the farmer cried. "Weren't the slogans written out clearly enough?"

The woman, who was busy scratching out her report, looked up. The first man looked like he wanted to give the farmer a good beating.

"He's right. It was all for shit," the short-haired girl suddenly interjected.

3

Now, with the heat close to fifty degrees during the day, Yuan Mengliu closed all the doors and windows in the house, drew the curtains and turned his room into a cave. Like an ant, he carried lots of food into his quarters, where he sometimes holed up for days at a time. When he looked out the window, he saw mounds of earth covered with weeds and small trees.

The past rose up before him with all the force of a hallucination. He saw bodies lying in a disordered heap on the ground. The sun scorched them so that the people were faint and dehydrated. Starved of electrolytes, they fell into convulsions . . . Everything was chaos. There were ambulances, gunshots, and the blaze of red flames filled the night sky. He had discovered that there was no solace for him, even in the arms of a woman. Lately, he had turned to Jesus, spending his weekends reading a hidden copy of the English Bible and visiting the city's magnificent churches. But he had overestimated God, and the result of his conversion to Christianity was simply that he discovered the strange hypnotic power of hymns. As he sat on the churches' pews, he entered into the same dream. In this dream, he was speaking in Round Square, surrounded by a crowd of people. The ferocity of his speech always jolted him awake. His face felt flushed, his eyes bloodshot, there was an icy pit in his stomach. After a vigorous "Amen," he would leave the church and aimlessly follow the dispersing congregation into the streets.

As he walked a complete circuit around Beiping Street, passing through the metropolis that had been attacked by financial crisis and turmoil, none of the city's attractions held any appeal for him. The trees along the roadside had grown thicker, the road was wider and prettier, and the people were well nourished and healthy. He bent his head and walked. The ground gradually turned red. He had walked all the way to the edge of the city. The water in the moat there was a violent scarlet stream. Dizzy, he leaned against the stone balustrade covered with engravings. The railings had been repaired so thoroughly that they were far superior to what they had been in their original state. The damage had been covered by a seamless reconstruction. Now that all the injury done had been compensated for, the events of a thriving life had taken over and filled in all the remaining cracks.

A faint smell of blood was detectable, sometimes seeming to come from the flora and fauna, sometimes from the sewer, and sometimes from a certain class of people who couldn't seem to rid themselves of it no matter how often they bathed, applied perfume, or covered it up with gorgeous clothing. Mengliu planted flowers, grass, fruit trees, but the poetic artificiality of the peaceful natural scenes could not rescue him from the restless feelings of the displaced. His spirit was never still. When he heard the night insects or a barking dog, or the wind howling in the dark, the sound was always interspersed with piercing jeers. His impeccable life had been calm as a brook, meandering through the plains and across the land, eventually to lose itself in the expanse of the sea. Now happiness had become shameful. He was filled with doubt, as if some conspiracy were brewing and a huge trap awaited him. He occupied his mind with research every day, seeking ways to better satisfy his physical needs. He went to nightclubs, hung out with a group of female doctors. He seduced the bridesmaids at his friends' weddings, or hooked up with female students on the train. Any consenting female was fair game. He would take women home, offering them his warmth and respect in exchange for the grave pleasure of having his way with them.

He placed women in two basic categories. There were those who liked revolution and those who did not. Women who liked revolution were energetic and restless. They liked to take the initiative, riding him for their own pleasure. Those who did not like revolution blindly closed their eyes and wore pained expressions. They secretly enjoyed being ravaged by him, and even when they reached a climax, it died on their lips. He could not say which group fascinated him more. Eventually he would think of Qizi, imagining her in his bed, and what it was like when the two of them were together.

It was a painful torment to him.

Each year at the height of summer, Yuan Mengliu was stricken with a strange disease, involving itchy skin, inflammation, muscle spasms, convulsions, and headaches, and his hallucinations grew more severe. He beat his body and bathed himself in hot water, soaking there until his skin was as red as a newborn baby's.

He had had a few lengthy relationships over the years, and during his bouts of illness he spent much effort convincing those innocent girls that he needed to be alone for a while in order to recover. None of them believed that his illness required him to be away for such a long stretch. Most were convinced that it was a cover for him to engage in an affair. Others, those with a deeper disposition who understood his personal experiences a little better, laughed at him for shouldering the burden of history, telling him that life was short and he should seize the day. One broad-minded girl gritted her teeth, pulled out a few of his white hairs, and tenderly warned him that he should pay attention to his safety. A secret spring brews in the hearts of women. When it bubbles into action, it is the recovery of all things, a sort of rejuvenating power. It is as unstoppable as the coming of spring, and the opening of flowers—and just as short-lived. He was not saddened by this. On the contrary, he appreciated it.

Mengliu believed Qizi was alive. She must be in some corner of the vast territory of Dayang, raising a family. So every year he went traveling, driven to find her by his gathering hysteria.

This summer he decided to go even further than usual, on the recommendation of a girl he had met.

After a long journey he came to a fertile land with exquisite scenery. He sat in a small café by the lake, where the well-endowed proprietress knew that the taste for delicacies was like going to the opera; the leading actors were the main attraction. Haltingly, she rattled off the names of the four specialties from the area around the lake. There was wild celery, wild artemisia, asparagus, and knotweed. She was like a procuress carefully reading off the names of famous courtesans in a pleasure quarter. The wild, the lovely, and the innocent—all kinds of beauties to please and entertain her guests, who had traveled such distances.

Mengliu went on a little binge, indulging in fried whitebait, steamed mandarin fish, and braised carp, along with the four regional specialties. The table was overflowing with delicacies as he drank his wine and gorged himself on the fish. His face was flushed all the way down to the base of his neck. Even his pores gave off the smell of alcohol. When he'd finished eating he felt a little sleepy and so he settled down to take a nap in the breeze. He was awakened by a sudden roar, to find several motorboats resembling tanks bulging with machine guns taking a colorful, noisy crowd to the island in the lake.

He pulled out his chuixun, thinking he would play for a while. He changed his mind, rubbed the instrument a few times, then slipped it back into his pocket. He peeled off a few garlic cloves and went for a walk along a secluded road as he chewed them.

The houses were scattered. The signs of people gradually disappeared. Birds flew low overhead, beneath brilliant clouds.

He continued to walk, passing over several hills and into less hospitable terrain. After a sharp turn in the road, he saw the white walls and gray roof tiles of a house. There were some domestic animals at its door, and a boat with its sail rigged was moored nearby.

There was something a little different about this lake and mountain scene. The lake's surface was an endless sketch of muddy yellow, a vast expanse. A white bird fell from the sky and struck a graceful pose on the sail of the boat. A spotted eagle dived into the water and speared a silver fish. When the clouds burned away, the water also seemed to burn, and the fishing boats in the distance could hardly be seen in the blaze.

Mengliu suddenly heard the screech of birds as they whizzed by like bullets overhead. He ducked quickly.

Now the scenery at the lake was beautiful and quiet. The path was overgrown with wild grass. The air was humid. The gardenia bushes were full of plump, white flowers. Thin gourds dangled on the loofa vine, alongside pink hibiscus blooms and bamboo shoots. Smoke hung over the house like the billowing sleeves of Chinese opera performers.

A pungent smell diluted the poetic effect of the scene. A fish hung on a bamboo pole, its eyes protruding. It wore the look of one who had died without finding happiness.

A fisherwoman in bright red garb stepped toward Mengliu, holding a harpoon. The blood-red color she wore had a dizzying effect. Her rough skin and dark complexion were in stark contrast to the color of her clothes. Her face, a black spot on a crimson bed, was that of a person who was content with poverty. Perhaps it was because of the dust, or maybe it was just a trick of the light, but her messy hair looked as if it were silver-plated, like a lazily floating reed.

The fisherwoman first looked frightened, as if she had never seen a stranger before. But once she realized that he wanted to charter her boat, she moved her bamboo chair over and offered it to Mengliu, then boiled him a strong brew of the fragrant local *leicha*, a green tea blended with sesame, peanuts, and herbs.

The house was old and seemed to sag just a little. The exterior wall was painted with red-lettered slogans.

In the distance the lake had a bewitching appeal. The breaking waves faded in and out. Waterfowl flew exuberantly into the line of fir trees that stretched to the horizon until it disappeared from view. The reeds formed an ashy clump of down that scattered in a thick cloud when the breeze blew.

The sun had ascended to its full height. Huge geese flew up like seeds sown in the sky.

Mengliu finished his tea in a single gulp. He was still chewing on the residue left from the brew as he boarded the boat. The rope was released, and the boat slipped out into the lake.

The sun was majestic, the white clouds puffy against the sapphire sky. Mengliu steered the boat past a wetland covered with a large patch of duckweed, blooming with flowers that flowed by like gold, slowly passing the low bushes, reeds, water hyacinth, and other plants whose names he did not know, stretching out into the distance. He could see a bird's nest in the reeds. The chicks sat there undisturbed by his presence, picking at each other's feathers. At intervals, he caught sight of cranes nesting on a single leg, curled up for a nap. Water snakes swam in lazy figure of eights.

With the boat drifting in the breeze, he pulled out his lady-charming chuixin and played a tune in the face of that vast lake. It was melancholy, solemn, and mysterious, and the water trembled.

When he grew sleepy, he found relief by reclining his head. He lay down in the boat, closed his eyes, and breathed in the pungent smell of fish.

4

Outside, flurries of downy snow began to fall. The basement windows were quickly sealed with snow, and the room in which their interrogation was taking place became even dimmer. Mengliu was so hungry that a constant rumbling sound came from his belly, making him feel uneasy. By now he had learned that the short-haired girl's name was Qizi. She was from the Physics Department and was twenty-three years old. Everything she said was interesting. When they asked her why she had joined the procession, she said it was because she'd broken up with her boyfriend and was feeling down. She had absentmindedly stepped into the street. Anywhere that there were lots of people suited her just fine. She didn't care anything for this shit everyone was talking about. She joined the procession because of love, and so she could breathe freely.

With the way that Qizi transformed filth into love, the atmosphere in the room suddenly became more relaxed. Even their captors started chatting idly about love. But before long they felt that they were getting carried away, so they turned back to the problem of the excrement.

The freckled woman said that ever since she was small, she'd heard her father talk about the animal kingdom. She knew a lot about hundreds of different species of animals and understood them better than she did humans. She said that gorilla manure was shaped like a fried twist of dough, not like a pagoda. Furthermore, the gorilla's excrement was important for the environment, so any attempt to protect the forest without protecting the gorillas was a mistake . . .

"Growing up with a father who talked so much about the animal kingdom must have been pleasant," said the first man.

The second, catching hold of the crux of the issue, ignored this proposition. "Why did that pile of dung shrink by ten percent after it was first reported in the news? Surely it didn't suddenly dry up?"

Everyone took this as a license to laugh. They wanted to ask the father of the freckled woman to offer his testimony. She said her father was just a humble scholar of the working class, not someone with a real academic background. Nor did he have any professional ties, so no one would believe anything he had to say. His speech and the belief of others would alike be of little use.

The first man's face squeezed itself into a worried expression. "If it's not gorilla shit, then what sort of trick are they trying to pull on us?"

The freckled woman knocked on the table, warming the two men to keep their roles here in mind.

After a while, some food was brought. There was only bread and water. The farmer, unused to eating bread, chewed at it awkwardly as he complained about the government's unreasonableness. "A man can't say a few words without being punished. All I did was carry a sack of peanuts into the city to sell, and I said just one word to support them . . . and now you're starving me to death, giving me nothing more than this rotten thing to chew on. My wife is still waiting for me to bring back the meager earnings from that sack of peanuts so she can attend a wedding reception. We need to buy clothes for the banquet, and I was on my way to the market to get a little fabric for my wife. We haven't finished with the arrangements, and now it's getting so dark that I can't go home anyway. I'm sure she's sitting at home cursing me, saying I went out squandering the money, drinking too much, and passing out on someone's doorstep . . . I just want to go back and tell her all about this shit business. She's sure to jump to her feet and give me a good telling off for talking such rubbish!"

The farmer raised his voice to a shrill note in imitation of the woman. "What? A pile of shit? What crap is this? You think that after all the years we've spent raising animals, I'll buy that? It might be easy to fool those hoity-toity city folks, but I'm no fool! That's like saying my dog's turned into a poet—there's no way!"

The words flew out of the farmer's mouth like bats from under the eaves of a house, a rapid stream in a strong rustic accent. When he'd finished howling, he glanced at everyone in turn as if looking for an ally. He licked bread crumbs from the corner of his mouth.

"I'm an honest farmer, always on schedule with my deliveries. Whatever the government asks me to do, I do. If they tell me to grow rice, I grow rice. If they say to plant hemp, I plant hemp. Everything is according to their plan. They set the price, and that's the price. If they don't accept my crops, then I let them rot at home. A fellow like me just wants to provide a simple house for the wife and kid, and to put food on the table. How could I have the time to accompany those who want to take to the streets to play their silly games?" When he'd had his say, the farmer patted his body here and there, then produced a flattened cigarette pack from one of his pockets. When he discovered that he didn't have a lighter, he reluctantly put the cigarette back into the pack and let out a long breath, just as if he'd actually taken a puff. "The plight of a farmer! Which of you knows anything about that, huh?"

The lamp was not working, and the rest of the house had been left in darkness. Only a faint glimmer from a streetlight fell in through the basement window. The farmer's voice made a circuit around the room, like the buzzing of a fly. No one paid any attention to him. After a while, his voice died down and he began to snore.

The detainees were released from the basement one by one. Eventually only Mengliu and Qizi were left, sitting at opposite ends of the bench. They could not see each other's faces.

"The Wisdom Bureau is so big . . . This is the first time I've noticed you," he said.

"I've seen you before. You're a famous poet. But it's good that you don't put on airs."

"Where've you seen me? And who are you calling 'a famous poet'? Is that supposed to be some kind of insult?"

"It's from the newspapers of course. Who doesn't know the poetry of the Three Musketeers? Your poetry, if you don't mind me being direct, I really like it."

"Oh, you mean you guys in the Physics Department are interested in poetry?"

"We have a literary society too. Unfortunately, the atmosphere at our meetings isn't much to boast about."

"You should join our literary salons. There are forums and poetry readings every week."

"Maybe I am an undiscovered poet . . . but I'm presently tied up in a scientific research project."

"Oh? Something relating to the use of a machine in place of the human brain?"

"A secret machine. The preliminary work will be done soon. I believe we'll see the results in the near future—at least, in theory. Are you laughing at me? To laugh at me is to laugh at science."

"I wouldn't dare! I hear that the Physics Department has quite a number of creative . . . geniuses."

"You can call me mad and I wouldn't care. There's not much to distinguish a madwoman from a genius. To a poet, scientific fantasies may sound weird. For example, would you believe there's a machine that can detect information anywhere in the world, even extracting human genetic information or accurately calculating the electrical power generated in a lightning storm? And that, harvesting the forces of nature, it is able to absorb data on the world's finest species?"

"I think your concept is worth admiring and exploring. But if there really were such a machine, it shouldn't be used to plunder . . . "

" . . . it also has an automatic conferencing facility that makes policy decisions, and holds think tanks to analyze the situation at hand and offer proposals about how to solve the nation's incurable diseases. It serves so many functions. It converses with people. Its methods are even more humane than a human's."

"Humane? Unless it has emotions . . . This machine, is it male or female?"

"How far we can progress is only limited by the smallness of our minds. Never doubt science, Yuan Mengliu." She used his own name to mock him.

"Yes, yes, yes. Humans wanted to go to the moon, so they went to the moon. And if they want to go to hell, they'll go to hell." Mengliu was rather enjoying himself.

But Qizi was taken away. Before long, he left the basement too.

The streetlights were dim. The people on the streets were wrapped up warmly.

The night mingled with the snow, a world of black and white.

5

The sky over the lake suddenly turned dark with rolling clouds and a freakish wind. The gigantic waves were like horses rushing out of an open gate, striking the hull of the boat with a loud crash, raising the bow out of the water and throwing Mengliu into the cabin, where he struck his head just hard enough to daze himself. The maddened clouds surged together, twisting in a fury into one great pillar that towered over the lake and drew it up into a funnel, leaving a spinning whirlpool at its center. The sail, caught in the winds, began to flap violently, and everything turned black before Mengliu's eyes. Both his body and his consciousness were sucked into the great black hole.

He did not know how much time had passed before he opened his eyes to see the clear moon overhead, looking like a round loaf of bread in the sky. The forest around him was dark and full of rustling sounds. The leaves of the trees reflected the light from the moon, as if countless pairs of eyes were watching. His body lay in the damaged boat, his legs dangled in the water. He was so cold that his teeth chattered. He cursed. The boat sank beneath his hand as he tried to push himself up.

He was soaked. He waded toward the bank, starting a bright ripple in the water that accompanied the sound of his splashing. Scrambling ashore, he shouted several times, but even his voice seemed dark and hollow. He wasn't sure whether his shivering was inspired by the cold or by his fear. The moonlight was cold; the shells strewn along the bank reflected its light. He was surrounded by a pale blue fog. He wrapped his arms around his body. He was barefoot and wore little more than tattered rags. He took each step cautiously, hoping to see some signs of habitation.

The moon was a dandy. As he walked, it followed him, mocking him for his beggarly appearance.

He was like a louse on an elephant's body, nothing more than a tiny insect in the forest. Branches whipped against him as he moved along, stinging his flesh.

As he crested the hill, the moon went into hiding. He was suddenly plunged into darkness. The strange nocturnal sounds made his hair stand on end.

As he walked on in the darkness, in an attempt to warm himself, he began to think of his most recent conquest. Suitang was a lovely girl. She chewed gum the first time she reported for work. She looked so much like Qizi that Mengliu had to catch his breath. When she took the initiative and asked to be his assistant, his mind became even more muddled. He compared her to a lily that flowed with a secret fragrance. He knew that Suitang would be completely taken in by this sort of elaborate but common analogy. At night, she would stand before the mirror, blushing, posturing, and preening, seeing the dazzling human world reflected in her dark eyes.

The next morning the sun shone into the forest and warmed the ground. Mengliu felt a tongue of sandpaper licking him all over. Opening his eyes, he saw a huge lion's head, and his whole body went limp. As he stared at it, he realized that the lion must be a benevolent creature, since it allowed birds to perch atop its head and sing. Another lion stood nearby grazing on a clump of grass. An antelope, an elk, and a kangaroo played close to them. The eyes of the animals looked happy, their ears moved like strings on a plucked instrument, and their tails were swaying gently.

It was a harmonious society of beasts.

Mengliu suddenly felt that everything was going to be just fine. He picked fruit from the trees and quickly filled his stomach. At a small brook, he washed his unshaven face. He wove a pair of sandals from grass and, leaning on a walking stick that he had made from a fallen branch, set out on a journey that would last several days.

It was not an easy forest for a hike. Sometimes he climbed like an ape, sometimes he rolled down, and sometimes he had to swim. He came to a strange place that seemed to have been burned. There was no flora or fauna, and no wildlife. All around were scattered hideous-looking glossy black stones, and the land was dry and desolate. The mountain peaks in the distance formed the jagged lines of a country mapped against the sky. One stone was particularly striking for its gigantic size. Its porous surface seemed to have retained warmth and was emitting an infernal gaseous substance.

He lay down to sleep. Before long, ants woke him up, and he found himself covered with countless red blisters. He got back on the track.

Ahead there was only one path to follow, through a weird crevice in the cliff like a huge wound that had scabbed over. He fumbled along, following the foot-wide trail along the edge of the cliff for a few dozen meters. He reached the crevice, and the path became even narrower. He eased himself forward. His skinny, shrunken frame seemed to be tailor-made for the narrow space. He smelled moss, followed by an occasional burst of floral perfume. He heard the sound of a spring, bubbling with girlish laughter. From its initial merriment, it grew more melodious. Suddenly, as if a car window had been thrown open, there was a sound like that of a beast's low, threatening roar. Before he could distinguish what it was, there was another roar and it leapt on him—a huge waterfall, seeming to fall from the sky, crashing down to the base of the cliff. Flowers grew wild on the rocky face, soaking up the spray from the waterfall.

He stepped forward, and his foot found only empty space. He plunged headlong into the pool below. The surface of the water was covered by large peonies. He felt that he had been dropped into a pot of hot dumplings. The waves buffeted him, and the spray from the waterfall hit him like tiny stone missiles, momentarily stunning him.

The grass looked soft. The sun lightly covered his body. The bird-song grew to a crescendo. Mengliu waded over to the bank and fell to the ground. He lay there motionless. Weak and somewhat dazed, he saw a beautiful girl walking toward him, her long hair hanging loose around her naked body, which was heavy with fruit like coconuts on a tree. She looked like Suitang at first, but as she drew nearer, she looked more like Qizi. The girl bent over him . . .

In his exhaustion, Mengliu had an erotic dream. When he woke, he thought of the vision of Qizi he'd seen in his dream. It had been over twenty years, but her likeness was engraved on his heart. It had not gathered any dust, nor had his love for her subsided in the least. He would never know such love again. Back in those days, Qizi and another girl called Shunyu had frequently made appearances in his diary. After the Tower Incident, Qizi had gradually come to play the central role. Mengliu visited the cinemas, shopping malls, and eateries in Beiping with the wealthy little princess Shunyu. Shunyu was infatuated with his friend Hei Chun, and Mengliu had fallen for Qizi, so the two had banded together for mutual entertainment and consolation.

The photo of the Three Musketeers he had kept depicted them as being full of vigor, self-confidence, and idealism. One look at Hei Chun's hardened eyes was enough to convince anyone of his influence. Bai Qiu's shoulder-length hair, full and ready to take flight, made him look romantic and elegant. Mengliu was the perfect image of a frail scholar, cool and reserved with his Adam's apple protruding above the neckline of his white shirt, hands held low and clasped in front of his body. The timid, rabbitlike expression he wore demonstrated his trust in and love for a peaceful society. He always thought he should have put his hand on Hei Chun's shoulder, or perhaps slipped both hands into his pockets, rather than letting them hang low, tightly clasped together, as if he were a football player afraid he was about to be kicked in the nuts.

The background in the photo was the double-tracked wall outside the Wisdom Bureau. The wall was covered with posters, all of which had later disappeared. The photo had faded, turning yellow and wrinkled. It was becoming more distinctly representative of its era. No one wore that expression anymore. It was the special property of the '60s generation.

This photo was a cherished memorial to his poetic past. He regretted keeping it, because of the memories it evoked. Yet, he was glad too, as it retained signs of the romantic youth he had experienced. If anyone thought a rift had developed between him and Hei Chun because of a girl, it definitely wasn't a crack in their relationship. No, it was more like a line of poetry. Thinking it over carefully so many years later, he still held the same opinion. Back then, the country was unsteady, dealing with economic decline, disorder, and rife with government corruption. The fate of both nation and individuals were uncertain.

Shunyu was a big-eyed, shy girl who could set off a storm with a furtive glance, but Hei Chun remained unmoved. Shunyu was worth remembering. In the end, she had been hit by a stray bullet in the middle of the chaos. As she waited in the long queue outside the hospital door, she died slowly from loss of blood. She died beneath the flag of Dayang, fluttering in the wind overhead.

Startled out of his reverie, Mengliu sat up. The sound of the water falling from that terrible height reminded him of the rumble of the tanks as they lumbered toward him.

6

The April following the Tower Incident, the flowers were in bloom but remained smothered under a layer of snow. The old acacia tree was covered in leafy green, its sharp points rising out from under its thin, snowy coat, bringing a cold hint of spring, flowing with life. Mengliu walked beneath the tree and considered going overseas. In an attempt to lure him into staying on board, the Wisdom Bureau had offered him a promotion and, before the venerable leader, he had made a show of being touched. He said he would think about it.

Mengliu pined for Qizi. The love buried deep in his heart flowed continuously like an underground spring. Only when he had written several poems about her could he find any peace of mind. To be fair, Qizi was a good girl, possessing all the beauty and frail delicacy of the women of olden times, just as she was equipped with the cool aloofness typical of the women of Dayang. Her career ambitions were quite exceptional. He felt ashamed when he recalled how he had treated her scientific ideas like crazy talk.

He remembered how she looked—pale, thin, short hair, pert nose, pointed chin, and a distinctive fragrance. Her demeanor as she spoke . . .

When the joy born of that memory revived, he got a bicycle and raced around the compound at the Wisdom Bureau, his head full of dreams in which he held her and kissed her, running his lips over her responsive breasts. He was pedaling so hard the bike was gasping and moaning when he unexpectedly came across his friend Bai Qiu near the entrance to the library. He was so startled that his lust fluttered away like a frightened bird.

Bai Qiu was dressed in an oversized military coat, the sleeves so long they hung over his hands. Mengliu slowed down, then put his right foot down to brake. Stopping in front of Bai Qiu, he exhaled heavily. His friend, apparently composing a poem in his head, was so stunned he took a step backward. Seeing it was Mengliu, he smiled as if in a trance but, quickly recovering, he commented that Mengliu's eyes were glowing so much he looked like a dog in heat. Though Bai Qiu had a keen mind, he appeared so slow that it was hard to believe that harsh words could come off his tongue, or that sharp verses could be penned by his hand.

They shared a few laughs by the roadside, lifting their spirits. Bai Qiu proposed they go to a bar. Mengliu's earlier hot-blooded state had cooled down now, and he put aside his thoughts of Qizi. He accompanied Bai Qiu along Liuli Street to the Green Flower Bar, one of their favorite haunts. The proprietor tried to be especially generous toward the poets with his home-brewed Chinese wine, often going so far as to offer them drinks on the house. Of course, if the poets occasionally received special treatment on account of the proprietor's daughter, whose name was Shunyu, the proprietor got something good out of it too. They held a variety of literary salons there, turning the Green Flower into a hub for Beiping's literati.

The Green Flower was in an old wooden house and occupied both the upper and lower floors. Inside, it was warm, with Chinese-style decor. It was said that the tavern's owner had been a soldier and had seen action on the battlefield. He had traveled to China and loved Chinese culture, Chinese food, and Chinese liquor. He had purchased several items at a private auction and had them shipped back to Dayang, bringing a Chinese flavor to the bar that included everything from the furnishings to the waiters' uniforms. He paid even more attention to the inner rooms. One room was furnished with an ancient wooden daybed and an intricately designed drinking table. Another had elaborately designed square tables, with chairs to match. The seats were covered with an eclectic assortment of brightly colored cushions, upon which the patrons could recline when they became drowsy with talking. Ancient calligraphy and paintings hung from the walls, and porcelain pieces from the Song through to the Qing dynasties adorned the shelves. Even the coat rack was carved wood. The literati gathered in the Green Flower to talk freely about politics, ideals, literature, and women. They drank until the small hours, then squatted on the curb and vomited. They talked bullshit and shared their truest aspirations, and at the end of it all, the old boys disappeared one by one into the cold still night.

At first, Mengliu and Bai Qiu sat in the main hall by a window with bowls of fried peanuts and seeds and nuts, assorted cold dishes, and shredded squid accompanied by warmed wine. They poured the wine into porcelain cups no thicker than a thumb and toasted each other with them. After they had had a few drinks, Hei Chun and some others lifted the curtain and entered the bar, followed by two girls, one dressed in black and the other in white. Mengliu took one look and froze. His gaze bounced back like a spring and his hand nervously reached for an ashtray. He pinched a cigarette and inserted it into his mouth, only to spit it out immediately after.

Hei Chun had already seen them and cried, "Cheers!" He hurried over and exchanged a few pleasantries, then invited them to join him in a room on the second floor where they could all catch up. They settled in, but the atmosphere had not livened up, and no one had yet taken up quarters on the daybed. They all looked like they had gathered for a meeting, propping their elbows on the edge of the drinking table. When the waiter carried their dishes up and laid them out, the profile of the girl dressed in white was visible through the crook of the waiter's elbow, allowing Mengliu a chance to watch her secretly. Soon he met her gaze through that same aperture. His heart was set on fire with a crackle like that of a newly lit match.

Just as they were warming up, the proprietor came in. He was in his fifties, his head sprouting a shock of silver hair and his cheeks as rosy as a tuberculosis patient. He lumbered over and plopped down on a stool, making it immediately appear small and frail. He did not employ his usual loud tone and seemed almost to be a completely different person. In a small voice he said, "Wine. You all drink whatever you'd like. Just don't talk politics, and don't make trouble."

After fiddling with the wine cups for a while, he got up. Walking to the door, he turned back and called, "Shunyu, come here. I've got something to tell you."

The girl sitting inside, the one in black, stood up. With a weary grimace, she reluctantly followed him outside.

Her figure wasn't bad at all, her appearance decent. She looked like a typical honor roll student, fit to be a civil servant or hold a job in education.

"Shunyu just joined the Plum Party. Her father has been a part of the literary movement all his life. He wanted her to be a poet but is also afraid for her to mix with the likes of us."

Hei Chun rubbed his palm over his hair, which was shimmering with grease. "Pity the loving parents! I guess we're just like chicken ribs. We're tasteless, but even if a thing is tasteless, it's a waste just to throw it out." Finished with his self-deprecation, he glanced around the circle and asked, "You all know each other, right?"

They glanced at each other, but before anyone could speak, Hei Chun pointed the girl in white out to Mengliu. "I guess you don't know Qizi, from the Physics Department. She's very talented. Her ex-boyfriend is from the Chemistry Department, a jerk called Dadong who helped someone with some research into the making of fake antiques a while back and caused an explosion that reduced the guy's house to nothing. He's been in the hospital for nearly a month himself, practically in ruins."

In large groups, Hei Chun always liked to preside over the small talk. Sometimes his talk was over the top, and he liked to season it with foul language.

The girl in white smiled in acknowledgement. She pulled off her white down jacket and hung it on the coat rack. Beneath, she wore a tight, black, low-cut sweater and low-waist, denim bell bottoms. It was quite revealing. Everything about her was petite and exquisite.

They all made the most of the occasion, laughing and enjoying themselves. Bai Qiu said he and Dadong had played a bit of soccer together. Dadong was a handsome guy but a lousy soccer player. He ran around the field haphazardly, committing fouls all the time. If a shot didn't ricochet off the goal post, it was only because it had sailed right over it.

They spent some time making fun of Qizi's ex-boyfriend as a source of merriment. Every idiotic move that could be made by a football player was attributed to him, and the poor chap's name was turned into dirt right there in the bar. But then, this was common practice. Any time they drank together, there were always a couple of absentees whose names would be brought to the table and dragged through the mud. Sometimes they would become the subject of a limerick, which would be relived at their next drinking session.

As they sipped at their wine, the conversation livened up.

Mengliu's expression gave nothing away, but his heart was fluttering. He was thinking about Qizi, and his joy once again broke down the door to his heart. It was as if he had entered a garden in full bloom.

He helped himself to the wine, noticing how dazzlingly white Qizi's skin was, like a spotlight aimed right at him. He longed for a moment alone with her, to hold her delicate hand, and to whisk her away to some secluded spot where he could express his affection to her.

Shunyu returned to the party. Their mockery of Qizi's ex-boyfriend came to an abrupt end.

Shunyu was young, with long hair, large eyes, a tiny mouth, and a flat chest. Her canines were perfectly aligned with an adorable set of jug ears. Playing host, she was in an unbridled state, constantly reaching out her slender arms to add tea or wine to each empty cup. With this wellspring flowing from her, her face became as rosy as the proprietor's, though hers was a healthier hue.

"My father just told me that he's heard news that some people are going to be picked up. It's best to behave ourselves, and also to avoid large gatherings." As Shunyu spoke, she took on the manner of a member of the Plum Party.

"Not again!" The tea was too hot, so Qizi sipped it carefully. "Don't worry. I was picked up last time. It was nothing."

"You were arrested? For what?" Hei Chun was taken aback.

Qizi stole a quick glance at Mengliu and said, "I was guilty of being in love."

The stolen glimpse at Mengliu was enough to establish a tacit conspiracy between them. The halo that seemed to surround her reached right into his chest. He thought she must have learned she could trust him.

Shunyu stared at them with eyes that had grown rounder than their wine glasses. This didn't necessarily mean that she was surprised. She wanted her lashes to seem longer, her mouth to grow smaller, and her face to appear sharp and thin, like an adorable cartoon character, in the hope that the boys would be fascinated. Specifically, it was all for Hei Chun's benefit. It was obvious that everything she did was motivated by concern for Hei Chun's wellbeing. Hei Chun pretended not to notice. He looked at Qizi, and after scrutinizing her for a bit, stubbornly returned to the topic of her ex-boyfriend.

"Dadong is not completely useless. The fake antiques he helped make were sold at exorbitant prices. Someone alerted the National Cultural Relics Protection Bureau, and he was almost thrown in jail for stealing and selling national treasures. If he'd put his brains to good use, he'd be fine. At the very least, he could apply it to his love life." Hei Chun tucked his feet in and sat in the Buddha pose as he continued, "Qizi, look around here carefully. Which of us can't measure up to Dadong? You could choose any of us. I think that punk just got lucky."

Even though it was clear that Hei Chun was joking, Mengliu cringed. He busied himself by gulping down more wine.

"Hei Chun, are you trying to hide something?" Bai Qiu asked. "Everyone in the world knows you've been bitten by the love bug. You hide under the covers at night writing Qizi's name in all the languages of the planet. Now that she's fair game, you can seize the opportunity to confess your love. You don't need to drag all of us into it."

They all ribbed him, growing more and more waggish in their jibes.

"Hey! What fucking nonsense!" Hei Chun's eyes flashed like the fluttering of bat's wings, but he quickly restored his bright countenance. Making an about-face, he began to expound on another topic of interest. "There's a good poem on the double-tracked wall. It says, 'Honest men die, while hypocrites survive; passionate men die, left to be buried by the indifferent.' The best kind of government is the one that does not make its presence felt. The next best is the one that makes its subjects feel close to it. After that, the one that uses administrative measures. The worst is the one that resorts to violence. What do you think?"

"Shh! Don't let my father hear or he'll kick all of you out. He told me so himself." Shunyu, really anxious now, turned her wide eyes on Hei Chun.

"Okay, okay, okay. Let's switch to the entertainment channel then. Mengliu, show us your unique skill. Blow us a tune to make us forget all our troubles. Make us believe all is well."

"I didn't bring it," Mengliu replied, suddenly nervous. He didn't feel like showing off in front of Qizi right now. Hei Chun poked a hand into Mengliu's pocket and went right for the lady-charming chuixun. "Unhappy with your performance fees, you little prick? Everyone, give him a round of applause."

A mix of applause and heckling came from the group.

"What do you want to hear?" Helpless, Mengliu wiped his instrument.

"Anything. Whatever you play is best," said Hei Chun.

"Then it'll be 'The Pain of Separation.'" Mengliu took a sip of water and wet his lips. "This is especially for the two lovely ladies, Qizi and Shunyu."

He fingered the flute and began to blow. Within seconds they had all been transported to hell, the music drawing out of them the great sorrow that lurked inside. It was the kind of mournful, melancholy tune that could break your heart.

When they left the bar, Shunyu's father gave Mengliu a thumbs up. "You play that flute divinely. Even better than I do."

7

As he pushed his way out from the dark mountains, across the thickly forested hillside, Mengliu climbed to the top of the hill to have a look. He saw a city, a real city full of mushrooming buildings, with spires sticking up like towering ancient trees. The atmosphere was solemnly quiet and mysterious, the air full of the aroma of buckwheat.

The sun was shining. A river ran down from the mountains and then through the city, stepping all the way down the slope like scales. Wild chrysanthemums swayed on the hill, dancing to their own tune. Church bells broke the silence, a ringing full of forgiveness and serenity, as if proclaiming to everyone, "All manner of sin and blasphemy will be forgiven. Don't doubt, just believe."

Mengliu raced like an escaped horse toward the city, his mane flying in the wind, eyes enlarged and nostrils puffing. He took wing, like a bird, the wind whistling in his ears, the trees falling rapidly away behind him. He shot forward like a bullet at lightning speed.

Of course, that was only in his fancy. In actual fact, he was squatting in front of a strip of engraved stone, carefully observing the text he saw there. The script looked like Hei Chun's writing, thin and aloof, strong strokes that added a lot of character to each word.

He saw that he'd come to a city-state called "Swan Valley."

Twenty minutes later he entered the city. It was extremely small, perhaps more appropriately called a town. The streets were deserted, and a mystical white smoke floated over the rooftops. The trees were low and tidy, their leaves thick and shiny. The buildings sprouting up in the midst of the trees were all of an identical style. Even the patterns on the windows, the door handles, and the stone steps were the same. None of the buildings were higher than two or three stories, constructed from beautiful granite stone. The joints were filled with plaster, and the walls topped with simple roofs resembling mushroom caps. White screens fluttered at each latticed window. The cloth on each screen was coated with a translucent oil, giving it an amber tint. The doors and windows were all wide open. The rooms inside were well lit and appeared clean and warm. They looked just like the sort of places where one might sit and talk of old heroic deeds and the current day's farm chores over a cup of tea or wine.

A white porcelain dish held pig's trotters that glistened in one room's exquisite glow, like a lotus blossom made of meat. In a short while, all that was left was an empty plate and discarded bone fragments. Mengliu cleaned his mouth with his hand as he looked at the house's decor. One wall was covered with a huge batik painting—the most eye-catching decoration in the room. It was a map that showed men, horses, bows and arrows, and deer, all in scenes of chaos and tension.

The dining table was formed by a few round wooden blocks. The edge of the table retained the shape of the original log, its surface made smooth, and the wood grain distinct. It was covered with script written in a child's hand, in what looked like the Latin alphabet. A cupboard held blue-and-white porcelain pieces, all beautifully crafted. They were covered with elegant patterns that gave them a historical feel. Rattan chairs filled the space with the smell of grass. Round baskets were hung around the room, each containing green Chinese wisteria plants dotted with blooming lavender flowers, giving one a sense of the owner's genteel, delicate tastes. Mengliu rummaged around for more food and ate a jarful of colorful cakes. He was not sure whether they were made from wheat or corn, or perhaps even some sort of ground soybean.

Without regard for manners, he washed and changed into a gray robe and black cloth shoes. The sun was bright but mild. He was bathed in comfort. Feeling that he'd entered a medieval atmosphere, he imagined people of that era, sheepherders spending their days out in the fresh air. They chanted curses when they got toothaches, and when they got tired of one place, they simply uprooted themselves and went on their way. They seemed to have just passed by.

Mengliu left the house and walked to a curved building. He found himself standing in an empty hall lit by stained-glass French windows. The floor was tiled with a red porcelain that made it look like colored glass. There was a curtained stage, with the walls on either side hung with paintings depicting the events of a fairy tale. The remaining spaces were hung with embroideries, paper cutouts, and paintings made with shells. A few musical instruments, having been polished, stood in a neat row. Passing through the building, he encountered a group of children playing marbles, wearing odd clothes and speaking in a strange tongue. The marbles rolled in the sunlight, setting off sparkles to rival the glow of their fancy jewelry.

Seeing Mengliu, the children stopped their game and began whispering to one another. After laughing strangely, they ran off. A boy of about five or six years, with short hair and brown eyes, was left behind. He approached Mengliu like a little raccoon, picked up the marbles, offered them to the guest, then turned and walked away.

The boy had given Mengliu dazzling diamonds, so bright they made him squint. He hid them nervously in his clothes, then left in haste.

When he had walked along a path for what seemed like a long time, Mengliu came to a square full of sculptures. Crowds of people sat on the grass. Some banners with slogans hung from the trees, while others lined the roadside. Everyone looked cheerful and relaxed, as if enjoying a barbecue while on holiday. People drank beer or other beverages. Several played pipes made from reeds, with a crisp lyrical melody that crackled with a fiery vitality.

The crowd was full of people of different skin colors. Their clothing was light gray and of a coarse linen texture, loose fitting, plain, and simple. Some were embroidered with complex patterns of fish, dragons, bamboo, flowers, butterflies, or the Buddhist swastika symbol, resembling clothing typical of Han Chinese, though not as beautiful. The men wore shirts with short fronts and baggy pants or open-necked long gowns, and their heads were either wrapped in turbans or left bare, exposing their curly hair. Their mannerisms and language were cultured. The women were distinguished by their colorful clothing, the sleeves had borders and the kimono-style collars were low cut, exposing their inner garments. Some wore their hair loose, some covered it with a black hairnet, others chose to put it all up, adorned with a few brightly colored hairpins. Some pulled their hair into a single ox-horn-shaped bun, situated on the left or right side of their heads. They tied their hair with something like flaxen yarn, of many different shades and patterns. There were also women who chose to plait their hair, curling the braids around their heads, inserting crescent-shaped combs at the crown to hold them in place. Others chose to pull their hair into spiral-shaped buns with scarves folded into hats at the crown, the neatly stacked ribbons flowing in the wind. The crafted shells used to secure the scarves shone like gems.

The women bloomed like flowers, and Mengliu was elated at the sight of them. He walked to the statue of a naked man and stood beneath it. At its base, he saw a plaque inscribed with a description in English. This was one of Swan Valley's spiritual leaders. He had created Swan Valley's language and led a life of hardship and good deeds. He established kindness as Swan Valley's most important virtue.

The spiritual leader looked like a woodcutter. He held a sickle or some sort of weapon in one hand, while the other was clenched into a fist. He was muscular, with ripples protruding all over his naked body. He exuded power from head to toe, and all of the strength of his being was centered in his phallus. It stood impressively erect, pointing straight ahead, like invincible artillery aimed at the very spirit of evil.

Mengliu thought, "What artist had the guts to take the clothes off his spiritual leader? Didn't he stop to think of how it would make all the women lust after him?"

A young man climbed nimbly up the statue. He hung a red banner with white lettering on the phallus of the spiritual leader. The slogans billowed outward in the breeze.

They were commemorating the spiritual leader's birthday. Bird-shaped flowers bloomed everywhere. Mengliu later learned that these were the spiritual blossoms of Swan Valley and stood for liberty and independence.

Enthusiastic applause broke out in the square. People beat on drums. The reed pipes belted out their sharp notes. The people, well trained, raised their voices in unison a few seconds later. Their timing was as precise and clean as the slicing of a knife.

On a huge electronic screen, a spaceship flew through distant stars and drew nearer. Its door opened slowly, and the image of a figure decked out in a space suit as it floated in the cabin was vaguely visible. It was impossible to tell its age or gender. The creature adjusted its position so that it faced the people, then waved and said in a robotic voice:

"Beautiful and highly intelligent people of Swan Valley, greetings! In our Swan Valley, where kindness is the priority, each person has the potential to become the new spiritual leader. Choose the better history, put into practice the precious right that has been passed down from generation to generation, these noble ideals: it is God's promise that each of us is equal, that all people may be free, and that everyone has the opportunity to reach the full measure of happiness. Thank you for your trust, your passion, and your sacrifice. Your insights and your upbringing are all influenced by the spirit of Swan Valley. You are all perfect, the pride of Swan Valley. We do not allow the soul to remain imprisoned. Now as your spiritual leader, Ah Lian Qiu, I will do my best for beautiful Swan Valley, giving my all, even my life . . . "

Mengliu did not understand the language of Swan Valley but did get some impression of the spiritual leader's meaning from the English phrases mixed into the speech, which used words such as "good," "spirit," "soul," and "freedom." He had no interest in the spiritual leader and his speech. With so many wonderful women in the gathering, he had, from habit, already been out on the prowl. In this area he had an innate sense, and he quickly homed in on a woman in green. She wore a simple robe, with the hem of her skirt, neckline, and waistband all embroidered in blue. Her blouse was low cut, her bosom full, and her neck smooth. Her black hair reached all the way down to her waist. Tiny feet peeked out from beneath the hem of her skirt.

His heart was like a car careening along a mountain road. The bumps and turns of it shocked him.

Just as he thought to go over and make his advances, he found himself surrounded by a crowd. They could tell he was a foreigner. According to their tradition, they were competing for the chance to take him into their care. He stood out like a cherry on a snowy-white cream cake. But they didn't speak to him at all. As if he were an animal that had strayed among humans, or an item in a bazaar, he was surrounded by heated debate, as if they were discussing whether to send him back to the zoo or release him into the forest. The dispute rushed on, punctuated by expressions of modesty and sincerity, and even some pleading.

Mengliu soon understood that he was the cherry to be plucked, taken home, washed, placed on a clean white plate, and stored in a warm, hospitable cupboard. He was all too used to seeing the cold and ruthless treatment of others, farmers going to the market with their bullock carts overturned and their bullocks slapped around; doctors who had not received red envelopes with payoffs inside sewing their patients' anuses shut; the elderly left to freeze to death on the roadside, the poor to die at home. People kidnapped children and sold them, demolished homes, abused animals. Now he stood here, a stranger, and he could feel the selfless love of these people. He was completely captivated by their show of friendliness.

They spoke Swanese, the language of the valley, occasionally mixing in English words. He did not know if this was just a fashionable mode of expression or if it was a regular part of their language. They also accented their speech with physical gestures and expressions, shrugging or pulling at the corners of their mouths. Sometimes they stood straight, hands folded at the center of their bodies. They occasionally lifted a hand, then lowered it back into the same place.

Mengliu only had eyes for the woman in green. He believed she was of mixed blood, with her wheat-colored skin and oval face, eyelashes like fans and narrow, chocolate-brown eyes. Her glances darted here and there, and her lips were like a half-opened rose. She wore a silver ring in her lower lip, and with her mouth turned up, her implied smile was full of meaning. When their eyes met, he felt that this woman and her exotic flavor eclipsed every woman he had ever seen before.

A handsome young man stood up and offered to mediate. In English, he said, "Now, please, choose anyone from this crowd. You may follow that person home, and you will be taken care of." He looked like a Mexican, dressed in a long shirt zipped in front, his head covered in short curly hair. His teeth were too white and too neat. They had a cold sharpness to them.

Without hesitation Mengliu pointed to the woman in green.

The young man dismissed the crowd and calmly swept his melancholy eyes over Mengliu, his expression like the dark billows of the sea at night.

Mengliu thought to himself, "This young man harbors some jealousy."

"Follow me," the woman said in English. Her voice warbled like an oriole's.

8

The woman in green pulled her hair back. Without a word she cooked and brewed tea. Mengliu was like a mute, sitting and waiting dutifully for the smoke to rise and the food to be served. At first, he was a little uncomfortable and his eyes followed the woman's movements closely. He wanted to ask her something—her name, age, occupation, interests—anything really, so long as it meant he could hear her voice and watch her expressions. But she showed no inclination to chat with him, as if he'd always lived in the house and had been a member of the family for a long time.

He looked around as if bored, taking the opportunity to get a reading of her body. Taking the measure of her with the precise observations of a doctor, he assembled a series of numbers for her height and weight. His estimates suggested that the numbers were in perfect proportion. He smiled, convinced that she was supple in every part of her body, and probably incapable of hiding her solitude and loneliness for long. Sooner or later she would become an exuberant she-wolf, breaking out of her confines and turning the whole world upside down. He concluded that she would be one of those women who liked revolution.

Her chest boasted a pair of loaded coconuts, uniquely lethal weapons with which to wage her revolution. They were a potent pair of aphrodisiac tear-gas canisters. Day or night, if she willed it, she could pull the pin and instantly fill the world with smoke. No one would be able to escape from her.

His fingers bounced in the air as if stroking the keys on a piano. On his fingertips was the warmth and smoothness of satin, the slope of the hills, and his touch made the flowers tremble.

The woman in green suddenly turned and looked at him. At her glance, his mind exploded like a spring thunderstorm, leaves whipping in the tempest around him.

She did not say anything. Her face remaining expressionless as she turned away again.

The leaves danced, and the noise subsided.

Mengliu meekly averted his gaze, reining it in. His heart pounded. He cautiously got a hold on himself, and with a flashlight's beam, he began to sweep the room with his eyes. In a situation like this where he did not know much about a woman, he was used to following external cues, reaching a conclusion based on various sources of otherwise irrelevant information, as if knowing that the body's systems were closely interrelated, and firmly mastering that knowledge, could help one to move the whole person. This was a strategy he called "the village surrounding the city."

The furnishings inside her home gave him a sense of déjà vu. If not for the different murals, he'd think he was back in the place where he'd eaten the pig's trotter. These buildings that all looked the same were also similar inside, almost the way rooms in a hotel have the same appearance. The only difference was in the detailed decor, like the arrangement of flowers, that revealed the owner's personal taste. This woman's home had a lot of flowers and plants. To the right of the door, there was a screen of plants lush with fresh foliage. On the ground were pots of various heights, and hanging baskets above, full of colorful floral vines. He recognized periwinkle, bluebells, marigolds, begonias, petunias, and the short blossoms of morning glory. The plant blooming in the living room window was like a curtain of falling water. On the dining table was a hydroponic orchid with one elegant flower in bloom. The open cupboard held stacks of candles and beautiful silver candlesticks covered with elaborate decorations. Atop them were half-burnt candles. On the floor were several blue-and-white porcelain vases, and a stone sculpture of an animal head. He also saw flowers that looked like birds. After the meal he learned they were called "bird flowers," "birds of paradise," or "birds of heaven," and their scientific name was *Strelitzia*.

Practically all the plants were in bloom. The woman in green was herself like a dragon tree, her long hair naturally loose, covering the slender stem of her body and drooping with a finely wrought leaf pattern. Filled with desire, his hands were scheming how they might minister tenderly to her.

His eyes turned back to the woman. Watching how she went about managing the household, he wondered how she could work without making a sound. He, too, kept silent. It was like a scene from a pantomime.

After a short while, she went into another room. When she came out, she held a stack of fresh clothes, shoes, and socks. She handed the stack to Mengliu and flatly asked him to bathe and dress. Her pronunciation in English had a loose quality, like wind stirring up all sorts of sounds in the dragon tree. It was a flavor all her own. When she uttered an *s* sound, she gritted her two rows of small pearly teeth tightly together and spat an ethereal wisp of air from her mouth, letting it float like a subtle fragrance. When she said "I am . . . ," her rosy tongue crept out and her eyes moved.

The smooth glow of her breast made Mengliu's tongue stiffen. He politely took the clothes, uttered a terse but sincere thanks, and turned his attention to bathing and dressing.

Incense sticks burned in the bathroom, saffron-scented, or maybe gardenia. They again awakened the desire in him. The wall was tiled with colorful mosaics and the window decorated with tinted wax. The lights were soft, and the room filled with purple flowers. Entering into this space filled with an air of feminine sweetness, Mengliu grew reckless, but at the same time felt the secret joy of such a privilege. His heart filled with sweetness, too, as he carefully set the clean clothing on the counter. Humming a tune to himself, he undressed.

When he went to urinate, he discovered that the toilet bowl was a chic matte golden color and gave out a cool, dark gleam. He leaned his head down and inspected it, carefully running his finger over the surface of the bowl a few times. He tapped it a few times more and gasped as he came to a tentative conclusion: the toilet bowl was wrought of gold. Taking upon himself the serious, responsible role of a scientist, he continued the exploration, squatting before the bowl and finally lying down and biting on it to test its authenticity. His sensitive fingers found the shallow tooth marks his bite had left behind.

He took the marbles the brown-eyed boy had given him from his pocket and rotated them in the light for a while, then cradling them in his hand, he created a circle of darkness around them just so he could admire their glitter. He did not doubt that they were genuine. He only found it hard to believe that the people of Swan Valley could value precious stones and metals no more than they would a piece of shit.

He stood for a long time, feeling emotional. Faced with the golden toilet, he felt an inexpressible pressure. The urge to urinate disappeared. He couldn't even squeeze out one drop. He dawdled as he began to bathe. Covering himself with shower gel, he thought of the hardships of the road, the strange things he'd encountered, the energy of the spiritual leader, the charm of the girls, the beauty of Swan Valley, the simplicity of the people, and he was overwhelmed with admiration.

Distracted, he finished bathing, his pores emitting the fragrance of the gel, dried his fit body, trimmed his mustache, dressed in the loose linen robe, then faced the mirror again. What he saw there was very pleasing to the eye. He felt that he had the look of one of the famed scholars of old. On his way out, he touched the toilet bowl again, rapping his knuckles against it a few times. He took a final look at the mirror and saw that he looked like a man going on a date. He wore a happy smile—the sort of expression a wife might see on the face of a husband who had been gone for a very long time and had now returned.

The meal was served, and a steaming aroma filled the air. In the center of the dishes of bamboo shoots and salted meat, rose soup, blood tofu, and vegetables was a vase of purple flowers. There were skirtlike blue-and-white porcelain bowls, two blue-and-white cups, and three pairs of chopsticks. The fragrance of the rice wine evoked a memory in Mengliu. He thought back to eating in a Chinese restaurant, where it was this same type of rice wine that had made Qizi drunk. He had taken her back to the West Wing and they had slept together on the same bed. Even in this state, she was alert enough to guard her chastity. His desire had boiled through the night.

The woman in green poured a milky substance into his cup. Placing it in front of him with both hands, she asked flatly, "Where does the gentleman come from?"

"Dayang. My family name is Yuan. You can call me Mengliu. I'm a surgeon." The chopsticks had a pattern painted on their upper ends. He privately wondered what the meaning of the third pair of chopsticks might be. There was a stiffness to his speech. He employed a formal mode of expression, hoping that would weaken his Dayang accent and add a bit of charm to his words.

"Oh, I guessed you were from there." The girl in green wore a gentle expression, but she seemed to be testing him.

Mengliu was surprised. At times like this, he did not want to waste his energy on polite matters. His heart was pounding with the sights and sounds of spring, his face radiant as if love-struck, like a bird rising confidently and joyously to greet the morning sun.

"It's actually a very interesting country," the girl continued.

"Yes, it is vast and overflowing with resources. It has a long history. Swan Valley is . . . ?" Mengliu tried to hide his embarrassment as he sought to gain a little insight into her place.

"You can call me Su Juli," the woman interrupted.

"Oh . . . that's a pretty name. Does it have any special significance?"

"My favorite number is seven, because God created man on the seventh day. Our poems have lines with seven characters. There are seven treasures in the Buddhist scriptures. The human body has seven openings, seven passions . . ." The woman in green hesitated, as if trying to think of what else might relate to the number seven.

" . . . There's the book *Seven Epitomes*, and there are seven continents on Earth. Which continent is Swan Valley on?"

"Mr. Yuan, what kind of book is the *Seven Epitomes*?"

"It's an ancient library catalog."

"China is a very mystical country. Look, this blue-and-white porcelain, that animal carving, they are all very ancient. I don't even know what period they come from."

Mengliu pretended to look at them. "They're pretty. But, I don't really know much about these things."

Unperturbed, the woman asked in a different tone about Dayang's legal system, the standard of living of its people, who its spiritual leader was.

Mengliu was overjoyed. He felt that this woman in . . . no, he should think of her as Juli—that what she had asked was intriguing, and humorous, but the expression on her face as she waited for his answer showed that she was not joking. He had to employ diplomatic tactics and recite at length from passages in his textbooks in praise of the motherland. He could not find the English equivalent to some parts, but he finally managed to express himself clearly—not fluently, but clearly. At a certain level, what touched Juli might not be her opponent's wit, but his awkwardness. Not everyone liked an eloquent person. Sometimes a person's charm emerged at a point between a pause and a hesitation. Mengliu strove to express himself in a more careful, mature manner, hoping in this way to attract Juli.

At the end of the day, he was a poet, and not a bad one at that. He was never at a loss with women. One might even say that this was his greatest strength. His accomplishments in literature and his interest in philosophy were embedded deep within him, and women always seemed to have a way to draw it out. He would rather waste all his talent on a woman than be hailed a hero by his ruthless motherland.

With an affected dramatic accent that made it sound like he was explaining a disease, he continued, " . . . With the ups and downs and changes in life, our people are wealthy now and very particular about how they live. After dining out on the weekend, they often go and listen to the music of a megastar, or see a play featuring some famous actor, or appreciate a world-renowned ballet. During the course of the evening they smoke Cuban cigars and sip on vintage wines. The women go for expensive beauty treatments, and their little purebred dogs visit pet salons . . . "

The longer he spoke the more outrageous he became. It was obvious his vanity was leading him into trouble as he took the upper echelons of society as the norm in his exposition. In fact, only about 4 percent of the population of his country enjoyed the lifestyle he spoke of, while 84 percent made up the bottom of the pyramid, mired in poverty and unemployment.

The woman in green spoke slowly, inclining her head slightly and clasping her wineglass, "We focus on liberal education, and our aim is a cultured people. We spend our time developing the mind, engaging in debate and the appreciation of the arts. For example, Esteban—he's the young man you saw today, the one who has been engaged in debate for three days and three nights—he admires the ancient Chinese philosopher Mozi. He says people should pursue plain living and seek after spiritual wealth, since pleasure and luxury are evil."

"Esteban sounds like a wise man." Mengliu returned the salute politely, then drank his wine. "Where does he work?"

"He has many identities. He trains future spiritual leaders, scholars, and poets." The ring in the woman's lip shook slightly beneath her pointed nose.

Her long lashes tickled his senses, almost beyond what he could bear. He released a little cry. He tried hard to make his "oh!" reflect admiration and feeling. Admittedly this was a difficult thing to bring off, but he did it easily. Going even further, he plunged straight into an elaborate, silent contemplation, and his silence was just perfect, for a long-winded man who sought to get to the bottom of things would have seemed boring and lacking in intellectual prowess.

Mengliu was smart, and he remained completely focused on the woman in green. At the most appropriate moments, he would say things like, "Do you engage in the art of dancing?" as a way of suggesting that her body was beautiful, or "You're like the goddess in *The Rhapsody of the Goddess of Luo*." In this way, he quickly shifted the atmosphere from a stiff awkwardness to more yielding ground.

"Oh no! No, I'm just a teacher. I teach sculpture and painting." She waved him off with a limp hand. "I'm just an ordinary woman. But thank you for the compliment."

Mengliu, sparing no effort, continued to employ his genteel manners in this nauseating play. The woman in green was obviously not the sort whose head would start to spin from the sound of a little flattery. If he did not appreciate the need for moderation, all his efforts would end up being counterproductive. So he used food to stop up his mouth, showing by his expression how delicious it was. He wasn't very hungry, but he was happy. His knotted feeling from a while back had disappeared, and he went about it all with an easy, carefree manner.

They chatted, and as they entertained themselves, the food diminished and the bottle emptied. With his body swathed in comfortable clothing, filled with the appropriate amount of wine, and faced with an appropriately fair female, everything seemed just right. He glanced at the foliage of the tree in the garden, and his heart overflowed with a special kind of wealth. Just then, the small raccoon-like boy he'd seen earlier jumped into the garden and trotted straight over to the woman in green. "Mom," he complained, "I don't want to wear these things."

The woman in green took the diamond jewelry off his body and threw it in the trash. It was as if she were picking strands of grass off him.

"Shanlai, this is Mr. Yuan . . . remember your manners."

One can never avoid one's nemesis for long. Mengliu mockingly prepared to accept Shanlai's greetings, but the latter gave him a supercilious look and ran out through the front door.

"As long as there's a debate going on, he doesn't bother about anything else." She spoke as a mother and didn't try to make excuses for her son.

"That was your child?" Mengliu knew he had asked a redundant question, but to push aside the surprise he was feeling, he quickly added a second question, "Those things . . . you just throw them away?"

"Things made of jewels and diamonds are just ornaments children wear to ward off evil." The woman in green started to put the dinner things away. "Let me clean up. If you'll wait for a while, we can have tea in the garden."

Mengliu bowed in her direction. From various details, he had deduced that this was a very well-mannered place, and so he, too, had become more courteous.

The garden was filled with the scent of flowers, and lots of fruit. They were green, red, yellow, round, long, flat—the greatest variety he had ever encountered. A hammock stretched between the trees alongside some lounge chairs. A stone table, carved with a multi-purpose playing board, was surrounded by four wicker chairs and two round stools. He sat in one of the chairs and watched Juli carry the tea things over. She was just like Chang'e, the famed Lady of the Moon.

"Along with their formal careers, all the people of Swan Valley learn a handicraft." She put the tea set down and opened the box of leaves. The scent of tea escaped from the box like a pack of demons. "I learned how to roast fermented tea over a fire, and how to pick the tea leaves myself. Those picked and brought back before rainfall have the best quality."

"It seems you get a lot of rain here in Swan Valley. I didn't know the weather was so important in tea-picking." Mengliu admired the cups and sniffed at the tea leaves with an affected panache, trying to demonstrate some level of expertise.

"I've heard that China's fermented tea is also pretty good. It has quite a long history there." She added plain hot water to rinse the tea set, put in more leaves, then brewed the first pot. "Our fermented tea comes from a different strain, but we use the same methods for preparation, heating, crumbling, soaking, and drying. It's not uncommon for us to store the tea in a cellar for more than five years before taking it out to drink. This has been kept for twenty years. Try it."

"I don't know much about tea. I like to drink sorghum spirit. Rice wine is also good."

"Swan Valley prohibits the consumption of spirits. Liquor is a source of trouble." She had made the tea and was waiting for its color to deepen.

Mengliu replied, "Alcohol is innocent. To put the blame on alcohol is like a conquered people putting the blame on women for the death of their country."

Juli said, "Your institution of marriage . . . "

"According to the law, it is one man, one wife. In reality, if a man's rich, he can have concubines, mistresses, bastard children."

She poured the tea into a small porcelain cup. The cup's surface glistened like jade against the golden hue of the tea. The aroma was light, though the tea was concentrated, and the bottom of the bowl was visible through the liquid.

The young woman was suddenly quiet, taking her tea very seriously.

"Have you seen an instrument like this before?" Mengliu pulled out his lady-charming chuixun.

Juli took the flute from him and inspected it for a while. "I know it's a *xun*, but it's the first time I've seen a real one. It looks very old. Oh! And your name is carved on it."

"Yes. It's an antique. At least six hundred years old."

"That's priceless. Where did you get it?" She returned the chuixun to him.

"My mom left it to me." It was the first time he had ever uttered this strange word "mom" in the presence of a woman he hardly knew. He was surprised by it. He almost went so far as to share his most personal information, that his mother had given him the instrument at the time when she abandoned him in his swaddling clothes.

To rescue himself from further embarrassment, he said, "You want to hear it?"

She nodded, and he began to play the soothing notes of his old favorite, "The Pain of Separation."

As he played the low, sad melody, the night fell quietly about them, as if the dark eyes of a multitude of small animals were peering from the shadows.

9

His bedroom was next to the garden. Its decor was simple and it smelled like it had been vacant for a long time. The smell of loneliness resembled that of a dried melon. But when Mengliu walked in, that smell disappeared, and the room became warm and pleasant. He paced slowly around it, a smile on his face, knowing that he already liked it here. He looked about him and noticed a moderately sized painting on the wall. It was of a white cathedral, its steeple covered in red tiles and its windows filled with gorgeous colorful images. The cathedral was surrounded by trees with golden leaves and white clouds billowing overhead. A bust of crude appearance sat on the wardrobe, its hair bristling and a rough beard curling beneath its protruding chin. Books rested on a small bookshelf, alongside a stack of blank paper. On the desk there was a framed photo, and the back of the frame bore the name Juan. Mengliu turned the frame around again and saw that the soldier had a commanding presence with his long face, deep-set eyes, bright teeth, and glossy dark skin, holding a hat under his arm. He was dressed in riding breeches and black boots, and his legs were very straight. He was young, about twenty-four or twenty-five.

His bedroom and that of the woman in green faced each other from opposite sides of the living room, which was filled with baskets of flowers. This put a fascinating distance of about fifteen meters between them. Mengliu left his door unlocked and stayed in his room for a while, but he did not sleep. He thought of the soldier in the photo. It must be Su Juli's husband. Was he alive or dead? How had he died? If he was alive, where was he? After a while, he became bored with these questions and picked up a book in English and flipped through it. His mind grew sluggish.

He lay on the bed. The sheets smelled of apples and his body felt like water spreading comfortably outward. He listened to the fruit swelling and the shoots popping out of the earth, like someone who was pulling a string and setting off a series of vibrations. Stirred by the wind, his orchard reached the climax of its symphony of sharp, bright, low, and short notes, all alternating in a pleasing mix of sound. After a soft adagio movement, the silence resumed.

Mengliu dreamed, and in his dream he saw three people playing basketball. It was a fierce contest, and when the ball fell into Hei Chun's hands, it turned into a pistol. Hei Chun pointed the pistol at him, forcing him all the way to the center of the court, where there was no way out. His assailant interrogated him, "Why didn't you participate in the poetry readings? Why don't you write poetry anymore? If a poet doesn't write poetry, what meaning is there to his life?" Bai Qiu suddenly appeared out of nowhere and blocked the pistol with his badly mangled face. His mouth was against the muzzle. He said repeatedly, "Poetry is no use; poetry isn't as fast as a bullet; poetry is not as cruel as the muzzle of a gun." Blood and tears flowed from Bai Qiu's empty eye sockets onto the muzzle of the gun. Blue smoke rose from the muzzle. The pistol turned into a white dove, its dark eyes looking gently at Mengliu. Seeing that the eyes were Qizi's, Mengliu's spirit soared. The dove circled the court a few times and with a cry rose into the sky, shooting upward like a bullet into the glare of the sun. People crowded around, looking at him contemptuously. He was so humiliated he wanted to die. His body became so light it left the earth, hovered in midair, then abruptly dropped to the ground.

When he awoke, he was drenched in sweat, even though his heart was chilled.

10

It was raining in Beiping. When the sun broke onto the scene, it warmed things up, and those who braved its heat soon had patches of sweat under their arms. They stripped off their jackets, showing off their physiques—strong, scrawny, stout, or slim—giving the spring a little more flourish.

Mengliu was in a bright mood as he cycled the ten miles to the Wisdom Bureau. He hovered at the entrance to the Physics Department library, a collection of poems clasped in his hand. He glanced over a few lines, then looked around. The peach tree in full bloom above his head occasionally let a few petals flutter down. He saw reflected in the building's glass facade his ruffled hair and finely chiseled features, and the beard he had specially trimmed for the occasion. His old black V-neck sweater was presentable enough, and his newly washed jeans had a slightly cloying soapy smell. They were a little long, so he had turned them up at the ankles, allowing the cuffs to rest on top of his canvas boating shoes.

To tell the truth, he was quite satisfied with his image.

Qizi was especially striking in the crowd. She wore a blue shirt with a gray skirt and black flat-soled boots. Her feet clacked as she walked down the steps of the library, clutching a large book to her bosom, blocking it from view. Her chin rested on the book, and it was clear she was lost in a state of mental and physical pleasure. Her skin was even fairer than it had been on the day of the procession, her short raven-black hair flowed around her face, and her slanting fringe especially captivated Mengliu. She was always so beautiful. He only learned later that the day they had met, she had just cut her hair. The way a girl wore her hair always had something to do with what was on her mind.

He stepped toward her and took the book from her arms. It was another book about physics. She was racking her brain over that machine of the future.

A group of young people walked by, laughing. They wore white T-shirts with the word "freedom" printed across their chests in black. Seeing Qizi, someone whistled cheekily. Mengliu smiled and raised his middle finger toward them.

"We're meeting Shunyu. She's got tickets to see a Chinese opera performance this afternoon at two," Qizi said, slapping his hand down.

"It's her father's idea, again. He worries too much. He's afraid she'll join in the march, so he gets her tickets to the ballet one day, a concert the next. This time it's a Chinese show." Mengliu shook his head, a wry smile on his face. "You and I won't understand it all. It's just a novelty, a way for us to have a good time. We'll have to make the best we can of it."

"Her father has good intentions. You're benefiting from them, but you act like it's a hardship. Don't you think you're being a little unkind?"

"Poor old man . . . We should hope that the unrest will go on for a while. Before it started he didn't even invite us to a movie. Once things settle down, that will be the end of our cultured lifestyle. I don't know if I could get used to that again!"

Qizi smiled and pinched him. "I've heard that a lot of people in Round Square have fainted from hunger. If the hunger strike costs someone their life, they'll be paying too high a price."

"Are they really going without food and water? That's playing too straight . . . They should sneak a bite, or is just sitting there quietly not eating or drinking supposed to be performance art?"

"You're talking nonsense again." She looked at her watch. "It's still two or three hours before the show. Where do you want to go?"

"Do you want to come back to the West Wing with me?" Mengliu blurted out. "You'll have to prepare yourself. It's a mess."

When he and Qizi appeared in the bar later, they were holding hands and kissing. Love blew on the spring breeze, and their happiness was like flowers bursting into bloom. It was as if their earlier intimacy at his place had propelled them all the way to the bar.

"Hasn't that plant ever known a woman's touch?" Qizi had been hit by bird droppings when she first stepped into the courtyard, and so had changed into one of Mengliu's thin sweaters. She stood in the doorway, her posture open and relaxed, watching him wash the bird shit off her clothing. She turned to the half-dead rose bush on the windowsill and started to toy with it, poking it here and there with a stick she had found.

"No. It has never flowered." The old acacia tree flourished in the courtyard. Mengliu hung the blouse out to dry, causing the wire to shake.

"Really?"

"Really."

"I'm the first?"

"You're the first."

Satisfied, she smiled. "Don't worry, I'll get it to bloom with fiery red flowers."

"What makes you so sure they'll be red?"

"I want them to be red. It's the color of passion."

"I like white ones. They're pure."

"Let's bet on it."

"Bet what?"

She leaned over and whispered a private message in his ear. Her words filled him with joy—a joy that lasted many years.

He took her and carried her back into the room. They made out for a long time, which made them burn with desire, but they conquered their carnal nature, and their hearts were filled with a sacred purity. He knew she was his, and he was hers. They belonged to each other.

"It looks like I'll have to wear your sweater to the show. It's so embarrassing. Shunyu is sure to laugh at me."

"She'll just be jealous that you're wearing your boyfriend's clothes . . . " He kissed her. "Ever since Shunyu went into the Plum Party, it's as if she's been brainwashed."

"She's still herself. If we don't go abroad, let's apply to join the Party too. What do you think?"

"I won't. I'm a poet. Poets have to be independent and free, without connections to friends or parties . . . But of course, I won't object to whatever you decide to do."

"I guess I can't put it off. To tell the truth, for scientific research, the environment overseas is a hundred times better. If our country were rich and powerful, everyone would be scrambling to come here. We wouldn't need to go anywhere else."

The sun fell on top of the acacia tree. A bird with a white head twittered in the trees. Patches of sunlight and bird droppings filled the courtyard.

A scarlet curtain was draped across the stage, with several spotlights shining on it. The café offered an array of snacks. The waiter moved to and fro between the tables, adding water to the teapots. After finding a good seat, Qizi downed half of her tea in one gulp. Mengliu focused on the playbill. It read *Lady Zhaojun*.

Just as he asked why Shunyu had not yet arrived, he looked up to see her lifting the bead curtain at the entrance and walking through it to meet them. She wore a Chinese-style outfit topped with a thin jacket lined with embroidery. It made her look like one of the actors.

From behind the curtain on the stage, the big gong boomed, accompanied by tinkles on the smaller gong, marking the beginning of the performance. They watched the actor spin in a full scarlet cloak, pheasant feathers in her hand, her arms snowy white and her costume shimmering. They were captivated by the glamorous apparel.

But that was all there was to it. Before long, the spectacle became boring.

"Traffic in Beiping has been blocked and the city is practically in a state of siege. I made a detour on a trishaw to tell you the news. Reports on the double-tracked wall say that people in the square will soon pass out from hunger. They are in urgent need of bread and water." Shunyu leaned in toward the center of the table and whispered. "The troublesome shit . . . Maybe there really is a monster out there."

Qizi waited for the actor to finish singing the line, "Even a huge pool of civilians is no use, and all the generals fight in vain," then asked whether anyone had sent food over. Shunyu said she didn't know. She had finished reading the news on the wall and then come straight to the theater.

The actress held a horse whip and walked swiftly onstage. She struck a pose, her gaze determined and the pheasant feathers in her hair quivering ceaselessly.

Mengliu, pretending to be very committed, would have rather stayed where he was and be bored than go and plunge into the events in Round Square.

"Are they all from the Wisdom Bureau?" Qizi rolled the playbill up into a cylinder, using it like a telescope.

"Most are. My father said something really bad is going to happen."

The actor sang to the climax, struck a pose, and won loud applause from the audience. When the scene came to an end, the scarlet curtain closed. The café burst into a small commotion.

The curtain reopened to the pathos of an *erhu* being played over a snowy background. At this point, Qizi and Mengliu abandoned Shunyu and left the theater.

"When we go abroad, don't get any funny ideas—not even out of curiosity—about those foreign girls. You can look once, or at most twice, and for no longer than two seconds. If it's more than two seconds, it means you've got some funny ideas in your head. If you've got those ideas, then just go with them. I won't stop you. But it'll be over between us."

Clumps of trees grew by the roadside. A well-proportioned foreign girl, fresh as spring, walked by with her breasts showing in a provocative fashion. Qizi, watching her as she passed one tree after another, elbowed Mengliu and said, "Hey! Did you hear what I said?"

"You're telling me what isn't allowed, while you're blatantly doing what I'm not supposed to do. Whatever you look at I can look at too." He purposely stared at the foreign girl for a good while longer. "Well . . . she's still not as cute as our girls."

"No double talk from you. I should wring your neck."

"I'm just trying to make a responsible, detailed observation. If I don't look carefully, how can I give an accurate analysis?"

"You're such a horny little thing."

"If I wasn't horny, how would I have been attracted to you?"

When they got back to the West Wing, Mengliu pulled a wallet from underneath his mattress, took out a few notes, thought for a second, then took out the whole lot, saying he would have to tighten his belt for a while. He put the money into his pocket, took Qizi by the hand, and they went to the supermarket to buy bread and water. From there, they went straight to Round Square.

Wherever they looked, the streets were packed with people. There was garbage all over the place.

A banner hung on a truck painted in bright colors. It read "Brothel Support Group." The bed of the truck was filled with prostitutes, all richly attired and heavily made up. They leaned over the sides, waving colorful handkerchiefs and calling cheekily, "Come on, gentlemen! If you've got money, spend it. If you have strength, then spend that. It's all in support of the Wisdom Bureau. Come on now!"

At the same time, they distributed scented flyers. "The feces issue is a hoax. The people demand the truth . . . Protest by petition, not by violence."

A voluptuous prostitute hung onto Mengliu and said earnestly, "Mister, dedicate your passion to the cause. Fifty *kuai* each time. Just put your money in the donation box . . . We can do it in the cab . . . Or we can go to a hotel if you want."

"Er, just fifty . . . to support . . ." Embarrassed, Mengliu remained deeply affected as he walked on. It took him a long time to settle down again. His mind kept going back to the prostitute's words. Why did she say it was in support of the Wisdom Bureau? Could it be that the Bureau had taken an important role in the rally?

As he pondered, he ran across another team, the "Writers' Support Group." In direct contrast to the prostitutes, they sat smoking, chatting, and casually wiling away their time among themselves.

One young fellow sporting a red bandana was carrying a banner across his body that practically screamed, "I am Yuan Mengliu!"

Mengliu walked over and asked, "Are you really Yuan Mengliu?"

The fellow ignored him.

Mengliu said, "I'm Yuan Mengliu."

The guy took a long, disdainful look at him. "Dude, stop pretending! Just take the opportunity to have a good time."

Mengliu and Qizi exchanged glances, then burst into laughter.

As they made their way through the crowd, it parted like water, then closed again.

In the square, Hei Chun stood, dressed in a black trench coat and with his legs splayed. His hair was tied in a ponytail, revealing the word "love" written across his forehead in red ink. As the ink dripped down his face like blood, he recited his new poem.

It's time, young people,
to let loose and sing!

Take your pain, your love
and spill it all on the page.
Don't hide your feelings of injustice
indignation and sorrow—
let the pain and joy in your heart
come out and be seen in the daylight!

In the face of your critics,
their accusations pelt you like rain
—only then will new growth sprout,
fearless in the sun's light!

My verse is a torch,
burning down all the world's barriers.

There was warm applause that lasted a long time. Some people took photos, some shouted, others whistled and threw hats, shoes, or empty bottles in the air.

The air was polluted, a mix of many different odors. Dizzy and headachy, Mengliu and Qizi went to an open space for fresh air. Then they saw a commotion breaking out, people running, shouting, and falling over one another. Suddenly all hell broke loose. The pair backed onto the sidewalk and sheltered by a tree trunk. They managed not to be separated by the crowd.

At that moment they saw people walking arm in arm, forming a tight horizontal line spread across the street to the walls of the buildings on either side. Like a bulldozer, the line advanced, occasionally issuing a brief, dignified cry. About ten meters behind them, another line of people followed, advancing in identical fashion. As they moved forward in unison, the street cleared. The afternoon sun fell serenely on the scene. In the distance, the boundless sky stretched as far as the eye could see.

11

Mengliu remembered very clearly how his newly appointed surgical assistant had taken the initiative to ask him to lunch that day. He had even gone out to the mall the night before and bought a new pair of red boxers—a girl had once said that when he wore red boxer shorts, it gave him an air of gentleness mingled with a ravaging sexiness, and he had taken it to heart. After that, he went to the salon for a haircut, shave, earwax removal, and trimming of his nose hairs. His nose hairs had never needed to be trimmed before. His overzealous approach illustrated just how important the date was to him. It was the first time since his relationship with Qizi had ended all those years ago that he had taken a date—or a girl—so seriously. He made a ritual of cleaning himself, taking longer than he ever had before. He cleansed himself inside and out and, just for the sake of it, abstained from eating garlic. But still his mind floated to Qizi, and he kept confusing her with Suitang. He even found himself wondering if Suitang might be an assumed name under which Qizi had come to test him.

He dug out a designer suit he'd worn the year he attended a medical school exchange program, matching it with a good shirt and tie, and polished his shoes. He remembered how he had once elegantly laid a young foreign girl face down on his bed, caressing her back, simply because it reminded him of Qizi's petite, pliable form. Just before going out the door, he changed everything, except the red boxers, taking pains to dress in a manner more in keeping with his professional standing. He was now dressed casually in sports shoes, white shirt under a black jacket, light gray trousers, and a subdued expression.

That day, Suitang similarly came without makeup, looking simple and pure. She was one of those girls who was all the more eye-catching in the simplest attire, like a pearl just pulled out of the water. The left side of her hair had a fiery red hairpin clipped to it. This tiny, seductive dot made Mengliu think of a widow dressed in black with a white flower pinned to her breast, but he quickly wiped that inauspicious image from his mind.

It was the first time Mengliu had gone to the restaurant. The waitress was dressed like a flight attendant, her face as welcoming as a spring breeze, eyes as brilliant as peach blossoms, her curves churning like waves, her mouth as fresh as the scent from a basket of flowers. She was respectful, caring, and humble—almost ingratiating—at every moment trying to satisfy the vanity of her customers. The charming waitress, knowing it was Mengliu's first visit, introduced him with a high degree of professionalism to the quality of their steaks, which were better than those he would find elsewhere. In their restaurant, meat from a single cow was served to only six patrons, and only the sixth and eighth ribs were selected, and after soaking for three days and three nights in the chef's special marinade, cooked over a fire.

"Do you know who our chef is? He is Chef Xieyong, who was employed by—!" The charming waitress uttered an intimidating name.

Mengliu asked what was so special about the sixth and eighth ribs. The girl smiled, her look as mysterious as God's would have been when creating humankind.

The French bread arrived on a luxurious covered tray, with little pieces of goose liver floating in glasses of wine, like beautiful girls lying on red velvet couches. The portions looked like they had been measured out for a cat, but it was all gorgeous and its extravagance was a feast for the eyes. They opened a bottle of Black Label whisky, poured it over ice, and slowly sipped at it. Suitang's pale skin gained a rosy blush.

The steak was delayed. Mengliu and Suitang's conversation sputtered. They talked on and off, sometimes seeming very close and sometimes very distant. The few topics they tried had short life spans, either because she killed them or because he couldn't manage to keep the talk up. Mengliu's eyes fell often to Suitang's cleavage. To call it cleavage, however, is only to describe his fantasy of it. In fact, only her collarbone was visible to him, slim and exquisite, just like the two curves of a peach on a canvas, inviting someone to add a few artistic strokes to it. Their conversation didn't wander beyond the confines of the hospital, and from beginning to end, everything was somehow connected to illness. Of course, everyone has their own circle of interest, and those inside the circle rarely talk about anything outside of it. Politics, war, economics, nuclear weapons . . . it was clear Suitang was not interested in those things. Mengliu had a feeling that there might be words sitting in Suitang's mouth, just waiting for her to find the right time to spit them out.

Finally the waitress came to them, poised as she swung her hips, balancing the plates. She arranged their forks and knives, gracefully poured the black pepper and onion sauces onto the few pieces of beef, her movements elaborate as those of an opera singer.

She asked, "Would you like me to cut it for you?" Upon hearing Suitang's reply, she set about with an impressive exhibition of swordplay, reminiscent of the murderous landlady Sun Erniang in Shi Nai'an's novel *Water Margin*. The knife whizzed as she attacked the meat, slicing through the flesh and leaving it in a pool of gravy.

Mengliu tasted one of the slices. When he offered his heartfelt praise, the waitress's chest swelled all the more with her pride.

The blues played in the background, mournful as a dying patient, the lingering phrases long and drawn out.

A man and woman sat at the table next to them, neither speaking to the other. They sat gloomily puffing on their cigarettes.

Several businessmen chatted on the other side. Their eyes also slipped slyly toward Mengliu's table to catch a glimpse of Suitang's collarbone.

When the waitress came to collect their plates, Suitang glanced at her retreating rear, wiped her mouth, and said, "Before, there was a man who always brought me here. I never got tired of the food, despite coming so often. Every time we ate, it was like tasting the food for the first time. I began to wonder whether they added opium to it."

"When love is sweet, the appetite will be good. In many senses, love is like a drug," Mengliu said casually, then sat silently, waiting to hear the man's name.

"I was pampered by him. He let me have my way in everything."

"A woman should be pampered."

"But there was one thing—"

"What thing?"

"Marriage."

"You were a mistress?"

"No, I was a third party."

"There's not much difference."

"There is a difference. A mistress is willing to stay a mistress. A third party has to work much harder to become a wife."

"When you put it like that, it makes sense."

"Shouldn't this also be considered as love? Is there really a need to brand us as fornicating dogs?"

"With love, you can never really say. As far as I know, the breakup of marriages is at an all-time high. That should be good news for a third party."

"He's got too much money. Divorce would bankrupt him."

"Maybe love will mean more to him than money."

"You tell me, do you think he loves me?"

"Maybe he's not even sure himself."

"Well, if he doesn't care for my feelings, I'm certainly not going to be the one to let things go. He thinks he's the king, a monarch who can bestow favors on whomever he pleases, a little here and a little there, so everyone will be happy and will remain loyal to him without any will of their own."

Does this mean Suitang is one of those women who loves revolution? Mengliu thought. But to Suitang he only said, "In times of revolution, one must revolt. The rebel has no choice but to rebel. But what will you use in your revolution? What sort of bargaining chip do you have? If his marriage is solid, then your attempts to break it will be like throwing eggs against a rock. Haven't you had enough of such teachings?"

"You mean all I can do is be led around by the nose? I'm a human, you know!" Suitang looked just then like a human rights crusader.

"That's right, you are human, but if you threaten his security, his benefits, his happiness, he'll have no choice but to cut you off and wash his hands of you."

"So now you're speaking up for him? You men, you always look out for each other's interests."

"To tell the truth, I've never been married and I don't know how married men think. But I do know that whether a person does good or bad . . . either way, it's natural and normal."

"Mengliu, do you think you're here to give me a lecture me about the Confucian Golden Mean? You've got no middle ground, only vul . . . vulgarity, no moral standing, no character. Surely you've been in love before."

Suitang's words were sharp as a sword. Overwhelmed, Mengliu paused for a moment, slumped back in his chair, and said weakly, "Of course. I've been in love. And I've been hurt. Heartbroken."

When he had finished, he straightened up again and took a sip of wine to wet his throat, as if he was preparing to let the whole story spill out.

Suitang's brow tightened. She stared at him strangely, as if a horn had sprouted from his forehead.

"Go on," she said, stealing another glance at him.

"With what?"

"Your love story."

"Even if I go on, you won't understand."

"You're so self-righteous. But, if Jia Wan hadn't overtaken you, maybe . . . " Suitang's tone was as casual as if she were polishing a nail, and just as casually, she unwrapped a piece of chewing gum and shoved it into her mouth.

"Jia Wan . . . ? That celebrity?"

Of course Mengliu was familiar with Jia Wan. In the year of the Tower Incident, just as spring turned to summer, the atmosphere had been tense as a guitar string. It took very little in such a charged setting to trigger an incident. Summer came early, withering the new leaves and buds, which were growing together on the same tree. At that time, there were poetry readings everywhere, with a major event happening every few days. The double-tracked wall at the Wisdom Bureau often attracted a crowd. On the trees, the wall, the iron railing—practically even hanging from the roofs—there were people everywhere you looked. As they recited Neruda, Miłosz, Whitman, Tagore, Jia Wan often made an appearance as well.

"Doctors are always getting involved with patients. How much do you know about him?" Mengliu asked.

"I have an in-depth understanding." She emphasized the word "in-depth."

"Strictly speaking, Jia Wan is not a poet."

"You're just jealous."

Mengliu did not say anything. He had never liked Jia Wan's poetry, and he liked the person even less.

"Of course, he couldn't compete with any of you. I've collected the poems of the Three Musketeers from the newspapers, and I've listened to your readings. Your poetry is like Whitman's . . . or *was*. Why did you stop writing poetry?" Suitang let him off.

"Whitman? Times have changed."

"'One's-self I sing—a simple, separate Person; Yet utter the word Democratic, the word *En-masse*.'" She recited a few lines. "Poetry will not hinder your life. When I chose to be your assistant, it was because I liked your poetry. It's a shame. If you don't write poetry anymore, don't you feel it's a waste?"

As she spoke, she smiled sweetly and tilted her head. The red hairpin flashed, catching the light's glare, and suddenly it was as if the sky were on fire. There was gunfire, fighting, killing, blood, tank-tracks rolling, and smoke.

Suitang smiled through the bloody scene. In consternation, Mengliu sat without making a sound. His expression resembled Round Square after it had been washed clean, and was suffused with a moist sheen of sorrow.

Driven by complex emotional forces, Mengliu left the Wisdom Bureau, went to medical school, and became a doctor. He intentionally distanced himself from his old acquaintances and soon lost contact with them. After that, he didn't form any new relationships. Patients, on the other hand, he had in abundance. They trusted him. In times of illness, patients and their families tried to curry favor with him. Their enthusiasm was often rewarded with a cure. Mengliu grew accustomed to the life. Occasionally someone would report him, accuse him of having a bad lifestyle. They especially questioned his past, pointing to some hidden errant political activity. Of course, that was all a load of rubbish. Even when they tried to get to the bottom of it, other than finding out that he had been quite a good poet, no one could come up with any kind of evidence.

All the same, he realized finally that sometimes you had to sell your soul to maintain your innocence. Being "without incident" didn't mean he hadn't had any pleasure or glory. He'd even endured some suffering. His leather-covered diary contained this entry: "I think that there is no such thing as a healthy person. The heartbeat of one person may thump in the chest of another. Some only have half a liver or one kidney. Some people are without uterus or breasts. Some are bald. Most have no conscience, and many are utterly wicked. The lungs of even the most upright person may be coated with oil like a kitchen stove . . . Even so, they will not, for the sake of some gain, give up the fight. They want to dominate others, they want love and sex, they want to take control of their lives and seem normal. I include myself in this. I'm a coward, just dragging out an ignoble existence, a louse lying on the gigantic body of the nation."

Sandwiched between the pages of his diary was a photo of the Three Musketeers. In the picture, Bai Qiu's arms were crossed over his chest, the very image of an independent, eccentric spirit, with a sort of uncertain, confused look in his eyes. A renowned literary critic once said of

Bai Qiu's poems that he heard a trumpet sounding in his lines, which was perhaps the most poetic appraisal that could be made of them at that time. Bai Qiu had an innate fascination with the grave, and his poetry was full of death, corpses, skulls, and other such imagery. For him, death was not something that came by chance.

On the afternoon of the dissolution of the Dayang Poets' Society, all five or six of its members slunk off to the Green Flower to drink in the gloom. Up until then Bai Qiu's poetry had merely served as criticism or warning, and it had not been appropriated by people who operated with ulterior motives. Now it was all completely banned—though the word "banned" may be too politically charged. To put it more precisely, no media source would publish his work. The editors stammered and stuttered, dodging behind various pretexts. Even those intellectuals who had previously valued Bai Qiu's poetry quite highly now began to have reservations.

"Hey, Boss, I've come to recite some poetry. Can you send a jug of wine over?" Bai Qiu said to the proprietor, as if nothing were out of the ordinary. He took a slim little notebook from his pocket. In it were three poems he had just composed. It was exciting then to listen to a poet recite his work, and many in the audience counted it an honor to have their photos taken with him. Poets were like movie stars. If a poet tried to board a train without a ticket, the conductor was likely to let it pass in exchange for an autograph. He would even try to arrange a comfortable seat for him, free of charge.

"The jug of wine is no problem, but please don't recite poetry here," Shunyu's father answered, surprising them. Everyone took it as a joke.

A few days later on a hot rainy afternoon, all sorts of rumors were circulating, and it was hard to verify which were true. Bai Qiu invited Mengliu to travel back with him to his village. On the train, he spoke at length about poetry, saying that death was the best subject matter for it. The next day just as the sun rose, they reached their destination. They walked along the narrow country lane, noting all the peaceful details of the village. Dewdrops formed on the tips of the grass, the vegetables and crops grew plump and full, the chickens and dogs were content. In the midst of this tranquil scene, a peasant woman sat at her door feeding her infant, her powdery white breast announcing that the world was sweet as a dream. The dream was limited, however, to this remote village. Mengliu had no inkling that this would be Bai Qiu's final farewell to him.

12

Wrapped around the outer wall and roof of the house were many creepers. In front of the windows, where there was no surface to attach themselves to, the creepers gave way to stalks of rattan, their shadows dancing along the floor as they swayed in the breeze. The faint fragrance of flowers floated all over the house. The window frames, timber doors, and the different pieces of furniture were carved with complex patterns, flowers, birds, fish, all sorts of living creatures, each showing traces of the Chinese Ming-Qing style. A pair of lion snouts with rings through their noses served as door handles on the wardrobe in the living room, looking dull and cold. The doors opened at Mengliu's touch, releasing the scent of sandalwood. He found himself faced suddenly with a hidden library set in a recess in the wall, with books placed neatly on the bookshelves and arranged according to categories. This huge library took his breath away. Some of the books' covers had been repaired, and others wrapped in craft paper. It looked as if they had been handled with great care, like the care a wounded soldier would receive from a nurse. They were arranged in terms of history, politics, literature, and philosophy, with not a single extraneous title grandstanding there among them. There was one work in the original English version. It was Su Juli's doctoral dissertation, and it was very thick.

When Mengliu had looked the dissertation over for a while, he felt a tightening in his chest and shortness of breath. Seeing that the window was closed, he pushed it open. The fresh breeze buzzed into the room like a group of lively young girls. He almost thought he could hear their laughter as they frolicked.

Feeling a little more comfortable, he looked out the window at the beautifully delineated landscape. Above was a pale blue sky without a cloud in it. A touch of snow covered the expansive green mountains, which were skirted with a thin fog. The color of the trees was well distributed too, growing in light yellows along the slopes, orange at the peak, and green near the base of the mountains. Most beautiful of all was the river flowing at the foot of the scene, a bright, sparkling ribbon—for Juli had rolled up her skirt and was wading in the water. Her smooth legs seemed to wade right into Mengliu's heart. He settled his elbows on the windowsill, rested his chin on his arms, and enjoyed the moving sight of her figure.

He saw her hair, with drops of mist clinging to it, and glimpsed the shape of her body through the sheer skirt as it dragged in the water. The light shone on her, highlighting the fresh round breasts that hung from her body. Due to the weight of the fruit it bore, her slender waist seemed especially pliable and strong, as she bent over and straightened up. As the skirt brushed against her skin it showed the curve of her buttocks. In this way, her shapely form rose and fell as she rinsed out the laundry with her hands.

"You aren't supposed to open the windows. The books will get damp." A voice emerged from the corner of the room.

Mengliu flinched, and the lust he'd harbored inside him leapt out of the window like a startled cat. He turned and saw a tiny figure sitting on the floor in the corner.

"Oh, Shanlai, you little scholar . . . what's that you're reading?" Mengliu closed the window, though the tender feeling inside him hadn't quite cooled. His theatrical tone was gentle and pleasing to him, and he instinctively felt that this was his chance to initiate a positive relationship with the raccoon-like child.

The little fellow propped the book on his knees, nearly covering his whole body. He didn't say a word.

"You want to learn to speak a foreign language? I understand some Chinese, Japanese, and French. I used to write poetry, then . . . "

"Poetry isn't something just anyone can write." The little raccoon, beady eyes fixed on the book, continued arrogantly, "It's much easier to be a doctor."

"You're right. It's not just anyone who can write poetry. You put it very well . . . Many people aren't suited to be poets. They would only tarnish poetry." Mengliu drew his right hand into a fist, stuck his thumb into his hair, and casually scratched his scalp.

"So are you not suitable to be a poet? Do you tarnish poetry?" The child turned to the next page of the book as he spoke.

"No, it wasn't like that. No . . . well, all right, let me tell you. I had two good friends who wrote poetry, and together the three of us were known as the Three Musketeers. Then, one died, and the other went missing . . . You tell me, what could I write after that? There's an old phrase, 'burning a lute to cook a crane.' If you do that, what's left that's worth writing? You don't understand, but I feel that everything is empty. What's the use of poetry?" Mengliu mumbled, but continued on, lost in his own ramblings. "For instance, say there's a horse-drawn carriage. If the horse falls, the wheels also fall from the cart. How can it move anymore? Where would it go? It won't go anywhere. It can't express anything . . . especially since when they needed me, I didn't stand with them . . . There's a sort of loneliness that you can't understand . . . "

Mengliu talked about the most enjoyable times with the Three Musketeers, the salons, the readings, the debates, and the beautiful girls . . . Unfortunately, the Tower Incident had ruined it all.

"Hei Chun wasn't handsome, but he had a certain charm. He was a bit like an ape, with a prominent forehead and loose, coarse hair. He played basketball pretty well. But the main thing was his poetry. Sometimes it was like a flame, burning you all over suddenly. Of the three of us, he was the only one without glasses. He had good vision, and strong teeth too. He could always see right to the essence of things, and his teeth seemed capable of cutting through anything, no matter how hard. He was decisive, and efficient. To illustrate, if someone slow to anger or with a soft temperament is a rowing boat, Hei Chun was like a speedboat, crossing the water in a burst of spray. He wrote poetry, read philosophy, and studied politics. He liked Rousseau, Plato . . . He fingered the pages of Thomas More's *Utopia* until the book was as fluffy as if yeast had been added.

"He said if he were president, he'd make sure everyone had food and clothes, not just an example here and there, when there is such disparity between rich and poor. If he were king he would govern by a system of virtue and punishment. Rebels would be cut down, and the law-abiding would be rewarded. The forms of punishment used in ancient times should not be discarded. He would bring back the old punishments like dismemberment, drawing and quartering, disemboweling, flaying of the skin, boiling in oil . . . For officials who committed petty theft or small-scale corruption, he would punish them with permanent scarring . . . Anyway, when he had some free time, he intended to write a book called *The Genetic Code of the City-State*. He said he would create a template for a city-state with excellent genes, and implement the reign of virtue . . . Sometimes, we would talk about criminal law, institutions, democracy, freedom, and so forth, talking until the middle of the night. Sometimes we carried on until well into the next day. Heh . . . I said that in his heart of hearts, he was a tyrant. Of course, the nature of one's blood—hot or cold, sticky or dense—is nourished by one's natural environment and the climate. All of us born in the '60s were born with a sense of responsibility, of throwing in our lot with that of the nation. We were born for hardship . . . Those who came after us were more individualistic, with nothing inside them except a desire for material gain. They were heartless. Then again, moral standards had stabilized by then, and the economy was more developed, the country bigger and stronger, and the people had grown fatter. It's only natural that the people felt they had nothing to worry about."

13

The canteen in the Wisdom Bureau wasn't the normal noisy sort of cafeteria. The food didn't look good, and the staff wore no expressions under their white caps. The ladle scooping the food was always precise—no matter how tasteless and bland the food was you couldn't expect to get a generous portion from that ladle. As a result of eating the canteen's food your appetite grew larger, and eating more left you feeling hungrier than ever. You grew hungrier, in fact, from eating there than from forgoing food altogether. Even the girls couldn't be bothered with good manners. Only Shunyu thought the canteen's food was all right. She especially loved the braised pork, saying it was even better there than in her father's bar.

The queue moved slowly. The only sound was the banging of metal on metal, like ping-pong balls bouncing back and forth, as the staff knocked their ladles against the edge of each plate after asking loudly, "Do you want *baozi* or *mantou*? ribs or braised pork?" The faces of the white-clothed, white-capped workers shone with an oily sheen. There was even more grease on their faces than on the food. Wearing plastic gloves, they proudly ladled out the food, scratched their chins, and handled the meal tickets. Rats' tails, dead cockroaches, wire, grass clippings, and hair were found regularly in the food, but for the young diners it was just business as usual as they made their way through the long queue.

The food at lunch was better than at dinner, when it was mostly leftovers. Meals on the weekends were simpler, since many students traveled home and others went out to restaurants. Only a few remained for the canteen to deal with, most of them "country folk" and some from a background of poverty. They insisted on eating *mantou,* or maybe pickled vegetables with rice. Putting all their efforts into their studies, they could often be found at the library, sitting until their legs were numb. They rarely went out.

The midday sun beat on the cherry trees, the flowers had already dropped from the branches, and the leaves were all new and shiny. Mengliu had just gotten his meal and was sitting by the window. The glass was covered with a layer of dust, forming a halo around the glaring sun. When he'd taken a couple of bites, he saw Shunyu walking toward him. She sat her tray down, took a seat, and said, "How come you're having tofu and spring onions again? Here, take some of my braised pork."

She was wearing a long-sleeved white silk shirt and a low-collared black cashmere Chinese-style unlined jacket, secured by silk ribbons tied in a bow at her chest. Her hair cascaded over her shoulders and almost into her plate. She used a finger to slip a hair band off her wrist and pulled her hair back into a bun, all in one neat movement.

"Your braised pork? You shouldn't try to bribe me. I don't know anything about what Hei Chun has been up to." Mengliu laughed. "These past few days I've seen him in the square writing poetry. He looked a little deranged."

Shunyu replied, "Don't secondguess my intentions. I saw you sitting here alone looking bored, so I came over to keep you company. Anyway, I'm also a part of the Dayang Poets' Society and share its joys and sorrows. If you feel you owe me, you can dedicate a poem to me some day."

"When it comes to writing poetry for pretty girls, Hei Chun is much better at it than I am."

Shunyu gritted her teeth and appeared ready to beat Mengliu over the head with her chopsticks.

"The most beautiful thing about you is that pair of canines."

"Don't talk nonsense. Do you think Hei Chun will get arrested? He would have to go back to sleep at the dorm, wouldn't he?"

"Even if he gets picked up, it's nothing to worry about. You go and check on him tonight. I bet he will be in his bed snoring."

"I'm just asking. I don't really care. It's not my business. He's so busy, he doesn't have time to waste looking after anyone else."

"Well, look who's showing her temper again! I'll organize a little dinner party to create an opportunity for you. After that, it'll all be up to you."

Shunyu glared at Mengliu, then took the braised pork from her plate and plopped it onto his.

Just as Mengliu finished up and was scraping his plate, Qizi came into the cafeteria. He waved to her. Her pale face suddenly turned an angry scarlet. She marched over to him, scattering everything in her path.

"Yuan Mengliu, please explain what's going on!"

As she said his name, she raised a hand and dropped a piece of paper onto his tray. It had apparently been torn from the double-tracked wall, and the glue still stuck to it. There were tears in her eyes.

Mengliu's mind was in a haze. He picked up the paper and looked it over. It was a list of activists in the Wisdom Bureau, the so-called

Core Group Unit, and his name was included. He was stunned. Then, in some confusion, he stood up and said, "What is this? I really have no idea what is going on!"

Qizi retorted, "You're lying! If you didn't agree to join the rally, why would they add your name to the list?"

Mengliu couldn't utter a word, but inside he was overwhelmed by a new sort of joy—as if his talent was being recognized—and also a little vanity. In no hurry to justify himself, he humored Qizi. "It must be that those sons of bitches liked what I had to say, and so they thought they'd just act first and then consult me later. They're a bunch of jokers. They play an autocratic hand, shouting about democracy all the while."

"You're still lying to me. How long are you going to keep on with this deception?" Qizi had raised her voice.

Shunyu tugged at her, signaling that perhaps the pair should move somewhere else and try to talk reasonably.

Qizi wore a brown hooded pullover that fell over her buttocks, brown canvas sneakers, and black tights, which made her legs look as scrawny as a little chick's. She walked along the green belt, a lonely and lost figure with tears rolling down her cheeks.

"If you really want to join the rally," she said, tears still falling, "at least you should discuss the matter with me."

"I never thought . . . I just gave them a few suggestions. I didn't expect them to . . . " Mengliu said softly.

"You know my father will be the first to object, and my mother will certainly stand by him. It will be no use trying to explain it to them."

"I won't join. I'll do whatever you want me to." Mengliu went to embrace Qizi but was pushed away.

"You wanted to go. Early on, I could already tell."

"If I wanted to go, I'd be a son of a bitch."

"You are a son of a bitch, so you wanted to go."

"What is going on here? I really don't know what I can say to you."

" . . . You lied to me. I can't trust you anymore."

"How come you sound like a housewife? So unreasonable, and so demanding?"

"Me? I'm just crude. Not good enough for an elegant poet like you . . . Let's end it here." Qizi, really angry now, jerked her arm from him and walked away.

Mengliu caught up with her. "Qizi, listen . . . No matter what, you have to believe me . . . "

They walked noisily along the path, tugging and pulling at each other. As he continued to explain himself, Qizi's anger faded a little. They reached a vine-covered walkway, but the long bench there was already taken by another couple, so they walked through to the lake. They sat on the grassy bank. A few young lotus leaves, not yet fully flourishing, hovered over the water, and the mandarin ducks swam between them.

"Qizi, when you get angry, my foot hurts." He showed her where he had twisted his ankle while teaching her to skate. He took her hand and went to place it on the injured part. When he saw that his sock was dirty, he put her hand back where he had taken it from.

In spite of his best efforts at humor, she would not laugh. The shimmer of the waves reflected on her face as she stared at the surface of the water, looking like she was about to make a momentous decision. Tears flowed continuously down to the tip of her nose and then dropped onto the back of her hand.

"Qizi, I've really been wronged. I'm really furious with those sons of bitches. It must be Hei Chun's doing. I'll go find them and tell them to take my name off the list, and I'll tell them that if they mess with me again, they better watch it."

Mengliu stood up. Qizi grabbed at him. Still looking at the surface of the lake, she wiped the tears from the tip of her nose.

"You ask other people to take this risk, but then you're so faint-hearted yourself. Aren't you ashamed?" She suddenly looked up and stared at him. "You can't say one thing and do another. There is no way out."

"I didn't say one thing and do another. You know I won't join an organization. Don't worry. I'll turn it down. I've still got a lot that I want to do."

"It's no use turning it down. Maybe you're already being monitored."

"Right now, I just want to kiss you. Let them watch us through whatever telescope or binoculars they want to use." He embraced her.

"We're finished," she said feebly.

"What do you mean?"

"Over."

"Breaking up?"

"Yes."

"Why?"

"There's no future for us . . . anyway, I want to leave the country."

"Of course. But Qizi, we planned to do that together."

"What I do is none of your business."

"You're my future wife!" He took her hand and pulled her around to face him. "Qizi, nothing is as important to me as you are. I don't want to lose you. I'll go and clear it up with them right now."

As she looked at him she slowly moved into his embrace. "I don't want to lose you either . . . I want to be with you."

As she buried her face in his chest, the friction between them sparked promises of love. The sparks lit up their faces and eyes like the midday sun. They looked at each other, eyes locked together, oblivious to everything around them. He held her tightly to him, as if he wanted to press her through his skin and into his internal organs.

He leaned down and kissed her hard, and everything between them was renewed in the kiss.

"I want to hear you play 'The Pain of Separation' again," Qizi said.

"I didn't bring it." His mouth was unwilling to do anything but kiss her.

She reached into his trouser pocket and pulled out the xun. "Everyone knows. Wherever you go, the flute is with you."

"Can't we do a different song?" he asked. He was thinking to himself, *We're so good together, why would we want the pain of separation?*

"No, play that one. It's my favorite."

"Why don't I teach you? It's actually very simple."

"I don't want to learn. I just want to hear you play."

"What's my reward?"

"See how well you play."

"First, just one kiss."

14

In his desire to speak to the little raccoon, Mengliu lost control of himself, as if he'd just run into an old friend he had not seen for years. He did not hope for any response from the child but simply said what was on his mind. It was like opening a release valve, letting out all kinds of grief, wallowing in guilt and a convoluted assortment of emotions. If the past were a woven garment, then Mengliu had found the end of a thread and was now unraveling it.

"Someone like you can't understand. Let me tell you, Shanlai, Hei Chun was the best poet, and he looked just like he does in that photo—he was his own imagined king, and imagined . . . all kinds of crimes. Some of his ideas had merit, but some were unconsciona-ble . . . Is he alive or dead? Has he turned to ashes? Who knows? No one knows, there's no news . . . I cleared out all his things, returned them to his parents, basically treated them like relics. We all thought this way, because he certainly wasn't the only one who disappeared. Hospitals, roadsides, funeral homes . . . we looked everywhere. The mothers of the missing youths were wailing day and night."

"Why did you run away?" the little raccoon interrupted, looking at him with cold questioning eyes the color of chocolate.

"Um . . . I didn't run away . . . " Mengliu couldn't explain clearly. He made a fist and slowly bit his knuckle, as if he could somehow find the answer there.

The little fellow put his book away. "You're a weakling. You're just a coward who's afraid to die."

Mengliu nodded his head woodenly, still lost in his thoughts. He folded his arms and rubbed his hands along his skin, as if he felt cold.

"You're right, that is the fairest, most accurate evaluation of me I've heard so far . . . My reputation in the medical community was all in vain. Those who lived by my scalpel were fewer than those who died under it. Publishing academic essays in authoritative journals, posing as a sanctimonious expert engaged in professional analysis, blatantly seeking publicity . . . All I did to achieve all that was spend a little money and buy space in a few journals. So we produce in abundance professionals without acumen and wicked drunkards. Authority? That never crossed my mind. And as for being a poet . . . Eh! I am very self-aware. In a money-minded society like ours, you can pass off fish eyes as pearls—there's always some rubbish mixed in with the good stuff. Just because it's gold, there's no guarantee it will shine. How many layers is gold buried under? What I'm saying is . . . there's too much garbage with this generation . . . there are no elite sensibilities. If you want to talk about strength of character, you're just trying to live on air, bone-chilling air."

Mengliu wiped his nose with his index finger. Resuming his posture of hugging himself, he continued to ramble.

"That was really a super-chaotic time. The greed of the masses was shocking. Toilet paper, batteries, clothing, electrical appliances . . . everyone was crazy. They hoarded everything at home, some even bought two hundred pounds of salt. How many years would they be eating that? I knew someone who bought eight hundred boxes of matches, and another who stocked up on laundry detergent . . . The stores did not dare to open for business, they just accepted payments through a gap in the door, exchanging cash for merchandise. While they queued, people cursed each other, some even got into physical altercations . . . And don't think I'm just making this stuff up. If you don't believe me, you can go and ask . . . er . . .

"Anyway, another ten years went by, and public morals were declining each day. I'm pretty clear about the hospital's business today. Patients should be careful when receiving prescriptions. It's like a private challenge, different from bargaining for the best price at a farmer's market. The buyer's the one taking the initiative there. What you're looking for, at the hospital, is a speedy and thorough recovery, and what drugs you get depend on the doctor, so you hang on his every word. You need to speak very cautiously, and not have any illusions about the doctor's kindness or compassion or integrity, or that he holds to some high-sounding code of medical ethics . . . Public health care has become a business. Individual officers scramble in pursuit of lucrative contracts. Whether through departmental contracting or single commissions, the rebates the doctors get from drug companies go toward their personal wealth. As long as something is profitable, then it's pretty much 'anything goes.' They opt for expensive drugs . . . meaning that cheaper, more effective treatments are now harder to come by. And then there are the substandard medications, which lead to malpractice. People have lost confidence in medicine. It's becoming a crisis . . . "

"It's as if you're saying that the country has gone bad because it's taken bad medicine." The raccoon-like child showed a change in attitude and seemed to be taking some interest in the conversation now.

Surprised, Mengliu stared at him. He seemed to have just noticed that the boy was there.

"If everyone is like you, then things will just get sicker," the little fellow said earnestly.

As usual, the weather was fine, and they ventured outdoors to enjoy the afternoon sun. The bright-eyed raccoon wore a sapphire-blue robe with a standing collar and the sleeves turned up a couple of times. He folded his legs under him on the swing, looking like a cat curled up before the fire and wearing a serious expression, making his fat baby-face look even more childish.

"Two thousand six hundred years ago, there was a ship that met with a storm and it was wrecked on a desert island. People from many races, including Chinese, the non-Han nationalities, the Miaos, and the blue-eyed people were washed ashore. Left on the island, they settled and multiplied. These were the ancestors of Swan Valley. Later . . . "

A young man with teeth as shiny as a steel blade came out from beneath the shadow of the trees, saying, "Shanlai, it's been a long time since I heard you tell these stories."

Shanlai, as startled as if he had heard a bomb explode nearby, dropped his feet to the ground, stood up, and said politely, "Señor Esteban!"

Esteban smiled. He was tall, stately, handsome. His well-proportioned build could stand up under any form of measurement, an impeccable specimen among humans, evoking a feeling of profound respect.

Mengliu was as confused as if he had been struck by a surging wave but, not forgetting his manners, he greeted the newcomer. "Hello, Esteban. It's nice to see you again."

The impeccable specimen conjured up a vague impeccable smile, offering it to Mengliu as if it were a sweet on a plate.

"Mr. Yuan, sir,"—Mengliu noted the use of "sir," both polite and cold—"I hear you are a poet. Poetry is the heart and soul of Swan Valley. It seems, sir, that you have come to the right place."

Mengliu's heart, like a sensitive scar registering a change in the weather, began to feel a dull, aching soreness. He looked around carefully, noting the dancing vine leaves, the falling pomegranate flowers, and the layer of red that carpeted the grass.

"It's more accurate to say that I am a surgeon," Mengliu replied, straightening his back. Then, somewhat dramatically, he added, "If I reluctantly admit that I was a poet, it is only because I have performed some artistry on the bodies of my patients. But the employment of medical technology does not require the daring application of the imagination."

"Between diseases of the flesh and sicknesses of the soul, which do you think is in more urgent need of treatment? Which of the two types of illness does more harm?" The gentleman seated himself on the swing. He lifted Shanlai, whose ears were pricked up, and seated the child on the swing beside him. With his feet against the ground, he gave the swing a push.

"Neither is as serious as the sickness that infects the state," Mengliu muttered, obviously preferring not to discuss the subject. He crushed the petals on the ground with his foot, watching them turn into powdered soil. Their fragrance blended with the smell of the earth and rose up in an aromatic blend of fermented grains. He knew Esteban had not come by to while his time away in idleness. From the first time they had met, he knew this was not a person who could be dealt with easily.

Esteban listened, then put his left foot on the ground, stopping the swing. He seemed surprised by Mengliu's answer.

"Surely your own country isn't terminally ill?" he asked, sucking in his breath as if dragging on a cigar. The swing started moving again as the child got down to give it another push, then clambered back up onto his perch.

"That's right! Their country has taken so much medicine that it has become even sicker," Shanlai said, one hand clutching the rope at his side and the other pointing at Mengliu. "And he is wallowing in the mud of cowardice!"

"Shanlai," said the gentleman, pulling the child toward him and putting an arm around his shoulder. "You need to listen first and only comment later."

Mengliu felt as if he had turned into a turtle, rolled up in its shell and tossed back and forth between two children. He was annoyed but controlled his irritation as he replied in his usual prudent tone, "There are idle people all over the world who sleep half the day. A lot of people spend their time gambling, visiting places of pleasure, amusing themselves to pass the time, without giving a second thought to society and those less fortunate than themselves. They don't have pity for their parents or compassion for their siblings. They don't have a soft heart at all. In their eyes, all that matters is their own gain . . . " Then he looked as if he wanted confirmation of his ideas from Esteban and Shanlai. "I think human nature is the same everywhere you go, isn't it?"

"That's not necessarily true, Mr. Yuan." The gentleman put his feet on the ground and steadied the swing again. His bright eyes bore the look of one who loved a good debate. "When a nation goes crazy, it wields the scalpel on intellectuals. There will be both natural and man-made disasters, culture will regress . . . " He shook his head helplessly, then continued in a despairing tone, "Do you know how lethal the Great Famine was, how many people it destroyed? It was the equivalent of more than four hundred and fifty times the number of people killed by the atomic bomb that was dropped on Nagasaki. It was a tragedy far greater than the Second World War. I'm not exaggerating, not at all."

Mengliu did not doubt the information, for this fellow had the sort of charisma that made people trust him unconditionally. His views, like his person, were real and tangible. But as the words came flooding out of his mouth, it was as if a spy had stolen state secrets and was putting them on display in front of you, in order to let you know how naive you had been to be deceived. It sounded like an insult.

"History, after the period when it was being dressed up in all sorts of fancy attire, will eventually reveal its true colors . . . "

Mengliu, trying hard to hide his inner turmoil, suddenly felt an inexplicable pain. It was as if he were a husband who one day came to hear from the mouth of another that his virtuous wife had been unfaithful to him for a long time. He had to express his confidence in his wife, not only in order to protect her reputation but also to preserve some sense of manly dignity for himself, at least in the eyes of others.

Mengliu felt extremely uncomfortable, like his heart was being scrubbed with a brush, and he said distractedly, "Mozi contributed not a small amount to cosmology and mathematics, but his asceticism was contrary to human nature. His impoverished approach to life was his own business, but to expect others to live like that was unreasonable. But then, the old gentleman thought that eating to one's satisfaction, dressing comfortably, living in a house with sufficient space, and having a car to get around in was enough. Everything that has no practical value, and excessive enjoyment, should be abolished.

That's not unreasonable. The problem is that during his time, most didn't have enough to eat or sufficient clothes to wear, so houses and cars were all the more out of the question . . . All kinds of health care, employment, education, and legal systems were imperfect . . . The public's grievances piled up . . . "

"You talk like a dumb government official." Shanlai jumped off the swing, landing on his tiptoes next to a dragonfly resting on a leaf. The dragonfly flew away, and the child watched it land on a leaf higher up on the vine. "The emperor made new clothes, just to make himself more comfortable. It kept him warm, it wasn't to display luxury or for showing off. When people make clothes, they use gold thimbles to guide their needles, and precious beads to make ornaments. That is living luxuriously. It doesn't help the state, and may even cause serious harm . . . There's materialism, moral decline, and everyone tells lies. Everywhere you go, there are false Christians . . . "

He jumped up and tried to reach the dragonfly, following it as it flitted away.

"Señor Esteban, Shanlai . . . does he know what he is saying?" Mengliu asked cautiously.

The gentleman once again offered an impeccable, sly smile, but this time something new was added to the platter—a look of disdain that was like a worm after feasting, lying on the leaf, mind blank while it basks in the sun and wind, lazily squeezing out a few blobs of black shit.

To link insect shit to the smile on that perfect, youthful face did not seem quite decent, but it was how Mengliu felt. Later, he came to understand that Esteban's smile held a much deeper meaning. In Swan Valley, a child of seven or eight often had the intellectual capacity of an adult. Their thoughts were fully mature before they turned ten years old. This was an amazing rate of brain development. It proved that Swan Valley's approach to genetic development was correct.

15

Swan Valley, with its pleasant and impeccable environment, was a good place to live. It was full of fine women and men of excellence. In Beiping, it was only at upscale nightclubs that you would see such neatly turned-out people—highly educated good-looking call girls, busy young gigolos with qualities that surpassed those of Alain Delon or Gregory Peck. If you were not a big spender their supercilious gaze might sometimes float by you as gently as a feather. Of course Mengliu was not a patron of such establishments. His interest in places of pleasure fluctuated, and though it sometimes grew into an addiction, it also became jaded after a while. Once, a patient whose outlook took a rapid turn after having his gallbladder removed, decided that he should seize the day and enjoy life, so he invited Mengliu to "a very special place" as a reward. It was a man's paradise, providing a range of services that included threesomes, foursomes, bondage, suspension, inversion, water treatment, air treatment, and of course the deflowering of a virgin. But when men come into contact with women who possess a cold charm combined with beauty, and topped by an overwhelmingly elegant disposition, they are reduced to the state of a weak country facing a superpower. Under such enormous psychological pressure, they often become impotent.

Mengliu was drawn to a particularly stunning woman and planned to take a room with her. When she told him that she drove a Ferrari, he found he wasn't up to the task. He couldn't muster the courage to engage such an extravagant and alluring creature, so he dug out all the cash he could for the woman and slunk away. From that moment on, he knew that he would always be like a fish out of water in Dayang's high society. It was infected with skin disease, and seriously ulcerated inside.

This was why he liked Swan Valley so much, its fresh fertile nature, its simplicity, innocence, and peace. Even the breeze seemed to bring with it a nourishing power. His skin felt moist and smooth, his mood was like a wandering shapeless cloud, free of the burden of the past. At the side of this beautiful woman, accompanied by an intermittently racing heart and the secretion of hormones, he lived every day as if in the early stages of love. A noble temperament was slowly taking over his whole being. The prospect of leading a selfless magnanimous life, away from worldliness and beyond the mundane, permeated the atmosphere. He found it in Su Juli's neat appearance and style of conversation, and in the calmness and accomplishment of the people of Swan Valley.

In the morning, like a married woman who had spent all night amusing and pleasing others, the sun was late in rising. It was nearly nine before it roused its lazy body, fatigued and weak, to glance at the world, before going quietly back into hiding to wash and dress.

Esteban had invited Mengliu to watch the rice-planting ceremony. The scenery as they walked along was glorious, and Esteban urged him to compose a pastoral idyll, in the hope that he would slowly recover his identity as a poet. He even recited one of his own and invited Mengliu to critique his composition.

Looking back at his own messy footprints as he trod along the muddy path, Mengliu thought what a foolish suggestion that was— to rattle off a few simple pastoral stanzas and recover his fucking poetic identity. Only the people of Swan Valley had the idle time to treat poetry—a bold and powerful mastiff—like a pug. Poetry was a raging fire, not a rhetorical game. When the Dayangese composed verse, they never went about it like a girl with her embroidery.

Saying nothing, he bent his head and continued walking. He had no power in his lungs to say anything.

The scenery was like nothing he'd ever seen, heard about, or imagined. It was perfectly suited to a dissatisfied government official turned hermit or recluse, putting up a hypocritical show of farming while, at the same time, waiting to hear the hoof-steps of a courier from the imperial government. On both sides of the road, the hedgerows were covered with tiny blossoms, punctuated by the occasional fiery-red wild rose. The sides of the ditches were scented with wild celery. The distant hillside was covered with flowers and grasses and white mushroom-shaped houses that popped up in the landscape here and there.

Mengliu refused to discuss poetry with Esteban. They had nothing to talk about. They silently passed a lotus pond full of blossoms and came to a gathering of fruit trees. Here in a sea of flowers, bees, butterflies, and birds fluttered about busily. The orioles were warbling, filling the air with the scent of pollen. It was like a produce market or some sort of meeting place; in the midst of the dazzle, all that was left to Mengliu's ears was a roar, the sound growing more intense and more immediate, as if it were pressing closely toward him and would soon roll over his body. Ashen-faced, he reached out and steadied himself against a tree, then leaned his whole body against its trunk. The petals upset by his movement dropped like snow, there were so many of them.

"Mr. Yuan, you don't look good. Is something wrong?" Esteban's voice didn't hold concern for Mengliu's person, though he seemed interested in the cause of his discomfort.

"Sorry, I'm just allergic to pollen." Mengliu recovered, pretended to sneeze, and tears started to form in his eyes.

Esteban turned up the corners of his mouth, putting on a smile that seemed to indicate an insight into how things really were.

Mengliu guessed that the other man must have seen through his lie. It wasn't that difficult, really. After all, he hadn't had any problem with the pollen at Su Juli's house.

Esteban continued to walk at a leisurely pace, as if he were deliberately torturing his companion. He picked a flower, curled his upper lip, placed it beneath his nose, and took a long sniff at it.

Wiping the tears from his eyes, Mengliu continued with an affected casualness, "It's not an allergy to every kind of flower. I'm not even sure which flowers are my natural enemies. It might not be just one kind, but perhaps a combination of several kinds. I haven't been tested . . . But it's nothing serious, just an allergy. It's not a big deal."

Esteban lifted the edge of his robe and strode across a gully. "From what I know, allergies are the body's exaggerated reaction to stimulation. Of course, that also includes mental stimulation." He stood across from Mengliu, looking at him with stormy eyes.

Just then the raccoon-like child jumped out of the forest in front of them. He stood in the middle of the path, hair strewn with petals and body covered in pollen. In his right hand he held a long stick, sharpened to a point. A fire wheel made out of green bristle grass wound around his left elbow. He wore an expression of superiority.

"Shanlai, did you go to see the peonies?" Esteban asked.

"Yes, the peonies have really opened up now. Those fellows are really plump," Shanlai answered.

Before long, Mengliu came across "those fellows" that Shanlai had mentioned. There were worms on the peonies. The "peony silkworms" were Esteban's innovation, the result of a breeding method he had discovered. Their silk was very strong, able to withstand fire, radiation, even bullets. It was lightweight and warm. And it retained the smell of the peonies themselves.

It was hard to believe that Esteban could be credited with this discovery, but such a thing should not have been surprising in Swan Valley. There was no distinction between farmers and intellectuals here. Every farmer was himself an intellectual, and every intellectual was also a farmer or a craftsman. Everyone was a manual laborer and a thinker. Occupational discrimination did not exist. Everyone was equal. They advocated learning and focused on nurturing a comprehensive sort of intelligence. One didn't just become an expert in nails and screws, or understand a specialized, one-dimensional field of knowledge, while remaining an idiot in all other fields. In Swan Valley, there was no monopoly on a profession or authority. They had none of that so-called authority crap, where everyone had to listen like a fool and take notes, without the ability to doubt or object.

The bulletproof peony silk made Mengliu think of artillery. The peony silkworms were manufacturing munitions for the citizens of Swan Valley. There was no need to pay them a salary or provide them with benefits or accommodation. There was no risk of these workers engaging in processions, protests, strikes, or violating law and discipline. The life of the silkworm ended when it stopped creating silk. From birth to death, they were the most law-abiding citizens in the world. He thought of Dayang's vast area and abundant resources, with so much land available to cultivate not just peonies, but chrysanthemums, peach blossoms, pear blossoms, lilies . . . assuming everyone wore silk made from worms living on these flowers, thin as the wings of a cockroach, they would all be invulnerable, and their personal safety, and their quality of life, greatly improved. They would even have time to spend researching the use of Chinese herbal medicines to feed the silkworms, and then who could say what sorts of cures they might come up with for all manner of diseases. It would drop a bomb on the medical profession. They could apply for a scientific patent for the findings. A Nobel Prize would be given, and a legacy would be born.

The two men made their way out of the orchard and across a terraced field where some girls were picking tea.

They were still wary of one another. They had nothing in common to talk about.

Women's voices raised in song wafted over to them. The bright clean voices melted the clouds and dispersed the mist.

"I'm sorry. We've missed the planting ceremony. They've already started," Esteban said.

Girls dressed in red and green were lined up in rows across a paddy field, singing as they planted. Their hands rose and fell, quick and smooth, with a steady whooshing rhythm. The splashing produced a metallic sound.

Esteban said, "Rice isn't the main crop. In Swan Valley planting is a leisure activity—please note that, it is for leisure. These 'farmers' are teachers, musicians, songwriters . . . They're not the sort of farmers who toil with their faces to the earth and backs to the sky. You can enjoy beauty and art in their labor, and in their happy lives. It's not just toil, and they are neither poor nor ignorant."

Dayang had a lot of people who spent their lives being neither warm nor well fed. They were only half alive. They had no money, and even when they died, they had to pay out of their asses to clear their debts. The demarcation between rural and urban brought with it discrimination, prejudice, injury, and all sorts of harmful consequences. All of these were compressed, hidden in the silent spaces of individual fate.

Reclining against a mound of earth and chewing on a stalk of grass, Mengliu asked the raccoon, "Shanlai, what grass does the lion eat? I hear that the grass lions chew on has healing properties."

The little creature had grabbed a handful of clay and was sculpting a portrait of someone. It looked a little like Esteban's silhouette. He answered, "It's hard to say what kind of grass lions like. There are lots of different kinds of grass in Swan Valley—Kentucky bluegrass, tall fescue, perennial ryegrass, Bermuda grass, bent grass, white clover, red clover, weeping lovegrass, Bahia grass, creeping dichondra . . . some kinds of grass don't even have names. The lion has to nibble on hundreds of them, and maybe the miraculous healing power comes from the mixture." The creature paused, then went on, "You're a doctor. You should learn from the legendary farmer god, testing hundreds of types of grass to find a way to cure sick people. If you keep thinking about reaping without sowing, you'll just be a good-for-nothing."

Mengliu spat out the grass. "That would be going back to barbarism. If all the good doctors went up into the mountains and started trying herbs together, then all that sick people could do would be to sit and wait for death. Moreover, hospitals have set procedures and a certain mode of operation. A single person can't be picking herbs and handling pharmaceuticals, as well as seeing patients and performing surgery . . . That's not practical."

"What I'm talking about is the *spirit* of the legendary farmer god. The spirit, you understand?" The boy finished sculpting the nose, picked up his work, and took a closer look, as if lecturing the face he had created. "What you lack is 'spirit.' You can't even discover the vast majority of illnesses, and when you discover an illness, you can't find a cure. For the illnesses you can cure, the patient has to wait a long time for you to treat them. With difficulty, he finally takes a number, then when he gets to see you at last, you don't even take the pains to cure him. Sometimes the cure comes just because the patient has endured the disease and let it run its course so the body can heal itself. But when the patient recovers, you get the credit for curing him. When they die, well, you've done your best. So it seems like doctors don't do anything."

The public cafeteria was housed in a stand-alone building surrounded by a gray stone wall covered with carvings of animal figures, water buffaloes, dogs, birds, and goldfish. The door was propped open, and the windows had colored wax drawings on their panes. The cafeteria wasn't large, and had timber walls, floors, tables, and chairs. The atmosphere was rustic and warm.

A stream of people wandered in and took their seats. Some poured rice wine from a large jug into smaller jugs, cups, or bowls. When the food was served, there were buckwheat cakes, corn on the cob, cubes of jellied blood, sour fish soup, bacon, fruit salad, salmon, sushi, and rice dishes. Mengliu had learned the names for many of the dishes. He liked the buckwheat cakes and salmon. He had been hungry for some time, and he eagerly took up his chopsticks and was about to pick at the dishes. But no one else had moved to do the same. As it turned out, there was a ceremony to be observed before the meal.

A man who looked like a pastor took a small book from his breast pocket. His beard quivered as he cleared his throat and began reading from his bible.

A young man beside Mengliu started playing a flute. It was a sparkling melody that brought to mind harvest festivities. The atmosphere was relaxed but dignified, and everyone spoke lightly as they ate. They were gentle and polite, and the sound of chopsticks striking against bowls was seldom heard. Some used a fork and knife. They conversed in Swanese, sometimes mixing in a bit of Chinese, such as the words for "soul" and "reincarnation" and the like. Their laughter, too, was typical of Swanese, used sparingly, with their merriment more evident in their soundless smiles. Occasionally there was a monosyllabic utterance, such as "eh," "huh," or "hey." There were dozens of diners, but it wasn't noisy or disorderly. Unlike Beiping, where restaurants were always full of a wanton clamor, everyone here ate and behaved moderately, with movements as careful as if they were meant for feeding a baby.

They discussed the soul and death, the spirit and its ideals. This was their version of small talk.

The raccoon-like child raised the question of the immortality of the soul. No one treated him like a child, and his question was taken seriously.

"God started with the body and breath. When he put these two elements together, the soul came into existence. When a person dies, the spirit goes back to God, and the body to dust. The Bible never records anywhere that the soul lives on after leaving the body and walks about here and there. The soul or spirit cannot exist apart from God's living power in the body," the man who looked like a reverend said.

The small fellow didn't even blink as he looked at the speaker, thought for a moment, then said, "Suppose I have boards and nails, and I hammer the nails into the boards and make a box. I have three things—boards, nails, and a box. If I take the nails out, I'll only have boards and nails again. The box will be gone because the box only exists when the nails and boards have been brought together."

The raccoon glanced at Esteban as if looking for encouragement or expecting praise, then carefully concluded, "The soul is a box."

"The soul is indeed a box," Esteban said, nodding in agreement. He commented that Shanlai would be a distinguished philosopher in the future, then, changing the subject, said, "Now let us listen to the great poet's thoughts."

He turned to Mengliu and said graciously, "Mr. Yuan, Buddhism teaches that there is reincarnation. What is your belief about life and death?"

Mengliu did not believe in reincarnation, but he could not deny that life was indeed a misery, and that both rich and poor endured suffering. When the mind became derailed, ideals vanished, then the spirit became an empty box, and no amount of talk could fill up this gigantic void. He did not want to lose face, so he began with the caution of a surgeon in an operating theater.

"Where there is life, there must be death. The Chinese philosopher Laozi says that every person must walk the path of life before he can attain immortality. Some people cling tightly to life, and they fear death. Sometimes, the value of life is to be found precisely in death. For some, beliefs are more important than life, and ideals greater than any individual. There's an idiom, *Some things are worth dying for.* For example, there's justice, enlightenment, democracy, freedom, and so on. That would be the best way to understand life and death . . . "

Mengliu had begun with an attitude of diplomatic sincerity, but as he spoke, numerous English terms welled up in his mind. They were like a red-hot iron poking into his bloodstream and making his whole body feverish. "Because of justice, enlightenment, democracy, freedom," he spoke so eloquently and expressed himself so boldly! He was moved by his own speech. Someone led a round of applause, and everyone joined in. The applause turned into a rumbling sound, a pressure closing in from all directions. He felt a bit weak, as if he were going to fall to the ground in a faint. He grasped the edge of the table with both hands. The action restored him to a more assertive disposition, and he steadied his emotions. His strenuous tone and attitude made what came out of his mouth next seem extraordinarily solemn.

"If you don't mind my asking, here in Swan Valley, has there ever been bloodshed and sacrifice?"

16

As Mengliu and Qizi approached the dorms in the Literature Department, they heard Hei Chun's voice talking about the current political situation, as it had arisen from the Tower Incident. The light in the room was dimmed by smoke filling the air. Cigarette butts were littered all over the floor. The people inside could only be vaguely made out, a pair of legs here, half a head there, and some moving shadows. It was a gathering of scruffy-looking ghosts.

Hei Chun hopped down from the windowsill and, as if passing through a smoky battlefield, walked across to meet Mengliu. He grasped Mengliu's hand and cranked it up and down several times. He smiled and said, "The Unity Party welcomes you," ridiculing him for hiding out at Qizi's. They could not find him, so they had to have the meeting without the VIP and hoped he did not mind.

The cigarette Hei Chun held had burned down nearly to his fingertips, so he threw the butt on the ground and stepped on it with the toe of his shoe, then turned to shake Qizi's hand. He observed her crimson cheeks, her slightly parted lips, and the length of her white neck where it met the boundless expanse of her alluring chest. His gaze could only go down. He stretched out his hand for hers, as if he were waiting for a hand to slide into a glove, a fish to swim into a net, or a bird to fly to a nest, like a young woman walking into her own house, which contains everything she loves and values. But the little hand he held bounced and jumped, shattering all of his fantasies. Qizi said, "Nonsense," and slapped his hand away, laughing at his addiction for meetings.

Hei Chun shrugged and ignored her. He invited Mengliu to take the seat of honor—the windowsill—saying that everyone wanted to hear him speak.

Mengliu had come to extract himself from the party, but before he could say anything, he had been pushed onto the seat of honor, and he found it difficult to get out of it. By this time, he had a clearer view of the people in the room and noticed a few familiar faces among them, though he could not recall their names. He was sure they were all from the Wisdom Bureau. He shook hands with Quanmu, who looked like he had been through a lot since they last met during the interrogation in the basement, and had become more experienced. Perhaps it was due to the lighting, but the eyes of everyone in the room seemed to glow, as if they had already been through an intense discussion or dispute. The air was still tense.

Mengliu thought, *Since I'm already here, it won't hurt to contribute a little wisdom. Qizi won't blame me.* But he didn't have a chance to discuss the matter with Qizi, for she had long since squeezed her way to Shunyu's side and both were busy whispering. So he sat on the windowsill with Hei Chun, propping one foot on the radiator and placing his elbow on his knee. Behind him, he could hear the leaves of the gingko tree rustling in the darkness.

"I don't think our meetings should be held in salon style like this. The Unity Party has been established, and the list of names publicized, so now it must create a structure and recruit talent. Democratic mechanisms will be the key to success," Mengliu began. "An organization must first learn how to hold meetings. This haphazard style—smoking, reading books, eating food, and everyone chattering on their own—it lacks discipline. There's no agenda, and it's just a waste of time."

The room fell completely silent.

After a brief pause, several people closed their books, put out their cigarettes, or put aside their snacks. They sat up straight and turned all of their attention on Mengliu.

Hei Chun voiced his approval. "This is our first party meeting, and we are all inexperienced. We need to develop a process."

"Right," said Qizi, "I suggest everyone read a couple of books. The first, written by an American, is *Robert's Rules of Order*, and the second is *Preliminary Comments on Civil Rights*, written by a Chinese. Both teach how to go about meeting to pass resolutions. When I was a junior at the university, I flipped through them, and found them very interesting."

"I've read those books too. I didn't know it took such a lot of knowl-edge just to hold a meeting." Shunyu raised her hand in agreement.

Mengliu, surprised and distracted, immediately adjusted his mood. "Shunyu, can you find those two books and give them to Hei Chun?" Shunyu blushed.

After he had spoken a little longer Mengliu slid off the windowsill. When he said he was leaving, the room was suddenly engulfed in a bright glare. All eyes were trained on him, and the spots, blackheads, acne, pimples, disappointment, surprise, regret, and discontentment on his face could all be seen clearly.

Quanmu was the first to stand up, his shadow falling across the floor. "Mengliu, we've all put our personal matters aside. You can't just go like this. The Party needs you."

Some people blocked the door.

Mengliu's eyes flew to Qizi and he said, "I came today to ask you to take my name off the list. I have never wanted to participate in any organization, or anything other than literature. But this does not mean I don't support you. If I have anything to offer, I will certainly tell you."

Qizi stood up too. "We're planning to go overseas. We don't have time."

Hearing this, Hei Chun's face suddenly went cold. He turned to look out the dark window. His hair formed a messy canopy around his slumped shoulders.

"Yuan, give it more thought. The Party needs your wisdom." Quanmu, with his high forehead and delicate handsome look, tried tactfully to persuade him.

"Those who escape are cowards," Hei Chun suddenly spat out in a strong Southern accent. "Who doesn't want to save his own skin? If the nation is rotten, how can individual lives flourish? And what is the point of feasting then? Of the young people now in Round Square, who does not have his own ideals and future?"

His words left no room for equivocation. Mengliu went off in a huff amid the smell of gunpowder.

He vented his frustration as they walked. "The most annoying thing is to have a person acting with a mysterious authority, and telling me how to live my life and how to do things. Now that he has set up the Unity Party he thinks he's quite a figure! He's lost his sense of direction. Am I just saving my own skin? Well, what's that got to do with Hei Chun? Who does he think he is? Why should he humiliate me in public like that?" Mengliu did not quite know where all his anger had come from, but it seemed to have been long repressed. "I write my poems and I mind my own business. I don't join organizations. I live my own life. Am I hurting anyone?"

Qizi felt his tirade was directed at her.

"I'm not putting my own neck on the line. I'm not joining the party, and I'm not staying here any longer."

He plopped down on the grass, legs splayed. The street lamp glimmered through the leaves, and a few fireflies chased one another.

Shunyu caught up to them. "It's not worth getting so angry with Hei Chun. I don't think he meant any harm. He just likes to talk in that sort of scathing, preachy tone. But you're right to resign. Let me tell you, your speech that night at the double-tracked wall was recorded. I've heard that the tape has been sent to the Security Board." Shunyu spoke cautiously. "You've got to be extra careful. My father won't let me leave the house. He gave me an ultimatum."

Mengliu breathed out between his teeth. "You're like your father, always thinking of how to take care of yourself."

"I'm doing this for your good. Why are you turning on me? It's really biting the hand that feeds you . . . I'm tired of looking after you. You're on your own." With that, Shunyu stomped off.

The night was black as water. Every now and then fish swam by quietly and the seaweed swayed.

Qizi was also unhappy. "Okay, you obviously want to join the party. Go ahead. You don't need to compromise."

"I've told you, I'm a poet. I don't want to be a stickler for any kind of form."

"Acting like this makes us seem boring. Everyone will look down on us."

"Everyone? You mean Hei Chun? You think I've embarrassed you. Well, isn't this what you wanted?" Mengliu was cynical. "Did you really read those books when you were a junior? You probably just saw the covers at Hei Chun's place."

In his jealousy, Mengliu could not make himself speak nicely to her. How could she flirt with Hei Chun right under his nose? Their familiarity with each other was beyond his understanding.

17

Mengliu had become used to the golden toilet, and his digestive system was now more regular than it had ever been. He toyed with the diamond marbles in his hand, his heart as forlorn as the baskets that were hanging on the wall, waiting for Juli's care. What annoyed him was her ambiguous attitude. He couldn't figure her out. She seemed like a wife of many years, placid and quiet, rarely meeting Mengliu's eyes when she spoke. All he could do was look at her limitless face, the long eyelashes, the distant nose, and eternal lips. She was cool, but not cold, like the low fence around the vegetable garden that was a sort of loose boundary and easy to step over. But Mengliu was acting contrary to his usual style and was also reserved and considerate, like a rabbit sensitive to the signs of a trap. He found that the one sure way to catch Juli's eye was to talk about his past. In order to win a glance from the beauty, he sometimes talked of Dayang's shocking political scandals or its human tragedies. Afterward he regretted it and felt like a traitor. Even so, just for the sake of bringing tears to Juli's chocolate-colored eyes, even just for the shadow of a glance, he would spare no effort, working out a draft of his presentation in his mind first, so that he wouldn't end up discrediting his own country while trying to win her favor.

Juli wanted to know specifically what made the machinery of a large nation turn. Was it flexible? Did the gears make a grinding noise, and what sort of lubricant was needed? Was wear and tear a big problem, and how did one go about replacing old parts? Or was it better just to scrap it all and start from scratch?

Mengliu kept leading the conversation back to medicine, saying that doctors had mastery over the machinery of the body. From ancient times until now, the body's organs and tissues had not changed. *The Yellow Emperor* and *The Compendium of Material Medicine* would never be outdated, and medical skills were essential for keeping all the two-legged creatures of the world up and running.

Juli was more concerned about the body politic and the diseases it suffered from.

Mengliu had a premonition of danger. When a beautiful woman developed her intellect, it could only lead to disastrous consequences for him.

It was a good day. Juli brewed the dark, fermented tea and invited Mengliu to play a game of chess. Distracted, Mengliu lost two games.

Juli's hair was arranged in two braids wrapped around her head and secured at the back with a shell clip. She wore clogs, and her toes were visible beneath the hem of her light blue skirt. The skirt was made of a soft, comfortable fabric that hugged her curves.

"You're playing too impatiently today. You are too distracted. You'll scare away the spirit of the tea."

She smiled serenely. It was a typical Swan Valley smile, temperate and lovely as porcelain. At that moment Mengliu felt the cherries had ripened, the coconuts were heavy, and the grapes on the trellis were surging forward.

"You're especially beautiful when you smile. Why don't you smile more often? When you smile, even the plants and flowers take notice."

Juli's smile broadened, as if she were granting some special permit for Mengliu to make an even more daring comment. Of course, this was just a small test. He had stronger motives within him. He was just waiting for Juli to issue a more relaxed smile. But Juli's smile came out like a bud in spring, showing signs of the flower, but not quite opening. Her liquid brown eyes solidified again and her thoughts took a leap.

"From your point of view, what could a scalpel bring to the nation?"

The leaves rustled around them, his losing game displayed by the distinctive black and white pieces on the chessboard.

Mengliu picked up his cup in two fingers and took a small sip of the tea. His movements were slow. He set the cup down and steadied it, then said, "Each flower is a world unto itself, and each tree a life. Perhaps I can give a sick person a new world, a healthy world that has emerged out of their experience of horror, blood, pain, and repentance." He paused, leaning back in his chair with his elbows resting on the armrests, as if talking about these things exhausted him. "You know, to open up a person's flesh with a knife is easy. Too easy . . . Sometimes, you cut out a tumor, or lance a boil, or remove a damaged kidney . . . just to save a corrupt official, a thief, or some other person who deserves to die a hundred times over . . . These people are the pillars of the nation, and taxpayers' money goes to salving their conscience and fitting them with prosthetic limbs . . . You don't know, but the kidneys of the poor, the bellies of the hungry, the various organs of the good—they all die helplessly at hospitals and at home. I can do nothing about that."

The last bit was spoken with great emotion. He surprised himself, not realizing he was so thick-skinned, as if he really did do his best for all living creatures, especially for those members of society who were subject to abject poverty and had no one to depend on. Actually, he had never cared about a patient's identity when he wielded the knife, and he had never felt real sympathy or compassion. He had just taken his salary and lived his own life. Or, rather, he relied on his own abilities to live out his life. Unbelievably, his eyes were actually wet. He was like a revolutionary talking about his failed experiences, occasionally revealing a certain will and spirit to start over again.

His expression touched Juli. She almost felt an impulse to take his hand and comfort him.

"People are always like this. When their desires reach a climax, their inner demons are released. The nation is like a person, always experiencing problems with its personality. But in the final analysis, wherever there are no strong values, things will end up in a mess." Juli sighed, then turned and said in a gratified tone, "Our hospital is like a beautiful historic site close to the mountains and water. When you see a doctor or pick up a prescription, it's all free."

"All free?" He was so surprised that he could not help but repeat Juli's words. He thought of Hei Chun's description of an idealized world, and now here it was right under his nose.

"Yes, the doctors are like our close friends or family. In the hospital, the patient enjoys warmth and care, as if from a member of their family. And the hospital's food is good too."

"You don't have to go under the table to get that sort of care?"

"We have state-of-the-art medical equipment. There are always beds and plenty of space."

"The key thing is, you don't have a large population, everybody is healthy and beautiful, and people rarely get sick."

"No, the key is that we have good genes." Juli stretched and stood up, then said casually, "The place Esteban took you to wasn't too bad, was it? When you got there . . . were you inspired to write poetry?"

"No," Mengliu answered decisively. "If someone's poetry cells have been burned to death, there's no way to resurrect them. They won't come back to life."

According to what Juli told him, the population of Swan Valley was strictly limited, and not heavily concentrated in the suburbs. The areas lying around the town made provision for only two thousand households, and the number of people who could live in each household was also limited, with the surplus moved to other places to pioneer new developments. For every one hundred people there was a church, its reverend trained from youth by special agencies. He was highly respected. He also held other executive offices, such as Head of a Hundred Households or Head of a Thousand Households. The reverend's wife had to be one of the outstanding women of Swan Valley. Criminals and the intellectually average were prevented from reproducing. Their propaganda slogans included exhortations like "Ensuring a Quality Population Starts with Good Genes" or "Let the Best Sperm Combine with the Best Egg."

Now imagine you are an insect, and you fly through a low-rise building to a grove filled with the scent of magnolias. Religious music comes from one of the windows. If you were to say that the scent belongs to the music, or that the melody comes from the scent, you would not be wrong. The streets are exceptionally clean, and there is no smog or noise pollution. The pureness of the air bears with it a trace of sweetness. In a colonnaded ring-shaped square, forty-five degrees to the east, you will see an old tree. It is called the Tree of Beasts, and it is said to be the patron saint of living creatures and has been standing since ancient times. Its trunk is amazingly thick and requires dozens of people to encircle it. The bough is wound tightly with dendrites, and the roots are engraved with animal shapes, inlaid with precious stones for eyes. When you see a python with blue eyes sticking out its tongue, there is nothing to fear. It is fake.

You lift your eyes a little and focus on a point two hundred meters away. There you see one black figure, one white, accompanied by a pair of shadows. It is Yuan Mengliu and Su Juli, walking away along a bridle path on the green slopes.

It was time to go to church, and Juli was dressed in a sober linen dress, with hem and neckline decorated with colorful feathers. She wore a necklace of exquisite workmanship. Her hair was in braids, coiled on top of her head and clasped with a crescent-shaped comb, so that it resembled a halo atop the Virgin Mary's head.

Following Juli's instruction, Mengliu wore a Chinese robe and cloth shoes. This style of dress suited him.

They met others going to church along the way, all wearing sober but kind expressions. They didn't speak but nodded to one another or waved.

Mengliu followed Juli closely, asking her questions from time to time in a soft voice. She offered short replies or responded simply with an "Ah." They looked like a couple after a quarrel. The man spoke carefully, and the woman was not very willing to entertain him.

The two figures made their way up the slope in this fashion. The wind suddenly gained force, and hair and skirts were sent flying wildly. Hiding his warm feelings, Mengliu looked around. The sun was dazzling and the distant stretch of river seemed to have donned a knight's armor, setting off a metallic glitter. He was not sure if this was the same river he'd seen earlier. A muddy gray wall rose from the ground, stretching for a hundred meters or so between each watchtower or crenellation, like the Great Wall of China. The river ran beside the wall. There were thick bushes growing at its base, with blooms reaching out over the river like they were playing in the water. They seemed to be offering the continuous reminder, *unless you are one of the hosts of heaven, you can banish all thoughts of attacking the city, given the defense offered by the river and this wall.*

Juli was downwind of him. Her breasts stood out pertly, and even her belly and the space between her legs could be clearly seen in the wind, like a naked body wrapped in a cloak. Her body's shapely and mysterious terrain was the main cause of the flames warring in Mengliu's heart.

For a short period of time Mengliu imagined the possible consequences of a surprise frontal attack. He even thought about blaming his actions on the surrounding environment, just as you might excuse killing someone because the hot weather had made you bad-tempered.

Of course he didn't do anything like that, he just watched as Juli turned around, her clothes bulging and then instantly deflating as she turned back to face the wind again. He didn't do anything at all except for maintaining the reserved, aloof demeanor of a poet, though Juli's skin was now emitting a bronze shine, smooth as satin.

He began to appreciate his poetic demeanor.

Turning to Mengliu, Juli said, "In 1876, the year the US celebrated a century of independence, an international expo was held in Philadelphia, with thirty-seven countries taking part. The latest British steam locomotive was on display and America's high-powered electric motors and generators, along with Germany's precision machine guns . . . Can you guess what China exhibited?"

Mengliu cited several things, such as porcelain, cheongsams, various kinds of facial makeup from the Peking opera, and so on. Juli said all were wrong, it was an earwax cleaning set made of pure silver, and embroidered shoes for binding feet. She was very interested in the bound feet of Chinese women. Such topics played right into Mengliu's hand. He immediately recited, in an exaggerated dramatic tone, a few lines from a famous poem by the Tang poet Li Shangyin, "Paper made from the river is the color of peach, with verses inscribed in praise of little feet." Then he followed with a made-up story similar to the one about the King of Chu and his obsession with tiny waists.

Yuan Mengliu could not be bothered with the location of the church. The steeple emerging some distance from the forest might be their destination, but he preferred to go about things in a rather nonchalant manner. Su Juli's skirt occasionally flapped against his legs, tapping out a playful rhythm. Several times Mengliu thought she was about to fall straight into his arms. His legs, having endured the onslaught of flirtation, felt fresh one minute, limp the next, and then perkier than ever, while his chest alternated between feeling full to the point of bursting, and completely deflated. His heart moved at a pace similar to that of a woman walking on bound feet, trembling and shaking all the way.

Judging by the constant changes in distance between himself and Juli, Mengliu guessed that her feelings must also be fluctuating. He noticed one small detail in particular. On the journey from the foot of the mountain to its peak, the distance between them had reduced from three meters to just twenty centimeters. From that progress, he anticipated that before they'd traveled another hundred meters, they would at last achieve an earth-shattering zero-distance.

But Mengliu's method of calculation proved not to be a useful guide. They suddenly pulled apart, for he had stopped, noticing a round object hanging from the wall, like a bell with a dangling tassle. The bell, rotating in small circles as it hung from the stone surface, suddenly turned to show a face, pale as a piece of paper and baring white teeth. Its eyes were wide open, and the blue eyeballs protruded, like glass orbs. He felt two rays of blue light on his eyes, then the face turned away again. Mengliu was a battle-hardened man, and he had used his scalpel on bloodied bodies, confronted dead men, and even watched some die, but this lonely hideous hanging head still gave him a fright. The unlucky, unpleasant piece of human debris struck him like a gunshot, scaring the fledgling of love from his heart and leaving behind only a few downy feathers twirling in the wind.

Glancing at him, Juli said blandly, "Actually, criminals aren't so readily executed in Swan Valley. For the most part the penalty of forced labor is preferred, since it's more useful to make them work than to kill them off." With her hand she pressed down her floating skirt. Mengliu caught a glimpse of a tattoo on the back of her wrist, a captivatingly beautiful poppy in bloom.

"That . . . why . . . " As he held out a stiff finger toward it, the human head turned around again, as if complying with his summons. The features, those of a handsome white man, were graced with a goatee. "What was his crime?"

Juli brushed her fingers along her forehead, where the breeze had blown a few strands of hair into her eyes. She continued walking then, as cavalierly as if she were talking about nothing more significant than washing up, or brushing her teeth, or making her bed. "Adultery. He was tied up and left hanging for two days. When he was barely alive, they cut him down and, while his heart was still beating, castrated him, dug out his intestines, ripped out his heart and lungs, then threw them all into the fire and burned them to ashes. Finally . . . " she turned and made a chopping motion in Mengliu's direction, "finally they dismembered him and hung his head on the city wall for a week."

For a moment, Mengliu's blood seemed to freeze in his veins. It was as if a blade had been jammed into his teeth. His whole body ached, and chills ran down his spine. On more than one occasion he'd heard

Hei Chun speak about how to use torture to achieve social stability. Allowing the masses to hear the condemned's screams and witness the suffering caused by the execution would be a warning that carried more impact on the inner person than any amount of moral education or effort on the part of the legal system. To be shot dead wouldn't be all that horrifying, since such a quick death would be painless. The criminal law's unique charm, its deterrent force, lay in its ability to make the public quake in terror, forcing them into submission.

What really terrified Mengliu about this case was not the method with which the criminal had been disposed, but the easy tone in which Juli spoke about it. She employed the same voice she might use if she were teaching someone to knit, "Loop the yarn over the right needle, insert the left needle into the loop, left, right . . . " It was as if she were talking about a ball of wool, a few needles, and the deft movements of the fingers as they manipulated them. He would need a strong constitution to keep his stomach from turning over when faced with such a casual attitude.

Mengliu was struck by the clear and sudden change as everything around him grew dark. A bitter wind attacked his flesh, and he wrapped his arms around himself.

Soon, he heard the comforting voices of the white-robed priests. With great relief he entered the church and turned his eyes up toward the giant vault, around which he saw thousands of candles burning. The flames restored the warmth inside him. The priests in their pure clothing had serene faces. The music accompanying the hymns of praise was like larks flying through the forest. He felt a sense of enduring freedom.

"No matter what," he thought, "with a girl like Su Juli, Swan Valley is a beautiful place."

Inside the church the pair stood close together. As his shoulder brushed against hers, he felt her tremble slightly. The warmth of her body moved him again, as if her blood coursed through his veins. He glanced at her. Her eyelashes touched her cheeks, and a drop of sweat inexplicably trickled down her nose. For reasons he could not express, he rejoiced in the sight.

The only other thing worth mentioning about the inside of the church is that this first little bit of physical contact between Mengliu and Juli occurred there. Afterward, in order to avoid retracing their earlier route, they followed a bougainvillea-lined path into the forest. Its floor was covered with a variety of flowers, the roots of the huge trees were blanketed with lush wild grass, twigs, and fallen leaves, and insects filled the air with a chirping sound from within the detritus. The deeper they went, the more moist it became, until the air above their heads was shrouded in a layer of fog. As he breathed in the rich odor of mulch, soil, and flora combined, Mengliu's heart once again warmed. He felt like he was walking along the paths of paradise, with angels darting in the folds of Juli's clothes and hair, and rustling between her legs with each movement. Sometimes he looked out at the tobacco plants growing on the hillside, or at the towering rocks, or to the spot where nameless flowers were in bloom on a strange tree. Otherwise his eyes remained on the creases in Juli's skirts, an absorption interrupted only by his sudden loud sneeze that startled the birds from their perches in the trees.

In a strong voice Juli said to him, "It's cool on the mountain. If you don't feel comfortable, we can go home."

He waved off the suggestion with his long slender fingers. He noticed that his hands were so pale they were almost transparent. Obviously his blood flow was slower than usual, and his breathing was ragged too. Still, he did not wish to abandon this journey, now that they were halfway to the "interesting place" to which Juli had promised to bring him. And so, with a pretended ease, he asked, "How many meters above sea level are we?"

Juli told him they were around 4,800 meters above sea level. Mengliu, having never been at such an altitude, suppressed his feeling of surprise. He made some amusing comment about the elevation, inducing a smile from Juli.

Perhaps it was out of boredom, but Juli began humming a tune to herself. It was one of those old folk songs with a melody that sounded like a Buddhist chant, making her voice bounce like a coiled spring. He instantly saw the angel's notes tumble to the ground among the leaves. He thought, "Doing it at an altitude of more than four thousand meters would be out of this world." Then an even more specific thought crossed his mind, full of possibilities about how he and Juli might enter an even more spectacular realm.

He pricked up his ears and listened. The notes were like a school of lively fish splashing out from Juli's throat. With their tails they created a stream of water, spraying the droplets onto his face. The melody flowed into his ears and entered into the cramped confines of his soul. There, in a sudden burst, green trees sprouted and a cluster of pink camellias bloomed. At this moment he knew without a doubt that he was in love with her. His rapid heartbeat was certainly not the result merely of altitude sickness. Then his body alerted him to the fact that it wasn't love, but lust, and that everything in and around him was waiting for him to take her.

But his mind sharply refuted the notion. How could anyone separate love from lust, any more than one could separate the flavor of chocolate out of chocolate ice cream? The two blended together to form one exquisite taste. He enjoyed this metaphor of his own that he'd come up with. Being with Juli had brought back to his mind a poetic sensibility, and he felt a strong lyrical impulse pulling at his heart. Without realizing it, his thoughts began to follow the rhythms of Juli's song, and some lines popped spontaneously into his head:

I am listening to someone sing
"God bless the people whose bellies are full"
and so I think of those without food
wondering whether they are like me
—bellies empty, but ears full—
For them are life's simple joys,
the morning dew on the grass
and a sense of piety in dark times

He got stuck there, and so stopped for a moment, bowed his head, and sought the next line. He wondered at his own gratuitous thoughts for the hungry, those who were too weary with life to change their own destinies—the silent majority, who had leapt right into his romantic imagination, squeezing their way into his thoughts. Each line of poetry was like a corpse laid in formation, here at 4,800 meters above sea level, waiting for him to review it. He looked down to the foot of the mountain, to the river where his memories of Qizi flowed and to the ghostly quietness there, and he felt himself to be a bell so large it needed several men to ring it, swinging back and forth in a slow, methodical manner.

Juli hummed her tune. The edge of her dress was dirty with mud and grass stains.

He bowed his head and continued walking. There was a layer of fine fur growing on the tobacco leaves, their edges made jagged by the artistry of tiny insects. Riddled with disease, the plant was gradually giving up its hold on life, like a weary, emaciated figure making its final prayers before death. Before he could sift through the rapid changes of emotion going on inside him, the next verse came to him, riding the rhythm of the insects as they gnawed the tobacco leaves.

Only the wind enters the wilderness
Beating against the farmer's gaunt form
Alongside the final rays of the setting sun
It sweeps over the tomb
There harvesting every last stalk

When the black cloth of night,
Completely covers weakness
Who, on his way back home
will contemplate the death of another?
By the time the rod is raised halfway
Destiny will cease its call for mutiny

Let us, like this, eat our fill
The sun shining on our bellies
We need no written word
To lord it over us
Each stage of life's cycle
Is a ringworm settled between my fingers
But I remain master of myself
My ulcer-racked body lying on the earth
Sees next year's cotton erupt
From my own navel

Then, we may all be blank slates
We will break the tyrant's muzzle
And slowly make our escape

"The tyrant's muzzle? Mr. Yuan, what did you say?" Juli asked.

Only then did he realize that he'd given voice to his song. The moment he looked at her, he realized it was Bai Qiu's poem. One evening years ago Bai Qiu had sat by the Lotus Pond at the Intellectual Properties Office and composed it all in one sitting. It had immediately spread far and wide. By the time the sun had gone down, a group of influential poets had initiated a movement in which they used verse to stir the soul of the people. In the spirit of the real Three Musketeers, they swore themselves to a common destiny in life or death, to honor and loyalty, and to action at the critical moment.

Juli did not need an answer from Mengliu, nor did she wait for him to speak. Pointing ahead as they stepped out from the cover of the forest to a rock that protruded over the valley, she continued, "We've arrived. That's it—"

Looking in the direction she pointed, Mengliu saw in the distance the "interesting place." Across the valley on the slopes opposite them were the green tiles and flying eaves of white buildings standing transcendentally among the vibrant hues of flowers and leaves. Green vines climbed the walls and roofs, and purple blossoms dotted the facades, scattered like stars across the sky. Down the face of the mountain beyond flowed a waterfall, which looked as if it was falling from the heavens, creating a mystical atmosphere. Rising through the clouds was a cylindrical tower constructed of beautiful red brick. As the wind blew and the clouds parted, they saw at its top a giant clock, which filled the valley with its music as it struck the hour of three.

"Oh, it looks like a lovely holiday resort." Mengliu gazed at it for a long time, then asked, "Does it have any special significance?"

"Upon reaching fifty years of age, anyone can live there." Juli's face wore an expression of longing. "It's the best nursing home in Swan Valley. I've heard that they have everything there—library, cinema, theater, chess matches, debating clubs, athletic events . . . or you can just laze about all day on a huge sofa in the café, listening to music and chatting while you consume unlimited supplies of fresh fruit juice. You will never feel like a lonely old person living there."

"Go into a nursing home at fifty years old? Things are very different in a welfare society," Mengliu said, laughing. "But, I'd rather work till I'm eighty, growing vegetables and rearing chickens in my own garden. I'd never want to live in a communal facility."

"But this is policy. It's all according to regulation." Juli picked a flower and placed it behind her ear. "Of course, it's also what the people want."

Seeing Juli's feminine gesture, Mengliu felt that her serious tone was basically just a pretense.

"The government is subjective. They don't care about what people want." He looked at the brilliant wildflower behind Juli's ear. It struck him that it would soon wither, and he felt pity for it.

"Everything is free. What benefit could the government possibly have?" Juli stared at him with a taunting attitude.

"What I mean is, simply put, it may not be quite what it appears on the surface. Furthermore, fifty years, just as a person's in his prime . . . "

Mengliu hesitated. Suddenly coming to a realization, he said to himself, "No wonder I only see young people here. The middle-aged have already been shut away in nursing homes. Don't they have any interest in the outside world anymore? Don't they come out and have a look around?"

"There's a small self-contained community in there," Juli said, ignoring Mengliu. Turning her head, she looked fondly and longingly at the nursing home. "Inside, there will one day be a famous old craftswoman, creating strange and wondrous things—and that will be me."

Mengliu climbed a few steps further up the rock, searching for a better angle from which to see more clearly, but all he could see was the outer wall surrounding the nursing home, blocking the view as effectively as if it were the Great Wall. He saw the old trees, the flying eaves, the waterfall and path, and the tower that seemed to disappear into the sky. Silence glided over the walls from the garden and came to rest in the mysterious forest behind them.

18

Cycling to the suburbs was Mengliu's idea. He said that people in love should not miss out on the spring, and he persuaded Qizi to put down her physics books and relax for a while. At dawn, they ate fritters, soy milk, steamed buns, and porridge, then took a pair of bicycles and set out through the bleary-eyed city to visit its outskirts. An hour and a half later, the thick white smoke released from the chimney at the brewery had turned to a thin wisp. The bustle of the city was blown away by the country air. The cycle path was covered with crushed black coke and the broken chips of red bricks. The two mingled colors resembled an abstract painting. As their bicycle wheels rolled over the path, they made a crunching sound. All around them were crops, vegetable patches, ponds, bamboo, birds in flight, animals, and people, with smoke on the rooftops and the yelping dogs serving only to emphasize the silence of the countryside when their echoes reverberated over the scene.

Happily humming schoolyard folk songs, in what seemed like the space of a breath they had cycled more than ten kilometers. They stopped at a roadside farmstead and asked for a drink of water. They chatted with some wrinkled old plowmen and saw from their expressions that they envied the young couple their youth and knowledge, and love. Qizi's face was like an apple at the end of autumn, flushed with a healthy rosy glow. Among the villagers were some who had traveled to the city and seen the crowds of people on the street. They were curious and eager to find out more as they sat smoking their morning pipes, one leg crossed over the other or a grandchild tucked between their knees. They talked about the city as if it were a completely different world.

Mengliu and Qizi answered them perfunctorily. Then, after expressing their thanks, they continued on their journey.

The pair now fell silent. The grinding of their bikes on the gravel became monotonous, and each felt the other's anxiety.

They had thrown aside their work, given up a wonderful play, rejected invitations to salon gatherings and parties, and at last they were experiencing a moment of freedom and beauty and tranquility. Neither of them wanted to destroy this unique opportunity. Their legs continued to pedal mechanically, perpetuating the crunching sound and advancing their journey. They stopped at what might have been an abandoned watchtower or church. Putting their bikes to one side, they gazed upward for a minute. Holding hands, they entered the building and were overwhelmed by the pungent smell of manure. They realized that the building was home to a tied-up water buffalo. It stood chewing on feed, staring at the intruders with red eyes as big as the rims of cups. They went up a rickety wooden staircase that had been reinforced with hemp ropes, and climbed right up to the third floor. As they climbed, the staircase shook badly, throwing off a lot of dust. They kept climbing, quivering all the way to the top.

The building was empty except for the water buffalo downstairs. Through the windows they saw the village they had cycled through. Neither of them knew why they had wanted to go up to the top, but there they stood, inside the dilapidated building, facing one another.

Mengliu kissed Qizi extravagantly, but even with his most dazzling gestures he could not move her. She wasn't in the least bit confused. Her expression was sober, her eyes misty, and there was some sadness in her smile. She put her hands on Mengliu's chest and slowly pushed him away, saying, "There's a demonstration this afternoon. We should get back."

Mengliu, burnt by her expression, suffered a moment of heartache. She was an intelligent girl. He was becoming more and more aware of that.

"Let's take a break first. We'll find a farmhouse where we can scrounge a meal. We'll fill our stomachs and then make a decision, is that okay?"

She was obviously a little tired. Leaning against him, she said in a soft voice, "I love you." He kissed her again, this time plainly and passionately, and he got more of a response. She returned his kiss, and he felt her melt in his arms, as if she were about to flow right out of his grip. He pulled her into a tighter embrace, feeling himself to be an infinite chamber, able to furnish her body, and her life, with riches.

After some time, she raised her head from where it lay on his chest and said, "I know you're concerned about the Unity Party business. Hei Chun was right, we all have a responsibility. Escaping is cowardice."

Her words pierced Mengliu like nails, setting off a burst of misgivings. He turned to the window and looked out across the distant assortment of trees, flowers, and farmhouses with a frown.

She leaned lightly against his back and said, "None of us knows what kind of feathers we wear, but at least we can make them as brilliant as possible."

He turned around. Her eyes seemed to have been washed clean by the pristine countryside. They were emitting a strange glow.

"So you want to forget about going overseas?"

She thought for a moment, then nodded in agreement.

"You won't regret it?"

She looked at him and said resolutely, "I won't regret it. I want to be with you."

He suddenly felt that her strength was propelling him toward the sunlight, and he felt bright and clear. Yet there was still a part of him covered in shadows. He knew that he was the only one who could drive the shadows away. He asked himself, *Does it have to be like this?* but he could not come up with an answer.

When they reached the city, the demonstrators had arrived in Beiping from everywhere.

Mengliu stood astride his bike on the side of the road, drooping as if he had been drenched in heavy rain. He hunched his body down, hands on the handlebars, and drew his neck into his shoulders, as if the rain were unbearable.

Qizi leaned her bike against the trunk of a tree. As she looked down the road, her expression was the same as Mengliu's.

They saw Hei Chun directing the contingents of demonstrators, with a strip of fabric tied around his head. He was full of energy and resembled a revolutionary from a film as he swaggered in front of the slogans on the banners that fluttered in the wind like flags.

Mengliu noticed that a darkness had fallen over Qizi's face, and her ears were inflamed. He signaled her with his eyes and, pushing his bike, walked in the opposite direction, away from the demonstration. Beside the mighty torrent of people rushing toward Round Square, he and Qizi were like a pair of fish swimming against the current, furiously shaking head and tail in their efforts to reach a buffer zone. By the entrance to the Green Flower, they saw Shunyu at the window watching the action. She winked and waved to them.

There was not a single customer in the bar. Her father was wiping glasses at the counter, wearing the expression of a man who was smoking a pipe. His eyes were half closed, and his teeth were clenched on one side. His hair flew and curled chaotically, and his face was flushed.

They sat at the window, their stomachs rumbling. Their morning meal had long since been burned up, but they had no appetite now.

There was an unceasing flow of demonstrators before the bar's entrance.

Mengliu could not look at the street any longer. Taking out his chuixun, he began to blow a few bars in his frustration, then put it back into his pocket.

Shunyu's father brought over some food, saying amicably that it was all free. After a while, he brought a jug of wine and said with enthusiasm, "I'm very happy to have a few glasses of wine with some young people."

Mengliu understood that this was his way of rewarding them for not participating in the march. He also wanted to take the opportunity to find out about the young people's "ideas for the future and feelings about life."

"I used to play the xun pretty well when I was young," he said pleasantly, sighing. "The life of a soldier is monotonous, and my comrades-in-arms would pester me all day to play for them. Comrades like to hear the chuixun, isn't this the popular taste? But the senior officer of our unit thought the tunes were negative and depressing, that they wouldn't boost morale, so I wasn't allowed to play anymore—though he said a harmonica would've been all right. Fuck him! That was only his personal preference. But he was the senior officer, and I was just a soldier. My fingers were itching to play, but I had to control myself and obey orders. The army is inhumane. It doesn't talk reason . . . So, look at those people outside. Processions, sit-ins, even if they create a greater disturbance, it'll all be the same. It's futile."

Shunyu's father rattled on. Some regular customers came in and called to him, and he hastily greeted them. When he came back, the alcohol made him all the more flushed.

"Shunyu said you two are going overseas to study. That's good. Such an opportunity isn't easy to come by! You'll definitely have a brighter future," he continued. Then he turned his criticism on his daughter. "I just don't understand, my girl, why you are reluctant to go abroad. Go add something to your life, like plating something with gold, learn from other people . . . To tell the truth, there's a lot of things worth studying overseas . . . Really, a lot." He munched on some roasted peanuts and, his face coming alive, he said as if to himself, "This fecal matter has been going on for several months now, hasn't it?"

Mengliu said cautiously, "Off and on for about three months."

The old man's nostrils flared, snorting out alcoholic fumes, and he took a hesitant sip of his wine. He seemed about to speak, but held back.

"I hear that representatives have met with the people, and they have negotiated. It seems they've agreed to find some experts to come and study the matter again, and to publish their findings about its DNA." Shunyu glanced at her father. Seeing that he didn't object to what she had said, she continued, "But there's still one condition the official representatives haven't agreed to."

"What condition?" It was Shunyu's father who asked, breaking his own rule that no one should speak of politics, much to everyone's surprise.

"Father, do you really want to hear about it?"

"Silly girl. If you're going to talk about the situation, at least do so clearly."

Shunyu said, "It's about admitting that people from the Wisdom Bureau got beaten up."

"The Wisdom Bureau people were beaten up?" her father asked.

"Yes, the newspaper made false claims, saying that it was the police who had been beaten."

Shunyu's father took a deep breath and then muttered, "The newspapers always lie, but it's hard to believe they would stoop so low."

No one replied to his mumbling, since he clearly didn't expect an answer. This was his usual attitude. He had his own way of dealing with things.

Just then, more customers came in and Shunyu's father left the wine jug but took his own cup. As he walked away, he reminded them, "Don't talk politics," then swung his large form around to welcome his guests. It was several of his regular customers, and he led them up to the second floor.

"Your father really loosened up on his restrictions today," Mengliu said.

"The main reason was that you played the chuixun well. My father takes you as a soul mate." Shunyu smiled happily. "In fact, there's no generation gap between my father and us. He likes to tell me about how things were when he was young. He did one thing once that was exceptionally absurd and romantic—"

"Shunyu, come here!" her father called.

"He seems to have a sensor. Any time I want to say something bad about him, he calls me." Shunyu stuck her tongue out and went to answer her father's call. When she came back, her face was flushed with embarrassment. She said her father's old army comrade had come, bringing his son with him, to discuss a marriage between the young man and herself. At this point, the tail of the body of demonstrators disappeared from the doorway, and Qizi's eyes suddenly looked vacant. "Maybe the negotiations will be useful. Then everyone's hard work won't be wasted."

"Yeah. Many of the leading intellectuals and celebrities are responding." Shunyu spoke excitedly, as if she herself were a participant.

"You act as if you're concerned about society, but really for you it's all about Hei Chun. This is called being blinded by love." Qizi smiled, looking at Mengliu as he refilled his wineglass. "You should seize the opportunity to tell him. If not, it's likely someone else will grab him."

In a panic, Shunyu looked toward the inner depths of the bar and seeing her father was still upstairs, she settled her nerves again. "Only if you're the one snatching him from me," she retorted.

"Shunyu, what kind of rubbish is that you're talking?" Qizi chided.

Shunyu's words had aroused Mengliu's interest. He had had a lot to drink, and the free flow of wine was going to his head. He looked red and hot.

"Hei Chun is talented, and there are certainly lots of girls who like him." His jealousy had provoked a cynical rivalry in him. "Especially when he goes up on the podium to speak, he looks so valiant. He speaks well, has a manly voice, and when the girls listen to him, they lose their wits." He turned to Qizi and continued, "Are you like all the rest? No? I bet your heart thumps at least a few times . . . Hei Chun, that son of a bitch. He just pretends not to notice the thousands of girls whose hearts throb for him. You're right! He's got his eye on someone, the bastard."

Shunyu stood up silently and left.

Mengliu realized that Qizi's face had darkened and her eyes were fixed on him in a murderous glare.

"You . . . What's wrong with you? Eh . . . why are you looking at me like a tigress?"

Qizi did not say anything but continued to stare at him until tears began to fall. The murderous look was extinguished. She snatched Mengliu's wineglass and swallowed the drink in one gulp. She drank so fast she choked.

Squinting, she said deliberately, "Hei Chun—right now he's out there charging the enemy lines! He's not spineless!"

"Are you calling me a coward?" Mengliu was getting worked up. "Qizi, you need to be clear about this. If it weren't for you, I wouldn't have gone on an outing at this time, and I wouldn't be sitting here like a pansy drinking wine now."

"I admit I've played some part in it, but you're giving me too much credit. You're making me the scapegoat for the sake of your own ego. You only care about your own future."

"Do you really think so? Have you no conscience?" This was going too far, and it stoked an alcohol-fueled fury in Mengliu. "You object to me joining the party, but then ridicule me when I sit here drinking. One minute you say this, the next that. I've been listening to you too much, going wherever you pointed, allowing you to weaken my will and disgrace me in front of everyone! And your father, that trump card, haven't you played that too? You tell me, at the end of the day, what the fuck am I supposed to do?"

"Stop pushing the blame onto me! In the final analysis, it's your personality that's the problem. You're indecisive and dependent." Qizi was disgusted with him for swearing. She had begun by wondering whether he could withstand her assault, but she became angrier with each word and, throwing caution to the wind, she continued, "You're a selfish prick. You live in the fantasy world of poetry. You are complacent, weak, and without any vision. You have no ambition. You're a hero in your own verse, but in real life, you're just mediocre."

Throughout Qizi's harsh speech Mengliu's pupils dilated until they were like flowers in full bloom. As the flowers reached the zenith of their life, there was a pause for several seconds, then they gradually turned dim and faded, shriveled, withered. He lowered his eyes to the empty wineglass, as if he had drained the wine with his gaze. Then he calmly stood up, negotiated his way past the chairs, and flew out through the door of the bar like a flurry of fallen leaves in a cold wind.

Mengliu walked sluggishly beside his bicycle with his head slumped forward. Drunk, he could neither see nor hear a thing. He bumped into people and trees intermittently, until finally he staggered back to the West Wing. He flung the bike carelessly against a wall, went inside, and plopped down onto his bed. As soon as he fell asleep, he began to dream. He was being chased by a biomechanical monster. He tried frantically to escape, but his legs were limp and he could not run. Eventually he took flight, but the monster turned into a huge bat with eyes as red and round as lanterns. It opened its ferocious mouth in hot pursuit. Just as the bat was about to catch him, Mengliu woke up, his body on fire and his heart heavy.

He opened his eyes and stared at the ceiling for a while. The cracks that spread over it made it look like a traffic map, with lines for highways, railways, and airlines winding here and there. He felt dizzy. Suddenly his whole life had become a mess.

Qizi's words echoed in his mind like a knife scraping against glass, grating on his ego.

He applied psychoanalysis to his wounds for a while and felt better. After a little longer he felt quite good about himself, confident he could carry on with his normal life. But soon the cold reality returned and he felt a terrible pain. He cursed the alcohol, blaming it for starting him off on the trashy talk. He wanted to apologize to Qizi and tell her he loved her very much.

Just as he was filled with tender feelings, he felt the sting of her remarks all over again. His heart hardened, and he thought she should be the one to apologize to him. He would not forgive her if she did not take back her harsh judgment of him. Instead he waited all night, hoping Qizi would suddenly appear, laughing and ready to bury the hatchet. But all he heard was the wind in the locust tree, the cat in the rafters, and the endless flow of the lonely night. He had a splitting headache, and only when morning came did his state of confusion pass.

The radio next door chimed 11 a.m., then began presenting the news. It reported an important meeting, saying it had been convened for the purpose of reexamining the feces. The issue would be researched and discussed, and a vote taken. Those who attended the meeting had a long list of impressive titles, which was read out in its entirety in the report. It went on to talk in detail about how they made their entrance to the meeting, the suits they wore, their expressions, the color of their ties, and emphasized the "thunderous applause" that had greeted them. Only at the end was mention made of an illegal gathering of people who had attempted to take the opportunity to cause trouble, and made a negative impact on the smooth running of the conference.

"In addition, at the entrance to the Catholic Church on Liuli Street, a young man claimed to have acquired some gorilla feces and ate them in front of the crowd, using this to incite the masses to gather at Round Square and support the sit-in. After this, a violent confrontation erupted; two people were seriously hurt and had to be rushed to the hospital for treatment."

Mengliu got out of bed and washed himself. The radio was now playing ads for laundry detergent. He went out and looked at the trees and the sky, and his spirits were revived slightly. He went to his landlord's shop for a drink of warm milk and a snack and to chat with the elderly man as usual. But the old man, buried in his own business, ignored Mengliu.

He left the shop feeling awkward. Seeing a trishaw parked on the roadside, he climbed into it.

"Where to?"

"Didn't I say to Round Square?" He saw that it was the same dark, thin fellow he had met when he went to the square before.

"You didn't say anything when you got in. Am I supposed to read your mind?" the skinny fellow said as he pedaled, the tassels around the roof of the trishaw trembling. "I can only take you to the top of Liuli Street. You'll have to walk from Beiping Street to the square."

When he arrived, he saw Hei Chun and a crowd of people gathered in a circle, their expressions serious as they discussed things. They were all very pleased when they saw him. Hungover, Mengliu looked at them without any interest.

"Why isn't Qizi here?" Hei Chun asked.

"Qizi? She . . . "

"Where is she?"

"I don't know."

"You had a fight?"

"Sort of . . . "

"Revolution always comes with the low tides. We have to be able to withstand the most severe tests."

"Yeah."

"A breakup is one way to prompt deeper feelings."

"That's easy for you to say."

"Women are like a strangely tangled knot. The more you struggle with them, the tighter they bind you. They only know they want this or that, but they don't understand what a man needs." Hei Chun was pulling him into the gathering. "Put aside your troubles with women and come, share some ideas."

19

From his long experience, Mengliu was aware that different types of women had to be handled in different ways. It wasn't wise to approach a woman carelessly without first understanding her history, education, habits, position, and other matters related to her background. If you didn't, you stood no chance of managing her. Up until this point in his stay with her at Swan Valley, Mengliu hadn't been able to figure Juli out. She was like a cluster of clouds he couldn't quite grasp. She changed shape as winds of unknown origin blew on her—becoming dog, horse, fish, lamb—sometimes singly, sometimes in a group. In an instant she would change into a plant, a tree, a spreading branch, or a flowering twig, and even the most solicitous bird couldn't destroy her peace. But relying on his instincts about women, Mengliu sensed that, deep inside, Juli harbored a suppressed assertiveness and lust. Moreover, he was sure that her lust had something to do with him, and with this thought he spent the whole night in a stimulated state, a torrent of heat flowing unceasingly through his body.

Imagine yourself as the sweet breeze of Swan Valley blowing into the window as Mengliu shaved. Follow his razor blade, serving as a sort of snow plough on his cheek, piling the foam in one corner, exposing the street-smooth greenish skin. He felt his cheek, scraped a few places again, then rinsed the razor and put it in its little box in the wall cabinet. He washed his face, then raised his head and checked his reflection in the mirror from different angles. He pressed forcefully on his skin with his left hand, like a masseur—or perhaps it was more an attempt to smooth premature wrinkles. His face followed the manipulations of his fingers, going askew as he pulled and poked. If you observed carefully, you could see clearly the traits of one who belonged to the '60s generation—teeth stained by tetracycline, a lack of calcium, shattered ideals, and a perplexed idleness—rather like a mirror covered with a layer of dust that made you long to reach out and wipe it clean. But you could also see that Mengliu had an open, well-fed look, the look of an official. If his waist had been broader with a more protruding belly, he would pass for a mid-level cadre. Only his eyes were still very clear, unclouded by worldliness. His stiff, detached expression caused his face to wear a cold glint like the blade of a scalpel.

Now, Mengliu was as careful about his appearance as a woman. He wiggled his eyebrows—rise, shoot, pinch, spread—like lively silkworms. He puffed up his cheeks, then opened his eyes wide, and his pupils suddenly turned dull, as if a bat had just flown past. The strange face in the mirror bore none of the romantic air of the poet. Years ago, his classmates said that his "every pore oozed with poetry," and he himself believed that each drop of his sweat bore the aroma of art. But the face in front of him now was characteristic of a professional, without the slightest trace of the poet, its pores emitting only worldly indulgence and aptitude.

How could a man who wrote no poetry, put in a place where the toilet was made of gold, go about pursuing Juli with dignity? This was the question that absorbed him now.

That night the moon looked pale as it hung above the forest. The look, so melancholy, made it seem like the moon was about to break into tears.

On Beiping Street a women's propaganda troupe appeared, headed up by Qizi. Holding a megaphone, she spoke to the crowd, making up jingles by substituting their own words for the lyrics of popular songs. A girl named Sixi played guitar as she sang. Sixi was from the Arts Department. She had a round face and dark red skin and was just over a meter and a half tall. Her raven-black hair was twisted into two thick braids. She wore the cotton print patchwork outfit typical of a minority ethnic group and jade pendants that jingled when she moved. She had a style that was simple and understated. She was healthy and fit, and her deep-set eyes were adorned with long lashes, like a row of reeds alongside a pond, which often cast their dark reflection on its surface.

Sixi could sing and dance, and she played the guitar beautifully. She had once won first prize in a singing competition for university students and had also participated in a nationally televised song contest and got good rankings. When Qizi and the rest recommended that Sixi join the Unity Party, she was unanimously accepted. As a contribution to the Party, she composed a theme song, "Tomorrow," and performed it on the spot.

The Unity Party had taken up its main position on Beiping Street, hanging up clothing and props for performances in the vicinity. An unsavory musty smell mingled with that of instant noodles and a mimeograph from which propaganda leaflets were being printed and distributed. Sixi sat at three square tables that had been joined to make a conference table, tuning her guitar. Her knees propped her flowery skirt up as she searched for the right key, then she sang in a solid voice.

At first, everyone looked at Sixi's fingers, lips, face, earrings, and floral dress. Then, as she sang the second verse, they closed their eyes and listened. Her voice was like a ball dangling midair in a fog. Sixi sucked in enough air to set her saliva splashing. She issued a string of groan-like trembling sounds from her lips, then bowed deeply.

She hopped off the table, put down the guitar, then said shyly that she had written the lyrics, but they had been polished and revised by a poet. Which one? Jia Wan. Some had heard that he wrote poetry and was especially good at political verse. The poet's face was round but held at an angle, with a dash of pockmarks. His nose was huge, and his eyes narrow. It was the look of one who had been brought up well.

Jia Wan had made an appearance at poetry salons but did not talk much in a crowd. He was relatively low-key. He was from the same village as Mogen, a writer who, though he was not well educated was very talented, and had been admitted into the Writers' Class in an unconventional move when he won a national award for a novella he had written. Later, he entered the Literature Department. Now he was an activist, diligent in his work with the Unity Party, passing messages, running errands, doing odd jobs, and generally making himself useful in any way he could. The Writers' Class was a place where people of unusual abilities could be found, who often quietly helped the Unity Party by drafting and writing slogans, making donations, or offering bedsheets to be used as banners.

As the result of a campaign speech made with absolute authority, Qizi had become the backbone of the Unity Party. Hei Chun was elected by an overwhelming margin to serve as the first chairman of its meetings.

Mengliu still had not joined the Party, but in order to see Qizi, he often showed up at their activities and performed small favors for them. Sometimes he bumped into her, but they exchanged no private words. They talked occasionally, but it was strictly on the level of comrades, as if there had never been anything more between them. All of their feelings seemed to have been transferred elsewhere.

The Wisdom Bureau's Freedom in Broadcasting Forum was an expansion of the Unity Party's Propaganda Department. Because of the unrest among the people and changes in its personnel, the Unity Party had been thrown into confusion. Some members were in hiding, others had fled, many kept farewell notes handy, ready to sacrifice their lives. There were also those who had the core members of the party in their sights, intending to weaken their positions. Hei Chun particularly was under attack, with people saying that he was a womanizer, and that he had used the funds raised by the Party on luxury-brand cigarettes, alcohol, and a life of corruption and vice.

One evening the previous week, in a dimly lit corridor where the whitewash on the termite-infested wall was flaking off in slivers, Mengliu had come out from the washroom and overheard a conversation between Hei Chun and Qizi. Hei Chun wanted Qizi to take over as chairperson, saying she was the only one capable enough for the role. He had written a letter of resignation and would inform the Party the next day. Qizi said he couldn't withstand the wind and rain, and that his heart became overwhelmed with anxiety at the first signs of trouble.

What made Mengliu's heart race was not that Hei Chun wanted to elevate Qizi, but that he had confessed his feelings for her, using this critical moment when she was vulnerable to express his affection. He bore with the unpleasantness and listened as Hei Chun continued.

"Last year in the twelfth lunar month, your long hair was awash in sunlight as you skated alone on the ice, eating candied hawthorns. I came up behind you, raced past, and caused you to fall. The candy stick flew from your hand and made me stumble too. I cursed, then turned back and saw you, looking like a penguin with your arms flapping as you tried to catch your balance. Your eyes were dark and your face clear and golden. At that moment, I forgot everything. I couldn't even remember that I had crashed into you. I asked which department you were in, and you asked if I was going to go to your department to apologize. I said I wanted to bring you a bunch of flowers, and asked what flowers you liked. I slid up next to you, and you recognized me then. You said my skating was much worse than my poetry . . . "

Mengliu kicked the base of the wall, knocking a shower of white plaster loose. He imagined the frozen lake, the sun shining on it, and Qizi's face like amber, with her dark eyes, looking irritated but lovely and innocent at the same time. The sky was a monotonous gray, and the trees were withered. Only she was alive with color. It was like an image from a film, developed in the darkroom of Hei Chun's mind.

"Qizi, everyone is very supportive of you. If I withdraw, it will be good for the Unity Party. Anyway, I've already achieved my goal."

"Goal? What have you achieved?"

"Actually, it's not exactly a goal. I do things out of interest. There's no reason. I don't have to be responsible to anyone."

"I won't be the chairperson. I oppose your resignation."

Qizi's recorded speech was like a newly unearthed weapon. Mournful, bleak, poignant, and tragic, it made spring at the Wisdom Bureau extraordinarily dreary.

Mengliu and Shunyu each carried a bundle of cloth, paint, and a bag of jingling objects. As they listened to the broadcast, they walked toward the basketball court, where there was plenty of space for them to work.

"Qizi's actually a very talented performer. Can you hear how sensational she is? She makes me want to cry." Shunyu pricked up her translucent jug ears and pursed her thin lips. "She is possessed. Her father is angry and wants to disown her."

Mengliu had slowed his pace and was looking at a speaker attached to the trunk of a tree. He began to envision angels running barefoot from the speaker, elves, roaring lions, snorting horses. Out of the dark forest came the thundering sound of thousands of horses and soldiers, the sad howling of wolves, the honking of a lone goose, and the whimpering of the north wind.

"On this sunny day, we are on a hunger strike. In the beautiful days of our youth, we cannot help but resolutely cast aside everything that's good. However, we don't really want to do that. We refuse to take it lying down!"

" . . . "

"Democracy is the greatest impulse for the survival of human life. Freedom is an inherent, natural right. Everyone has a right to know the truth . . .

"We do not want to die! We have a vision for the future, because we are at the most beautiful age of our lives. We do not want to die! Our motherland is still so impoverished, and we do not have the right to cast it aside. Death is not our aim! But if an individual's death, or the death of a few, will enable more people to live a better life, and to create prosperity for the motherland, then we have no right to hold on to our own lives!

"When we are hungry, our mothers and fathers, do not mourn. When we say farewell to this world, our uncles and aunties, do not shed tears. We only have one hope, and that is for you to have a better life. We only have one request: please don't forget, we are definitely not pursuing death!"

"What are you looking at? Idiot!" Shunyu swatted Mengliu with the cloth.

"I was listening to the speech. It was really good. Earth-shattering."

"A talented literary work? Did you play any part in it?"

"She has plenty of talent to deal with this sort of thing."

"What's going on with the two of you? Are you still planning to go overseas?"

Mengliu could not answer Shunyu's question. He thought back to what had happened two days earlier, when he had worked overnight assisting the Unity Party. His stepfather had come and could not find him, and had lain on his doorstep all night, waiting. As soon as he saw Mengliu, he caught hold of him, but in his anxiety he could not get his words out. He wanted Mengliu to go back to the village and lie low until the trouble was over. He said, "Don't join this damn rebellion."

Mengliu asked him, "Who's rebelling? It's just a petition. But I'm not even signing that."

His father had scolded, picked up a book, and started to hit him with it. After a while, his attack weakened, leaving him tired and helpless.

Mengliu was overcome by a burst of sadness.

"Why are you in a daze? Why don't you say something?" Shunyu said, elbowing him.

"If Qizi starts to create literary works, she will certainly be an excellent writer," he said.

"She's very smart. It's like she's from another world."

"Both of us have low IQs. Why don't we get together?"

"Don't flatter yourself. My IQ is much higher than yours! Someone as beautiful as me is only fit to be with a hero. Who wants to make do with you, Mengliu?"

He knew her hero was Hei Chun, but even though it was just a joke, it still stung. They had idled the time away together in mutual sympathy. They no longer felt like going to the theater, and they had no interest in concerts. They bumbled around a few antique markets, and finally grew tired of that too. They were bored with the blandness of it all, watching their friends rush like soldiers to the front line of revolution. In the end, they were conscience-stricken, thinking they should at least show their sympathies. It was because of this feeling that they had begun doing these errands for the Unity Party.

With Mengliu's excellent penmanship and Shunyu's nimble handiwork, they stitched up banners and wrote slogans, listening to the radio as they worked. After Sixi's theme song, the Freedom Forum came on air. The guest, a well-known intellectual, brought explosive inside information, saying there was an intense internal struggle in the Plum Party, which had split into two factions. One of the factions wanted to take advantage of the demonstrations to raise a public outcry, hoping bigger trouble would be stirred up.

Mengliu spread out the cloth, indicated his approval of the tailoring, and took up his paint brush and began writing. The paint fumes caused him to sneeze and his eyes to water, but by the time the Freedom Forum ended, the words had emerged from the black background he had created for the banner.

"These are the biggest words I've ever written in my life." Mengliu stood up and massaged his knees, feeling like he was no bigger than a toothpick in front of the black banner.

"Will you go to Round Square tomorrow?" Shunyu looked at the black banner spread out on the ground.

"We'll see."

"When you were doing the poetry reading at the bar, do you remember what you and Hei Chun were fighting about?"

"I didn't fight with anyone."

"Hei Chun said it doesn't matter if poetry is romantic and graceful, so long as it is passionate."

"Since when have you become his spokesperson?"

"The Three Musketeers should unite for the power of poetry. It boosts morale."

"Poetry, apart from inviting trouble for yourself, is utterly useless. Aren't Bai Qiu's poems banned now? What use are a few lines of rhetoric?"

Mengliu thought of Bai Qiu's death. He was like a bird, flying down from the roof of the Wisdom Bureau, his last words folded neatly in his pocket. His death had nothing to do with anything, except that he despaired over this damned generation, confused between right and wrong.

"Bai Qiu was always a poet." The wind lifted a corner of the banner reflected in Shunyu's eye. She whispered, "I admit that I like Hei Chun, but I don't have the courage to stand with him. I am weak."

"Your loneliness serves you right, then." Mengliu used stones to weigh down the corners of the banner, then checked to see if the paint was dry.

"I kind of hate Qizi."

"What do you hate her for?"

"She always plays hard to get with men."

"Doesn't seem so to me."

"Why don't you apologize to her?"

"I . . . didn't do anything wrong."

"A man should be a little more magnanimous."

"If you think that Qizi is the roadblock between you and Hei Chun, you're wrong."

"I like him, and that's my own business. It's got nothing to do with anyone else," Shunyu said.

Mengliu stood up straight as a flagpole and replied, "Shunyu, you can extract sweetness from the bitterest root, and that's a real talent. I, on the other hand, suck bitterness from a sugar cube. Our perspectives are different, and our tongues don't detect the same flavors. But why don't you compete with Qizi? You're also very pretty. Don't you have a long line of suitors behind you? Why are you only entranced with Hei Chun? Let me tell you, he's a selfish bastard, and a bit of a playboy. When is he ever free? The rumors about him never stop, and he likes to read love letters from his female fans in public. He's not good enough for you. You should look for a guy who's more . . . "

Shunyu was kneeling on a white banner outlining the words "Long Live Freedom." Her brush suddenly stopped. She screwed up her face, looked up at him and said, "However bad Hei Chun is, I don't mind. Even if he were in prison, I'd bring him food every day."

"What? Are you really that far gone?"

Ignoring Mengliu, Shunyu dipped her brush into the ink and continued to outline the words.

Just then Sixi ran onto the basketball court, her clothing dazzlingly colorful. Two others trailed along in her wake, Jia Wan and Mogen. Neither said anything, they simply rolled up and neatly stacked the banners that had already dried and checked to see how many more strips of cloth were left. They went to work turning them into banners, Jia Wan commenting on those that had been filled with words, saying which strokes were too thin, where the ink was too light, and which characters should be written in a way that looked more imposing. He almost completely negated the effort that had been put in by the others.

Shunyu tossed her brush aside and looked at Jia Wan in exasperation. Mengliu knew she did not like the fellow, and he also felt there was something sordid about him, like a painting in a vulgar frame. He always wore a suit, as if he thought it would make him look classier. Instead, it only proved he had no taste. From Shunyu's point of view, a pretentious poet who wore a suit every day, as if he were in a hurry to attend a banquet, wouldn't be able to write anything worth reading.

Tired and with an aching back, she didn't even attempt to be polite to him. "What do you think you're doing, coming over and pointing here and pointing there? You don't like it? This is the way I do things. Why don't I go buy some cloth and you rewrite it all?"

When Jia Wan heard these angry words, he realized he had offended Shunyu. He smiled obsequiously and said, "No, no, no. Don't be angry. I didn't mean to criticize. I just think we should pay attention to every detail, so that we will be taken seriously. These banners and writings are the voice of the people, and can be taken as the face of the Wisdom Bureau."

"So you're saying that I'm making everyone lose face? What were you doing all this while? Go back to the press conference and talk to the reporters. Why bother coming back here where all the dirty work is done? It doesn't do much for your image!"

Sixi interrupted, "Don't bicker. We're all doing our best. Jia Wan has joined the Unity Party. He's in charge of publicity and logistics, and he's just trying to fulfill his responsibilities."

"Oh, is that right?" Shunyu said. "If I'd known I was working for him, I wouldn't have come even if there were eight sedan chairs waiting to escort me here. I would rather be at home lying in bed, reading a novel."

The short-haired Mogen said, "Our fellow student here seems a little biased. Actually, you aren't doing this for any one person. We are all working for the country, for the good of the people."

This just stoked Shunyu's anger. "Are you trying to make a fool of me? I don't want to hear it. You tell me how many people really have the best interests of the country and the people at heart. Aren't they all after a little power? What is it about the country, or the people? Do they need you to be in charge?"

Once Shunyu lost her temper the insults flew from her mouth like daggers, and she wouldn't relent on anyone's account. Mengliu knew that her heart was in turmoil because she was completely lovesick over Hei Chun. He led her away from the basketball court, listening quietly as she vented her frustration.

"Just look at him, with his slip-sliding eyes. I think it's pretty clear he's not a gentleman. He joined the Unity Party, and next thing you know, he may bring the whole thing crumbling down." Shunyu wiped vigorously at the ink on her fingers. Walking past a cluster of willow trees, she said, "Let's go to Round Square. Maybe we'll find something to do there."

"Let's not. I'm worried about your father." Mengliu pretended to object, but actually he wanted to see Qizi.

"My father donated two thousand kuai to the Unity Party yesterday."

"That doesn't mean he allows you to participate."

"Let's just go. I'm bored."

"I guess I could go and help construct the broadcast station."

"I'll come with you."

"Well, I'm not your father. I can't stop you."

"Yuan Mengliu, you asshole. Are you being cheeky with me?"

"Sure I am! If I'm the one who has to look out for you, doesn't that make me your father?"

"You're incorrigible. Hey—do you want to hear one of my father's romantic stories?"

She told him the story as they walked towards the square. "It's from when he was in the army. Of course, he hadn't met my mother at that time. My father's company rested in a village for a few weeks. He got a little stir-crazy, so sometimes he went to the river to play the chuixun. Because he played so well, a beautiful girl was fascinated by the music. He taught her to play the xun. On the night before he was to depart, my father and the girl went into the bushes by the river and, you know . . . He also left the xun with the girl."

"What sort of xun?"

"He didn't say."

"What happened next?"

"There was no 'next.' My father only knew her nickname, something like Little Liu. Maybe she was the sixth child in her family, so they called her *liu*."

"Your father really was a romantic, seducing a village girl while in military uniform." Mengliu pretended to be preoccupied, but he was thinking of all the rumors he had heard about his own father. He took out his xun and looked at it, noting where his adoptive father had seen the engraved words *meng liu* and taken that as his name. Could there be some relationship between these two "sixes," these "lius"?

Impossible! Inwardly, he laughed at himself. It was too fantastic. How could he even entertain such a ridiculous notion?

Shunyu spoke on her father's behalf, saying he had taken the thing he loved most and given it to Little Liu. "That xun was the only thing my father cherished. It was an heirloom."

"At least he had a heart. Go back and ask your father, what did the family heirloom look like? Was it an oval xun, a bottle-gourd xun, a grip xun, a mandarin duck xun, an attached xun, a cow's head xun, or was it like this . . . a lady-charming xun?" He thought a moment, then laughed. "Well, for people with low IQs like you, it's too complicated. How about this—you take my xun back to your father and ask him what era it comes from."

20

Dark clouds swallowed up the moon, the bird of the night let out a scream as if the sudden darkness had bitten into it, deepening the surrounding shadows until everything became indistinguishable patches of blackness. Mengliu quietly listened to his own heartbeat for a while, feeling bored. The constant sound of turning pages came from the room opposite, where Juli sat. He felt that she was summoning him. She had left the door unlatched and slightly ajar. The light in her room was soft.

To express his loneliness, Mengliu put on a show with the chuixun for a while. He sat quietly for a little longer, then stood up and walked straight across to Juli's room. He stopped in the small strip of light in the doorway, allowing it to split his body in half. The rhythm of his fingers on the door were like a bird pecking. When he got a response, he opened the door and let the light pour onto him.

As he went into Juli's room, he found himself insufficiently prepared. He was stunned, as if he were standing beneath the vast sky with the lake and mountains shimmering in the distance, and the foliage stirring nearby. The sun shone on her golden face and chest, the low neckline of her gown emphasizing the two mysterious mounds that rose like graves there. His spirit was sucked toward the sight, but he bravely tore himself from the grip the specter of the graves had on him and returned to the warmth of reality.

He pretended to sweep his eyes across the furnishings in the room, a pear-carved table, chairs, and wardrobe in the Chinese style. There was a bronze glow over everything, and tassels hung from the edge of the purple linen covering the bed. On the wall above the bed hung a needlepoint depicting Japanese ladies in kimonos. Juli knelt there beneath it. Her long skirt covered her legs, exposing only her feet, which peeped out like the paws of a cat lying on its belly.

Seeing that Mengliu did not speak for some time, Juli straightened her legs and laid her book upon her lap. His eyes immediately fell to the book—or, rather, to her lap. Juli thought for a moment, then sat up and moved to a chair. She wore a pair of white cotton slippers, which looked very comfortable.

"You can also have a seat," she said. The light fell on the side of her face, illuminating the fine hairs on her neck. Her ears looked like a fried snack, golden and crispy thin.

He felt as if he had taken a drag of marijuana. His legs were floating, and his eyes felt as if they had tendrils growing out of them, crawling like ants across the floorboards and stopping at Juli's feet to gaze up at her.

"I . . . don't really need anything."

He and Juli sat at a round table with a porcelain vase of white lilies on it. He stared at the flowers and added, "I just . . . wanted to talk."

Juli smiled gently, revealing four small shell-like teeth. At night, he could see how black her eyes were, and unbelievably soft.

"Are you still thinking of the nursing home?"

"No . . . no! I feel like there's a caged beast inside of me." He seemed to be describing an interesting dream. "This wild beast keeps roaring, and trying to crash through the cage it is shut in. Oh! It is going to rush out of my chest!" He rubbed his chest, as if to appease the unseen beast. "It's nearly crushing my heart."

Juli frowned in confusion. "What? There's an animal inside you? What should we do? That's so strange." She did not understand this type of analogy at all.

Mengliu looked at her, shocked. He had deliberated on this piece of poetic expression for a long time. But perhaps the beating around the bush only served to magnify the difference in the thinking processes of their different countries. His head was buzzing. After Qizi, Mengliu had never really tried his hand at seriously falling in love. All those years ago in Dayang, in that time of economic development and obsession with liberation, it was easy to get one's hands on a girl. Each knew she was master of her own body, and as the animals awoke inside of them, they let them loose to play and run wild. Love at that time, like poetry now in Swan Valley, overflowed. No one took it too seriously, and all the young people lived in a state of confused ecstasy.

For a moment, Mengliu felt helpless. Juli's thin linen nightgown gave him a clear view of the body inside it, provoking the wild beast inside him.

Suddenly he got up and stepped decisively toward her, grabbed her chin in one hand, and kissed her. Juli's surprised expression was at first like a tightly shut bud. But under Mengliu's quick attack on the lips, the bud suddenly blossomed. In plain terms, Juli did not resist. Instead, she plunged quickly into this act of rash wild kissing. Mengliu half expected that his rude behavior would incite a slap on the face, or perhaps worse, so he was a bit taken aback by Juli's response. He paused, pulled her into his arms more carefully, and began to kiss her more meticulously and fervently. He felt her firm body warming quickly against him, becoming as hot and floury as a baked potato.

All at once he knew how to strip the skin off the potato and consume the soft flesh inside it. He resorted to an indefinite kissing, while planning how to achieve his goal. He carefully followed Juli's body movements, but the fingertips of his mind could not find the exact location of the tender button amid the complex tissues of her brain. He became completely disoriented.

Mengliu thought the hot potato in his hands smelled just right, that it was expanding to readiness, but as soon as he attempted anything further, it turned to a hedgehog in his grasp, offering sharp resistance to his moves and reestablishing certain boundaries. He redoubled his patience and, very gently, plucked the spines out one by one, hoping she would let her guard down, but also taking care not to get pricked. *Women all over the world like to play this game, he thought to himself.*

He had undertaken a huge, indefinite, but not disappointing project. This was like a major operation, and it required a long-term approach and much preparation. He took a careful but tough approach, covering her mouth with his, slowly making his way down to her breasts. He took his time, making her feel that her whole self was in those breasts, and that she could entrust them to his warm palm. He had never been a pig who would swallow a woman whole; he prided himself on being a master of good taste. He wanted to show her how much he appreciated her body, as if his whole world were contained there.

Finally Juli succumbed. She lay down on the bed before him, and Mengliu breathed a sigh of relief. But when he saw her lying there stiffly, it made him think of a patient on an operating table. With his free hand, he brushed aside the hair on her forehead and asked why she seemed so nervous. Juli looked at him like a patient addressing a doctor, with trusting, begging eyes that seemed about to say something. But her mouth only opened like that of a fish out of water, and issued no sound.

Considerately and cautiously, Mengliu began kissing her again. He saw her liquid chocolate eyes, blazing with the reflection from the light, gazing at him from her flushed face, and was moved by such genuine beauty. He unfastened her gown and as he slipped it off, she rolled over and he saw a large butterfly tattooed on her back, its forewings extended out over her shoulder blades and its rear wings over her hips, wrapping around her buttocks. Her waist was delicately thin. She lay there quietly with her back to him. The butterfly seemed poised to fly away at any time. Without stopping to study the tattoo, he stroked her curvaceous body with his skilled surgeon's hands, inspecting every crease and crevice. A hidden torrent welled up, violently pushing and shoving through his fingertips, pounding his nerves. He was like an arrow on a bow, ready for release; within seconds he had removed his own clothing. But just as he leapt toward Juli, an alarm sounded in the room.

"What's that?" Mengliu stopped and asked.

"It's a warning for us." Juli brought her legs up toward her chest, and turned to lie on her side. She looked at Mengliu with a provocative smile.

"I don't understand . . . "

"You still don't get it. Swan Valley prohibits sexual intercourse."

"You're very funny." Mengliu's body quivered with merriment, and he bent to kiss her.

The alarm sounded again, this time issuing a more severe warning.

"I'm not joking. It's true. Every room is equipped with a special sensor. This is a code-yellow warning. If intercourse begins, it will move to code-red. Ten minutes later, you'll be picked up." Juli looked up at him, her expression charming. "You aren't afraid of having your head hung on the wall, are you?"

"You mean . . . everyone is being monitored?" He was shocked, but kept his face calm.

"Monitored? You have a crude way of putting it. It's concern for our well-being. A way of taking responsibility for the individual." Juli looked at him, her expression that of a patient begging a doctor to tell her the results of a procedure. "Am I worth that sort of risk?"

Completely carried away, Mengliu now sought to cool his still thumping heart. He tried closing in on Juli, but the alarm sounded again. He had to believe what she was saying.

"All sexual intercourse is illegal, even between husband and wife." Juli lowered her arms across her breasts, smiling at him as if she were the beneficiary of this policy.

"Hang on . . . Swanese people, you mean they've all jumped out of cracks in the stones?"

"No, we use artificial insemination. A clean, painless little procedure."

"Artificial insemination . . . " He could not keep from laughing. "That's crazy! Why even bother?"

"Mr. Yuan, you're not taking this seriously. Swan Valley advocates a scientific approach. We use genetic research to produce quality in the population. Each person's body has its optimal period for conception, and before artificial insemination is performed, the physiology of both parties has to be subjected to a lot of calculations . . . "

"Oh?" Mengliu felt like he had seen a ghost. "Precise calculations? Scientific operations? But what about human feelings?"

"We pay more attention to the higher spiritual life. For unlawful sexual intercourse, a man may wear a gold shackle and go into servitude, or even have his head cut off. We don't punish the women . . . but you know punishment of the soul is also a torment. If a woman commits the blasphemous act of intercourse, her soul is corrupted forever . . . "

The feverish flush had faded from Juli's face, and her complexion was returning gradually to its calm, golden tone. Even the lights in the house were becoming more rational again.

Mengliu remembered the way Juli had made the chopping gesture by the wall that day, and he shuddered. A chilly wind invaded the space between his legs, and he grew limp there. He needed a dignified way to retreat, but he looked at her with strange eyes and said, "To use your body to fight the system is tantamount to throwing eggs against stones. A variety of historical facts have proven this. You probably don't know how many young people, a whole generation, have foolishly paid an exorbitant price because of this belief . . . many were killed, but the worst was the punishment that came later. You can never escape the hand of judgment. Even less should I, a mere stranger."

Mengliu, unable to control his emotions, now appeared neurotic. Either he had nothing to say, or once he started talking, he was like a pebble rolling downhill, unable to stop. "I have an acquaintance, he tried to hide and survived on roots and tubers for many years in the mountains. It finally caught up with him . . . there has never been a party more vengeful, or more thorough and ruthless. Some people were expelled from their homes, leaving their loved ones, living in exile . . . in fact, all rulers' temperaments are the same. The only difference between them is their height, weight, and hair color."

"You should treat the ruling institutions like chastity. 'Don't touch' is a good rule of thumb." Juli picked up her gown and covered her chest, then resumed her position beneath the embroidered picture. Her lower body was still exposed, her legs long and slender. "When people make decisions, they need to have the support of a belief system. You're right, defying the law with your body is like a moth playing with fire."

Looking at her now, Mengliu realized he was still naked. He was already flaccid, and now he was ashamed. He dressed slowly, his actions full of the sadness and helplessness of a mourner. In an attempt to hide his cowardice, he finally spoke as if offering his condolences. "May I ask, has Swan Valley conducted a public opinion survey on this matter? Is this something the public agrees to? Is it the result of a democratic consensus?"

"Let's not talk about this in my bedroom," Juli said faintly, using the tone of someone resigned to the death of a loved one, and talking respectfully to those offering their condolences. "You can express your views freely at the weekly salon."

"Juli, I'm just a foreigner." Mengliu looked at her, using a dark tone and expression, tuned to a funeral environment, as he once again expressed his grief.

"Don't worry. Before long, you'll have citizenship here in Swan Valley." The light caught her eye, making it glow.

"What?" Mengliu yelped. "Citizenship? I can't live here. I want to go home."

"You mean that place where there's no democracy, no freedom? What is worth remembering about that authoritarian place?"

"It's my homeland."

"Once you set foot in Swan Valley, you belong here. It's just like you were born here."

"I don't even know where I am, or how I got here. Or whether I'm just dreaming."

"Swan Valley's citizenship is not issued indiscriminately. You have exceptionally good genes. Your wisdom and potential will be developed here."

"No matter what I am, no matter what happens, I won't stay in a place where sexual intercourse is forbidden."

Juli smiled, and her legs writhed sinuously, like a snake spirit.

"Actually, it's not absolutely prohibited . . . If you're willing to explore the policy and find the loopholes, you'll see that if you write a good poem and recite the poem loudly for it to hear," she put one hand on her private parts and pointed the other at the alarm in the corner of the room, "it will be quiet."

She sat up slowly and hugged her legs to her, breasts squeezed between her knees. She spoke in a tone that struck Mengliu as a confusion between begging and seduction. "At least . . . write one for me, won't you?"

Mengliu kept staring at her wheat-colored flesh. As if struck by its luster, he squinted involuntarily. He issued a string of bizarre laughter. "Ah . . . so it's sex for poetry? You want to enlist me in the sex trade? Why would you want to treat lovemaking as a commodity? You're as crazy as they are!"

When he finished saying this, he turned away and rushed back to his own room. He slumped onto the bed in a mess. His body had cooled down, but his heart was still hot, like boiling water stored in the cold steel shell of a thermos. The more he thought about it, the more absurd it seemed. He had been blown by a foul wind to this strange place and to a woman who, at the height of his passion, had told him that, in order to ensure the quality of the population, they didn't allow sexual intercourse. As soon as he drew near her, an alarm went off, but then she said that if he wrote poetry he could sleep with her. He suddenly sat up in bed, laughing. The Dayang Poetry Society had dispersed years ago. He did not write poetry anymore. He could not write poetry, and did not take life so seriously. Now he despised himself. His body had denied the fact that he could do anything for the love of women. He dared not risk his head to have sex with a woman, and he was even more loath to use poetry in exchange for a woman's body. That would be to blaspheme poetry. It was an insult to his history with Bai Qiu and Hei Chun.

The candle had burned down and went off with a whiff. As he was feeling drowsy with sleep, he heard the sound of a wooden latch sliding. The sound was hesitant. It paused a few times. The latch seemed to be thousands of miles long, never reaching the end, like a carriage bearing a great load up a steep slope, where the slightest interference would spook the horses and stop them in their tracks. Mengliu's ears were alert. He hardly breathed. Darkness enveloped him. He could see Juli coming out from her bedroom, and hear the swishing of her gown. The wind blew from the forest, rattled the coconuts on the palm trees, filling the air with their fragrance. In the garden insects struck up a chorus. She came in, sinking onto the edge of his bed. She was holding a sharp knife. Her hair was disheveled, her eyes bloodshot. He could feel her breath on his face. The tip of the knife reached his chest, but it was warm, more like a fingertip than a blade. Ah, Juli's fingertip pressing, two fingertips, three . . . all of them on him, like a flock of tame creatures. They stroked the grassland of his face, nibbling at the stubble there. Slowly, the fingers straightened and her palms pressed on his face, like a little beast sprawling on top of him, its warm belly pressed against him. All of a sudden, the liquids beneath the earth became torrential, his body tightened like a taut string. When he reached for her there was a crashing sound, and he fell from the bed, waking himself from his dream. He got up and walked out of the house into the darkness. Laughter echoed in the blankness of his mind.

As dawn broke, he returned in a cloak of mist, extremely weary, and went back to sleep. When he awoke, his emotions were still in a tangle, making his chest feel bloated and hot. Everywhere he looked he saw images of Juli. With the precise observations of a surgeon he concluded that he was in love with her. This woman turned the glue-like substance secreted in his heart into something stickier than any chemical. What he was feeling went beyond science.

It was said that Juli's husband was a diplomat, an ambassador, young and personable. Only a few people had seen him. It was also rumored that he had disappeared during his travels at sea. In Mengliu's imagination he was himself a criminal, thinking of ways to get away with a crime. After he had slept with Juli, how could he act normal, clean up the scene of the crime, clear all signs, erase all suspicious clues . . . the feeling of success a criminal had did not come from the crime itself, but from the ability to escape being caught. His mind wandered, and he began to taste the excitement of committing adultery. He wanted to have his way with Su Juli. At the same time, he was thinking of how he would escape from Swan Valley.

21

In Round Square there were no songs and no slogans, no bustle, just a mass of bobbing heads. Black flags waved against the bleak sky. People were losing consciousness from hunger, and many had to be carted away in ambulances. The shrill sound of their sirens, like the buzz of a chainsaw cutting through oppression, solidified time and space, like a hand squeezing the light in a tight grasp. The weak light escaping between its fingers brushed past the faces that had suddenly lost their joy. The bodies reeling left and right were wilting like flowers. The number of supporters had increased. People had come from all over Beiping just to sit in Round Square without eating or drinking. The original plan for a rolling schedule of fasting had been jeopardized. There was chaos, disorder, a loss of control. Someone took a loudspeaker and requested that the crowds follow all the organizational arrangements, so as to avoid injury. A headquarters was established and a commander-in-chief installed. Qizi was dressed for the part, wearing a white headband and white mandarin jacket. She hopped up onto the scaffolding of the small broadcasting station and related the developments of the past few days. When she got emotional, she became teary-eyed and her voice filled with a generous grief.

At night, the street lamps cast their glow over Round Square, creating a dreamy warmth there. The temperatures were much lower after dark than in the daytime, and many of the protestors were turning blue with the cold, their lips gray. They were like baggage unloaded from a long-distance bus, thrown untidily together, covered in dust and mud. Early in the morning the square resembled a battlefield that had fallen silent once the fighting was over, with bodies all over the field and the dilapidated flags shrouded in a smoky mist. The clouds were stained, first gray, then pale orange, golden yellow, then a mix of yellow and red as the sun rose to expose its own gray face, blanketed by the fog.

Sixi's voice sounded over the radio, reading poems by Pablo Neruda. Another voice, belonging to Fusheng, a professional broadcaster, joined in. They had hit it off the first day they met.

Mengliu was kept extremely busy doing odd jobs in Round Square. Hearing Qizi's voice, he looked up and noticed she had the word "sorrow" printed in huge letters across her back. He took some comfort from this, but the word also gave him a sense of foreboding. He was not sure when it had happened, but he was no longer angry with Qizi. A familiar joy glowed in him again. His affection and hunger were still alive, telling him of the suffering and pain she had undergone since they had parted. She had lost weight, but at the same time she had been through the forge and had absorbed the essence and strength of darkness, breaking out of the door finally like a brilliantly shining gold coin.

He needed to speak to her.

He hung his megaphone on a flagpole and went back to the broadcasting station. He bent low and stepped into the tent, planning in his head to wait until the busy period was over to apologize to Qizi. He would accept any punishment from her, and the two would make up and engage in a dizzying embrace. But when he finally found Qizi, she was sitting with her back against a tent post, with a bag of fluid hanging from it. She was on a drip. They were holding a meeting. She was listening, brow furrowed, face pale, chin sharp as an awl. She had grown thin. Mengliu almost didn't recognize her.

She didn't even look at him, or if she did, she showed no response. He wondered whether she recognized him. What were they involved in—a great cause? a brawl? It was because of their breakup that she had joined the demonstrations in a confused state. Could she be going on a hunger strike now because she had fallen out with him? Mengliu was absorbed in his conjectures when Qizi suddenly pulled the needle out of her arm and stood up.

She uttered something that shocked him—it was about self-immolation. She would use her death in exchange for the lives of the hundreds now on hunger strike.

Mengliu forgot to breathe. He was saying to himself, *Qizi, you're crazy.* As if answering him, she said hoarsely, "I'm not mad. I am very composed. This is the only way we will awaken the conscience of those indifferent to our plight . . . " Her voice quivered and she dropped to the ground.

Each man's death diminishes me
for I am involved in mankind
therefore do not send to know
for whom the bell tolls

It tolls for me, and for thee

In times of fear and trembling
I want to make my life real

I must make this confession public
exposing my own hypocrisy
and that of my generation

As Sixi recited the poem on the radio, Hei Chun entered and interrupted her. He brought several important announcements and wanted to broadcast them immediately.

"There are no substantive negotiations. They are filibustering, obviously stalling for time." Hei Chun sat on the table, a cigarette in his hand.

"That's a pain. I heard that many people in the headquarters have fainted and are now in hospital," Mengliu said to him. He had been left in the tent with Sixi.

"I know. Who is in charge of directing in the meantime?" Hei Chun asked.

"Fusheng. He's got experience in organizing."

"Damn it. Heaven is against us too. A heavy downpour on a sick crowd. I hope it won't become an epidemic. The Red Cross has donated medicines that we should receive in the morning. There are also a thousand tents, and a transportation company has given us fifty buses at no cost. If it continues to rain, we'll have places to shelter in." Hei Chun ran his hand from his forehead to the back of his neck.

"How about everything else?"

"No casualties, but still bad enough."

"I heard the hospitals are full."

"Quanmu is ferreting out the inside information. The situation is more complex than we ever imagined."

Hei Chun lit his cigarette. He watched the match burn down almost to his fingertips, then blew it out.

"Anyway, I believe history will give us our due." He took a deep drag of his cigarette, and let his eyes fall on Mengliu. "Guess what the bigwig had to say. He said, 'As a member of the Plum Party I never conceal my views, but today I'm not going to say anything. In any case, I've pretty much stated what I think.'"

Mengliu couldn't help but laugh.

"They are so insincere. They said they wanted to visit and talk to us directly, but then they wouldn't communicate with us because they couldn't get to Round Square." Hei Chun hopped down from the table, then crushed out the cigarette he had just lit. "It's nothing but nonsense! The really bloody sacrifice is just around the corner. The death bell will begin tolling for this generation."

"Hei Chun, I think we should retreat . . . "

"Retreat? Why? Are you crazy?"

"You should understand their attitude better than anyone. Why should we slap ourselves in the face?"

Hei Chun was startled. Just then, there was a pelting sound. Someone was throwing stones at the tent.

Jia Wan burst into the tent with a single stride, dressed in his usual suit. He said, "Headquarters has announced an end to the hunger strike."

Hei Chun was shocked. "End the hunger strike? I don't believe it. Everyone has stuck with the strike for eight days. Why should they stop now before any real progress has been made?"

Outside, a group began a chant of, "We won't eat! We won't retreat!"

"Come on, let's go to HQ."

The headquarters was located on board one of the buses. The windows had been smashed, and shattered glass covered the ground. Qizi and several others were on the bus discussing strategy.

Hei Chun strode onto the bus and asked, "Why did you announce an end to the hunger strike?"

Qizi had already begun to look like a paper doll, and now it seemed like she had been cut even thinner. It was difficult for her to swallow her own saliva. Her hair was messy as a bird's nest, and she was enveloped in a confusion typical of the homeless. Hei Chun must have remembered how she used to look, pale in the sunlight with dark eyes.

He did not dare to look directly at her. "Why should we betray the efforts of all those who have suffered through the strike?"

Qizi did not reply.

"Well, I'll explain it to you." Quanmu stood up. He was dirty too, and there was a trickle of blood on his forehead. "I have heard from reliable sources that they will declare martial law soon. Most likely tonight, tomorrow morning, this site will be raided. We held an emergency meeting and decided that it was best to break the hunger strike."

Boom. A brick pelted the bus.

"How will that convince them? The people who have suffered and worked over the past eight days don't have the right to cast their sacred vote?" Hei Chun's tone relaxed a bit as he continued, "If we undermine democratic procedures, we damage the reputation of everyone at headquarters. Do you want the people to look down on us?"

Quanmu did not reply but stood there like a shabby beggar unable to squeeze a coin out of anyone.

"We need to vote on the issue again immediately." Hei Chun took the microphone, ready to use the broadcasting equipment to convene a meeting of all the representatives.

Qizi snatched the mic back, like a hungry tiger pouncing on a lamb. "You aren't authorized! I'm the commander-in-chief, and I am responsible for everyone."

Hei Chun was stunned. He looked at Qizi like he had never seen her before. Her face was lit up, flickering like a candle before it finally goes out.

He turned around, got out of the bus, and disappeared into the crowd that had gathered around it.

Mengliu looked into the vehicle, weighing the situation. He raised a stiff leg, held on to the door, and pulled himself into the bus.

"Hei Chun is trying to maintain democratic procedures. As far as I know, the majority still insists on the hunger strike, but I think you're doing the right thing."

Qizi didn't speak, but her mouth trembled. Mengliu could see her inner turmoil.

"Any further delay will be life-threatening. I have to look after them," she said.

"You should probably discuss a more comprehensive approach." Mengliu wanted to persuade her to retreat but couldn't make himself say the words.

"Actually, we have already resigned ourselves to death, if need be."

"Qizi, you're a good . . . leader. You're responsible. I think you should retreat. Withdraw." Mengliu finally said it, surprising even himself. "You don't need to sacrifice everything here in vain. Qizi, I also want to say, I'm sorry about all that nonsense that day. I'm sorry for what I said. Can you forgive me?"

Qizi looked at him blankly. "I forgot about that a long time ago."

"These last few days, I keep thinking about you. Let's go. Don't be angry. Let's get out of here, just like we planned before. Let's leave."

"Liu, I'll admit I was a little angry with you at first, but after that, I wasn't anymore. Now even less so. I can't leave. Even if we decide to leave Round Square, I should be the last one to go."

"There are some things we would prefer to believe, even if they are unbelievable." Mengliu felt a sense of foreboding.

"No. Everyone is watching us. If no one is willing to make the sacrifice, how can we face that? I'm ready to die, just like I said in the speech I wrote." She had already thought the issue through.

"Qizi, what about your parents? You've got to think of them. They were already forty when they had you. You are their life. If you die . . . they . . . "

"They will hear the words I wrote. 'I can't be loyal and filial to both country and parents.'"

"Have you really forgotten how we felt for each other?"

"My feelings for you haven't changed." Her face and tone were very calm.

"Then as soon as all this is over, we . . ."

"I don't have time now to talk about trivial personal issues."

"I believe this will all be over soon. Let's . . ."

"You should go. If you think this is all meaningless, then just leave now. I don't want to pull you down with me."

"I want to be with you. Qizi . . ."

"I'm not lonely. There are plenty of people with me." She spoke in a rush.

For a flickering moment, Mengliu caught sight of the spirit of love. She was a nimble, dark spirit, and she was running in the moonlight, emitting a varicolored light. She fled to the flag and hid herself behind it.

He felt that he was walking further and further away in Qizi's view. Like a lonely figure in a landscape painting, he was now nothing more than an ant-sized inkblot.

He left the bus in silence, like a passenger reaching his destination at the end of a long journey.

"Your poem 'For Whom the Bell Tolls' was very well written. I hope you'll stay and continue writing."

Though he seemed to hear Qizi's comment, he did not look back. He may have paused momentarily, but maybe not. An early half moon hung in the sky. He felt a little cold, like a man lost in the wilderness.

22

When Mengliu left Round Square, Sixi and Fusheng were going through a wedding ceremony. Their marriage certificate had been prepared by Hei Chun. He printed both names and birth dates on a sheet of paper, covered it with the red Unity Party stamp, and gave it to the couple. The broadcast had declared the protestors' refusal to retreat, and the people brought with them a passion for victory when they gathered to witness the wedding ceremony. They were rowdy, surrounding the group of hungry protestors who were staring out of vacant eyes at them as they danced, turned somersaults, or performed martial arts. Hawkers sold melon seeds and peanuts and smoked mutton kebabs. Pickpockets blended into the crowd, couples cuddled together. Mengliu stepped over the obstacles and wove his way through the lively atmosphere, filled with the smell of beer and urine, and finally disappeared like a bubble into the air.

All he could do was walk back to the Wisdom Bureau. There were sounds of fighting as he walked the streets, and he occasionally encountered injured, bloodied people. One young man was refusing treatment, unbuttoning his clothing to expose the wound and declaring his own willingness to shed every last drop of his blood. Mengliu lowered his head and quickened his steps. Sweat soon covered his face. He ran into an old professor from the Department of Medicine and was about to hail him, but the professor just glanced in his direction, then walked away suspiciously. He suddenly felt desolate, like he was falling to pieces. When he got to the Wisdom Bureau he sat under a tree for a long time. He finally came to a conclusion—he would leave the country, never to return. Wherever he went, he would find a girl and marry her, and would raise a brood of foreign citizens there, where he and they could live freely. He stood up decisively, smoothed his trousers and his collar, then said to himself, *Finally you understand, Yuan Mengliu. This will be the right life for you. You are no hero, and you weren't cut out for earth-shattering deeds. And as for love, that's just an illusion too.*

He looked around at the old gray office building. It was silent, and the countless empty windows looked back at him with a profoundly solemn light.

Jia Wan came by, wearing a gray suit with his shirt buttoned all the way up to his Adam's apple, defying the heat. His shoes were covered in dirt, making him look quite shabby. He was surprised to see Mengliu and asked why he wasn't at Round Square. His voice was thick with accusation. Mengliu answered patiently, "None of that is my business."

Jia Wan was surprised. "You're just being modest. Your poem 'For Whom the Bell Tolls' is very good. It's a particularly powerful call to action."

Mengliu replied, "I didn't write that."

"The poetic styles of the Three Musketeers are distinct," Jia Wan said. "Hei Chun's poetry is direct, while Bai Qiu's is romantic and graceful. No one but you could have written that kind of poem."

Mengliu admitted to himself that Jia Wan's analysis was accurate enough, but he didn't want to change his position simply because of flattery. He knew he hadn't signed the poem, and he didn't want to be associated with it.

He said instead, "Professor Jia, aren't you a member of the Unity Party? Why aren't you there?"

He noticed that a lanky fellow with a sharp profile stood behind Jia Wan. He was lighting a cigarette, and Mengliu thought there was something very familiar about him.

Jia Wan said, "The Unity Party is suffering from internal chaos. I've resigned from my post. I don't want to struggle for fame and fortune, and all this politicking has made me lose confidence in the organization. Just look at Qizi. The international media has really taken to her, and she's always in the headlines. Her reputation is skyrocketing above everyone else's. She is envied by everyone; there was even the staging of a fake kidnapping. Her infatuation with the mic in her hand is an infatuation with power. She doesn't even realize it herself . . ."

Mengliu saw that the lanky man behind Jia Wan was growing impatient as he smoked his cigarette. Jia Wan looked around, then whispered, "It's best not to go out at night."

"Why?" Mengliu asked.

He answered mysteriously, "There's no harm in staying home."

"They're going to be cleared out?"

Jia Wan patted his shoulder. "Just listen to what I'm telling you and you'll be all right."

Mengliu pondered this as he walked home. Jia Wan had never been a close friend, so why believe him now? What was his motive?

He stopped at the entrance to the West Wing. Sadness, riding on a heart-piercing wind, stabbed at his chest. It was as if it had been lying in wait and had attacked him with an iron bar. The pain almost doubled him over. He was breathing heavily, and tears escaped from his eyes. He was being ground into the earth. His heart cried out, *Qizi! Oh, Qizi! What am I going to do?*

His legs felt like they were filled with lead, and his head with water, which swished as he walked with twisted steps, his shoulder rubbing against the wall. The slogans that had been painted there had already run, were no longer fresh.

"I'm tired, so sleepy. Yes, sleepy, and thirsty, and hungry. I want to bathe. I want to have a restful sleep. I don't want to think of anything. The birds, the wind, the shouting, the radio, love, democracy . . . just shut the hell up! Don't talk to me about any of it anymore. I don't want anyone to bother me. I just want to have a good night's sleep."

He had no idea how long he had slept when the door opened and woke him. He saw a girl standing in the doorway, the sun making her face blurry and her body luminous, like a white angel descended to Earth. It took some effort for him to focus, and then he discovered that the girl was tall and well built, and her head almost touched the top of the doorframe. It seemed as if she was stuck there. He did not know a girl as imposing as this one was.

She leaned forward and entered the room. The halo dissipated, and the body ceased its glowing. Seeing more clearly now, Mengliu realized it was a man, Shunyu's father.

The older man's hair was a curly mess, his clothes dirty and in disarray. He wore a strange expression, staring at Mengliu but saying nothing. Two minutes passed like that, then, with a ghastly pallor, he said, "This . . . you hold on to this first. The issue of the chuixun . . . wait until you come back and we can discuss it then." He carefully placed the lady-charming xun on the table, then turned and gave an extraordinarily grave, secretive command. "You must leave Beiping immediately."

"Why?" Mengliu asked, frightened. "Why should I leave Beiping?"

"They opened fire . . . " Shunyu's father's voice trembled, and there were tears in his eyes. "Last night, they opened fire. They brought tanks in and started shooting indiscriminately. There's blood everywhere. Shunyu . . . she, she caught a stray bullet . . . She's dead."

Mengliu felt a bomb exploding in his head. "She's . . . dead?"

"Here is a train ticket, and here's money to use on the road. It should be enough. It should be safe in the countryside. Lie low. Go, and wait for word from me." Shunyu's father was suddenly overcome with emotion.

Mengliu didn't hear him. He rushed out, disheveled, and Shunyu's father grabbed after him. "Don't go back there. They've declared martial law."

"But no matter what, I need to go and see . . . there's still Qizi. God, Qizi! Where are they?"

"They were the first names on the wanted list," said Shunyu's father heavily.

"It can't be. I've got to go look for them."

"The list is growing, and if your name is on it, it will be too late." The old man was filled with anger now. "Do you want your father . . . to bear the pain of losing a son too?"

Mengliu's heart sustained another heavy blow.

No, it couldn't be true. It was a dream. He stared at Shunyu's father, waiting for him to break into a rosy smile. The man couldn't be angry if he had been playing a cruel joke on him.

But Shunyu's father stood helpless and sad, his eyes knotted with a scarlet web of blood vessels. He clenched his fist tightly, then quickly went away.

Mengliu was left in a foolish daze, not quite able to come back to reality. In his trance, he saw a touch of red on the rose bush at the window. He rushed over and inspected it. A shy, fiery-red bud peeped at him, like the eye of a sleeping baby. It was the answer to the question he and Qizi had bet on. They had used their bodies as stakes in the wager. She chose red roses, and he white. She said if he won, she would give her body to him, but if she won, he had to give his body to her, with one added condition—he had to remain committed to poetry, no matter what the situation, and never give up writing. At the time, he had laughed at her condition, feeling it bore no weight. He was a poet, and it was instinctive for him to write poetry, it was the very meaning of his existence. He looked at the delicate bud and almost laughed. But now the bud looked like it had been dipped in blood, and the color was spreading. His mind suddenly became exceptionally clear.

He had to find her.

PART TWO

1

They had a good breakfast of preserved meats, pickled vegetables, fried eggs, and rice porridge. Mengliu washed the bowls, cups, plates, cutlery, and pans and put everything away. He couldn't see any change in Juli. The sky outside the window was as blue as before and the birds in the garden still sang as happily. It was only Mengliu's heart that seemed to be missing a piece, like a hole where the roof tile has broken, allowing the cold wind to enter. He took the diamonds out from under the edge of his bed and held them toward the light, trying to draw some warmth from their glow. He bathed and dried himself, then pressed the green button on the wall and received a spray of perfumed toner. After he had put on a silky white dressing gown, he turned one of the golden taps and filled a glass with beer. With his mouth still full of the taste of malt, he went to the living area and spread himself out on the sofa, his feelings for Juli over-flowing. He heard music and at first thought that he had imagined it. Then he suddenly remembered the cavity in the wall that housed the alarm and realized the music had come from there. The Swanese people listened to the same song all the time. He did not know what else was behind the hole in wall. Listening devices? Monitors? A pair of eyes? The melody was like an eraser, wiping the image of Juli from his mind, turning the vivid thick watercolor painting of her into a gray, filmy form. Qizi and many other women swirled in his mind, and before long they disappeared, too, as if sinking into deep water.

Now he was sucked into the moving green waves. Distracted, he lay on the sofa like the man of the house and rested a moment. Then he put on his robe and shoes and went out the door.

On the road, he encountered a funeral procession. The deceased, covered by a white cloth and laid upon a board, was carried by four men in white clothing. There was a musical troupe, priests, and a group of sympathetic citizens, and they all sang in a soft chorus a poetic narrative of the life of the deceased. It was a calm, serene song, untouched by sadness. Mengliu watched as the funeral procession started to ascend the hill. He could no longer hear the band playing when they stopped and formed a circle, like a wreath worn on top of the hill. They seemed to be holding some sort of ceremony. The blue sky extended beyond his line of vision.

Mengliu headed east, through the deserted streets, to the foot of the mountain. There he found himself facing a complicated gray building. Two spires were raised like swords toward the sky. The heavy wooden doors were open, and on the arch above them was a carved relief. There was a stained glass window above the arch, with red and blue the dominant colors, and window frames of exquisite craftsmanship. He stepped inside. The hall was bright and spacious, under a cathedral-like dome engraved with an elaborate pattern. Light fell through the stained glass windows, and the soft glow was reflected on the tiled floor. There was a solemn, religious atmosphere in the building, and a cold, lonely air about the hall. The crude columns were painted with dragons and phoenixes, and the carved images of curly-haired heads were distributed about the four corners of the room. The aisle stretched out straight ahead, as if it were a long tunnel through time and space. Mengliu moved deeper into the hall. The temperature suddenly dropped, and he began to shiver. Gradually, he felt the building changing. His footsteps sounded with a metallic echo, as if he were walking through a tin box. Then he seemed to sink, and the sounds were gone. The light dimmed, his vision blurred, and he was finally plunged into total darkness. The air was filled with a strong taste of the sea. Suddenly he felt dizzy, as if the hall was moving rapidly. This feeling lasted for several seconds, then he bent over and vomited. After what seemed like half an hour, his stomach was completely emptied of its contents. A hole opened up in the wall of darkness. His vision became clear, and a strong light fell on him, as if the sun was shining so brightly it made the surroundings dreadfully pale. His eyes were bursting with pain, and he covered them with his hands to block out the light. He heard the sound of a machine clicking. When he opened his eyes again, he was in a diamond-shaped space. The strength of the light above him had weakened and turned into the soft light of a blue sky. Music floated like snowflakes through the air.

"Mr. Yuan, we welcome you to Swan Valley," said a robotic voice. At the same time a metal pipe with a coin-sized opening projected out from the wall and stopped right in front of Mengliu's face. "You can see me through this periscope."

Mengliu froze for a moment, then took hold of the metal pipe and peered through it. He saw, as if in a reflection on water, a blurred image of a machine control room. It exuded a charming orange glow and was filled with green plants. There were buttons on the wall with mysterious writing under them. In the middle of the room was a large desk and what looked like a sofa with a person perched upon it. The person gestured to him and told him that if he adjusted the dial beneath the periscope, he would see more clearly, and in even more fantastic colors.

As he adjusted the focus, Mengliu saw a figure sitting in a chair, with hair as green as seaweed. A white veil covered half its face. Its body was glistening, as if it was wearing golden armor.

The robot seemed to laugh a little, then reached over and pressed a button. The periscope retracted.

Mengliu heard a whirring sound from the machine as it went through its operations. All around him, various sorts of equipment now began to go into action. The instruments, meters, valves, and control panels had all been polished until they shone. Electronic numbers jumped as the red screen flashed, and data was generated. A body of glowing spherical electronic bulbs rotated slowly on a screen as the robotic voice issued from it.

"Please have a seat, Mr. Yuan. I am very sorry that I haven't had time to meet you until today."

A man came out from a gap in the wall, his bald head shining. He pushed forward a Chinese-style armchair, then stood to one side, his body stiff and his hands folded at his waist.

"Who are you? Why did you bring me here?" Mengliu was not willing to sit. He looked around suspiciously.

The robot laughed and said, "Mr. Yuan, your tone is a little unfriendly. You should feel honored to come to our beautiful Swan Valley. You are timid and weak, and you lack ideals. But you also lack spiritual support. You need a resuscitation, so we can change your shortcomings and flaws. You will become a poet with impeccable character."

"If I am good or bad, what is that to you? I'm just an ordinary man, and of no value to you." Mengliu felt that the machine spoke with a style that was vaguely familiar.

"Ha ha ha ha. Put aside your old ways of thinking," the robot continued, laughing. "If you have any questions, feel free to ask and I will answer."

"Who are you?"

"I am Ah Lian Qiu, the spiritual leader of Swan Valley."

"You are a woman?"

"Sorry?"

"A woman?!"

"It does not matter."

Mengliu was silent for a moment, then asked, "Why is sexual intercourse not allowed in Swan Valley?"

"A single person can color ten million years of history. That is to say, one good, great, perfect person is more beneficial than countless handicapped people, and those with lower IQs. Swan Valley strictly regulates fertility according to scientific principles. It guarantees a quality population, and that we will not produce useless citizens. So . . ."

"So you seized upon excellent food, laid claim to blue skies, and captured perfection in humans . . ."

"That is blunt, and rather unfriendly."

"You strangle human nature . . ."

"It is logical to be inhumane. What use is humanity? Humane feeling is just a vat of paint. It will make a mess of everything. I am sure you can see how affluent Swan Valley is, how orderly. The people's intelligence, their knowledge and spirit as well as their attitude toward life, are all to be commended. There is no desire, no greed, no selfishness or distraction, only good deeds. Swan Valley will be the most ideal place on Earth."

"Yes. There is no resistance, only compliance. There is no self, only manipulation. People have been turned into robots. It is no different from castration."

"In Swan Valley, where everyone has ample food and clothing, how could there be any unhappiness? Who would object to such a comfortable and agreeable life?" When the robot had said this, it laughed wildly several times, as if it had reveled in this pleasure for a thousand years.

"Then what do you want to do with me?"

"To save you. To let you start over again as a poet."

"I am not a poet, and I don't need saving. Please, let me go home."

"As far as I know, you are a good poet, but you are not the least bit patriotic."

"Nonsense. You would have no way of knowing what my feelings for my country are."

"Mr. Yuan, if you were patriotic, why didn't you join the protests all those years ago?"

"I don't know what you mean. I have my own way of expressing my feelings for my motherland. Moreover, things were not the way you think they were. What everyone knows is just their view . . . "

"You are wrong. One has a clearer perspective as an observer.

"You are like a frog in a well."

"I'm sorry. I meant to praise you. You keep away from messy complications. You are wise."

"I do not need to talk to you about such things. You've violated my personal liberties."

"I wonder. You live like farmers in a village with no church, and yet you talk to me of individual rights? Maybe you are thinking of that girl, Suitang? Don't worry, we can invite her here, and hope that your genes match hers. Sometimes a prodigy . . . "

"No, I've got no relationship with her," Mengliu said, raising his voice. "I don't want to get married, and I certainly don't want to father a prodigy."

"Ha ha. Mr. Yuan, don't be so quick to reject the idea. You will come to love Swan Valley, and you will make a comfortable life here."

"Frankly, I do not feel your goodness. You deprive others of freedom as a means of entertainment."

"You are so stubborn. But you will come to understand."

"I just want to go home."

"We are prepared to make you a cultural officer, and you still want to go back? You'd rather be a zombie, entangled in self-condemnation and guilt?"

Mengliu was secretly surprised. The robot seemed to have completely mastered both his past and his hidden inner world. Yes, he admitted to himself, he did live in a spiritual prison, and he knew beyond a doubt that he had no chance of being set free. He still remembered the day very clearly. Shunyu's father had brought him the devastating news. The red rosebud appeared. He did not board the train and leave. He had gone in search of Qizi. If she was alive, he wanted to find her, and if she was dead, he wanted to find her body. There was no one at the Wisdom Bureau. The guard's eyes were red. The horrors he had witnessed that night reverberated in his trembling words. He described the sounds of gunfire, the tanks, the fires, and the hand-to-hand combat, the wounded and the dead, the ambulances, and the chaotic spectacle, like something out of a movie. He bade farewell to the guard, then ran to other places where she might be found, but discovered nothing. The streets were full of people in uniform, patrols searching and cross-examining people. He went to Liuli Street and found it empty. The walls of the Catholic Church were full of bullet holes. The mouth of the injured street had been stopped up—the birds didn't sing, nor was there a sound from the empty darkness of the broken windows. Beiping Street was even worse. The pavement had collapsed under the weight of the tanks, the surface of the road had been destroyed, stone structures and traffic signs ground into powder. Smoke-charred vehicles stood abandoned along the road. Some of the trees beside the road had been uprooted, and bullet holes filled the walls of the buildings on both sides. The tree trunks were covered in blood. He wanted to go along Beiping Street to Round Square but was stopped by a man in uniform. He remained resolute and got a blow from his gun butt as a result. He created an uproar. He wanted them to arrest him. Maybe if they did, it would be like the previous time, when he was locked up with Qizi. He begged them to take him, but they just chased him away. He was unkempt, one foot bare and the other shuffling along in a slipper. They thought he was crazy. In a daze, he sat down on the road beside a motorbike that had been crushed to a flat, paperlike form stuck to the ground. He looked at it like it was a piece of meat. He knew the odds were against Qizi.

When he returned he just sat in the West Wing waiting for someone to come and arrest him. No one came for him, because the old landlord had told the police that Mengliu never left the house and stayed in all day every day sleeping. On the third day, he went to the Green Flower, but the bar had been closed and Shunyu's father arrested on charges of harboring and abetting wanted criminals. No one knew where he had been taken.

Nearly two years later Mengliu received a letter from him. It was his dying testimony.

Unfortunately, we have no way of discussing together the question of the lady-charming xun. I promise you, it has been passed down from generation to generation in our family for six hundred years. The words on its base, "meng liu," were inscribed by my own hand. "Meng" means to miss someone, and "Liu" was a girl's name. I had hoped we would be able to meet again . . .

The letter had been sent from a prison in the outer provinces. The envelope was postmarked with a date six months earlier.

So Shunyu's father was the chuixun player his mother had met beside the river . . . Every time Mengliu thought of this, he felt suffocated and could not speak.

When your innocent relatives were killed by the guns of the nation, your own life had been taken over too. You were no longer yourself.

His voice softened. It was no longer so self-righteous. He did not want to go back to Beiping, but he was filled with a disgust that he could not quite understand. It didn't matter if the robot of Swan Valley could capture the thoughts of people and understand a person's past and future; the spiritual leader's words still needed to be considered. What man did not want to possess power, status, and prestige? He would hold to his sense of dignity, though.

"Don't try to tamper with my emotions. Even more, don't slander my brothers and sisters. Whom you choose to breed with whom is your business. All I want is my freedom."

"You do go on and on! Today's conversation ends here. Goodbye."

The robot was annoyed. With a crackling sound, the machine ground to a halt. Then all was silent.

2

On Saturday mornings, there was usually a public academic report, followed by an open salon, where everyone could listen or speak as they pleased. Mengliu surprised himself by showing up at the event. He was in a daze and did not remember how he got there. He recalled what seemed to be a conversation with a robot but could not figure out if it was real or a dream. He saw a flat space hewn out of the mountain, and on it an oval table encircled by bamboo chairs. Many young people were sitting there, and some he knew, like Esteban and Juli. They had serious expressions on their faces, which were as hard and cold as stones in winter. He noticed several girls of about sixteen or seventeen, including one with blonde hair and pink skin, a full figure, and long eyebrows above her wide eyes. She wore an indifferent, proud expression. There was also a handsome, elegant-looking young man. His facial features were perfect, delicate and gentle, with idealism flashing in his eyes. They called him Darae, and from time to time, he cast an appreciative glance at the blonde-haired girl.

The mountain breeze blew gently through the leaves on the trees along the slopes, making them sway, with the birds bobbing up and down on their branches. A mighty burst of drums sounded, as Darae presided over the reading of the conclusions of the academic report. The contents were in praise of the beauty of Swan Valley, though there was also mention of a handful of cases of theft, adultery, fornication, and other immoral actions.

"These came about because people were unwilling to change their bloody values, and some even treated gold or diamonds as treasure. Such decadent ideas would seriously affect the development of civilization in Swan Valley, hindering it in its quest to become the world's most ideal place to live.

"In some countries, there are fucking awesome princes, gold-dealers and loan sharks, and those who do not think of the good of the country or have any sense of crisis, and they all live an aimless, useless, bloody extravagant life. The wealthy all work hand in glove, making unauthorized use of the name of the state for their own bloody profit and enrichment. They exploit the poor, and the laborers and the carpenters and the farmers all have to toil endlessly. They are like bloody beasts of burden, barely making enough money to make ends meet. Their lives are a fucking misery. They suffer worse treatment than animals, but without their labor the country couldn't survive. Even the beasts of burden are given a time of rest. They need not worry about the future. And what about the humans who are worse off than bloody animals? They labor and suffer, gaining nothing, and have to suffer pain and poverty in old age. But fucking hell, Swan Valley will never repeat those mistakes. Everything the government does is for the citizens of Swan Valley, for the citizens' fucking lives, to do good, be optimistic and proud of the knowledge we possess. As long as everyone is pure and perfect in their spiritual life, this poetic lifestyle will be a reality in Swan Valley."

"Fucking" and "bloody"—such words kept popping up in the academic report, and Mengliu was stunned to hear them, even though he could not help but nod, the smile of a sleepwalker fixed on his face. He observed the others carefully, his eyes finally falling on Su Juli. She always looked grim, but at that moment even her hair was shining with the glory of idealism. He felt that on some nights her body must have trembled with wild joy, and that however sated she was on polite conversation, she too earnestly looked forward to the coming of midnight to lie with a man. On those hidden occasions her face shone with the elixir of love. Her hair was as smooth as silk. She would have taken off her lip ring way ahead of time, in preparation. As he thought of her warm moist lips, his body stiffened, but he immediately broke free of his absurd imagining.

Esteban seemed to have grown thinner, and looked slightly worn out, but was still in high spirits.

Like Darae he was filled with all the arrogance in the world.

The green-haired monster emerged in Mengliu's mind, along with the robot, and the metallic flavor of that place. "I saw a green-haired monster," he confided in Esteban.

"What . . . monster?" Esteban asked.

"A green-haired monster. Your spiritual leader."

The academic report had ended. It was time for a short break.

On the round table sat a teapot with a spout that resembled the male genitalia. The golden glasses had long stems inlaid with diamonds, and mouths that resembled female genitalia.

The blonde girl picked up the teapot and appeared to pour out a stream of pearls. All that could be heard was a shrill tinkling sound.

Mengliu was thirsty, as if his whole body were on fire.

Before the start of the discussion, Esteban introduced Mengliu to the gathering, calling him a poet. He made particular mention of the fact that he was a carrier of excellent genes.

Still in a daze, Mengliu learned that the blonde girl's name was Rania, and that she was one of Juli's students.

Esteban finally introduced Darae as the young artist who had crafted the naked sculpture of the spiritual leader.

Mengliu shook hands with Darae and was secretly amazed at how soft and smooth his hand was.

In a flash, he thought of Hei Chun, Bai Qiu, the years they had shared together, and the girls.

He sat down, feeling shaken.

"Mr. Yuan, you don't look well. It seems you need a rest," Rania said. The syllables blew from her teeth and lips like a breeze over the valley. Behind her, the blue sea sparkled.

"It's like you've not quite woken up." Darae's tone was suspicious.

Juli's face was impassive as she looked at the bundle of papers in her hand, occasionally correcting a line with her pen. She appeared quite confident.

"Let's continue with the discussion," said Esteban. "As for crime, let's say someone goes into another person's garden and steals some peaches, or chickens, or perhaps even kills a person. Everyone would agree that these are crimes, and that the criminal should be punished. But when one country invades another, destroying their ancestral temples, snatching treasures, and killing millions of people, it is not considered a crime. On the contrary, it is celebrated. But the nature of these two acts is exactly the same. Both are unjust, both are crimes . . ."

"Only people who are dissatisfied with the status quo are eager to rebel, and then dispossessed people make trouble, taking every opportunity to gain something from the chaos," Darae interjected.

"Some governments will try to suppress the confusion by using torture, plundering and kidnapping, thereby reducing the people to beggars. If all the people in the country are beggars, then the whole nation becomes the private property of a small group or elite, much to the sorrow of the people."

Mengliu's mind was a little foggy. "You are all the private property of the green-haired monster!"

Rania hesitated for a moment but did not alter the course of the discussion. "If the country is private property, it is an autocracy, like a person running their private business. No matter how many workers he has, the benefits all go to the business owner, and the workers are under the supervision of the owner alone. But if you look at it another way, it's like a joint venture, and the people are the shareholders. As the company suffers losses or gains profits, the shareholders will be affected. Everyone has a right to have a say in the company's operations, and everyone has the obligation to give to the company."

"You are all the private property of the green-haired monster. She told me so herself!"

Esteban suddenly turned to address Mengliu. "I hear that the crime rate in some of your cities is particularly high because of social dissatisfaction and hatred. What do you think of this situation?"

It seemed no one had heard what Mengliu had said. But he was still thinking of the green-haired monster.

"Do you have hatred in your heart, Mr. Yuan?" Esteban asked, one hand playing with his teacup.

"What hatred?" asked Mengliu.

"Maybe toward women, such as . . . "

"No."

"I heard that your people like fancy clothes and elaborate dressing, but that very few think of their spiritual adornment. They never look up at the sun or moon or stars but are entranced by the sparkle of jewels. Do you think this makes people more noble, Mr. Yuan?" Esteban continued.

As he listened to Esteban's undisguised sarcasm, Mengliu's blood was stirred.

"Of course not. I don't deny that there are a few who live in great luxury. We can't expect everyone to live on bread and water. Since you find it impossible to see nobility in outer displays, then what does it matter if some dress freshly and brightly? You can wrap the same body in linen or silk, but it won't change the spirit of the person. For me, I think a life written in blood is the most noble. Perhaps you want to say that people taking off their hats or bowing to you can't really make you happy. They can't cure rheumatism or correct vision either, but I think no one is really all that concerned about who wears a fur, or how they kneel before a diamond. After all, it is the person wearing these things that they pay respect to."

He spoke quickly, like a burst of machine-gun fire. He suddenly felt that his own words were fresh, and nicely expressive of his thoughts. Because of the pleasure his own remarks gave him, he no longer felt that this sort of discussion was as ridiculous as talking about poetry in a meeting of doctors.

Esteban was very gentlemanly, but his words were oppressive. "When the state is rich, there are massive construction projects everywhere, money is spent, and things get done. The government has shown results, but poor taste. To put it plainly, the emphasis is on showing off wealth. If the whole country is this way, no wonder the people . . . "

"There is indeed a phenomenon of the sort you speak of, but you shouldn't generalize. In any case, the government is always there to serve the people, for the benefit of the people . . . " Having said this, Mengliu's voice grew noticeably weaker.

"Serve the people?" Rania laughed, leaning her head over. "Will those in power serve as nannies to the people? Do you really believe such a childish pack of lies?"

"Mr. Yuan, I'm also inclined to think you are joking," Darae said confidently, touching the buttons on his cuffs. "In democratic countries, you shouldn't have to wash the people's diapers."

"I think that the type of government should suit the type of citizens in a country," Esteban said.

Rania retorted, "No. The type of government determines what type of citizens a country has. What type of chicken you have determines what sort of eggs you'll get."

"That's also not necessarily the case. An ugly chicken may lay double-yolked eggs. Some chickens have beautiful feathers, are gorgeous and elegant, but they still lay small ugly eggs." Darae laughed smugly at his own development of the metaphor.

A small bird landed on the table and began combing its feathers with its beak. It hopped happily a couple of times, then flew onto Juli's shoulder.

3

At night when he thought of the crime he planned to commit after stripping Su Juli of her clothes, Mengliu's body felt engorged, as if all its energy were gathered in the root of his manhood. That part of his body was a restless little beast. Fattening itself up with loneliness, now it was robust, protein-rich, and ready for action. He was not sure when it had grown so fat. This newly gained power was inconsistent with the psychological sluggishness he was experiencing. His body was betraying him, was filled with a vengeful desire. He was a stocky, well-nourished middle-class man with a sparkle in his dark eyes. The scars of history had faded from his gaze, replaced by the charming moderation of Swan Valley.

Like a tree that grows and flowers that bloom, Mengliu opened himself up to enjoy the morning light. He was wearing a navy-blue robe. He stood up from where he was seated and, walking with an easy stride, saw Juli tending the garden, picking off dead leaves, loosening the soil and watering it. He could recognize some of the plants—Holsts snapweed, spotted leaves of Chimaphila, single-flowered wintergreen grass, calyx, purple loosestrife, willow herbs, hickory grass, hibiscus, mock strawberry, butterfly beans . . . He thought that this woman with no sex life could only pass the time by tending her flowers—not unlike a widow scattering and gathering coins in the middle of the night—the various heights and different colors of flowers, growing in the ground or hanging from supports, with the wind blowing casually over them as they climbed, as if struggling and full of pain.

"What is this flower?" Mengliu pointed to a snowy-white blossom, making idle conversation.

"Camellias. Boy-faced camellias . . . Unfortunately, when they're most beautiful, they fall." Juli's expression was simple and natural as she said this.

"Not fall, they wither, or die, or fade. You can say that when a woman passes the age of beauty her breasts and buttocks fall," Mengliu teased cautiously.

"Can people also be said to fade?" Juli did not understand what he implied.

"Yes. For example, a woman dies, like a wilting flower. You can say she has faded."

"Esteban is waiting for your poem." Juli did not smile, nor did her voice become more gentle. "He thinks highly of you."

"I'm a doctor. I stopped writing poetry long ago."

"You can write any time. It's not difficult for you to do."

"I don't want to write."

"Why?"

"What use is poetry?" His eyes suddenly grew dark, as if darkness had fallen over the garden. Juli frowned, unsure how to answer.

"Juli, can I ask you a question?"

"Go ahead."

"Throughout the long night . . . do you ever want that kind of thing? Do you want . . . to know what it's like?"

"What?" Juli still did not understand what he was getting at.

"Have you seen the current spiritual leader?" Mengliu reined in the hints, fearing he might annoy her.

"Yes," she said, her brows still knitted.

"With your own eyes?"

"On the electronic screen. She used to appear once a week. Sometimes she talks with the leading scholars about science and poetry, and sometimes she chats with people about domestic issues."

"Is she pretty?" Mengliu asked.

"Maybe. She isn't tall, and she likes to wear veils of different colors."

"Does she have green hair, like seaweed?"

"Sometimes, but not always. It depends on the light."

"Then I'm not dreaming. I've seen her and talked to her," he said in a single breath. "I've seen her moving about in a room, talking on a phone. She mentioned you, Shanlai, Esteban. She praised all of you . . . "

"These days she doesn't appear on the electronic screen. She has gone on a world tour," Juli interrupted gently, burying the leaves that she had nipped off in the soil. She calmly continued clearing the ground, her movements causing her hips to swing and her buttocks to quiver, as if there were an animal under her skirt.

Mengliu wanted to continue talking about what had happened to him, but Juli had lost interest. He stood alone in the bright sunlight, watching as her body was absorbed into the dark shadows of the house.

It was midday, and Mengliu was walking along the road in a hurry. The diamonds in his pocket knocked against his body. The people resting by the side of the road smiled at him, and he saw in that smile a much deeper meaning, as if they knew he wanted to escape from the place. Their expressions told him they saw a terrapin trapped in a screw-top jar. He realized what a stupid thing he was doing, so he slowed down and crossed his hands behind his back, walking unhurriedly as he tried hard to recall the path he had taken into Swan Valley that first day. Strangely, he could not remember. His memory had been cut off at that point. He felt like he was standing on the bank, looking at the wide expanse of water, with no trace of how he got there. He hoped to evoke more of the memory as he walked. He assumed a casual air and wandered a long way. He had come to the engraved stone when suddenly he fell, rolling head over heels until his body landed against a heap, some soft object, at the base of the slope. When he came to his senses, he saw two lions looking at him with kind eyes. One of them even raised itself and gracefully offered him its place.

His first reaction was to check the diamonds in his pocket. They were all there, not one missing. He could barely stand. He had pretty much always known there was no way out but had needed to test this for his own peace of mind. After his fall, his restless soul quieted. He rested his head on the lion's back, feeling himself no different from the birds, reptiles, and other animals. He had no language, no voice, and no one would ask about his disappearance or death. He was the most common sort of creature and easily forgotten, naturally base, not even in need of a sheepdog to look after him. Where everyone is the same, they all become one big organism.

With a faint heart, he got up and walked toward the mountains. The poplars were scrawny, their leaves sparse. Birds' nests sat in the V between their branches. Thorns were growing in bushes. White flowers bloomed and scattered, like a girl's jacket, giving off a light fragrance. Before long he heard the sound of a stream. Walking along its bank, he came to a body of water. The pond was small, about four or five meters across, and of a dark blue color. The current chased the fallen leaves to the side of the pond, constantly shoving them into a tight spot. They had no choice but to jostle with each other for position.

Mengliu fished the leaves out and placed them beneath a tree.

He thought, "Every stream flows to the sea. If I follow it, I will get some results."

Sure enough, before it was dark, he had come upon a river, about twenty or thirty meters wide. It wasn't deep, and its surface was placid. Bushes covered the opposite bank, and in the distance behind them he could see the boundless mountains, a touch of white at their peaks, stern and bright.

He went into the water, intending to cross the river. He remembered wading ashore on that first night. He looked around, but he couldn't see the remains of a boat, so he raised his head to look at the sky. There was no moon, and night was closing in.

He tasted the water and found it salty. Thinking he must be near the sea, he grew excited. The water was cold and seemed to suck the warmth from his body, making him shiver. His condition also had something to do with the thing he had stepped on, a hard object like a skull, covered with slippery moss. He rubbed the eye and mouth cavities with his toes and very clearly felt two rows of sharp teeth. He thought he must also have stepped on some ribs.

The water was up to his thighs now. It was not completely dark yet. All around was hazy, with only the snowy tops of the mountains clearly visible. Schools of fish swam by him in the water. He had never seen this kind of fish before. They were oddly shaped and not as long as a finger. Their bodies were almost transparent, and they gathered at a spot about a meter from him and halted, as if waiting to accumulate a larger school of fish in this one place. If not for the ripples on the surface of the water, they would have been difficult to detect. Together they were soft, like a cloudy body of fluid, or like seaweed floating back and forth, constantly changing its formation. Attracted, he reached toward them in the water. The fish scattered, then disappeared. Calm was quickly restored to the surface of the water.

As he continued to make his way across the river, he felt a sting on his left leg and immediately realized something had bitten him. It was followed quickly by another hard bite. He turned and fled back to the shore. He saw two wounds on his calf, flowing with blood like a spring. As he was thinking of how to bandage the wounds, he saw Shanlai looking at him.

It seemed Shanlai had been by the river watching him the whole time. He was chewing something as he casually walked over, spat a bit of foamy grass into his palm, and applied it to Mengliu's wounds. The bleeding stopped.

"The squids in the river are very powerful. Within a couple of minutes they can chew you to bits, leaving only a pile of white bones." Shanlai carried a small bamboo basket. His eyes flashed in mockery.

"You're kidding. Man-eating squids?" In response to the extreme exaggeration, Mengliu's facial features enlarged to several times their normal size and looked a little grim as they stood out in the darkness.

Shanlai swung his head, motioning for Mengliu to come back with him. "Every time there is a river burial, you can hear the ghosts of humans struggling in the water at night. The river churns like it is boiling. Actually, it is the squids snatching food, emitting an eerie sound." He turned back and looked at the man behind him. "Many millions of years ago, there were man-eating squids. You see them in all of the cave drawings of the early humans. They were very vicious." He reached behind and knocked his basket a couple of times. "If you stir-fry some of these fellows up with a bit of corn, it's a dish to die for. I've got a few here. They are ferocious, but stupid enough that, with a little light, you can lure them into your net."

Hearing this, Mengliu grew a bit queasy. Limping behind Shanlai, he encouraged the boy to put the squid back into the river.

Shanlai acted like he didn't hear. He switched the flashlight on and swung it back to look at Mengliu's calf. He saw that no new blood was oozing and said, "If you are pure, God will heal the wound . . . "

Thinking that he had almost been turned into a pile of bones by a bunch of squid, Mengliu shivered slightly. Not daring to act rashly, like an innocent child meekly listening to an elder's nagging, he followed in Shanlai's footsteps. Even the snap of dead branches beneath his feet made him flinch. As they moved away from the stream, they pushed their way through bushes with fat thick leaves, into the forest, where they were surrounded by a moist fragrant scent, which mingled occasionally with a rancid odor. Mengliu felt something was wrong. The fear of not being able to get out of the forest enveloped him. The forest at night reminded him of the scene so many years before, when young people grew like trees in Round Square, waiting for rain to come and cleanse them. The forest was silent and furious, bearing great sorrow and helplessness, as if a beast were being held back, waiting for release under the cover of darkness, when it would rush out and devour them. Qizi was like the owl perched on the tree there, eyes bright and vigilant.

"I don't understand. What were you doing at the river?" Shanlai asked, shining his light on Mengliu's face for a few seconds before he turned away, letting the beam play on the forest again. Someone went fleeing by as if holding something in its hand.

"I . . . was checking to see how deep the water was." Mengliu's answer wasn't very convincing. There seemed to be baby cries coming from the forest. "Listen," he said. "What sort of strange bird is that calling?"

Shanlai did not immediately answer. They reached a point where the forest was less dense, and the half-moon shone down between the trees. A bat flew low through the light of the fireflies. "That is a waste disposal site over there," he finally replied. "Some people come to discard things, and the vultures call out. They are pleased."

Mengliu was still not clear about what he meant. They had crossed the hillside, and the quiet face of the town lay spread out before them. He was so surprised he was speechless. The path that had taken him all afternoon to walk took less than half an hour on the return journey. The pain of his wound and the blood trickling down his leg again let him know that he wasn't dreaming. He set aside all the strange questions that were troubling him and filled his mind with the pleasure of returning to Juli's side. His heart was as warm as ever. He did not want to leave her.

4

When Suitang first saw Jia Wan's poetry and photos in the library, she dreamed of meeting the handsome poet, but she didn't imagine that it would happen years later in a hospital. By that time, Jia Wan was no longer youthful and suave, but he still retained a sort of romantic elegance, the wrinkles on his face enhancing the attraction Suitang had first felt for him. Having just entered society, she was now in the first blush of adulthood, perhaps in part because of the positive experience of her affair with Mengliu. The feelings she had for him were easily transferred to Jia Wan, being a poet as he was, and because of his Cadillac. In Jia Wan's eyes, she saw a desire for power that excited her. The old gifted scholar and the pretty young lady wasted no time falling into each other's arms.

Jia Wan had heart problems and needed to undergo surgery. The insurance company was even more concerned about whether he lived or died than his own family was. To begin with, there were problems with his pharmaceutical company. Some patients had died from taking medicine produced by his factory, so Jia Wan was in trouble with the legal system. Suitang said she had tried everything humanly possible to set her man on the right path, but Jia Wan was like a deeply rooted tree, unshaken by any tempest.

When Mengliu learned that Suitang was pregnant with Jia Wan's child, he felt his head would explode.

Suitang's affections were nothing more than a youthful whim, not to be counted on. Jia Wan promised to give her two million yuan, provided that she abort the baby. Jia Wan's wife had dark thoughts regarding the issue and wanted to wait for Suitang to abort the baby, and then not give her anything. She had to prevent Suitang giving birth to the child, for fear she would demand a share of Jia Wan's fortune. Though Suitang was enduring the discomforts of pregnancy and pretending she wanted to keep the child, she went quietly to the hospital and had an abortion. Then the injured bird landed in Mengliu's garden. Imagining it was Qizi, he took her into his warm nest and nursed her back to health, until even her feathers glistened again. When she had recovered, she talked about her fascination with poets once more, mentioning Bai Qiu and the poem in his suicide note. "I see soldiers with their bayonets, on patrol in my verse, searching everyone's conscience."

Sometimes she wore a long pink chiffon dress as she sat in one of the lounge chairs in Mengliu's garden, reading his poetry or looking toward the distant mountains in a trance, as if she had not walked out of the shadows of the past.

"Qi—no, Suitang, let me tell you about Jia Wan," Mengliu said, the alcohol perhaps making his speech a little incoherent. "You don't understand him . . . Hei Chun might still be alive . . . It's hard to know the truth."

He looked at Suitang's face. She seemed very interested in what he had to say.

In the story of Jia Wan's infidelities, according to Mogen, the betrayal of his motherland and of certain political beliefs were smaller matters than the betrayal of his friends.

The summer following the breaking up of the protest in Round Square, the atmosphere had been sensitive and fragile, and everyone was on edge. Summer arrived early, many of the flowers refused to open, and the trees remained bare of leaves. People were very interested in poetry readings, which occurred often and were well attended. The most sensational was the one held in a small garden near Round Square. There had once been grassy mounds there, where the bodies of the dead had been buried, but it had since been covered with concrete. Most of the reciters were students. They read poems by Neruda and Miłosz, Whitman and the Three Musketeers. Later, a young man rushed onto the stage and recited what was in effect a letter of resignation. He was scrawny as a flagpole. Sweat covered his forehead, and he was nervous, his face suddenly turning brick red. He said, "Being obedient citizens under a tyrant's reign is immoral . . . " This phrase pushed the atmosphere to a climax. The young man worked at the Propaganda Unit and was known only by his code name. Somebody shouted that it was time to take care of the headaches, and time for the young people to give their lives for their country. The people's emotions were stirred. Things got out of control, grew chaotic. One of the less famous poets recited poems as he undressed. Then most of the poets began to strip until they were naked, turning the poetry reading into performance art. Later, when the police came, those who were naked and those who were not, poets and non-poets, were all taken into custody and charged with disturbing social order. They were detained for fifteen days. The inquiries did not address the undressing; most of the questions were about the content of the poetry. More pointed investigations revealed that it had been aimed at inciting the people and instigating a reactionary movement. This was especially true of the resignation letter, and his use of the word "tyranny" brought the young man, Xiao Guang, a good deal of trouble. He remained incarcerated longer than anyone else, and it was at this time that Mogen met him.

It was finally over, but the situation remained tense. Many had been caught, punished, and even put to death. Many more remained under "close observation." Mogen fled to his hometown on a remote island to hide. Jia Wan went to great trouble to find him, bringing him news of the death or disappearance of many of their classmates. Of course, he also brought cigarettes, liquor, and books and kept him company as they drank, discussed poetry, talked about ideals, and analyzed the current situation. Mogen felt that, even as the world collapsed around him, he had gained a valuable friendship. He decided he would continue working with Jia Wan for the sake of their fallen classmates. Mogen acted anonymously, while Jia Wan used his numerous connections to help him find work in the district, procuring materials for the manufacture of illegal cigarettes. Mogen still felt uneasy. When everyone else was living in hiding, why was Jia Wan completely unaffected? He even seemed to be a little too successful. But then, one night, Jia Wan drove for more than two hours, rushing back from the provincial capital to vent his frustrations to Mogen, cursing the authorities and informing his friend that he had resigned from the Plum Party. Mogen gained new respect for Jia Wan and started treating him as a confidante. It was on that night that Jia Wan brought up the idea of setting up an organization to carry out underground activities. He would be responsible for handling the money, and he asked Mogen to find trustworthy people. First, they would start an underground newspaper for publicity and the enlightenment of the people, and at the same time, they would correspond with related overseas organizations. He even had the audacity to say that everyone should behave like the poets had.

Hot-blooded Mogen once again found meaning in life. He immediately started preparing and, not long after, got hold of a place for the underground press, pulling trusted compatriots together from all over the island. However, Jia Wan's promised funds never materialized, no matter how long Mogen waited. One day, Xiao Guang, the reader of the resignation letter, suddenly appeared before Mogen and asked him about his relationship with the overseas organizations. He had stolen a secret document and said it might be valuable. Skeptical, Mogen asked him why he should risk imprisonment. Xiao Guang said that, for the sake of their companions who had shed their blood, he had always hoped to be able to do something to help. He could not just stand idly by. Mogen treated the matter casually at the time, but he did tell Jia Wan about it. Jia Wan was overjoyed and told Mogen to get his hands on the document. Mogen thought Xiao Guang could not be trusted and did not want to be fooled by him. Several days later, Jia Wan drove to Mogen's residence, and the two of them discussed Xiao Guang in detail, finally deciding that, even if he wasn't very reliable, he was at least harmless. Three days later Jia Wan again brought up the document. Mogen remained hesitant, but Jia Wan demanded that he get it within three days, because he had already mentioned it to an overseas organization. Two days later, he came to Mogen's residence again, enraged this time. He said five people from the overseas organization had already come to see him, and he did not want to keep them waiting as they had many other matters to attend to. If they did not establish trust from the beginning, there would be no way to work together in the future. He tossed his cigarette butt out the window and bunched up his face. He wanted Mogen to pick up the document immediately, then go to the hotel to find the people from the overseas organization.

Mogen got the file from Xiao Guang and went to the hotel in the city and met Jia Wan, but there was no sign of the members of the organization. Jia Wan told him it was not convenient for them to meet him at the moment, but that the file would be passed on to them.

Actually, the so-called "overseas organization" was just one of Jia Wan's fabrications. He was also the one who had paid Xiao Guang one hundred yuan to read the resignation letter, then paid him another hefty sum to be part of this "document" scheme. As soon as Mogen left the hotel, he was arrested by plain-clothes police officers and immediately sentenced to five years in prison for leaking state secrets. After his release, he could not find work, nor would anyone publish his articles, so he was left destitute.

Jia Wan, who had rendered meritorious service on the other hand, was transformed. He started up his own business and married the daughter of a senior official. He wrote lyrics praising the political apparatus, and his talent for flattery grew and grew. Using the rotted-out ladder of poetry, he climbed his way to the top through the black chimney of conscience. Hearing that Mogen had fallen on hard times, he secretly contacted him through influential friends, hoping to patch things up by using his wealth to redeem himself for past wrongs.

"No matter what, Jia Wan is more powerful than you. There's nothing he won't do, no crime he won't commit. He knows what he wants." Suitang's sleepy voice did not lose its harshness. "But you? You don't write poetry anymore. What do you want? Where are your ideals?"

"After Bai Qiu's death, poetry became hypocrisy, showing off, meaningless." Mengliu's face darkened. "Rows of sentences are just row upon row of corpses. It's all ringing in the ears, and hallucination."

Suitang's eyes closed as she lay on the lounge. She seemed to have fallen asleep.

"Yes. The Three Musketeers are either dead or castrated. Everyone thinks that romance with a doctor conforms more to reality." She lazily opened her eyes and said leisurely, "A hot-blooded fellow could soar higher than the wind, higher than any victory ever experienced, transcend the most beautiful utterances in the history of the world. We have left that time behind, and we have learned to crawl. Armed men couldn't break down the security doors. Only a few men with long hair were left to dwell in Beiping. It is impossible to know whether they feared bloodshed. I still want to believe that, besides shouting and singing, our flesh was also hardened. I am waiting for war, to bring back my homeland. The wolves are growing old and perishing in the wilderness, they have nowhere else to go. I am not a thug. I just want to marry a poet."

Seeing that Mengliu had no response, Suitang straightened up and said slowly, "Those two sentences about war and wolves . . . would you know who wrote them?"

Of course he knew that the poem was written by Hei Chun on the evening before the bloodshed. The poem had circulated underground. Everyone who read it was struck with sorrow. Those who died would not live again, and those who had disappeared were still missing. The Green Flower had been closed down, Shunyu's father captured. Mengliu did not want the pressures of his past to bear down on his present life. In particular, he could not bear to let a girl as lovely as Suitang know the cruel weight of history. But his more secret reason was the fact that he had not played the part of a hero at the crucial moment. He didn't have enough of that quality to fascinate a young girl. He said casually, "I'm a doctor. I only care about the life and death of my patients. I do not bother with who writes what sort of poetry."

5

As Juli applied medication to Mengliu's wounded leg, it was just like the first time they had met. She didn't say anything as she squatted before him, her face a distant landscape covered with a light fog. Mengliu felt like a fish, protected in her aquarium, but also limited, barricaded in. He was willing to give her up—he refused to write poetry, and she did not deliberately do anything to make it difficult for him, but his heart was very troubled, and he was sometimes suddenly filled with remorse. But then he would insist that what he was doing was right. If neither his repressed poems nor his body could be liberated, everything was meaningless to him. He thought she should understand this logic. When he had gone to bed with women, the bodies of both parties were free and uninhibited. It had always been this way. In his own room, doing whatever he pleased with his own body, who was there to bother? He looked at the stud flashing in Juli's nose. Every so often she would get a different part of her body pierced. Her ears had been pierced until they resembled sieves, and even her navel hadn't been spared. He thought that sooner or later she would become a human quiver, carrying arrows in the various holes on her body. Yet her natural orifices didn't allow anything to penetrate.

In the dull silence, after she had wrapped his wound in white gauze and told him about the effects of a squid bite, she said that if he tried writing poetry, the distraction would make the healing process go faster. The poetic impulse had a secret property that stimulated healing, causing the body to secrete regenerative cells. Most people, relying on natural healing, would only recover 50 percent of their health. The wound would continue to fester, the new flesh to decay, and the patient would eventually die of infection.

"I'm going now to the opening ceremony of an exhibition at the art museum." Juli wore a knee-length black coat over her gray robe, her hair braided and fastened at the back with a red clip. She was transformed into an emerald-hairpin, spiral-bun lady, an independent petal. When she spoke, he felt like he was surrounded by blooming peach trees and green willows. "If you are interested, you can come and have a look at what is going on in the minds of today's young people, and see how things have changed."

Mengliu envisioned her naked body, her skin the color of golden wheat, the nectar rippling in her full, round breasts. He thought of all the women he had sampled as water, flowing wild and wanton during sex. At the moment of climax the buns in their hair would uncoil in a sudden burst, their bodies blossom, and their greedy throats utter a baby-like sound that hummed in his ears. They gripped his hair, raising their bodies and biting his shoulder, and he did not hold back. Sometimes after they had recovered they expressed sweet feelings of love, or politely exchanged stories about their background, laughing together over interesting people or experiences. But he had never again fallen in love with a woman.

When Mengliu pulled himself back to the present, there was nothing in front of him but a fleeting trail of scent. He looked to the door through which Juli had walked, up the gravel path that cut through the grass, and out onto the empty road. He saw that it was an overcast day, as if rain was in the offing. His feelings grew dull, and the pain in his leg became more noticeable. He brewed a pot of fermented tea, then hung around the house sipping from his cup. The green plants that crowded the living room seemed to make the air more stifling. He went to the window to get some fresh air and in the distance saw flashes in the clouds. He knew it was raining there, and that the bright flashes were moving in his direction.

The art museum was four kilometers away at the foot of the mountain, about a twenty-minute journey in an environmentally friendly electric vehicle. Mengliu set out to walk there, giving himself time to think. In this way, he could stop if he changed his mind, take a piss, then return home. The bushes gave way to pine forest, and the pine forest to wheat fields. He sat down on the edge of the grass near a field of wheat. Observing closely how the wheat resembled the color of Juli's skin, he plucked a spear and tested its sharp, hard edge with his fingertip. Suddenly the sun came out, and it was as if a brush had swept over the fields, turning them a bright, glaring yellow. They were like a desert, and his gaze was drawn to a straight row of trees in the distance. Perhaps it was an illusion. When he set off again, he could not remember if he had stopped at all. On the left were rolling hills, covered with tall old trees, oak, elm, chestnut, and beech, all clustered together under the rolling wind and extending far into the distance. As he traveled the road between the wheat fields and the hills, he felt he was passing through emptiness. Suddenly, everything was gone. At the same time, two sentences escaped from his mouth:

"My corpse is here."

"My spirit is there."

He took out his xun and, after polishing it with his fingers, started playing "The Pain of Separation." The tune howled like the wind.

A small road veered to the right, passing through the middle of a forest, sheltered by trees on both sides, the sky visible in the interstices between the branches. The sun shone on the leaves as they were blown by the wind, reminding him of the rustling of the crowd that had filled Round Square. For all this time Mengliu had not been able to picture the moving armored vehicles in detail. His imagination collapsed completely at some point. But the cold wind at this moment seeping into his oxygen-filled brain from across the vast wheat fields made him realize that it was harvest time. To the beat of a cheerful, pleasing rhythm, the rows of wheat were falling in succession, the farmers' faces full of a festive spirit. The earth would be left empty as the sun turned red, leaving only the low-flying egret to watch over it. Where were the sheaves of harvested wheat? At the celebration, the wine would be thicker than blood, sweet and sticky. A spilled glass of wine would flow like a river, and a word would transform into a corpse. Right or wrong, man or woman, old or young, innocent eyes would open, large and round, silently swept into the rolling, invading waves and returning with them to the sea when the tide turned. Every summer, all of the world's wheat lowered its head, the flowers withered, fruit remained underdeveloped, insects were more rampant year after year. Summer was meant to be like a woman in the throes of love, wet and thunderous. At this moment, his imagination and the wheat fields were alike bathed in golden radiance, and poetry soared like the birds of the forest.

He leaned against a tree and closed his eyes.

"Hi! Wake up, Mr. Yuan. What are you doing snoozing here?" a girl's voice asked. As if in a trance, Mengliu found himself still sitting by the road, facing a seemingly boundless wheat field, leaning back against a birch tree that had been stripped of its bark. An ant was walking in circles on his sleeve.

"Oh, it's you . . . " He stood up, a little embarrassed because he could not recall the girl's name.

"I'm going to the art museum. Would you like a ride?" Her hair was golden and her skin pink, and her dress a little unconventional. She straddled her bike, balancing her toes on the ground. She had a wicker basket full of scrolls. Her elongated features wore an expression of sneaky arrogance.

"No, it's all right. Thanks," Mengliu said. *A plump girl*, he thought.

"You seemed to be brooding . . . " The girl cocked her head to one side in a way that made her look like a fat bird. A cloud of curls was flying around her. "Are you cooking up a poem or something?"

"No, no." Mengliu did not want to discuss anything related to writing poetry.

"God, you mean sitting across from such fine scenery, you're really just sleeping by the roadside?" The girl straightened her head and peered at Mengliu.

"Being able to sleep any time, anywhere, means you were good in a past life and have no regrets."

"Sounds like you're talking about a pig," she said bluntly.

Mengliu looked at her carefully. "More or less." He didn't want her to go on.

"That's right. I see that you aren't like a poet anyway." The girl snorted, threw him a contemptuous look and, with a whoosh, the bike was gone.

As if someone had slapped him, Mengliu sat stunned for a while. Using the force of his back against the tree, he pushed himself up and the friction rubbed off some debris. He wanted to scold the girl, but the view of her riding off on the path between the mountain and the wheat field stopped him from doing so. The girl was nothing like Qizi. He had only to see a girl on a bike to think of her, though. Sometimes when he saw a bike, or any turning wheels, he would think of her. All young girls would make him think of her.

He lowered his head as he walked, as if he were looking for something on the ground. After a while he came upon an electric vehicle, which was enveloped in youthful laughter. He remembered then that the girl who looked like a fat bird was Juli's student Rania. She had a sharp tongue and enjoyed bandying about all sorts of political rhetoric. Mengliu had a very bad impression of such women. It could even be said that he hated them.

Seen from a distance, the Swan Valley Art Museum looked like an egg sitting horizontally, a gray stone shell wrapped around it, free of all attachments, making it seem aloof. The square outside was full of nude sculptures of strange shapes and sizes, and both sides of the path leading to the museum were lined with national flags. It was noiseless, so silent that even the sound of footsteps was swallowed up. Mengliu sat on a wood-colored bench. The wound on his leg was hurting, and he began to worry that it would continue to rot, right through the flesh, leaving only a skeleton's leg. Bai Qiu had long ago turned to a skeleton in the earth. His poems had been authorized and published. People read his poetry, but no one questioned why he had died. Mengliu smelled the mixture of sunshine and fresh grass and felt confused by his own presence at this place. Groups of gorgeous men and women walked into the art museum. Some of them waved, seeming to recognize Mengliu, but he ignored them, immersed in his own emotions. When a colorful bird descended with a screech and perched on a statue's head, he remembered that he had followed Juli here. He stretched his legs and stood up. All of Swan Valley's exhibition halls were free of charge and open to the public, so he went straight down the promenade covered with a red carpet that led to the museum. There was applause, as the opening ceremony was just ending, and the crowd began to disperse in an orderly way.

Mengliu thought it was a sealed egg, but then he found that the inside of the egg was brighter and more spacious than he had thought. He could not figure out where the light came from.

The huge space had been constructed out of many scattered pieces, and light broke at various angles through these pieces. There were various types of paintings, sculptures, photographs, and craft . . . some pieces hung, some floated, and there was space for animations, films, and videos. His attention was captured by a cluster of oil paintings. On the canvases were pictures of a snowy scene with a dilapidated old factory, cold chimneys, a steel ladder, and footprints across the quiet, depressed landscape, the traces of poor, humble lives. The strings of steel between the trees were laden with tattered children's clothing blowing in the wind. Amid the abandoned train tracks, rusty ventilation pipes, and boundless snow, he seemed to be able to see things beyond the canvas. He felt he had been in this remote town, perhaps in his youth or childhood, perhaps in a dream. Anyway, he was familiar with the scene, and his heart was touched. He wanted to say something. There were people around him who likewise stood in melancholy silence for a moment before the group of paintings, then moved on with blank expressions. They had no desire to speak. There was no Hei Chun here, no Bai Qiu, Qizi, or Shunyu . . . The wound on Mengliu's leg started aching again. He leaned over and checked with his hand to see if the area around the wound was swelling. The skin was very hot to the touch. At this point two pairs of feet stopped in front of him, and their owners held a whispered conversation.

"Darae, if pigs take an interest in art, how interesting can it be?"

"From a philosophical perspective pigs do not think, but if you want to know whether pigs think, maybe you should ask a pig . . . "

"Hi, Mr. Yuan!" The toes turned toward Mengliu. He straightened up, his head almost bumping against the girl's chest. It was she again! "What a coincidence. Do you think . . . a pig can take an interest in art?" Rania smiled as she spoke. Her fertile body crowded his space, and he felt himself being pressed into a corner. He didn't retreat. It was his first close-up view of the contours of the girl's face. It looked like it had been carved out of dough. The eyes were light blue amber and the lips red and sexy, and naturally a little mocking. Darae was positioned between Mengliu and Rania, forming the third side of an equilateral triangle. He obviously did not know where "the pig" had come from. The two men shook hands, maintaining the distance between them.

Mengliu still had not spoken. Juli and Esteban suddenly appeared from behind another screen.

"I heard your leg was injured. Are you all right?" Esteban wore a brown robe with a straight, standing collar. He had shaved his head, leaving only a short beard encircling his mouth.

"Never mind. It's much better now," Mengliu said. Seeing Juli and Esteban appear together, he was filled with a wave of jealousy, yet he could not help admiring the way Esteban spoke so compellingly, with a gentle suggestion of arrogance. Mengliu praised Esteban in his heart, but at the same time felt that he had endured some sort of invisible persecution at his hand. Esteban was a man with a burning purpose. Like a candle in the dark, he would turn everything around him into shadows.

Not wanting to be made a shadow, Mengliu turned and continued viewing the exhibition on his own.

"Mr. Yuan, seeing these pieces of the students' art, you must have an opinion, no?"

Esteban walked a few steps with him. "Would you be willing to be interviewed, or perhaps write some articles on the works?"

"Thanks, but I am just a doctor. I know nothing about art," Mengliu waved his hand. "I am just filling in time, and casually browsing . . . " He paused, then continued, "Señor Esteban, may I venture a question? Do you feel that Swan Valley is perfect?"

"If you would write a long poem, that would be perfect." It was as if Esteban had not heard a thing he said. "That is what we lack, good poetry, and a great poet."

Mengliu eyed Juli, and she raised her chin slightly, as if sensing rain falling upon it.

"I always have a hard time believing the great poet's background." Rania put her hands in the pockets of her fancy dress, as nonchalant as a cat after a meal. "People in shackles can only write shackled poetry."

"Chaos isn't freedom. Freedom comes from order," Darae interjected.

Esteban turned his back to a snowy scene three or four meters long. His brown robe was silhouetted against the white snow. "I think that a great poet's drive should come from a noble, pure spirit. You know, people are like trees in a forest. They need each other so that they can get air and sunshine. Then each tree can grow up straight and beautiful." His mouth flicked to the right, like a breeze blowing the flame on a candle, revealing the trace of a smile. "Those trees that are separated from one another grow up crooked and tangled."

Mengliu glanced at Juli again. He did not want to talk about poetry. He wanted to escape from such conversations.

"You and Darae go and have a look at the sculpture exhibition. There are a few parts of it that need to be tweaked," Juli said to Rania, and the two young people bustled off. "Would either of you object to a drink at the café?"

"Good idea. I am a little tired." Mengliu raised his injured leg.

They passed through a maze of corridors. The café seemed to float in the air. Beyond it, the vast expanse of golden wheat spread to the horizon, meeting the sky in the distance. Clouds were scattered overhead.

A waitress with a flower-trimmed apron served them onion rings, french fries, corn-breaded calamari, and coffee.

"Of course, human nature, this crooked piece of wood. It is impossible for us to make anything absolutely straight." It seemed that Esteban wouldn't eat anything until he had finished speaking. He crossed his legs, stretched his hands along his robe, smoothing it out, and looked toward Juli.

Juli took a book of poetry from her bag, saying that such fine weather and such a perfect moment would be ideal for reading. Opening the book, she slowly read, "'When I think of the things

I regret in life, plum blossoms fall, like seeing her swim across the river, or climbing to the top of a pinewood ladder . . .'"

Each time she read to this point, she went back and started again. After reading it several times more, just as she was about to reach her momentary pause, Mengliu blurted out, "Dangerous things are sure to be beautiful. It is better to see her riding back . . . " He seemed to be possessed and continued reciting without taking a breath, his face turning red and his eyes ablaze. He stood up, faced the endless wheat fields, and recited the final lines, "I need only think of the things I regret most in life, and the plum blossoms will fall on the southern slopes." Tears welled up in his eyes amid the silence of the abrupt ending. When he turned back, his face was pale again, and the light had gone from his eyes. The three of them stared at each other.

"Your voice proves that you are still a good poet. You have a very strong feeling for language." Esteban was excited, and it broke his usual calm, arrogant demeanor.

"Esteban is right. Maybe you are not even aware of it, but your appeal just now . . . " Juli's two chocolate eyes stared at Mengliu. Her speech betrayed an obvious lack of confidence.

"They eat human flesh, but in the end, they will be eaten by humans." Mengliu picked up a piece of squid from the bamboo basket, sniffed it, and put it back again. "I am a doctor. I recommend that you all eat a healthy diet."

6

That night, Mengliu was a little sad. He thought of Suitang. In the pink of health, she was like Jupiter hanging in the night sky before his window. The moon in Swan Valley was always round, sometimes golden and sometimes silver. Sometimes she was covered in fine hair, sometimes she was more like cold rock, sometimes like a big sesame seed cake, and sometimes she did not look like anything other than the moon. She was always three-dimensional, often making him feel that he would see her back if he stood on tiptoe. He believed Suitang was there, her white face tightly clenched, chest bulging, black eyes rolling, as if she were always searching for some misplaced item. She was absent-minded when she cared for the sick and caused her patients a lot of distress. Once, she was responsible for a patient's death, but of course the incident was only known to a few people. The hospital had to protect its own cadres if it wanted to avoid developing a bad reputation that would harm its ability to generate revenue and to contribute to the nation.

He knew that Suitang had greater ambitions than just to be an anesthetist. Her lifestyle was on a much higher level than her career. She was an artistically talented girl. Her calligraphy was beautiful, and she produced inscrutable paintings. Society needed more unfathomable works to be produced. All people were doing these days was comparing who could draw the roundest circles. And she could carve. Her desk at work was covered with the carving of a strange creature. It was hard to tell whether it was an animal or a plant, and on closer inspection it was hard to make out anything other than a few scratches. But the identity of an anesthetist was too strong to be surrendered. The role was part of the mainstream, and as it surged, it washed her clean of everything other than her anesthetist's pale face. Mengliu loved the part of her that had been obliterated, like that of an angel that had passed through death. He found it difficult to extricate himself from her gaze.

Now it was Qizi's face that was imposed over the moon in the night sky, making him feel several centuries had passed. He had in fact already forgotten her face, but every time he grasped the feelings he once had for her, he felt she had grown into a polyp, or a gallstone, or a kidney stone, something like that. He wished the polyp, or kidney stone, would start burning. God, I can't feel my own body. The moonlight poured over him, venturing east. The birds and insects glided in the wind as if surfing on waves, like black meteors passing before his window. He stroked his major organs one by one—heart, liver, lungs, gallbladder, spleen, stomach, large intestine, small intestine, bladder, kidneys, eyes, nose, lips, ears . . . finally he remembered his genitals. Ah, my testicles, my penis. Poor little things! They were like refugees, beggars sheltering under the eaves of a great cold house, wrinkled and filled with a malaise. How they wished for a meal with precious delicacies! They waited for a glorious release. He worried about this ligament, that his muscles would deteriorate and he would develop other sorts of dysfunctions . . . He wanted to soothe his hungry cock. Its body was gradually waking up with the warmth of his touch. It was standing up energetically now, looking at the world. It saw the moon's flowing in the soft night. It stood up and strutted, flapped its wings and cried out to the moon as it soared heavenward. He saw Qizi. She had just finished bathing and was walking out of the moon's palace, her hair wet, lips red, dressed in white and holding a rabbit in her arms. Her chest swelled, flowers bloomed in her eyes. She had become a celestial being, was transforming into the rocks that covered wild places.

Mengliu thought of the surgery. Perhaps there had not been enough anesthetic. He saw a tear roll from the corner of Jia Wan's eye. His will had been torn by his lawful wife. Practically all the wives of the world's wealthy men would have been venomous, ready to take down their husband's lover. Mengliu had thought heroic love had once again appeared among humans, when it came to him and Suitang. When Jia Wan died, the teardrop wrapped around Mengliu and Suitang, and they turned it into amber. Millions of years later it would find a place on some antique collector's shelf. When Mengliu realized he had killed Jia Wan, he fled. He tried hard to recall the scene, but his effort was like breathing on a mirror. His past was becoming more blurred. He kept confusing Suitang and Qizi in his mind. His past was gradually disappearing. Now, he had completely forgotten his youth.

7

The weather had turned even colder, and the early morning fog blocked all the paths from the house. Visibility was low, and the atmosphere pervasively damp. The creatures of the world were unusually quiet. The silence was like a saucer, with nothing to crack it. Water dripped constantly from the ends of leaves, a cozy, soft but sad rhythmic accompaniment to the silence.

Mengliu walked in the fog, his hair falling in sticky white lines. On this morning his body was hard and faced rigidly frontward, like a gun on a ship. He needed an animal to hunt and aim his gun at. The beast inside him had an urge to feast. He walked along Juli's well-worn path. A few minutes earlier, she had picked up a basket of clothes and headed toward the river. She liked washing her clothes in running water in the morning, just as she liked bathing at night when she had finished her dinner, and reading a book in bed before she fell asleep . . . She must have other habits, he thought, like preferring a certain type of underwear or her responses during orgasm. His intuition was that she had been with a man, and that there were certain things she had done surreptitiously. How did she overcome her feelings during ovulation, her desire? Was her eccentric personality the result of this long-term suppression? His own body experienced an indescribable excitement coupled with tender feelings of pity for her. He held his gun resolutely, not weakening even for a moment.

Peering around, he saw he had entered a forest, which was fairly covered in fog. He heard his own pulse, the sound of his blood flowing, the bitter secretions of his gallbladder, and the infinite wind blowing through the silence. He felt like a monkey who wanted to climb up the tree and pick Juli's solid coconuts, and lay her down whether she resisted or obliged. He was almost lost in the foggy forest, but the faint sound of her rustling clothes guided him, like a bell or drum sounding from some unseen place in the distance. He believed she was calling him, and that her already-damp body was waiting for him in the mist. He became urgent, resolute, and, deciding not to turn back, followed Juli's trail of white chrysanthemums, his hair dripping and his clothes mottled with damp stains. Juli's laundry had already been packed into a bamboo basket. She sat on a bench reading a paperback, her rose-colored robe revealing ornate shoes beneath, embroidered with plum blossoms.

He came to a stop five meters from her.

The fog cut them off from everything, as if they were in a secret room. He saw her hair was put up casually, a messiness that revealed her anxiety. He guessed she was reading the Bible. He knew what he should do in order not to startle her. So they were at a stalemate for several minutes. Just as he intended to turn and plunge back into the fog in order to make a new entrance, she looked up. She was smiling, and her smile was bright. She was not the least bit surprised at his appearance, as if she had asked him to come.

She seemed to have become a different person. He felt her change. This time she was like a math problem that wasn't too difficult, and he thought it wouldn't take him long to solve her. She looked at him with interest, like a little girl. Like the sticky juice from a fruit, when she blinked, sweetness flowed from her eyes, along with a kind mockery. He noticed an awkward feeling in himself, like a stifled young bird. They could not find opening remarks. The shifting shroud of fog gently enveloped them in an even more profound silence. He slid swiftly toward her.

"Juli . . . what a coincidence. You're here too." He ran his hand over his hair at the same time as he realized that his gun was no longer there, and felt a timidity that came from knowing he was unarmed. "I heard noise here, so . . . What book are you reading?" He held his hands behind his back and bent his body to look at its cover.

She closed the book, and he saw its title, *The Gulag Archipelago*. He sat down beside her. She read aloud, "'June 3, radio stations in Novacherkassk broadcast the dialogue between Mikoyan and Kozlov. Kozlov did not weep. They made no further promises to identify the perpetrators among those in power. As they spoke, they only mentioned that the incident had been incited by enemies, who would be severely punished. Mikoyan said that the Soviet forces had not authorized the use of dumdums, so those using dumdums were certainly enemies. All those injured had not been accounted for, and none had come back. On the contrary, the families of the victims were sent to Siberia. Those others who were implicated, those who were booked, or who had been photographed, all faced the same fate. Those who participated in the marches were arrested and put through a series of trials . . .'"

"Hey, Juli, you looked really beautiful when you were reading, like a bird singing." Mengliu interrupted cautiously, settling on the point to sweet-talk her. His feelings returned to being pure and simple. "I remember the first time I saw your face in the crowd. You were like a lonely century plant, your long hair fluttering. You could not have known my feelings at that moment—just when I thought I would never see another human again, I saw you." He looked at her intently. Her face was damp, her lips parted as if in surprise.

She closed the book again and put it in her pocket. Just the right size, the pocket looked like it had been made especially for holding a book. "Yes, you dared to go with me then, not afraid that I was some monster who would eat you up in the middle of the night," she said, stretching her hands along her skirt.

He continued teasing a little. Feeling that she had already got up onto his wagon, his own speech became a bit more presumptuous. "I wanted to be eaten by you. The best is if I could watch with my own eyes as you ate me . . . "

She did not seem to understand the lewd direction of his conversation but said that he was lucky, since the Swanese were not cannibals. They were silent a moment, and he tried to think of a way to lead her a step closer to his meaning. "Have you seen a wild lotus? The other day I wanted to pick one and bring it back for you, but it was very strange. As soon as I touched it, the petals scattered." He shook his head with regret. "I think they are the most beautiful flowers in the world. It was just like a folktale, something seen by very few people. I was lucky."

Juli grew flowers in her garden, and she recognized many varieties, but she knew nothing about wild lotuses. This ignorance inevitably made her feel uneasy. "What color was it? What flower was it most similar to?"

He pondered for a moment, then said, "White, or pink, and the petals were thin as a grain of rice. But up close, it looked very different . . . It's difficult to explain, but it was amazing."

She struggled to picture what the wild lotuses might be like, but gave up. "No, I have to see what this exotic flower really looks like." She jumped off the chair. "Take me there now."

He liked the way she leapt up, like a wayward girl. "What reward will you give me?"

"Are you taking the opportunity to blackmail me?"

"Would a hug be too much to ask?"

She looked at him, acquiescing.

He stood up, his arms in a wide circle, like a gambler about to pull in the chips he had just won. She snapped into his embrace, and he raised the gun again. Their embrace grew tighter, neither releasing the other. Everything around them grew quiet, as if immersed in the pleasure of their embrace. Her body was soft, and he pressed against the fullness of it. The parts that were bony made him think she would break if he exerted just a little strength. But when he lowered his head to kiss her, a terrifying scream sounded overhead. A vulture was circling above them at a low altitude like a model aircraft. Their embrace came to a sudden end.

He led her deeper into the forest. They began their walk apart. But after ten minutes, they were clasping each other's hands. He had no idea where they should go. He was looking for a comfortable patch of grass where he could lay Juli down and show her what a wild lotus really was. She seemed to be very patient and didn't ask him about their destination. There wasn't any sunlight along the way. The trees were wet, and when the cold fog dripped down her neck, she cried out.

"Tired? Rest here." He pointed to a fallen tree. He felt this place was all right, concealed enough, and completely safe. "I seem to have taken a wrong turn. I remember it was near the river . . . "

He braced his feet and sat down on the trunk. Juli looked at him but said nothing. He reached out and pulled her toward him. She stood between his legs. "Have you seen that bit of hazel wood before?" He took her hand, looking at her wheat-colored fingers and the white crescent moons in her fingernails. "I forgot which hillside it was on. There are so many bushes."

Her buttocks leaned against his thighs, and he naturally put a steady hand around her waist. Her chest was at the height of his mouth. His passion ignited again, and he buried his face in her cleavage, his body burning. He grasped her. Juli was like a plastic doll that emitted a strange sound when he squeezed. At that moment, as if he had pressed too strongly, the doll popped out of his grip. She looked like a deer standing still there outside his legs, her hair mussed. She said, "I still want to see the wild lotus!"

She was full of an unfathomable vivacity today. He felt that he was a penis, stuck in the ground and unable to move. "I have one more condition." He reached for the hand tucked into her pink jacket sleeve. "I want you to kiss me for a minute."

He also had a puzzling waywardness about him, as if they were two innocent childhood friends.

"Come on," he said. "Just for a minute."

She stared at him, not making a sound.

"Okay, then, I'll kiss you." As he spoke, he stood up, feeling surprised at how free-flowing his performance was, whatever he said. There was no monitor, no alarm. He got to kiss a real woman, then broke off to breathe, but she did not release him. Feeling she was on board now, his restless hand began daring moves. He decided to take her right there and then.

A crow cawed twice, quite rudely. As if she had heard an alarm, Juli suddenly released Mengliu. She could have been waking from a dream. She tidied herself quickly.

"No, it's not safe here." She covered her face, leaving only her eyes revealed. "Nearby there should be a garbage dump. The people who go to dispose of things will pass by and see us."

Mengliu remembered that Shanlai had also mentioned the garbage dump. Right now he wasn't interested in figuring out why they chose the forest as a disposal site. His body was about to explode, and that was the only urgent consideration.

They renewed their search for the wild lotuses. He clutched her hand firmly, his nose sniffing out a more secluded spot. She followed closely, like a runaway. Sometimes they climbed a slope, sometimes they moved on at a trot. He felt that with a woman like Juli, he needed to be clearer in his intentions, since she did not understand his hints. She was an elegant woman, and also infinitely spiritual, a vestal virgin. Of course, whether she was really a virgin he had no way of knowing.

"Wild lotuses only open under certain conditions. I don't know how our luck will be."

When they reached a sheltered place behind a small hill, Mengliu stopped. He thought that, whether from a physical or a psychological perspective, this slope was very suitable for lying down on. The grass was dense and clean and wouldn't soil Juli's dress.

"Don't you want to know what conditions are necessary for the wild lotus to bloom?" He turned to face her. He was glad the fog was still thick, like a curtain hanging around them.

She watched his face, hesitating.

"I do know. It opens when there are illicit sexual relations," she said, laughing triumphantly. "I also know there's no such flower."

"Eh?" Mengliu's heart sank in awkwardness. "You . . . ?"

"Look at the flowers on this tree. I want you to pick me some." Her voice was still innocent. He pulled down a branch that held four or five blossoms. She sniffed. "I think this is called a wild lotus."

"Huh?" Mengliu was taken aback. The situation had suddenly taken a one-hundred-eighty-degree turn. He was the passive one. His mouth was now covered by Juli's, and the crazed passion that came from her was not at all by his design, which made him feel that his careful schemes had been quite childish after all. He reflected on the situation. She had pretended to be confused. This discovery was unexpected, and also beyond his contemplation. It greatly stimulated his animal nature. All he wanted to do was press himself to her, to prevent any further interruptions. Their bodies intertwined in passion, they fell to the ground, and he felt the slope of the earth beneath helping as he eased himself into her. Without further ado, he began undressing. But suddenly, the sun shone directly on them with the glare of a spotlight. Juli's body retreated instinctively, and even Mengliu was stunned. They stood up again, watching in amazement as the fog shrouding them disappeared. In the blink of an eye the air was crystal clear and they were standing not in woods, but in an open space, with only an old tree towering impressively overhead. As if grasping at the dissipating fog, there were two screeches from the sky and a pair of vultures rushed downward into what looked like a meteor crater.

This omen destroyed Mengliu, completely defeating his spirits. He wanted to know what was in the crater. "Let's have a look," he said.

"Don't," Juli held herself tightly, almost begging. "It is the waste disposal site. There is nothing good there. We should go."

"Wait here. I will take a look. I'll be right back."

"I'm telling you, don't. Really. If you look, you will be sick."

The sky was like blue glass. There was not a speck of dust in the air. There were all sorts of weeds and flowers everywhere on the ground. The old gingko tree stood straight up, like a burning torch. Mengliu glanced back at Juli. Her words energized him, and he ran to the pit. She watched him stand there, then quickly turn away, bending over as if his stomach was cramping. She knew very well what he had seen, and that he would be vomiting for the next few days whenever he recalled the sight, expelling everything he ate.

8

At the thought of vultures pecking at the vacant bloody wreckage of the child's flesh, Mengliu's stomach did churn. He felt less and less like a doctor who had opened up the flesh of others and more like a fragile girl. He had thought there was nothing left that could disgust him, whether death, politics, poetry, or desire. He wanted to vomit but could not. He had gone for two days without food and was feeling drowsy. The child seemed to be alive. He watched the vultures snap at its throat, devouring the innards. They pecked at its flesh, staining their feathers with the child's blood, their eyes grim. No one told him why the pit was called the waste disposal site. Both he and the topic were unpopular. Even Shanlai would not explain it to him. He drank fermented tea, which made him hungry but also calmed him. The intimacy between him and Juli had disappeared, as if it had all been of his own imagining. He could not get any confirmation from her. She remained as polite, civilized, and indifferent as ever. He could not imagine her involved in debauchery any more than he could imagine Esteban, stern as the emblem of the nation, in that hidden moment of ecstasy, face twisted as he climaxed and ejaculated.

A week later, it was arranged for Mengliu to stay elsewhere, apart from Juli, a couple of kilometers away in a small house with a garden, built exactly the same as hers, though the plants in its garden were disorderly. The furnishings were exactly the same, with a painting of a forest on the wall in the living room, replete with snakes, butterflies, and all sorts of creatures. The bedding was new, the batik linen embroidered with drums surrounded by groups of birds facing each other. Between the birds was a snake, which in turn held a gourd. Butterflies flew out of the gourd, filling the spaces between the snake and the birds. The room had an ambiguous wedding-night sort of atmosphere. Mengliu walked numbly in a circle around the bedroom then back to the living room. Juli's student Rania was there, as if she had dropped from the sky, her plump body stuck in a wicker chair. Her golden hair was piled into a high beehive atop her head, her skin was pale, and she had a cold, aloof look in her eyes.

"Where did you come from?" His meaning was clear. He was not happy about being disturbed.

"This is my home," she said deliberately, getting up from the chair to replenish her cup of fermented tea. Her fingers, pale and plump as maggots in contrast to the black tea, created a strong visual impact. "Surely you cannot be completely ignorant."

Rania had the charm of a noble lady today and looked like the Mona Lisa, wrapped in a large, loose scarlet robe with pale-pinkish-purple pajamas underneath, which left her full bosom half exposed. Even so, Mengliu felt she was too young, with that unique naivety of wayward girls. "I would appreciate more information." He could not keep the note of sarcasm from his voice. "I'd like to see what fresh tricks there will be."

"Have a good look at this. If you don't understand it, I'm obliged to translate it for you."

Rania took an envelope from her robe. Its sticky seal had been carefully opened so as to preserve its original appearance. Mengliu looked inside. It was an official document issued by the Swan Valley Council, a marriage-gene document. He was so shocked he felt the fear of someone about to be executed on the spot. He closed his eyes, as if he were waiting for his throat to be cut. At that moment his mind was in chaos, with red files surfacing above the mess, each as murderous as a bullet, with the list of the condemned giving off a charred odor, and birds like ashes flying in the sky.

The document was handwritten, a lean script on white paper. There was a fresh, woody scent, and he could tell careful attention had been given to the document's format. It was beautifully laid out, impeccable. At the top, in the center, was a line of text in red and in a bold font. "Regarding the decision to arrange the marriage of Mr. Yuan Mengliu and Ms. Rania Fu . . ."

Mengliu started; the blood was rushing to his head. "Ha!" he laughed, then said strangely, "Arranging for Mr. Yuan Mengliu and Ms. Rania Fu to be married?"

Rania sipped her tea indifferently. Mengliu's mouth gasped as he continued reading. The document not only contained detailed information and explanations about the decision but also described their race, height, weight, blood type, eating habits, hobbies, and included a variety of genetic data. The data was very precise. Scientifically, he and Rania were a perfect match, and their offspring would be a 100 percent prodigy. At five or six, or even younger, the child's thinking would be as mature as any adult's. Their union would bring about the most perfect creation in history, a genetic legend. The document contained many more theories, such as that strong genes build strong countries, that when a country is involved in international conflict it is a contest based on the quality of the people and their knowledge, that riches and power begin with good genes, grasping the spirit of education starts from birth, and so on. At the end, it said, "We have not created a new society because we are better than others, but only because we are simple people with simple human needs. We want air and light, health and honor, freedom and spiritual pursuits. Our impartial behavior is innate. We, the fine citizens of the new nation of Swan Valley, will capture the world's attention in a few years."

"Absurd! Absurd! Absurd!" Mengliu shook his head repeatedly. "What a cock-and-bull story! Can you even believe this nonsense? Are you obeying it?"

Rania's face was like a full moon, like flowers in full bloom protected by strong leaves from the freezing wind. She wiped tea from the table, her clothes rustling with the movement, without showing any response.

"Rania, we do not like one another, and yet we are commanded to become husband and wife. Don't you find that ridiculous? If I haven't guessed wrongly, the person you like is Esteban. You should tell him. We should each pursue our own happiness."

Mengliu felt that this beautiful girl was like a medicine. Nourishing, adding supplement but not too overbearing, gentle on the liver, stopping pain and harvesting sweat. It was difficult for him to view her as a flower, but maybe this was her misfortune. She was the opposite of Juli.

Swanese girls were not rash. At this critical moment Rania remained quiet and calm.

You could say she was confident, or apathetic, or just dispassionate when she said, "Happiness is in the heart. You do not need to pursue it, or even seek it. Whom one likes and whom one marries are different matters. There is no conflict. You Dayangese are used to taking good things for yourselves, turning beauty into something ugly, whole things into something broken. As a result, everything is ruined, and you become disillusioned. You say you want to become a monk, or to migrate, but in fact, you just want to escape."

"Rania, don't you have anything to say about this arranged marriage?" Mengliu was deflated. "I'm a layman, not at all a part of your world . . . If you don't know that love can sometimes demand one's whole life, then you can never understand real love . . . "

"Who says a marriage has to have love? For you the world is big, but not as big as your heart. Is there nothing, or no theory outside the heart under heaven?" Rania had a point of her own to make.

"Your system in Swan Valley, whatever your observances, has nothing to do with me. I want to choose the person I love and marry her. That is my right."

"Well, it seems you really don't know anything. You've been appointed the Head of a Hundred Households. I want to congratulate you on your official position, your contribution to Swan Valley. Your Certificate of Citizenship and letter of appointment will be issued soon and sent to you." Rania's nostrils flared and she snorted. "I really do not understand what use Swan Valley has for a washed-up poet. But anyway, please be less selfish and think more for the collective good."

"Official? You think marriage is for the collective good?"

"You don't love Swan Valley?"

"I love my own country."

"But your own country doesn't love you."

"You're talking nonsense. I won't marry you. I don't want to create a child prodigy." He thought of the raccoon-like Shanlai becoming a miniature wizened old man, with the verses rotting in his belly and causing indigestion, gallstones, kidney stones, intestinal ulcers. His blood would cease to flow, and he would no longer be able to hold the knowledge inside. They would use a scalpel to dig it out, opening the diseased organ and removing tens of thousands of archaisms and countless useless words.

"It's just pride on your part. The match is right. Forget other women." Rania thought for a moment, then added, "Do you know what I'm talking about?"

Mengliu's angry exit from the house brought an end to their unpleasant conversation, but an hour later, when his feelings had calmed, he found that Rania's attitude had also changed. She was respectful toward him now, and more careful with her words, and even her silences expressed a more reverential obedience. She referred to him as Master Yuan, and she looked like a perfectly submissive wife and a good mother.

"I think I offended you earlier. Never mind if you write poetry or not, I should still show you the respect I would a poet. I have not done so, but now I know what I should do." Rania offered him a pile of clothing, and a scarlet mandarin robe, its collar and cuffs embroidered with birds and flowers. On its hem, the swans were so finely sewn that the wings looked alive. She held up the new robe, and Mengliu involuntarily opened his arms and slipped them into the sleeves. As she helped him dress she said, "This was made especially for you, a combination of styles befitting the Head of a Hundred Households, and a bridegroom. You don't know this, but the position is only given to those who are highly respected, so it's an honor. I believe you will be able to take the lead in dutifully doing good deeds."

As if under a strange hypnosis, Mengliu began to feel a little smug. He looked at Rania as she buttoned his robe. As she clasped the next to last button she squatted down, and her breasts swelled as her knees pressed against them. When she finished, she twitched the hem and stroked the birds that were embroidered there. Perhaps because she had squatted down, and her blood flow had been blocked, her pale face was flushed. Her hair was flowing. A red shell hung between her breasts.

Mengliu stepped back, spread out his arms and looked down at himself. His body was covered with birds with strange eyes and gloriously overlapping feathers. It was like a magical robe, and as he wore it, he felt a burning sensation in his chest. His mind was in chaos, and his legs seemed to float, as if he were in the clouds.

"Tonight at the bonfire party we are to take the lead. We need to arrive on time." Rania's expression was submissive, like a humble wife's, a lowly sort of humility.

Once it was dark, she was a different person again. She wore a white wool dress, spread her wings, and flew out the door, bouncing like a Mona Lisa and singing the wedding march in a shrill voice. He did not know this dance of hers, whether it was tap dancing, or a tango, or line dancing. It was a bit like all of them, and also unlike each. It was dissipated and yet restrained. It stopped as it reached a frenzy. It was a rhythmic pulsing, like waves of flesh. She danced wildly all the way, bringing Mengliu to the square.

There were lots of people there. The fire had been lit and the drums were beating. It was a masquerade; many of the people were dressed like savages and wore animal masks. Women suddenly exposed their flesh, draping branches over themselves, leaves dangling as they shook their breasts, twisting their bodies in madness and desire. Some people were using metal skewers to roast rabbits, seasoning them with marinade or sprinkling them with herbs. They were also cooking squid, chicken wings, pig hearts, potatoes, onions, cabbages, sending up fragrant aromas.

Mengliu spotted Juli. Even though she was wearing a vulture mask, her eyes were uncovered, and dazzling. Her hair fell like a waterfall, and her painted body was glittering in the light of the fire. Her breasts were clasped in two melon shells, and she wore a string of red cherries around her neck. Her lower body was wrapped in a skirt of corn husks, and her legs were smooth and as sinuous as a swimming dragon. Earlier, when Rania had told him that at parties of this kind the Swanese people were allowed to abandon all modesty and engage in wild pleasure, he did not expect to see such scenes. He wondered what a carnival among these aesthetes, the Swanese, would really be like and what the limits of their revelry would be. The beauty of the women and the smell of the food stimulated him. The music was lively, the drums and flutes were playing with abandon. Men and women alike were stirred into action, whipped to intensity, their legs flailing and hips gyrating in a danse macabre. They leapt into any space that became vacant, rubbing hips and shoulders against one another in play that was rough and wanton, full of provocation and seduction, like a grand orgy.

"Head of a Hundred Households, today is a double celebration. Why are you looking so glum?" Esteban pulled off his tusked mask. His lower body was encircled by a leopard skin, and he carried a spear.

"I am appreciating it." Dressed in his official robes, Mengliu replied briefly. "What is this dance?"

"The Infinite Dance. It was invented by the Chinese. During the Spring and Autumn period, when the Emperor Chu died, his disciples wanted to pursue his woman, and they invented this dance to tempt her."

"Oh, so that's the Infinite Dance. I've heard of people dressing beautifully for it, and eating elegant food to make them radiant . . . but with you this is . . . "

"Yes, the food must be elegant, and the clothing beautiful." Esteban gave him an arrogant smile. "But to the Swanese, clothing would only cover our perfect bodies."

As the pair was talking, Darae came over carrying a metal skewer with a roasted animal on it, saying, "Mr. Yuan, this is the rabbit king. Yesterday, it bit off the water buffalo's neck, and a hundred rabbits devoured the buffalo."

Lions that ate grass, squids that ate people, rabbits killing and eating a buffalo. These unusual things in Swan Valley no longer seemed strange to Mengliu.

"Mr. Yuan, Darae's cooking skills are superb, just like his sculpting skills. Why don't we watch him use his knife on the rabbit?" Esteban waved his hand toward the square, exclaiming, "Please play 'The Mulberry Song.' Everyone continue dancing!"

Darae took the roasted rabbit off the skewer and sat at the communal table, on which there were laid out knives of various sizes. He took one and applied it to the meat. It was as if his actions were a dance timed to the music. The petals of meat flew in the air like plum blossoms, and their aroma lingered. He paused, changed knives, then took up the dance again, cutting through the muscles and dismembering the animal. Mengliu heard the tearing of the flesh as it was stripped from the bone. The rabbit meat was oily, with a strong taste. With the last note Darae gracefully put the knife down, the process of butchering the rabbit and the song ending together.

"Ah, that's amazing. There's nothing better than watching a skillful butcher dismembering an ox." Mengliu was filled with wonder. "How have you mastered such skills?"

"Darae holds in high esteem the chef who butchered oxen for King Hui of Liang," Esteban said, smiling. "Everything is an art. Does its beauty match that of a good poem?"

Mengliu rubbed his hands, trying to restrain his excitement. But Esteban had mentioned poetry again, and this spoiled the mood a little for him.

Rania, having had enough of dancing, was like a bun that had just come out of the steamer. Her expression showed that she was enjoying herself. She stood to one side, her eyes filled with pride.

Someone brought lotus-leaf cakes, cucumbers, garlic, sweet sauces, hot pepper rings, and carrot sticks, placing them in a huge circle on the table. "Will you please, together with your wife, taste the rabbit?" Darae said respectfully, not at all carrying himself like a great artist.

Feeling himself like an emperor in his robes, Mengliu involuntarily fixed a more dignified expression on his face. As he chewed the delicious rabbit meat, his face remained ridiculously stiff.

"In another forty minutes, the couple will enter the bridal chamber." Esteban ate a few cakes, then got up and left his seat. "Someone will bring you to the hospital. Everything has been set up."

"Hospital?" Mengliu swallowed the last slice of meat. "But why should we go to the hospital?"

"Artificial insemination," Esteban said, without looking back.

Mengliu felt like the chair had been kicked out from under him. His face fell.

"You really don't know much," Rania added. "That's the regulation."

9

The light of the sun rising in the east fell diagonally across the fence and into the garden. With the fresh seed growing in her body, Rania had the look of a new wife. She was like a pregnant cat, and seemed even more elegant when she walked. The old rebellious, naughty, mean edginess had disappeared. She had begun to tend the plants in the garden as she waited for the seed in her body to germinate in the sun, to flower and bear fruit. Mengliu felt it was a dream. His feelings for her had grown even stranger to him. He had no idea what she was thinking, and feared he would never figure it out. He felt the people of Swan Valley were like robots running on a program. In the face of instruction they offered unconditional obedience. And yet it was as if everyone here was a philosopher, denying personal desire with their lofty spirits and the depth of their insights about life.

The wound on Mengliu's leg had still not healed. In fact, it was just as they had said, regressing again after it had begun to improve.

Now that she was Mengliu's wife under the law, Rania used a mysterious potion every day to clean his wound, murmuring as she did so, as if she were saying a prayer before a meal. Since the absurdity of their wedding night, Mengliu had continued to struggle. All the way to the hospital he vowed not to submit to their arrangements, even to die fighting them. Upon reaching the hospital, he and Rania had been separated, and he was brought to a secret chamber with warm lighting and mural-covered walls. The elaborate frescoes with their quasi-religious symbolism moved him greatly. He skirted around green and red mountains, meandering rivers, plains, hills and forests, and a barefoot flying god. Above the giant lotus blossoms, men and women engaged in intercourse, employing all kinds of positions. As the light shifted, they seemed to move in a very lifelike way. Meanwhile members of the hospital staff stood in a corner playing sensual tunes on reed flutes, while a woman chanted passages from a book, as if calling him enticingly to bed. Obscene sounds seemed to come from the people in the pictures. Under such stimulation, poor Mengliu's resolve and dignity crumbled together. A young nurse, smiling with admiration, brought a glass bottle over, and he was happy to pay his debt in pent-up seed. They planned to use an instrument to inject the fresh sperm into Rania. Now he saw that the figures on the lotus were the Hindu god Shiva and his wife. They weren't moving after all. Perhaps the obscene images had been the product of his own imagination. The last image he saw was of a woman, upside down and with legs spread apart, a plant growing out of her womb.

Rania was a woman who was easily managed now. After marriage, she was idle and dull, brightening her days by sipping fermented tea, cleansing her organs along with her libido. All distractions had been washed away. She had become as pure and innocent as a baby, her mind a vast empty space. Touched by the orange of the sun, Rania's sunflower-like face looked eastward, filling her fertile body with the sun's warmth. Mengliu saw the germinating sprout pushing her belly outward. A strange tenderness filled him, brief but sweet. In a way, this unexpected family life had struck a chord in his instincts, as if a candle had been lit in a dark chamber, allowing him to study himself. He was still unable to find clarity—without poetry, his former life had collapsed. It was past. He had often thought about how, in this morass, he could rebuild his world, but it was all in vain. The whole world had caved in.

Mengliu felt a little fondness for the serenity before him. A woman he had never touched, pregnant with his child. He hardly knew her. Her civility toward him gave him a sense of dignity and self-worth. He could appreciate the simplicity and perfection of this kind of relationship, like prescribing the right medicine for a specific illness.

Sometimes he missed Juli acutely, and the distant Suitang, and Qizi, though he did not know whether she was still alive. Rania did not mind his moodiness at such times. She gave all his belongings a good cleaning, even destroying his wallet—credit cards and all—without his permission. She said it was all rubbish, not needed by the Swanese, and therefore cumbersome. The spirit could not be measured in Arabic numerals. People could not live by figures alone. It was a waste of time to fight for worldly possessions. She said the spring has flowers while the autumn has the moon, summer has breezes and winter snow. Having nothing to do is the best season. You could write poetry, study, or meditate, with nothing confusing or surprising happening, no improper thoughts; you needed only to feel cheerful, because the family and the nation were prospering. She related everything to the politics of the nation, turning a flea into an elephant with her descriptions, or a crocodile into a gecko. It was her responsibility to assist Mengliu fully in his role as Head of a Hundred Households, and possibly even as the future Head of a Thousand Households. A dutiful wife should naturally push her husband forward in this way.

Rania was bathed in sun, her hair pulled back into a bun, her forehead white and shiny, idealism crystallizing in her features. Her arms lay on the armrests of her chair, as white as porcelain in the sunlight. She looked like she could break. Her fingers were plump as maggots, their nails rosy. Mengliu had never known their texture or their warmth, their desire or even their curiosity. They had never known the plains of his body, and yet they belonged to him.

His eyes narrowed as he looked at Rania's dazzling white face. It was a leering expression, as if he were calculating how he might seduce her. Since he could not do anything with his own legal wife, except perhaps one day escape with her to the forest for an illicit liaison, he now understood how seriously wrong the situation was.

"Where did you put my bag of marbles?" he asked, thinking of his diamonds.

"I threw them away," she answered.

"You tampered with my stuff again? That was a souvenir Shanlai gave me." He was angry, and distressed about the diamonds.

"Are you still talking about 'mine' and 'yours'? Yours is mine. You forgot that this authority was conferred on me by Swan Valley," Rania said casually. "I was assigned to be your wife according to the document."

Having nothing to say to that, Mengliu turned to the garbage bin, but he could not find the bag of marbles. "You should marry your Swan Valley. It is more suitable than any man to be your husband. I want to annul the marriage right now."

"I know. If you had married Su Juli, you wouldn't say this. But I should remind you that only genes can be a basis for annulment."

"You don't need to bother about who I might have married . . . Swan Valley's ban on sexual intercourse, its reliance on artificial insemi-nation—creating geniuses—don't you find these things contrary to human nature?" Mengliu turned his back to the sun. His body was covered by a soft layer of dust motes. "Rania, as a human, as a woman, do you really not have an opinion about this?"

"No. They're the rules."

"There's always a place not exposed to the sun. A little bit of shadow is nothing very unusual . . . but now, this sort of thing . . . "

Rania smiled quietly, as if to say he was making a fuss over noth-ing. She turned and went into the house, and when she came back out she carried a tea set. "Many years ago we had an artist who went to China and returned with many relics. Look at this purple clay teapot. It's said to be a thousand years old. Try it and see what is different about our fermented tea when it is brewed from Swan Valley's water in a Chinese purple clay teapot." She was very particular about her tea making, not the least bit perfunctory as she spoke. "Smoking is bad for one's health. Smoking is not allowed, and tobacco production is prohibited. Tea drinking has been designated the national pastime because tea cleanses the heart, promotes goodness, and fosters a peaceful environment."

Rania did not speak like a big-hearted, empty-headed person, and Mengliu had some respect for that. "If people maintain a preference for a single flavor, there will be nutritional imbalance. The provisions in the tea referendum seem a little overbearing.

"In some places, good tea is ruined by common hands, just as a good landscape can be ruined by a mediocre artist, or good students made poor by inferior teaching. Swan Valley does not have such terrible problems." Rania took a sip of her tea, testing its flavor with her eyes closed. "Mr. Yuan, don't be a nitpicker. You have admitted that your own place is quite imperfect. Your pitiful attempt at democracy crushed by the government and left to die . . . "

"You bitch, don't try to change the subject," Mengliu interrupted rudely, having gulped down two cups of tea. "This tea isn't so special. The one who brewed it didn't put her heart into it, so there's no soul in the tea."

"You're right. I was distracted. I kept thinking of a question. Did you . . . " she stared at his face. "Did you *do that* with Su Juli?"

"Do what?" He pretended to be innocent.

"Okay, I'll say it directly. Did you go to bed with her?"

"No," he said coldly.

"You are my husband. I will not betray you."

"It's true. I didn't."

"Then Esteban? Her relationship with him?"

This was something Mengliu also wanted to know, so he gave a mysterious knowing smile, deliberately provoking her. "I can't say. You should ask the parties involved."

"Mengliu, I feel we should have no secrets between us." She had changed, and was now calling him by his given name.

"What? No secrets? I hardly know you. I wouldn't even count you as a friend." Mengliu suddenly wanted to mess with this woman.

"You did not see the requirements in the files . . . Of course, we shouldn't talk of requirements, but I really do want to be your friend . . . your confidante . . . your wife."

"You don't need to offer sweet talk. Of course, if you have a good attitude, I will change my view of you." Then Mengliu added abruptly, "Let me ask you. What sort of place is the waste disposal site in the forest?"

Rania's face darkened. She stammered and said she really did not know, as she had never gone roaming about there.

"You're still not honest enough," Mengliu snorted. "I was testing you. You just missed a chance to earn my trust."

Rania was embarrassed, and her face was mottled, as if crisscrossed with the shadows of tree branches. She looked as if she were suffering from vitiligo.

10

No one had given Yuan Mengliu a concrete idea of what the Head of a Hundred Households should do. Life in Swan Valley was based on virtue. They didn't need to lock the doors at night, or keep watch on the roads. The more leisurely an officer's life was, the more it proved that the society was stable, like a smooth surface on a deep lake, free of waves. There had never been sit-ins, poster campaigns, riots, or any such thing. There was a regular flow of inactivity, with everything kept calm and quiet. Of course there could be no substantial change in Mengliu's relationship with Rania either. They were still two unconnected wells, each with its own patch of sky. They always seemed courteous enough to each other. As for a marital relationship, Mengliu was secretly inclined to feel that marriage practices here were more civilized than in Dayang, and of a higher nature. Dayang's marriage customs were more hypocritical. He remembered Suitang's evaluation, how she had said that most married men kept another woman on the side. The wives' forbearance, tolerance, magnanimity, and the so-called idea of their being sensible all allowed the root of their husbands' vice to grow stronger and thicker. A wife had no power to lessen the drive of the male in her husband, and she certainly wasn't attractive enough to increase it. And yet, she emphasized, this was society's mindset, its immovable way of thinking, and marriage was its highest form of self-deception. The male temperament was never as humble as its root, aware as it was of the demands of the situation. His spirit was more like this wretched root, full of wrinkles and folds that would house filth. But men were never as frank and sincere as their own dicks. They could put on all the trappings of a eunuch—falsetto voice, ambiguous discourse, and all—then read *Playboy* when they were alone and get off with the girl next door after dark. It was obvious that Suitang's explosive verbal power was something Jia Wan had given her. But Mengliu thought that her argument, though a bit extreme, wasn't unreasonable, and was useful in bringing him to terms with his own sense of absurdity.

Their house was full of poetry books. Rania would readily pick one up and start reading. It was if she read the poems full of sexual content especially for Mengliu's hearing, to stir his tired body. To begin with, as soon as he heard her reading poetry, he would leave the house for long enough to become exhausted. There was no way to coexist peacefully with her. He had submitted a request for separation, but it was rejected by the Genetics Governing Body, so he ended up writing a confession letter instead, and here his attitude toward poetry became even more ambiguous. He knew Rania was trying to stimulate him, to stoke his desire and inspiration for poetry, but her efforts were futile. She was overly concerned with whether or not he would write poetry, and this lead him to feel it was all a conspiracy, including the marriage. The doubts snowballed in him. As he thought of the mysterious unknown spiritual leader, of the landfill in the forest, the strange pension system, he often touched the edges of a memory that remained a huge blank patch, like a hole where a tooth was missing. It was chilling.

In the midst of this boring, tedious stalemate, he thought of organizing a meeting or holding a spiritual forum. This would also be the best way to keep out of Rania's way. First he would call together the leaders or heads of the various households, then choose a suitable theme for the forum. They would settle on a place with attractive scenery to stay for a few days and send the conclusion of their discussion to be published in the news so that everyone could learn from it. The first meeting went well, the baptism of spirit reflected in their gloomy but energetic faces. Since no specific problems had arisen for them to solve, they had to come up with plans for possible rainy-day scenarios. The meetings began on a monthly schedule and soon moved to once a week, running for two or three days at a time. They were held in various parts of the country, with large or small groups as suited the situation. The groups might include a director of social studies, a chief bodyguard, a medical foreman, the Head of a Thousand Households, and multiple subordinate leaders under the Heads of a Hundred Households. It was mandatory for those invited to attend, each submitting their thoughts over the past week, giving spiritual reports on the public, asking questions, and making suggestions. They put special emphasis on investigating and researching those whose spiritual condition and interests were of a low level.

Individual counseling and exchange would be carried out based on gender and place, with the development of a spiritual model and benchmarks for future members to learn from.

Mengliu's work was impeccable. From a life of leisure he had suddenly become very busy. He ran an efficient operation. In just a short time he solved all the spiritual crises that might arise over the next fifty years. They were stockpiling, their minds steaming forward. They were bending over backward to advance the spiritual work of Swan Valley. The influence of this attitude was widespread, and a lot of people from different places came to learn from them. Darae was the hospitality and logistics manager. He preferred cooking to sculpting, and he often greeted guests with a display of "Darae's settling of a rabbit," while privately practicing his next feat, "the settling of a sparrow." He was preparing to show off his skill at the annual work report. Mengliu and Darae worked well together. But then a rift occurred, because a group of important officials was coming to do an inspection. Mengliu panicked and ordered a vigorous city-wide urban sanitation, whitewashing, road repairs, planting of trees and flowers, and the preparation of Darae's specialities for a hospitality banquet.

"What is a specialty? What's a banquet?" Darae was already against lavishness, and he could not quite adapt to Mengliu's changes.

"A specialty is something different from the norm," Mengliu said solemnly, stroking the embroidery on his robes with his fingertips. "In my opinion, we should kill a lion, and prepare bear claws, tigers' testes and penises, sharks, whale meat . . . "

Darae exclaimed loudly that the Swanese never ate such things. Mengliu said they should serve everything fresh. He wanted someone to be sent to the woods immediately to find hunters, and then to the wharves to look for fishermen, to tell them what to deliver. Darae said that no one in Swan Valley hunted or fished. Mengliu broke into laughter. "Can any place be without hunters and fishermen? Darae, in order to be an excellent chef, in addition to your rabbit you must know how to cook a variety of rare and valuable animals. A chef must possess the skills to cook anything in the world. He should even be able to make timber taste like pork fat. Of course that's just an illustration, but you do know what I mean?"

"Mr. Yuan, this is your wish, but people cannot eat just anything," Darae replied. "I know you're trying to manipulate the laws put in place to prohibit the killing of animals in order to satisfy the extravagant tastes of the rich and powerful. That is a performance that has no boundaries or beliefs." Darae would not pander to the dignitaries. He believed that as long as a person was sincere what they ate was secondary. He had recently gone to painstaking efforts to learn a few new dishes, different from those he had cooked in the past, and he would put these on display. Darae's suggestion allowed Mengliu to back down gracefully, so he relented. He asked him to list the names of the dishes. Darae explained in detail how each was cooked, the nutritional value, the color and taste. He went at full throttle for a long time and didn't seem to be talking about recipes but about the gospel of good health. He put his ideas into the preparation of his dishes, hoping that the diners would feel that they were not just eating food but culture.

"Of course, if dinner included poetry slams and readings, then the characteristics of the feast and the flavor of the food would really emerge." Darae was adamant in his ideas. "Mr. Yuan, you are a poet, a cultural official. If you don't object . . . "

Mengliu didn't say anything. Afterward, Darae really did as he said he would, so Mengliu claimed he was unwell and went home. He could hear the rhythm of the recitations, like the solemn rich beat of a watchman's drum, filling the space around him.

The following week, this outstanding model of "the meeting" was promoted all over Swan Valley. Mengliu was elevated from Head of a Hundred Households to Head of a Thousand Households. He was given a new robe. Its collar and cuffs were still covered with a bird motif, but this time it was a phoenix with gorgeous feathers in a noble pose. Mengliu couldn't differentiate between dream and reality anymore, as if he were starring in a drama. After frolicking about in his robe, he went to Su Juli's house and found her inside drinking tea with Esteban. Although they congratulated him, they seemed somewhat indifferent to his success. He sat for a while but felt bored and could not find anything to say.

When he returned home, Rania's expression pleased him. She was obedient and thoughtful, and meticulous in her attentions. They even began to chat calmly about life. When Rania suddenly put her hand to her mouth and rushed into the bathroom, her face flushed, he knew immediately that she was pregnant.

"The government's aim is accurate." He followed her and, standing outside the bathroom door, took a nonchalant stance.

She stopped retching. "What aim?"

"Hey, it's highly efficient. There's no excitement, no frustration, no prelude, and no climax. Everything is cultivated successfully according to the will of Swan Valley." Mengliu leaned against the doorframe, smiled cheekily, and said, "But having a child without putting effort into the creative process is really shameful. You see, Swan Valley has played me for a fool."

More retching sounds came from Rania and she flushed Mengliu's words down with the fresh vomit. When she had finished, he had to accompany her to the hospital for a checkup, filling in forms and waiting for the government's birth permit. Rania stuffed her mouth with cranberries and started reading Rousseau's *Emile*. She chatted about the child's name and education. As soon as she placed her hand on her abdomen, Mengliu became red-faced and breathless, as if she were clenching his heart.

At night he grew inexplicably anxious. He was unable to concentrate on a single thought without the pockets of blankness appearing in his mind. He walked on the darkened streets. The moonlight flowed around him, and where the bushes grew he could hear rustling sounds. Experience told him that a couple must be involved in illicit sexual relations, secretly enjoying the freedom of sex as they did the freedom of the moonlight. The moistened bushes were disheveled, and the trees stout and carnal, creating an indulgent atmosphere.

The moon painted the streets and houses in a poetic mist, but one that was also rational and calm. Getting a taste for this impersonal kind of romance, he found himself close to a demonic blue light that rotated and flickered. He chased after it, and the beam of light seemed to play a game with him, stubbornly keeping at a certain distance. Without realizing it, he had walked into the forest, and the blue light rotated three times in quick succession and charged at his face. His head exploded into a white cloud, and he lost consciousness.

When he awoke, he was seated in a Chinese official's chair, surrounded by the familiar machine room. He immediately stood up and shouted, "Hey! Listen to me. I'm just an ordinary guy, not one of those big brains with superior intelligence. I'm the kind of scum who'd take the taxpayers' money and do shoddy work. You should be out looking for the high-level people. They have a sense of justice, conscience, ideals, patriotism. They are so heated up with enthusiasm their blood burns. Frankly, their excellent genes are much more suitable for your plans. I can give you a list. Men, women, fat, thin, educated, politically motivated—I know them all. I can take you to Dayang. I know every building on every street. The people there trust the state, they trust ideals, and they trust other people. I think it is safe to say they could quite easily be taken away."

"Mr. Yuan, you really shouldn't say anything." It was the robotic voice again, languid, full of disdain and mockery. "You are the one our machine searched out, the man with the highest quality of genes. Of course, you can be suspicious of anyone, but you have to trust science, and you have to trust the machine."

Mengliu assumed the robot would give him the periscope, as it had done before. He really wanted to have a better look at the woman with green hair. But apparently the robot did not plan to do so. "That can't be right," he replied. "There must be a problem with the machine. Someone like me is just rubbish, not even worth mentioning."

"Ha! Mr. Yuan, you were born a Swanese. Humble, low-key, with the virtue of not being proud of your special talent. You can win a much better reputation and status . . . "

"I don't need it. You can't possibly know what it is people need!" Mengliu shouted, his voice lingering.

"Don't worry about that. I know exactly what the people of Swan Valley need. We won't be tarnished by the modern pleasures of life, the decay, the erosion of principle, the moral turpitude, the spiritual emptiness . . . human life is limited. We won't create waste or let crises brew. Our practice is to allow each individual to be innately elite, genetically so. We must improve the quality of the human race."

"That's just subjective fantasy. Winston Churchill said that Western society has two things that were least flawed. One is democracy and the other is a market economy. From what I have seen, Swan Valley has two things that are most flawed."

"Oh? May I ask which two?"

"Abstinence and politically arranged marriages. Since ancient times, humans have seasoned food with spices to satisfy their taste, used the fragrance of flowers and grass to cultivate their sense of smell, and created art to satisfy our eye for beauty—but you want to put restrictions on all human feelings and imprison people in their bodies. And as for excellent genes . . . "

"Mr. Yuan, you greatly underestimate an elite race's tenacity of will. Immorality caused the death of nations even in ancient times. Lowly personal desires only exist in vulgar people. The citizens of Swan Valley are broad-minded, they hold manners and virtues in high esteem, and focus on noble spiritual pursuits, so how . . . " The robot was talking slowly.

"This is a perverted illusion of peace. I know that not long ago there was a man who went missing. And a girl committed suicide—she was forced to death by what you think of as nobility but others call insanity. You lied and said the man lost his mind and fell into the river and was eaten by squid. The girl who committed suicide was just following her own beliefs . . . "

"For maintaining the normal social order and institutional dignity, death is the most common deterrent."

"That is a fallacy. It is disregard for human life," Mengliu interrupted.

"Wrong. Your mind is overgrown with weeds. You need to cleanse your brain, clear away anything that hinders the operation of the machine. But then again, you are doing a good job with the forums. Evaluating the psychological state of the people and reporting on their thoughts—very impressive. You have ambition, and you know how to use power to serve the people. This is an excellent quality." The robot took a deep breath. "The direction of all human activity, whether political, economic, or cultural, is not something that can be decided by individual intuition or feeling. A machine is selfless, it pays attention to data . . . Oh, by the way, let me congratulate you. You are going to be a father. The government will send a professional to take care of the expecting mother. The food has been arranged scientifically to ensure good nutrition."

Mengliu wasn't listening to the robot. He noticed the fluorescent blink and alternating colors on the machine nearest to him. There were oddly shaped controls that made clicking sounds. He reached out and pressed a purple switch with his finger. The lights faltered in a drunken chaos. He began moving both hands frantically over the machine, as if playing an instrument. All he could see was a crackling burst of fiery light, as all the machines began to shake and then to roar like frightened, crazed beasts. Their parts jostled, and there was a great confusion of noise, as if he were in a huge workshop. The robot's angry voice mixed with the cacophony. "Ruined! You've broken the machines! You've dared to destroy the machines, and you will be hanged, fed to the squid . . . The machines are failing. The information is confused! The data is incorrect . . . You've acted in ignorant recklessness. It will lead to numerous miscarriages of justice."

The temperature in the room had suddenly increased. Sure enough, the machine in front of him was manically producing statistics, filtering data, creating analogues, and clicking away like a typewriter. The data printed out continuously, faster than a newspaper press. It piled up, full of strange hieroglyphics. Mengliu found himself blocked in. He climbed over the stack of paper, intending to flee, when he saw a sheet headed "A Comprehensive Report on the Swan Valley Mind, and Spirit Data Chart Statistics." Printed in red were the names of people with mental defects and other diseases. His name was there, like a centipede, bloated with blood, crimson and plump, wriggling its numerous feet. It suddenly turned into a huge monster, its mouth open to bite him. Mengliu went limp and fell to the ground.

11

The officially brewed recipes for pregnant women gave special attention to nutrition. There were three vegetables dishes, one or two meat dishes, and a soup, and in addition to these regular meals, there was a flexible supply of extras. If the pregnant woman vomited, complementary foods were to be taken immediately, and it was considered a traitorous act for an expecting mother to refuse food. Noble dedication would quickly overcome the symptoms of morning sickness, and the pale-faced Rania, each time she vomited, placidly ate another meal, only to expel it again in an ongoing cycle of eating and vomiting. She remained calm and maintained her appetite. She no longer minded the sounds or uncomfortable poses that her retching produced; she acted like a filter. Food and fresh fruit juice went into her mouth and were deposited in the golden toilet bowl very soon after.

She lost weight very quickly, and her face grew sharp and her shoulders narrow, like the Mona Lisa morphing into Lin Daiyu, the willowy heroine of the sentimental tragedy *The Dream of the Red Chamber*. Her pale skin was suffused with green, her plumpness disappeared, a gaunt look took its place. The poor girl suffered the sacrificial pains of motherhood; she underwent a severe testing of her patriotic doctrines. Mengliu did not bother about any of this. He was immersed in his musings about the robot and whether it was a dream or a real place he had visited. Perhaps his auditory hallucinations, or his perceptual problems, had become more serious. He was always in a daze, unable to recall even the names of Hei Chun and Bai Qiu, much less a line of their poetry. His permanent place was beside the window where he could see the mountains and the river and the herds grazing on the slopes, and hear the playful voices of the people floating by, as if he were seeing characters taken right out of the Old Testament. They had land and cattle, and God was always with them. He longed to talk to God.

The government and the scientists were very concerned about whether Mengliu and Rania's offspring would be a genetic wonder. They took great pains to provide the necessary culinary and nutritional care, assigning Darae to be Rania's nutritionist. When the weather was bad and there were no meetings, Mengliu was surrounded by an unshakeable sense of melancholy. Darae was the only friend he could talk to. Every time he saw him, it was like grasping at a life preserver. Darae brought Rania his newly created dishes: Snow Fox (fried pieces of squid), Battle of Bosnia (cabbage and black mushrooms), Running My Fingers through Your Hair (pig trotters stewed with seaweed), and Small City, Unique Talent (a mixed salad). Mengliu said that the mix of hot and cold in this menu, eroticism and war, was not a bad combination. Darae thought that eating was an art, requiring a certain level of genius when it concerned the appetite of a pregnant woman. Mengliu was shocked to hear Darae's view of Rania's pregnancy. He said that depriving a young girl of her vitality and making her conceive was inhumane and, to put it more seriously, was almost equivalent to raping her. He had been naive not to have anticipated this sort of thing. He asked if there was a girl Darae fancied. Darae remained completely silent for a long while before he finally said no.

It was hard to say what brought about the miracle. Morning sickness didn't interfere with Rania's appetite anymore, and she was able to suppress the vomiting with the strength of her willpower. Her skin regained its color and her body returned to its plump state. She was praised as the pacesetter for pregnant women and invited to travel around giving lectures about her experience in controlling morning sickness, turning the lectures finally into a bestselling book. Her message was "Will determines everything." Nailed to Mengliu's lintel was a golden sign emblazoned with the words *Home of a Spiritual Pacesetter*. He felt like he was a fake Christ being nailed to a cross, full of unease. He could not break through the shell of Rania's spirit. She focused all of her attention on her budding career and her abdomen. Her skin glowed, once again white and lustrous as porcelain.

But during this time, something wasn't right with Rania. Her temperament was eccentric, flaring up from some unknown source, making Mengliu irritable in his turn. He read that pregnancy could affect the sexual functions of a woman, but Rania's actions were also very odd. This Lin Daiyu would break plates in her anger, which was swift and fierce. Sometimes she seemed completely out of control, suppressing her vomiting one minute, weeping the next, making a mess of her whole face. He didn't know whether to stop her or simply let her vent her unhappiness. He didn't understand women at all, especially not pregnant women. He felt like he was watching someone else's wife, wondering what sort of husband she must have to make her so unhappy, thinking he must be a real piece of shit. He also wondered whether the woman had a mother or father, siblings or friends. The government sent servants to care for her, but could they really make her happy? Could they meet all her needs?

Mengliu's expression, at once innocent and stupid, further intensified Rania's emotions. She scolded him, this stranger who had come to ruin her life. When the government had been unable to find her a genetic match for a parenting partner, she had been quite happy, since it left her free to participate each day in intellectual debates. Not to say she was all that good at it, but she had developed something of a reputation. She didn't want to marry and have children; she just wanted to pursue knowledge in order to sharpen her tongue in the debates. She could be subtle and underhanded. The government arranged for her to marry someone she liked, but she found out that he was another woman's man, and hypocritical to boot. In the end, she thought that Mengliu must be her lucky star. But since he had appeared she'd gotten herself into all kinds of trouble. He was the one who had turned her into a fertility machine.

As her accusations against Mengliu grew more fierce, he grew happier. He preferred her like this. It meant they could really talk.

"You wrong me when you blame me for turning you into a fertility machine. That is your beloved government's doing. I was abducted by Swan Valley and have also become a reproductive machine. Maybe you don't believe me, but the people of Swan Valley are nothing more than data, a bunch of guinea pigs." Mengliu took a considerate attitude toward Rania, hoping to catch her at a sober moment. "In fact, I'd love to go back to Dayang. If you could help me, I will remember you forever. As for the child . . . it's also not what you and I want, and moreover it will be raised by the government. Anyway, you and Su Juli, you Swanese women do not need men. Rania, let me say it again, I was kidnapped and brought here. I will leave Swan Valley sooner or later, and whether or not you choose to believe that is up to you. I simply don't care about this damned official post, I would rather go back and be locked up in prison than stay here . . ." As he said this, Mengliu suddenly stopped, wondering if it was really necessary for him to go back and sit in jail.

Rania flushed. "You . . . are the most sordid man I've ever met."

Mengliu responded cheekily, "Since this is how you feel about your husband, you should apply for a divorce. I will certainly cooperate. I'll present you with all the support you need. Does that sound all right?" He was mostly sincere in saying this, as he had no desire to quarrel. Rania did not understand. She said he was narrow-minded, making concessions out of condescension toward a pregnant woman. She called him a villain and said he would never understand the breadth and height of the spirit of Swan Valley. Then she resumed her gentle obliging state, using polite speech to shame Mengliu. He was at pains to smile bitterly as he responded. "Tea cleanses the mind and calms the soul. I'll brew a fresh pot of tea."

During this time Mengliu's skill at brewing tea had improved, and he drank it like an addict. It was difficult to imagine how his meetings could be carried on without the beverage. Holding the cup, smelling, sipping—this series of actions could divert attention and demonstrate his leadership qualities. They contributed to the pretense of being serious, churning out ideology reports, digging up a batch of ideas wrapped in spirit, thrashing it out before the others, arguing, holding up their souls, which were purer than snow, as they cried out.

Rania sat down, looking dignified with her knees touching the underside of the round wooden tea table, her skirt falling over them to the ground. She wore a pale pink lined jacket. Her neck was slender, with no sign of wrinkles. It was such a waste to use this unblemished youthful body to carry a fetus. Her maternal instinct was still hidden; she exuded a powerful sense of youthfulness and innocence. You could easily think of her as a competitive young girl. Mengliu was visualizing her in this way when she said to him, "Let me tell you the truth. I'm not pregnant with your child."

Mengliu was not as shocked as she expected; his expression was cold. "Nothing strange about that. I've always doubted the government's workmanship. In a place where abstinence is practiced, this sort of confusion isn't surprising. But I don't understand why you are telling me."

"If you expose me for having premarital sex, you will be promoted."

"But I don't care."

"That's not being magnanimous. It's cowardice."

"Even if it's cowardice, that's how I feel."

"You don't mind at all?"

"Rania, we are husband and wife in the legal sense, but we have no emotional connection. Still, what do you need me to do? I'll give it my best shot."

"Please expose me."

"Why should I expose you? What benefit is there to you?"

"Do you really want to go back? I know a secret passage."

"Huh? A secret passage? Why haven't you escaped yourself then?"

"Whether I'm to live or die, I won't leave."

"Even if they're all just out to test me, they shouldn't have sent a novice like you to try."

"Mengliu, I haven't been sent by anyone to test you. I only want to know what you want. Even if I was pregnant with your child, you wouldn't care about me. You're the most cold-blooded man I've ever known."

Mengliu handed her a glass of water. "Rania, the debt of bearing this child is best paid by Swan Valley." When she had calmed down a little, he went on, "I want to tell you something serious. Can you guarantee that you won't tell anyone?"

She nodded.

"This may sound a bit strange, but I'm sure you're not from here. You're from somewhere in Eastern Europe, such as Germany, Poland, the former Czechoslovakia, Hungary, Romania, Bulgaria . . . your parents and siblings and friends must be there. Think about it. Isn't that so?"

"I don't remember."

"I suspect that your memory has been tampered with. Tell me, what is the earliest memory you have? What year? Where?"

She thought, then shook her head.

"I believe we can get to the bottom of this." Mengliu felt he could talk to her about the robot. He told her about his meetings and conversations with the machine and the circumstances surrounding them. "You have amnesia for a reason. And it's not just you. It's Juli, Esteban, Darae. They all have this problem. Perhaps after a few years I will be just like you, forget the past, my family and friends, and think of myself as Swanese. This is a frightening prospect. We will all be like fruit from a tree, picked and put in a basket, never knowing which tree we've come from. We're alive, but our names are already recorded in Hades, we're dead without having seen the grave. Our relatives grieve over us. Have you ever wondered why Esteban is dark-skinned, Juli appears to be of mixed Indian blood, Darae looks Korean, and you seem like someone from an Eastern European aristocracy? There are people here from all sorts of races. We all speak English in our own accents. It's obvious we come from different countries. I can't explain how. You say you are a child-bearing machine, and I'm just a breeding stud. We're like grasshoppers on a string."

"I can see you are bewitched." The yellow leaves rustled as Rania spoke, coldly. "And quite sick."

12

The meetings had become boring and were eventually replaced by debates. Esteban was always a major figure at the debates. On this occasion he was leaning against one of the pavilion's pillars, watching the decorative fish in the pond as if he were one of them, a fish that had left the school and was swimming alone. Perhaps he had something on his mind, something he could not say to the fish, because the fish population was the incarnation of morality. He could only blow bubbles in the midst of the fierce ideological turmoil within him and think of a plan while facing the bubbles as they floated constantly to the surface.

Mengliu threw a pebble into the pond, startling and scattering the fish. The lone black koi swayed its tail a few times, not moving from its spot. When Mengliu finally spoke to Esteban he said, "Who knows what fish think? When two of them swim together, can they be considered a couple? Do they have any concept of a family connection? Do they shed tears?"

He went on to say he was tired but he couldn't sleep well. He woke up in the middle of the night and stared at the stars. He felt tortured. God had too many suffering souls to look after, and the devil was given free rein to go about at his pleasure. "What should I do, Esteban? Tell me, Rania and I . . . don't you think it's just too absurd?"

The black carp started swimming away, looking for a more secluded spot. It stuck its head under a rock, leaving its rear exposed to the world.

"Mr. Yuan, to tell you the truth, you are the nastiest person I have ever met. You know it to be true, too, but you don't want to admit it."

Talk of the spirit and that sort of thing was like a drug to Esteban. Once it had taken effect, a rosiness emerged from the darkness of his face. It was hard to describe that sort of radiance. It looked like he had activated some sort of impenetrable shield. No language or culture or onslaught of cannon or gunfire could shake his inner faith.

Mengliu remained silent for a while. Other than feeding the black fish with bits of the bread he held in his hand, he could think of no word or act that was consistent with his inner world.

But then he resumed. "I'd very much like to know where you are from. One day when we all return to our own homes, we should remain in close contact, and visit one another often. We may even become brothers in adversity. Actually, I've had a lot of brothers who've been through trials and tribulations with me, but you wouldn't know. They bled, died, disappeared, fled, sought refuge elsewhere . . . but me, I have escaped through the gate of history, and I have lost contact with my brothers."

Mengliu's words felt fuzzy. He was like a koi blowing bubbles, with smooth, spangled scales, perfect lines of muscle. He could not be singled out as he swam among the fish. The school made him feel safe and secluded. It was a quiet group of fish. They swam as one, playing by the rules. He became completely caught up in his recollections of the past. When he looked down again, the black carp had disappeared, leaving only an empty crevice and a confusion of young shrimp learning how to jump.

Several days of unusually heavy rain left Swan Valley in a state of disorder and darkness.

The rain showed no intention of stopping, so Mengliu took an umbrella and went out. The rain beat on the umbrella like a drum, creating waterfalls at its edges. He was like a rock, a wasted log, a huge ship, his heart turning in agitation. Later, the rain let up a bit, and a misty red strip of cloud appeared in the sky. The sun poked its face out, still half-hidden by the clouds. The light rain looked both alive and tired in the sunlight. He walked to Juli's house, his shoes and socks getting soaked. It was just like the first time they had met, with Juli bringing clean clothes for him to change into. They started to talk about the rain. The great inconvenience it brought also had its benefits. It was as if Mengliu had come specifically to discuss the rain.

Juli took his damp clothes to dry, then casually went about making tea, her movements haphazard and her eyelashes sticking to her cheeks, her speech cool and courteous. Mengliu felt like they were looking at each other from opposite sides of a river. With the waters between them surging, he grew somewhat bored. The distance made him sad. It was as if they were being pushed apart by some unseen hand. He hoped Juli was hiding something, that she was in fact about to collapse and would soon be throwing herself into his arms in tears. The porcelain teacups had three painted herrings swimming in them, with a muddy yellow line running around the sides of the cup. Juli knitted her brow, her eyelashes trembled, and her hands shook. She spilled the tea.

He felt that she was fatter than before, her face was like a Buddha's, full of meaning. From time to time she would break into a crazy laugh, creating a tense atmosphere in the room. When she wasn't speaking, she was like a mushroom growing in the crevice of a cliff, lying low, wet and preoccupied. He wanted to talk to her about something more than the weather, like artificial insemination, or a marriage ordered in red ink by forms from the state, or the present, or the future. But Juli's unbreakable quiet elegance prevented him. He took a book from the table and flipped through it idly. He remembered a topic that interested her, grew animated, and decided to end his dilemma.

"Let me tell you something interesting." He put the book on his knee, caressing the cover with his palm. He wanted to see a renewal of life in her eyes, and so he paused, waiting for her to ask him what it was.

But there was nothing urgent in Juli's demeanor when she asked flatly, "Is it a funny story about the Three Musketeers? Or is it about the leaders? You shouldn't rely on the same old material all the time. Come up with something fresh."

"This is something I've never talked to anyone about. It's a secret about Hei Chun and Shunyu. Shunyu was always in love with Hei Chun, but his heart was just not inclined that way. Love is unfathomable, sometimes it is able to attack a long-standing fortress and topple it in an instant." Mengliu stalled again. The house grew dim, as the sun set behind the slight misty rain that fell on the trees. "At that time, the crowds on the streets had carried out a sit-in that lasted almost a month. One day, there was a conflict between the civilians and the military on West Beiping Street. A military vehicle was smashed up. Hei Chun took a brick and, in anger, threw it at the pile of scrap metal. Suddenly he saw a girl in a white dress digging out two bricks from the doorframe of the public toilet and slamming them at another military vehicle. It was Shunyu. Hei Chun was very surprised. He thought her posture had perfect revolutionary style when she threw the bricks, and he was enchanted. He trotted over to her, grabbed her hand, and ran. Shunyu said, "What are you doing?

Leave me alone. I'm not a party member. I quit the Plum Party." Hei Chun said, "You better stay in the Plum Party. I want people to see how I do a Plum Party member."

Juli lowered her head, as if the story stimulated her and gave her the shivers. "That's barbaric!"

"Sometimes savagery is romantic. They ran into the nearest alley. Hei Chun pressed her against the wall, raised her skirt . . . that son of a bitch! You know, Shunyu loved him. Even if he tried to have her killed, she wouldn't resist."

Juli's body retreated instinctively.

"It's all true. Nothing that happened was unusual at that time. That was Hei Chun's revolution, and his romance. He said when the conflict ended he would marry Shunyu . . . " A light fell on half of the living room as the rain stopped completely and the setting sun floated in. Mengliu squinted, paused for a moment, then said, "After Shunyu died, Hei Chun went missing, and the conflict ended."

A person can close his eyes, but not his ears. The sound of flowers opening, night falling, birds singing, bones shattered by bullets, machine gun chatter, explosive missiles hitting glass, the pulsing moans, and the fires punctuating the dark . . . these sounds were like a symphony that was both passionate and cruel as they blared in Mengliu's mind.

Juli wiped water stains from the table with a towel. "You are still alive. It's a pity you have run out of ideas."

Mengliu didn't speak. He felt blood on his tongue, and he tasted its salt. When he went out the door, the sun splashed over him. He heard Juli say, "The walking dead," and his leg injury began to ache faintly. He walked alone, slowly, not knowing where he should go. Since moving out he had lost all sense of belonging. He still burned for Juli, but she didn't display a trace of warmth. The ground was wet, the air cool. A curved rainbow hung over the hilltops in the mist. The golden forest stretched to the horizon. It was autumn, and there was a hint of a chill in the air. Mengliu sat under an acacia looking into the distance at a cluster of clouds on the mountains, watching the occasional fall of a yellow leaf. He looked at the wound on his leg. It had healed; now the pain was mostly in his mind. He was overcome with sadness and had to breathe in deeply.

The appearance of Shanlai cheered him. He wore a dark-colored lightweight jacket. It had been many days since they had met, and he had a new sense of maturity and calmness, as if he knew all the secrets. He met Mengliu with the warmth of an old friend. Mengliu had much he wanted to say, so when he saw Shanlai, it came pouring out of his mouth.

"Shanlai, you once said the soul is a box. Where does this box go after we die?"

"It turns into a star." Shanlai pointed to the sky. "When a meteor falls, a soul has disappeared."

Mengliu looked at him. He turned into a fish, a mysterious black-and-white, speckled, furry fish. Its tail swung eerily, and its chocolate-colored eyes flashed slyly, seeming to taunt the human inability to understand a fish's world. Mengliu rose from his sadness, as if he'd suddenly remembered he had a meeting to attend. He was willing to go on sitting here, perhaps sitting forever. But he thought, *You little shit. I'm treating you as a good friend, but you don't understand the complexity of the world . . .*

"Head of a Thousand Households, the world is indeed complex, and always surprising." Shanlai seemed to read his mind. "They asked me to look for you and take you immediately to the hospital. I've heard that the machine data was mistaken, and that you and Rania are not the perfect couple . . . "

Upon hearing the machine had made an error, Mengliu was so happy he nearly laughed out loud.

The distant snow covered the mountain like a veil on a demure bride. The sky was so thin that a fingertip could poke through it. The moon floated out, transparent as a soap bubble, shiny as a coin. If one blew at it, a string of silvery whistles could be heard.

13

Mengliu had no interest at all in procreation. He considered his own life quite terrible, and always lived in confusion. To bring a child into this world would be irresponsible; even without considering the fact that the world was only getting worse, there was pandemonium and pollution everywhere. He had seen a lot and he was sick of it. He would rather be alone, free to come and go as he pleased, without care. It wouldn't matter if he lived or died.

He was not anxious to go to the hospital and dallied on the way there. He wondered what Rania being at the hospital had to do with him. She had Swan Valley, an omnipotent, meticulous, and all-embracing government. It gave her the warmth of a husband, the dignity of a father, the omnipresence of God . . .

He seemed to see her lying on a white hospital bed, with a family of doctors and nurses for companionship, holding her hand, examining her body, stroking her forehead, their smiles calming and comforting her. So he was superfluous. His only value was that he had carried the genes and provided the sperm. He was special material. But someone like him would not be particularly favored in Dayang for this reason. Dayang didn't care for such things. They just wanted mediocrity, so long as you were servile enough and stayed firmly fixed in your place until you were rusted on there. Even if you were versatile, useful, full of ideas, if you weren't obedient you'd be ostracized until you were broken and then allowed to drift away.

From this point of view, living in Swan Valley was a blessing. Mengliu came to this conclusion for a moment, and the beauty around him deepened the conviction, as the clean air scrubbed the bitterness from his heart and emptied his mind. His light, transparent body floated, as if the wind were carrying him on his way to the hospital.

The hospital was cool and quiet, shrouded by trees. A stream flowed under a wooden bridge, seaweed swaying and leaves floating on its surface like boats on a voyage. The courtyard was warm and orderly. In the garden, patients in pink-striped garments were strolling, reading, or telling stories to each other in controlled voices and looking good. Mengliu walked through the garden and a hundred-meter-long hallway hung with paintings, past an art gallery, library, and concert hall, and finally along a narrow path full of flowers. He arrived at the obstetrics ward. A scent like that of a lady's bedroom surrounded him and irritated his nose. He sneezed several times, as the sound of his footsteps disappeared into the sky-blue carpet.

He pushed open the door to the ward and ran into a tall nurse who was just coming out. A pair of big black eyes gave him a fright. He had been engulfed by a dark sky with two lone stars twinkling in it. She looked like a giraffe, with her too-large eyes blinking as rhythmically as wipers on a windscreen, though in slow motion, which made her look lazy and arrogant, and somewhat knowledgeable. She knew who he was, and she forced him back a little as she closed the door before saying his name. Her speech was gentle and easy-going, and she said she had been hearing his name for a long time, and that she counted it as a privilege to meet him. She admired the fact that he was humble and unassuming, even though he carried good genes. And she adored poets. She rambled on, not allowing him to interrupt. Finally, in a whisper, she revealed a secret, some of the parties concerned had come to the scientific conclusion that she and he would provide a perfect combination of genes. As she spoke, she donned an expression of academic rigor, then turned to open the door and made him sidle through the narrow opening into the ward.

Rania lay there, face paler than the wall, hair disheveled. She looked as if she were being ripped apart. Her eyes remained closed. From the expression she wore it wasn't obvious that she was enduring pain. She seemed calm and detached when the convulsions passed. Mengliu bent over and looked at her face, asked how she was, and what had happened. Rania opened her eyes no wider than a seam. They looked faint and scattered. She said nothing, but then her face suddenly tensed and her body doubled over. She did not make the slightest sound. He thought she looked like a giant shrimp, convulsing and then returning to stillness, and he almost laughed. Actually, he did laugh in his mind, but he stood still, waiting for her to finish convulsing, then asked again how she was. She didn't try to open her eyes this time. It was as if she were dead.

At that moment, the tall nurse came in. She said that this sort of pain was normal after labor-inducing drugs had been injected, and that after a few more hours, after the fetus was out, things would be back to normal. Mengliu was shocked. "Induced labor? Who dares to tamper with this government-sanctioned child? This is illegal."

The tall nurse took a document from the bedside table and handed it to Mengliu. It bore the red stamp of the Gene Department. The content of the file was quite lengthy, but the gist of it was that the data produced by the upgraded version of the machine showed that any offspring produced by a combination of Mengliu and Rania's genes would create a child with an IQ of less than eighty, which did not meet Swan Valley procreation requirements and was contrary to genomic principles. To ensure a quality population, the pregnancy had to be terminated immediately.

Rania convulsed a few more times.

"I am Head Nurse Yuyue. If you need anything, just press this."
The tall girl pointed to a red button on the side of the chest of
drawers. Her figure was slim but curvaceous, and checking her out
required Mengliu to climb up and down some mountains. She looked
quite naive, her bob-cut hair was black and smooth, as if covered in
water drops. She took the file with her and seemed to smile back at
him as she left.

Mengliu gazed at the woman on the bed waiting for her contractions. The head nurse's attitude showed that Rania's "normal labor
pains" were hardly worth mentioning, and that pity would be wasted
on her. If it meant bidding farewell to an unpleasant identity, then
Rania's pain was a positive thing. Mengliu thought of what he had
read in the file. The clear implication was that he and Rania would
soon be released from the bonds of marriage. Like someone who
had been tied up for a long time and then released, his body was
still numb, and he was not quite sure what to do with himself. He
poked through the books on the shelf, picked up the one that seemed
most interesting, and then sat down on the sofa beside the bed and
flipped through it. He felt warm and comfortable, his blood resumed
its smooth life-giving flow, and he became absorbed in the book.
Occasionally he looked at Rania as she maintained the fixed rhythm
of expression and convulsion, and noted nothing especially out of
the ordinary.

In the dark room Rania's face looked paler under the lights. She
couldn't eat anything. Even drinking water was a struggle. At seven
or eight o'clock, Nurse Yuyue, lips shiny, returned to check on her,
apparently satiated with dinner and complacent, as if she was doing
everything on autopilot.

"If you don't eat, how will you have strength to carry on? You've
got to force something down," she said to Mengliu in a professional,
authoritative manner. She paused for a moment, then putting on a

pair of rubber gloves, she told Rania to lie flat and began poking around inside her body with her fingertips. She wrinkled her brow and grumbled, "What's this? You're still not dilated." She took off the gloves and threw them into the rubbish bin, then went to consult the chief physician.

Before long, some people came in, led by an elderly man with fluffy white hair. It seemed he had been drinking excessively, for his face was flushed. Without a word he put on a pair of gloves and began his investigation. His face grew tense. A young intern clumsily repeated the same procedure. No more than five minutes after they had come in, they all left the ward. Rania was like a pile of refuse discarded there. Her convulsions continued. Sometimes she opened her mouth like a fish, but she didn't cry out.

Yuyue told Mengliu that in order to maintain a peaceful, cozy atmosphere in the hospital, they often needed to inject patients with sedatives. Howling was detrimental to human dignity, and the hospital would be turned into a place of terror. She wrote something on Rania's chart, slotting it back into the clipboard when she was finished and returning her pen to her breast pocket. She said there were complications with Rania's situation, but that he should rest assured she would be fine by the next morning. Yuyue sat down on a rotating stool and turned a full circle. Then she spread her legs and planted them firmly on the ground. Evidently she wanted to have a heart-to-heart chat with Mengliu. She took a small book out of a pocket in the side of her uniform. In it were the poems she had written over the past couple of years, more than a hundred of them. She had never let anyone see them before, but because he was a poet, she wanted him to be her first reader. She didn't use words such as "ask" or "edit," assuming the pleasure would be all his.

He opened to the title page and saw a photo of her there. She was pure as jade, only eighteen years old. She wore faded jeans and a tank top. She was like a giraffe. He handed back the little book and said that he didn't understand poetry, nor was he interested in it. He stood up and looked at Rania and asked if there was any way to alleviate her pain more quickly. Yuyue put the poetry book back into her pocket and explained that when it was really time to give birth to the child, the cervix would dilate to the width of five fingers. Her current pain was nothing, he shouldn't worry, the fetus would certainly come out the next morning.

Mengliu said, "You mean she will have to suffer like this the whole night?"

Rania replied, "Everything is normal. You can go home and sleep. The nurses will take good care of her."

Rania reached out for Mengliu, as if she was on her deathbed. Understanding her meaning, he nodded to indicate that he would stay, but he didn't take her pale hand.

Rania's continuing contractions grew dull and monotonous throughout the night. The hospital was lonely and silent, and there was a romantic orange light glowing outside the window. Mengliu read, but he felt drowsy and could not help dozing off. When he did finally sleep, he slept like a dead man, not even waking when Nurse Yuyue came in to check on the patient in the morning. Rania's contractions continued. Her forehead was sweating and her mouth was open, as if she were dying.

When she came in again, Yuyue donned her gloves and checked Rania. This time, she looked puzzled. Rania's cervix was still not dilated. She checked the time and said the patient needed to eat something. Mengliu immediately got up and went to the hospital cafeteria to get breakfast. Breakfast was served buffet style, and there was a huge variety of options available—bread, cheese, smoked fish, porridge, steamed buns, dumplings, noodles, fruit, milk, coffee . . . A card on the buffet table read *Please do not waste food*.

Mengliu ate hurriedly, then carried some steamed buns and porridge back to the ward. The white-haired old man led a team of doctors around Rania's bed. Their expressions and gestures were the same as the previous day. Before they left, the white-haired man said, "We'll observe her for another three hours. If there is no change, we will have to crush the fetus and then do a D&C."

Mengliu helped Rania up and tried to give her some food. She was only able to take a couple of bites between the bouts of pain. Even chewing was difficult. When Mengliu had been through a similar situation with Qizi long ago, she would playfully bite the spoon and chopsticks, giggling. Lost in thought, he asked Rania if she was in great pain. She closed her eyes, waiting for the contraction to pass, then nodded slowly. Feeling she needed all her strength to wrestle with the pain, he didn't speak again, but fell instead into the steady rhythm of feeding her. After half an hour, she had only finished half a bowl of porridge and half a bun. She could not eat any more and needed to lie down in order to deal with the attacks of pain. But before long she started to vomit and her stomach was emptied of its contents. Her body drooped over the edge of the bed, like a wilted vegetable robbed of all its moisture. Mengliu lay her back on the bed, covered her with the quilt, and wiped the sweat and tears from her face. She experienced another violent contraction, then calm was restored. She was very tired and slept finally. He looked at her childlike face, recalling her unruly manner of speech, her sharp arrogant words, her bike speeding away, her unbridled state as she strutted around . . . and now she was just a helpless infant, manipulated by others. She had never been master of her own body. He sighed. Her face was drained of its color. He felt time was frozen in her face. Gradually a creamy layer formed on her lips and turned to a dry crust. He realized that she needed water. He took a glass and went out to find it. There was a dispenser at the end of the corridor. There was mineral water, fruit juice, and instant hot tea. He took a cup of mineral water.

When he returned, he found Rania sleeping soundly and could not bear to wake her, so he stood holding the cup of water as he looked down at her. At this moment, he inexplicably felt a sense of responsibility toward her. No matter what, she was a fragile little girl with a high IQ and a good heart, and had done her duty toward him. He, on the other hand, was cold and often cynical, bickering with her for any reason—or even without reason. He never trusted her and always thought of her simply as an agent of Swan Valley who was trying to get him to write poetry. When she endured suffering, he was insensitive and didn't offer any comfort. Thinking of this, he felt some remorse. He sat down on her bed and clutched her hand. It was very cold, like the hand of a patient who had died on the operating table. An ominous feeling came over him, and he pressed her hand harder. She did not respond. At the same time he felt that he was sitting on something sticky. He stood up and discovered blood. Pulling the blanket back, he saw that the lower part of Rania's body was lying in a pool of blood.

She was dead. He was almost pushed out of the door by this realization. His chest felt cold, as if his own heart had stopped beating. He stared at Rania as if he had murdered her.

14

Grief is like a perennial frost in the heart, but no amount of grieving could cause an avalanche in Mengliu. He still maintained a doctor's cold rationality, and his regret and self-condemnation remained buried under the ice, though to alleviate his conscience he continued to blame Rania's death on the government. The media and the public all thought it was an accident, and there were even some reporters who wrote euphemistically about the couple's dereliction of duty, saying that they had been immersed in reading erotic Japanese novels at the time of her death, highlighting the apathy between them. This united front of gossip made Mengliu anxious. They had concluded, ridiculously, that it was the marriage, not medical malpractice, that was the cause. The more gossipy magazines began to exaggerate even more, expounding on men and their family responsibilities, and then the moral arrows really started to fly at Yuan Mengliu. For a time, he was a very hot topic.

Swan Valley gave Rania one final glorious moment. Her funeral was carried out to the highest specifications in the most prestigious church. She was laid out among fresh white flowers, her cheeks rouged, her body covered with the Swan Valley flag. A high-ranking government official delivered the eulogy, during which his voice choked several times. People wept silently with a controlled sadness, passing by her coffin to place flowers and say their farewells in an orderly fashion. Then they went out of the church and on with their lives. After a couple of weeks had passed, people mentioned Rania from time to time, saying what a pity it was to have lost such superior genes and such a talent from Swan Valley, but no one bothered to trace the loss back to its source. When he thought of Rania's corpse among the fresh flowers, there was a dull pain in Mengliu's mind. Guilt and anger wrapped themselves around his heart. He resigned from his post as Head of a Thousand Households. He wanted to move back in with Juli.

He imagined that he would be released from his old shackles and allowed to put on new ones, but everything was different now from what it had been before. Rania's death gave him a fresh start. He was polite to people, but behind it there was a quiet kind of alienation. He thought that if he lived with Juli again it wouldn't be like the last time. Back then fantasies of temptation flew about the house like butterflies, and the atmosphere was one of quiet joy for both of them. His mind then had been like a notched arrow, waiting to fly at the first sight of a suitable girl. But now it was as if he and Juli were coming together again after decades of separation.

They often didn't have much to say to each other as they went about their business. Even Shanlai didn't disrupt this scenario, as he came in the door without a sound, sometimes carrying a few books, sometimes turning out his pocketfuls of wild berries and leaving them on the table. They no longer discussed the soul or art. The two of them gave off an air of religious detachment. Esteban came to visit on his own initiative, occasionally looking in on Mengliu as he passed by. When he visited, he was often with Darae or another young person, and they always talked about Rania with regret. Her memorial inscription was an elegiac couplet that Esteban had written, wrought with distress and pain. They did not criticize Mengliu. He tried to avoid them at such times, sometimes going out to check on Rania's grave to see if the grass had grown on it, sometimes to visit the mountains. Once he looked for the waste disposal site, but he did not find it. He could never quite figure out the state of the roads, and could find no trace of the places in his memory, like the place where the robot had spoken to him or the slopes covered with wild lilies. The weather was as temperamental as a menopausal woman. When it was about to rain, the sky would be unusually bright, and sometimes covered with a layer of haze.

On this day, a heavy rainstorm had just passed and the company was again talking of Rania's death, about what might have been if she were still alive. Mengliu walked quietly away, not wanting to recall the sight of her dying right there before his eyes. The air was fresh and damp in the mountains, the valleys quiet and the narrow path he walked on empty. A scattering of black fungus grew on the side of the path. The leaves on the trees appeared disordered by the storm. Dark, thin clouds floated high above, and the vegetation on the hillside changed at intervals, sometimes grass, sometimes bamboo, and whole patches of azalea bushes. There was not a breath of wind. Mengliu's shoes were soon soaked and the sweat was flowing off him. He didn't know where he was going. Everything around him seemed desolate. The wind ripped into the warmth of his body. His lips started to quiver violently, and his teeth were knocking together. He wrapped his arms around himself and began to run in this awkward posture. Sweat ran down his face, and his feet exploded the puddles and snapped the twigs beneath them. He was running through the Wisdom Bureau's sporting grounds. The cries of the girls were ear-splitting as they cheered Hei Chun on. He wore a blue-and-white sweatshirt and looked supple as a stallion. He galloped along, stirring up waves and clouds of sand, leaving Mengliu in his wake. He always lost to Hei Chun. This was an indisputable fact. He just didn't possess Hei Chun's desperate passion. They had fought once for the sake of a poem, and he had suffered a hard blow from his friend. Hei Chun told him why he had hit him—he believed that fists could make fools a little cleverer, at least for a while. Mengliu had never questioned his own intelligence. His proof lay in the fact that he had been admitted to the nation's top schools and finally to the Wisdom Bureau itself because he was a champion of the arts. Hei Chun said it was just a silly exam that propelled a stupid fellow like Mengliu to a high position, but he couldn't change his fate and become just a useless mediocrity. For some time afterward Mengliu drank alone in crowded bars, not talking and not thinking, just listening to the complicated strains of jazz that wove through the contorting bodies that surrounded him, like the sound of a stream flowing past. He sat there, indifferent. Then the sun would come up and the people dispersed. They had their work, their health, and their sobriety. Their eyes were bright, and they lived contented lives, while his heart was cramped with a sense of loss. Sometimes he thought Hei

Chun might be right. A high IQ was nothing in some circumstances, and could lead one to live an impotent life.

But obviously Hei Chun was mistaken, and Swan Valley was proof of that. Not long ago, he had risen to the position of Head of a Thousand Households. Those who prepared the spiritual briefing materials wrote them in a more interesting way than he was used to. They knew he was a poet and were happy to rack their brains and modify their style to try to find an interesting way to express themselves. In the meetings they read the reports as if they were reading poetry, intentionally breaking long sentences into manageable lines, carefully pausing at the right spots and for the right length of time. They put a lot of effort into getting the emphasis right, and they were studious in displaying rich emotions. Some used body language or exaggerated expressions, raising the government work conference to an unprecedented level of literary and poetic showmanship. People loved this format, and some started writing poems themselves, furtively showing them to Mengliu and asking him to "feel free" in his criticisms. He quickly drew every kind of poetry fanatic to himself, and the meetings were transformed into poetry readings. Darae was especially affected. Both his temperament and his talent were like a replica of Bai Qiu's.

Mengliu recalled an unpleasant confrontation with Darae. Like Bai Qiu, Darae believed that revolutionaries were the greatest poets. Mengliu said that revolution was not something to toy with. From ancient times until the present, many people had gone crazy for revolution, but even after their sacrifice, nothing had changed. "You'd be better off going for a Nobel Prize for Literature like Rabindranath Tagore, Neruda, Miłosz . . . "

Darae smiled quietly. "You're right. When the fascists undertook a war of aggression, Tagore was outraged, ready to sound the battle cry for the fight against the beast in human skin. When the Spanish War broke out against the fascist dictator, it was the outcast Neruda who said, 'I must take to the streets, shouting until the last moment.' And as for Miłosz, when the Second World War broke out, he chose not to flee but stayed to take part in the resistance movement."

Rania had interrupted at this point, saying that a poet could not just sit as a silent observer of life.

Mengliu felt a little ashamed. He thought they were setting an ambush for him. Then Darae said, "Some poets are trees, rooted in their own land. Others are birds, flying all over the earth. I wish I could be a bird, living everywhere in exile." Against his own conscience, Mengliu said his comments reflected the thinking of a naive student, an expansive fantasy, pure and ignorant idealism. Not being able to return to one's home was not romantic. Nobody wanted to taste that sort of bitterness.

Streaks of fog were creeping over the hilltop, like the bent backs of a stealthily invading enemy, slowly passing over the weeds and through the dead trees. Mengliu made his way down from Rania's grave, his face wet and his hair knotted in mist. Thinking of taking a shortcut, he made his way east. He was sure there was a way out there. He was now more determined than ever to leave Swan Valley. He became more and more convinced of its urgency and grew desperate, scratching and scrambling where there was no way through, rolling and crawling, and when the path was clear, hurrying to push ahead. He did not believe in the secret passage Rania has spoken of, but he needed to find the way by which he had come in. He saw a gray wall in the distance and the glow of the meandering river, with white flowering branches from the bushes dangling over it. The familiar scenery encouraged him. But he couldn't get any closer to the wall and seemed further from it the more he circled the place. Eventually, he couldn't see the other elements either, as if they had all been a hallucination. He continued walking through the woods, but he had lost his way.

Just as he was about to look for a place to rest, he heard a strange sound echoing through the forest. Suspecting it was a wild beast, he hid among the trees. The continued rustling sound brought three dark figures into Mengliu's view. One was in front and two behind, as if they were transporting a prisoner. The person in front looked like a nun, wrapped in a black gown that brushed the ground and was caked in mud.

She limped, and her head was wrapped so that he couldn't see her face. The two people behind followed closely and seemed anxious and mistrustful. Mengliu thought that the one in black robes had caught a glimpse of him. He retreated and glued himself to the trunk of a tree. He dared not move or breathe. He heard them stop and talk.

"Little brothers, I am telling you the truth. Please believe me. I can't go back. That is not a retirement home. It is hell!" a quivering voice groaned.

"Please compose yourself. Don't talk such nonsense or I'm afraid we'll have to send you to a mental hospital. You're old now. Why don't you want to enjoy the blessing you've been given? Why should you degrade yourself like this?"

"I had to escape . . . listen to me. This is a place where they burn you alive . . . See the white smoke from that huge chimney? Beneath it is a crematorium. They stick living people under anesthesia in there . . . Oh God, I'm hurt. My leg is broken. Let me go to a hospital. Please, I'm begging you." It was the same shaky voice.

"Looks to me like you asked for it. Our job is to take you back to the nursing home. The hospital there is better for you than conditions on the outside. Everyone out here is terribly envious. I've never seen anyone willing to leave the nursing home . . . It's too bad we have to wait twenty years before we'll be eligible to enjoy it."

"To go in . . . to go there is to die, little brother. It's a big scam . . . they take sick and elderly people and throw them into the furnace alive."

"God, all you old people ever do is complain. It would be better for you to cooperate. Let's get moving."

"Let me relieve myself . . . I'll go to the side of that tree there."

"All right. Let him go. He's limping. He can't run."

There was the sound of dead wood breaking underfoot and the person who wanted to relieve himself walked close to where Mengliu was, then back after a moment, taking up his long-winded pleas with the pair once again. When he was rudely interrupted by the younger men, he finally closed his mouth. They quickly left the scene.

Staring at the quiet path shut in by the forest, Mengliu thought what he witnessed must have been an illusion, but a white envelope under the tree where they had stopped was proof that someone had come this way and had deliberately left a clue. He picked up the envelope and saw it was just a neatly folded piece of paper. When he opened it and started reading, his expression changed completely.

15

With great difficulty, Mengliu made his way out of the woods. The sun fell as lightly as silk at his feet. He had long ago begun to feel weak in his legs and knees. Resting on a bench, he saw the young nurse Yuyue. Though she wore no makeup, her lips were rosy, and her bobbed hair was shiny and smooth. Her black overcoat was unbuttoned. She wore a pink turtleneck sweater inside, her curves obvious, with a black A-line skirt and boots, topped off by the natural black of her eyes. She looked very fashionable. Mengliu's heart was swayed. If it were not for the critical matter at hand, he would find a way to be with Nurse Yuyue at least once, he was sure of that. The night he had gone to her office and found her on duty, she had hinted that he could manipulate her. She dared to defy the world's opinions for the sake of love. This girl's temperament was very different from Juli's. She was always ready to get cozy with a man, as if sex were her only joy in life. Mengliu had known women like this, but they couldn't compare with Yuyue. She was not the sort who would burn out too quickly. She possessed a kind of faith that was beyond doubt, and would act like a closed clam, but when her heart was touched . . . Mengliu's mind became clouded, and he momentarily forgot the mission that was driving him.

Yuyue had come especially to bring a message from the hospital. Michael, the director, wanted to talk with him. She had her hands in her coat pockets and was standing before him in a relaxed pose with a compelling look on her face. He hesitated, then stood up and followed her. She walked quickly, but this did not affect the pace of her speech. She said the hospital had had several patients die with similar symptoms, and they suspected it might be the outbreak of an infectious disease. He said a surgeon wouldn't be any help against an infectious disease. She retorted that he should never underestimate the power of the human spirit. A poet could have a positive impact on a patient's mood. Sometimes poetry was medicine. "Do you need a doctor or a poet?" Mengliu asked.

Yuyue answered, "There's no real difference between the two."

He laughed. "If a poet were to wield a scalpel and a doctor treat sickness with a sonnet, then the world would really be perfect. Money may be no problem in treating the sick in Swan Valley, but in some places, the poor can't even get through the door of a hospital. They ignore their minor illnesses, and cannot afford to treat their major illnesses, so many people lie on their beds and just wait to die. In any case, I'm no longer a doctor, and I'm certainly no poet. I am just a foreigner who got lost." He went on to ask Yuyue to get him out of this maze he was in and point the way home.

No ripples appeared on the two deep, cold pools of Yuyue's eyes. She was a perfect inflatable doll. There was no response to his words. Her eyes narrowed, like curtains falling over a window. The wind fluttered the curtains as she mused. She said that they had just received a lame patient who was dressed in black. He had a high fever that would not subside and was uttering nonsense, saying that the nursing home was a slaughterhouse. It sounded horrible, and they had to give him a sedative to shut him up. She thought for a moment, then noticing that Mengliu seemed distracted, continued cautiously, "Hey, it's not the plague, is it? You know how the medieval plague was carried by the fleas on rats, and the rats carried the fleas across the English Channel and spread them all over England, and there were countless deaths in rural areas? The city garbage and sewage were handled by ignorant sanitation workers who didn't understand what was happening, and so the illness was passed along even faster. Doctors exhausted all of their options—bloodletting, smoking, burning of the lymph nodes—but still people died. Some Christians thought the plague was the result of human depravity, and a form of divine punishment. They paraded through the towns and cities of Europe, using whips lined with metal barbs to scourge confessions out of one another. In Germany Jews were treated as plague-spreaders and were burned alive. A lot of Jews were massacred. But there also awakened in their minds the possibility that it was being spread by animals, so they killed their livestock too . . . "

As soon as Yuyue started speaking she became long-winded, but it was not just useless rambling. She was intelligent, well read and well mannered. Sometimes she came up with a smile that seemed to indicate she didn't care how many people had died. She was calm. She spoke as if the rhythm of her speech was guided by punctuation. Commas would make her pause, but it was a half-beat shorter than the pause for a period. When she met an ellipsis, she would look at the distant landscape attentively before going on.

When she came to the next ellipsis, Mengliu suddenly quickened his steps and walked in front of her.

"Miss Yuyue, lives are at stake. We must go to the hospital as soon as possible."

Soft chuckling came from behind him, as if leaves were rustling down. "Didn't you say you were neither a doctor nor a poet? What can you do if you go there?"

He turned back, stunned. He saw that she had draped her coat over her arm. As she stood there in her charming pink sweater, her face suddenly looked as if it were covered in rouge. Her dark eyes were watery above a graceful smile, dark as night, with a solitary star shining in each one.

"Are you joking?" He felt that this was a game of cat and mouse, and he was annoyed. "How can you joke about a thing like that?"

"Of course it's true." Her face perked up, restoring the look of the inflatable doll. "I was just wondering what you would do."

"There is nothing I can do." He suddenly felt his tone had been too harsh, and was sorry.

"Michael, our director, must have been indoctrinated, to put so much hope in a washed-up poet."

"I will say it again. I am really not a poet. Definitely not a great poet."

The hospital loomed before them, its door framed by a pair of trees, all their leaves fallen. A blackbird flew out from its nest in the branches of one, and sounded strange.

Michael's office was at the end of a corridor. Mengliu walked in to see his fluffy white head bent over the desk, and a magnifying glass sweeping back and forth over a book, as if he were making a careful examination of an antique. The bent head raised itself, revealing the flushed face of one who had had too much to drink. Mengliu had seen him before, but had not known he was the head of the hospital. In the Dayang National Hospital the director rarely went to the wards, being too busy with meetings, overseas study tours, dining with his wife, sleeping with his mistress . . . and, most importantly, maintaining a decent, dignified image. This old man seemed to have long ago passed the age for entering the nursing home, but in reality he had just turned fifty. The Swanese were all like this. They didn't exactly age prematurely, but they were a special breed.

Three of the walls in the office were covered with floor-to-ceiling bookshelves, and the books there stood in neat rows.

"Have a seat. You're a poet. Have a look at this. How do you explain it?" The old man handed him a bunch of records. His accent was from the west of England.

Letting a poet look at medical records is to treat him like God! was what Mengliu thought, but he simply said, his manner not lacking sincerity, "I was just a surgeon at a small hospital. I've not studied infectious diseases. I don't dare to offer a professional opinion."

"Don't be so humble. Michael has never been wrong in his judgment of people." Yuyue leaned her rump against the desk, propping her feet on the floor, making herself seem extraordinarily slender.

Mengliu guessed her relationship with Michael wasn't strictly professional.

"Dr. Yuan, modesty is not a virtue. It will only affect your ability to judge."

The medical records all displayed similar symptoms—cough, fever, chills, black blood, and some had blisters on their bodies.

"It looks like a new infectious disease. If we can locate its point of origin, it will be easier to deal with." Mengliu wished to be done with the matter. He felt it was a smoke screen, and that the really important information was to be found in the nursing home. "You have to find the source and learn how to control it, and then at the appropriate time inform the people about the epidemic, then you can begin to limit the spread of the disease by disseminating information on prevention, and following up with frequent reminders."

"Several of the newly admitted patients have identical symptoms. Besides the fever and cough, they experience vomiting and diarrhea and other symptoms similar to food poisoning." Yuyue now sat on a wicker chair, with her arms draped over the armrests. With her knees pressed together, she angled her legs in a glamorous pose. "The patients are unconscious or confused, unable to say anything coherent." She finished and smiled. She was a queen.

"Hundreds of years ago, a village tailor in England received a piece of foreign cloth. Four days later he died. By the end of the month, six were dead. A swath of fabric brought the plague into the village, and eventually led to the death of all the people there. So we should consider whether this situation might play out in a similar fashion." The old man picked up his magnifying glass and slowly swept it over his book again. His manner was unhurried. "The seriousness of the situation should not be underestimated. Dr. Yuan, I'm putting you in charge of this matter. Your room has been prepared. Yuyue will send you the relevant information shortly. You probably don't know, but the status of a poet in Swan Valley is on par with that of the Dalai Lama in Tibet." He raised his head and, with an effort, looked at Mengliu. "If you tell the patients you are a great poet, they will conceal nothing from you. That is the main reason I wanted you to be involved."

Mengliu felt his hands and feet grow cold, as if he were in the grip of a nightmare.

"I feel it is necessary that we perform a test, so that we can eliminate inferior individuals. This would be consistent with how the natural world works." Yuyue straightened her legs and stood up from the wicker chair, as if she were going to see a guest off on Michael's behalf.

The director's flattery and Yuyue's sudden fierce opinion left Mengliu dumbstruck. He stood there in embarrassment and, with great difficulty, spoke his mind. He asked to see the patient who had been admitted that day, the one dressed in black. "While the patient is awake and can speak, perhaps we can get important information from him."

But the answer he received was that the patient had died suddenly and had already been cremated.

16

The smell of pinewood and pale green smoke was scattered throughout the city. In the depth of winter, all of the fireplaces were astir. Regardless of whether it was freezing rain or snow falling outside, the ward was warm and dry. The soft mattresses imparted a saffron and orange scent to the air. It was as if the patients were living in their own homes. The books on the shelves were changed at regular intervals; the patients could also go to the hospital's library to read or to borrow a book themselves. There were different patterns on the curtains for the patients to choose from; each room had its own private bathroom, fitted with a white porcelain toilet and basin, a half-length wall mirror, and anti-slip floor tiles color-coordinated to match the wall tiles. A small closet held earthenware art, and sandalwood or lavender incense was lit on a stone shelf, eliminating all unwanted odors. Here a patient's stay was undoubtedly a pleasure. Wealthy Swan Valley might have some aspects of life that were not quite satisfying, but no one would mind too much. They all had it rather easy. There was no pressure, and no worries about money. Everyone tried to outdo the other in artistic, spiritual, or moral excellence.

The windows of the ward offered a variety of views. The yellow rays of the sun shone obliquely from the sky and entered the forest, where a thin fog shimmered like the heat produced by the sun. In fact the sun had cooled long ago and was left there without warmth.

An unfamilar bird hopped among the dead wood and dry leaves, uttering a shrill, sad, horrible cry, *caw caw caw*, as if it wanted to rip the human heart to shreds. When the birdcall ceased, the world outside the window seemed to fall into a decayed submarine state, with the living creatures swimming about in it in a slow and orderly fashion. The wildflowers that opened there held a trace of loneliness. Mengliu thought of the girl Yuyue. She and the wildflower alike could blossom or wither and it wouldn't matter. It only mattered that they were lovely now. Every morning and evening she washed her face with fruit juice. She was a vegetarian and did not touch fried or spicy foods. She read the Bible, and was like a lotus springing up out of clear water, exuding a fruity fragrance.

She was waiting to record the patients' histories, but she had discovered nothing. Some of the patients talked nonsense and looked at the doctor with disdain. She repeatedly hinted that he should reveal to them that he was a poet, and he brooded over this for a long time, but he never had the courage to say "I am a poet," or anything like it. Asking an accomplished doctor to proclaim himself a poet in front of his patients seemed to Mengliu humiliating and awkward. When he was young he had already become aware of the fact that people no longer respected poets. They suffered a worse fate than the common people. They were even regarded as rogue elements, who were fanning the anti-revolutionary flames. They were good-for-nothings, and that's why many remade themselves as businessmen. Now they were bosses, entrepreneurs, and merchants, burying their poetry beneath their pillows, not bringing it even a half step out of the bedroom. They were duplicitous all day long, expressing scorn for poetry when they were out drinking with friends, except perhaps for a line of coarse doggerel. All art was just a sick pretense. They gradually fell in love with this life; business was the main disguise they wore. They maintained an ambiguous attitude—and a discrete distance from the affairs of the nation, holding on tight to their women and children, while they watched the stock market as if their lives depended on it and engaged in a little antique collecting, or calligraphy, or landscape painting. They never bothered to open a book, unless it was the passbook to their bank accounts.

Mengliu took off his stethoscope and mask and walked out of the ward, feeling that his cooperation could come to an end now. Infectious disease was like poetic inspiration—he had no wish to catch either. He would have to tell those superstitious people that poetry was rubbish, not even as useful as a rag. He was angry, and as he took off his white lab coat, his tight black sweater looked like it was about to burst. Yuyue chased him outside, her feet were moving quickly. She was like a hovering fairy, with a calm expression and not a strand of hair out of place in her bob. He thought she was going to stop him, but she smiled sweetly, showing her teeth, as if she appreciated his actions. He was surprised she was on his side, and a little flattered. If he had met a girl like this earlier he would be thinking happily now about how to get into her pants, but he just said sternly, "You confuse me, Yuyue. You're on the wrong side."

He abandoned her to go his own way. These days a stay in the hospital had the flavor of house arrest. But Yuyue stuck to him. He needed to get rid of her as soon as possible, to find Juli. She was the only one he could trust.

"I don't want to call you Mr. Yuan anymore, it's so formal." She followed him down the corridor. "Are you going to see Michael? He's not in today. Don't worry. I will speak to him on your behalf."

Mengliu pondered her words as he walked. She was unpredictable. Why should she help him?

Her attitude kept him guessing. Later, when they had returned to the entrance to the hospital, a flock of birds had gathered in the trees. Yuyue reached out to bid him farewell. Mengliu took the pale soft hand, and her fingertips seemed to scratch his palm. He saw her smile, her eyes dark pools, as if saying, "You really can trust me."

His hand seemed stuck to hers. He wasn't able to detach it for a moment. He wondered if he told her what he had seen in the woods, revealing the contents of the letter, what her scream would sound like. Of course his motive wasn't to frighten her. In the end he suppressed the desire and didn't say anything. Yuyue's hand was like the kitten he had raised in his younger days. When she withdrew it, he felt a sense of nostalgia. It was at such moments of loneliness that one was most likely to commit an error. So he looked back at her. She stood motionless, hands in the pockets of her white coat, like a newly built snowman. It was the first time he had smiled at her. He had not smiled in such a long time he felt his muscles had grown stiff.

"Maybe we can go some place interesting." Yuyue stepped forward again, hands still in her pockets. "There are some rare creatures to see. I am sure you will like it."

He didn't immediately reject her. Since the person in black had died, things could slow down a little. If that letter really was just mental trickery, and he took it seriously and went to the authorities, he would be a laughing stock. He did not want to lose face in front of Juli. When he thought of Juli's description of the nursing home and the look of longing on her face, his heart dropped. So he stayed where he was and waited for Yuyue to change her clothes in the office. A sort of excitement like elopement brewed in him. Not long ago the two of them had been relatively cold toward each other, and now they were planning a sightseeing trip together. Although it was difficult to adapt to all the changes, he found it fairly easy to fall into step with his emotions. He didn't know what sort of battle awaited him. How would things progress with Yuyue? Was she one of those who liked revolution? His thoughts now turned toward such questions with the same liveliness as his sperm. When he saw Yuyue in her casual clothing, like a bluebird in flight, he almost thought they had been in love for a long time.

They each took a bicycle from the hospital garage. Their wheels turned in unison, the silver rims ran over the hard gray road. A brightness swept over the snowy mountain slopes. The sun and the moon were both overhead. The clouds looked like a sandy desert swept clean by the wind. The air was very pure.

"Yuyue, how old are you actually?" Mengliu asked, slowing down as they reached a flat stretch of road. He knew nothing about her.

"Me? I turned twenty-one today," she said.

"Go—" Mengliu braked suddenly. He had not thought she was already twenty-one. "Oh. Your birthday."

Yuyue stopped her bike and said, "Twenty-one years ago today, my mother was successfully impregnated via artificial insemination. The moment the sperm and egg met is considered my birthday. The day of my birth was my mother's Day of Suffering, and was also Mother's Day. We have a special celebration. It's a custom in Swan Valley."

"That's very humane," he said. "But where are your mother and father now?"

"My father passed away, and my mother is in the nursing home." Yuyue sat herself happily on the saddle again, her pale blue jacket and white skin blended with the sky. Perhaps the sky was too bright. There seemed to be a halo around her.

Her mention of the nursing home coincided perfectly with what was on his mind. He caught up with her and said casually, "Why don't we go to the nursing home now to visit your mother?"

"Staying there she is like an immortal, with nothing to worry about." Yuyue laughed easily. "Hey, it's as if you believed that patient you saw. Poets love to imagine things, but life goes on as usual. It's very rare that anything extraordinary happens."

"You've never been to see her?"

"No." Yuyue shook her head, and her hair flapped against her face. "She writes to tell me how things are going for her. She's happy. Last year she even entered her 'second spring' there, and fell in love like a teenager."

"Why haven't you thought of going in to have a look?" Mengliu knew the Swanese were independent from the time they were small and never relied on their relatives much. They were not sentimental, but surely they must have some curiosity about this mysterious place.

"I'm not interested in a place where a bunch of old people live. And in order to get into the nursing home, you need a special pass that requires you to go through a physical exam, get approval stamps, and then there's a long waiting period. Who wants to go to such trouble?"

"When did she go in?"

"A few years ago."

They began pedaling uphill, with the last few meters becoming so strained that it seemed impossible to move forward. After ten minutes of pushing, they reached a downhill slope a few hundred meters long. They slipped between endless rows of birches, their golden leaves rustling all around them. There was no path through the trees, but there were plenty of ways around them on every side, though they had to deal with their bikes getting stuck, and avoid falling. Their previous conversation had been interrupted. Naturally, in such bright sunlight, among the trees and bushes, in the forest air, with a beautiful girl by his side, Mengliu forgot his interest in the nursing home. He kept the talk with Yuyue light as he tried to avoid the stones and other obstacles in their path.

Playing cards, drinking, and traveling are all quick ways to excite the feelings, especially traveling. By the time they reached the dilapidated old house, they were as unrestrained as two old friends. The old wooden building had a Gothic spire reaching to the sky and blurred stained-glass windows. Its windows and doors were shut tight, and leaves covered the steps. A railway track buried in weeds ran past the door and disappeared into the depths of the forest. This place must have been a small train station in the past. From time to time a lone traveler must have got off the train, or on the train, coming home or leaving it. Mengliu thought of the noisy stations in Beiping, always crowded and with young people from everywhere hopping off the trains to head straight to Round Square, some wounded, some humiliated, some dying in their dreams.

"Let's rest here a while." Yuyue brushed the fallen leaves aside, exposing the wooden steps. When she sat down, her movements were a little jerky, as she rested her elbows on her knees and intertwined her fingers. "Listen," she said, "someone is reading."

The sound came from inside the house. It was speaking Mandarin with an accent. Judging from the person's rhythm, Mengliu thought he must be reading a Chinese rhapsody. At the same time, he recognized the voice. It was Shanlai.

Surprised, he opened the door and went in. His eyes were momentarily unable to adapt to the dimness of the room, but a skylight allowed some natural light in, and he could see it was covered in dust. The building was full of sacks of grain, and there was a layer of grain on the floor too. A huge millstone occupied the remaining space. A person with white hair and beard and dust all over his body was working the millstone. The gold crown on his head glittered. He was like a negative film, flashing in the glare, then retreating into the darkness. On the other side of the millstone, Shanlai sat on a sack, his legs dangling and a book perched on his knees, its pages pure white. Dust motes hovered around his head like a band of mosquitoes.

"Those who strike in hatred will be sadder in the netherworld." Shanlai stopped reading and asked the person grinding, "Why is it called the netherworld?"

"Legend says there are nine levels of heaven above, and nine levels of hell below. Among the odd numbers the greatest is nine, and the netherworld is the deepest of the nine levels below. All who die must go there."

"Wherever you go, I will go too," Shanlai said. Then he continued asking about the book he had been reading, "The poet Yu Xin was a great deserter, and forgot his loyalty to the aspiring politician Wang Shao. Should he be considered a pathetic coward?"

"This . . . you can ask Mr. Yuan." He continued grinding as he replied, turning the millstone in circles.

When he once again passed through the pillar of light, Mengliu saw that the person with the white hair and beard was Esteban. Noticing that Mengliu was too surprised to speak, Esteban stopped and used a cowhide brush to sweep the flour off him, from head to foot. Like the cold and snow disappearing from a person who comes home on a stormy night, the young Esteban stood there, black hair poking out from the thornlike golden barbs of the crown around his head.

Mengliu secretly wondered why Esteban was doing a mule's work. Why was he wearing a golden crown, with his hands bound in golden chains, dressed like a prisoner? Had he committed some crime?

"Mr. Yuan, was Yu Xin a coward?" Shanlai asked.

A shadow of embarrassment crossed Mengliu's face. He wanted to brush Shanlai off, but Esteban seemed to take the question seriously. He was watching them and looked calm as he waited for the answer.

"Well . . . in a sense it could be said that he was a coward, abandoning his armor . . . though even if he stayed, he might not have been able to keep them from destroying his home city . . . he was miserable and his family ruined and three of his children were executed," Mengliu said.

"He was miserable? He lost his country? Wasn't he eventually roped in to be an important government official?" Shanlai responded quickly. His comment gripped Mengliu.

"Yes. He was in great conflict and suffered all his life. He developed a split personality. One side of him hated the rebels who invaded his homeland, the other gratefully sang the praises of its new rulers, then he hated himself for it late at night when he was alone. Of course, if he had been killed in battle you would not now be able to read such compelling poetry," Esteban said, renewing his work of grinding the grain, still with a calm demeanor.

For a while no one spoke, they just listened to the sound of the millstone. The white flour fell slowly from it, covering the whole room.

"Shanlai, many things are not as simple as they seem. We might have been less decent than he was. Yu Xin's mental suffering is hard for outsiders to understand. A single poem could not alleviate his pain." Yuyue had walked into the room, breaking the silence. "But if he had not written about it, nor found some other release, he would have gone crazy."

"I cannot like anything written by a deserter," Shanlai said. "Some people stop writing, and seem to manage to live happily enough without suffocating."

"Oh . . . because the lies of a contrary spirit can never become good poetry. Some people need a long time to think things over . . . " Yuyue was like a fire extinguisher.

"A real poet would not use poetry to spread lies . . . It's all about attitude." Esteban came back from the shadows into the light.

Mengliu had not expected the arrow to be pointed at him the whole time, but now he understood that he was in a trap. They had not come to this place by chance. Perhaps the rare creatures Yuyue had spoken of were these two people, Esteban and Shanlai. Together they had captured and trained a fly to recite poetry, and whenever they got the opportunity, they let it out to buzz in his ears. They were crazy. Regardless of the time or place, they would talk about poetry or the spirit and make him feel awkward. He would rather talk to them about the basic needs and freedoms of the body, or why Esteban was wearing golden chains and pushing a millstone. What crime had he committed, he wanted to ask, but he suddenly found it was too private an issue for the level of friendship he shared with Esteban, not to mention the fact that the atmosphere didn't suit the change of subjects.

He stood there stiffly. Now his mind was pounding with the sound of sloshing water. *Which of you is worthy to talk to me about poetry? You sprouts in the greenhouse, you people of talk and no action, have you seen its blaze, or heard its roar? None of you have touched the soul of poetry and its wounds. None of you have tasted it. There isn't anyone who is above the material attractions of the world. Our last great poet died nobly. He stood in the night as a testament. You're just a bunch of busybodies full of useless knowledge.*

17

It seemed Juli had gone missing. The stove in her house was cold and lifeless.

From time to time Mengliu took out the letter he had found under the tree in the forest. The initial shock it had caused now turned to suspicion. Increasingly he came to feel that the allegations it contained regarding the real business of the nursing home were quite impossible. How could it be like that? The letter was full of deranged comments. He recalled the strange scene in the forest, but whenever he tried to expand his memory of it in an attempt to verify the experience and put it into perspective, it was like fishing for the moon in water. When he lowered a finger to its surface, the moon dispersed.

He could not even confirm where the letter had come from. Perhaps it was a novelist's discarded draft, or a drunkard's ramblings, or the product of a random graffitist's whim. He put a pot of tea on to steep. He thought about the contents of the letter as he drank his tea. He was still troubled. He did not feel grounded. But he stopped feeling that way after drinking half a cup.

The sky was very overcast. The cold pierced him like a knife. Mengliu stoked the fire in the fireplace with dry wood and noticed that it was now snowing outside. The snowflakes hit the ground like beans, making the leaves crackle. After half an hour, it turned downy and continued to fall. Soon, other than the great white snowflakes, there was nothing else to see outside.

It was the morning of the third day before the snow really stopped. The sun shot out through a layer of ice, the cloudless sky was a thin transparent blue. There was a sharp tranquility to the cold wind. The earth was swollen with the snow cover, making the black strip of the river seem thinner. The silver hair of the willows floated on the wind, and the hills looked like a sleeping woman, her curves rising and falling.

When Juli came back at last, Mengliu was warming himself by the fire as he read. Perhaps because she was wearing so many layers, she looked plump, thick around the waist, and a little clumsy. He stood up quickly. The tip of her nose was so cold it was red. She looked at him dully, her eyes like solidified chocolate, as if a layer of autumn ice had formed over a pond. There were no withered lotus leaves in this landscape. There was only a clean vastness.

"Where did you go?" He wanted to ask her why she had vanished without a word, but he suddenly remembered that he was the one who had been drawn away to the hospital, so he couldn't blame her. He changed tack, saying he had almost registered her with missing persons. Looking like someone who had just returned from a long journey and was extremely tired, she sat on the sofa in front of the fireplace and closed her eyes. He didn't say anything else but took a blanket and covered her. He noticed that her face was also slightly swollen and felt that she must have been in a great deal of trouble.

"I thought the squid must certainly have eaten you this time. I didn't think you'd survived," Juli said, with barely enough strength to smile. "It's a miracle."

Hearing her speak, Mengliu was very happy. "What would you like to drink? Tea? Milk? Or rice wine?"

"Give me a cup of warm milk. If you can add a couple of eggs, all the better," she said bluntly. Of course, since this was her house, there was no need for formalities. She spoke lightly, but it still knocked him senseless.

"Actually . . . I'm pregnant," she said.

He had just turned around to prepare the milk. He spun back to face her and stood mutely for a moment. Finding nothing to say, he went back to boiling the milk. A few minutes later, carrying it over in a pot, he said, "Your husband?"

She did not say anything.

"Your government made you undergo artificial insemination?"

She shook her head.

"I see," he said. "You acted freely . . . adulterously . . . and are in big trouble."

Her expression surprised him. She was smiling. "I won't die. Esteban surrendered himself, so at least the child can be born."

Mengliu suddenly thought of Esteban in golden chains, but his consternation was only momentary. His attention was completely focused on the child. "Oh . . . if it is allowed to be born . . . then it's not all that bad," he said mechanically.

"Yes. It's not that bad . . . but I have to comply with the National Planned Parenthood Non-Matching Data Policy . . . this will determine whether the child will be allowed to live, but first it must pass a test, and be soaked in alcohol for half an hour."

"What? Soaked in alcohol for half an hour? Isn't that infanticide? They might as well do it as quickly as possible . . . " Mengliu lost control of his voice and was unconsciously shaking the pot in his hands.

"No, Shanlai also survived this test. When he was a year old, people found his mother's body next to the river, her lower half eaten by squids. A poor Cuban woman."

In his mind, Mengliu reached out for the wound in his own leg. "You mean you are not his . . . ?"

"I brought him up . . . I like children, and I definitely don't want an abortion." She paused, then said, "What's more, this is love . . . "

Love. She was talking about love. That was fresh! Now he was really uncomfortable. He would prefer to think it had been a moment of passion, so he could tell her that losing control was a virtue, that he was glad her body was awakening to the freedom to be used as she chose, that he liked her courage to resist in secret, and that her suffering now would be his, he would bear the burden for her. But she insisted it was love, and moreover, it was Esteban she loved. He did not believe she knew what love was. A citizen who allowed the government to decide their marriage did not have the capacity for love, because love required freedom, and freedom came at a cost. He thought, *What was all that ambiguity in her conduct with me? That night in her bedroom, and later in the forest? Wasn't that almost "love"?* He wanted to slap her "love" a few times, yet he was grateful for this moment. They were talking deeply for the first time, almost like good friends.

She ate the milk and eggs as if she didn't have a care in the world.

The house was surprisingly bright. He thought hard, looking for something to say, like a fly searching for a crack on an eggshell. But even though he crawled over the surface several times, he couldn't find a suitable opening.

"You know Yuyue, right?" He knew this was rather roundabout.

"Yes. She has very exotic genes. The government can't find a match for her genetic data."

"Her mother went into the nursing home a few years ago, and she has never gone to visit her. She said her mother often writes . . . " He frowned, remembering the white smoke from the chimney. "I wonder if she didn't die long ago."

"Hm. There are all sorts of talented people there, so it's entirely possible there are ghostwriters too. But from such attention to detail, you can see that the nursing home must be a warm, humane place."

He had no answer for that, given that her thinking and his on this issue were so much at odds. But he wanted to continue talking and felt obliged to engage her, to clarify the situation for himself.

"You remember the waste disposal site?"

She finished the milk, her expression showing that she was satisfied now and ready for battle. "All the flawed, rejected babies are discarded there . . . "

Though her words only confirmed what he already suspected, they made his heart thump. "I understand now, altering the quality of people by starting with the genes . . . I just don't know what to say . . ." He reached into his pocket. Perhaps it was time to talk to her about what was in the letter.

"He will hold on." She patted her stomach optimistically.

"I want to show you a letter," Mengliu said. "Maybe you will feel it is all nonsense . . . "

"If you've got something to say, go ahead. Why did you have to write?" Her tone indicated that she was thinking, *There's nothing new under the sun.*

"I didn't write it. I don't even know the person who did. He died recently."

"You think reading a letter from a dead person you didn't know is good for the baby?" She was a little harsh, as if she didn't care about anything except what she carried in her belly.

Hesitatingly, he took his hand out of his pocket. He thought she had a point. Sharing the contents of the letter, which had nothing to do with her child, with a pregnant woman, could be a bit dangerous and might be met with disdain. From his experience with Rania, he knew that pregnancy could make a woman a little slow, mentally, as if she had turned into a primitive female animal.

"Well . . . okay," he said. "I will make an exception and read a poem for him instead . . . it was written in Round Square a long time ago by my friend Hei Chun."

The fire crackled busily. He reached out his hand, warming it for a moment in front of the fire. He noticed that her eyes had suddenly lit up.

Standing by the fireside, he recited the poem.

autumn has come
I am in this wheat field
and you are in that

the poor children are looking for fruit
the fields are covered with scars
inflicted by their torturer

I have brought a porcelain bowl
to collect the blood that won't sleep

I believe only in the night
the sins of darkness and its wounds
unhealed, even after many years

a child wanders on the outside
waiting for the snow to melt
from his mother's forehead
he drives his dagger into the salt

you live at the bottom of a stagnant lake
I have come to the end of my journey
while you smile, guarding the fire

in a time of confusion, let me die as I wish
in a sweet embrace
leaving a black seed behind

18

Mengliu went to see Yuyue to get her input on the question of soaking a child in alcohol and its surviving. As she skipped a piece of ice across the surface of the river, she answered him, saying that it was something no one could answer with any certainty. In short, she was not very optimistic. The ice danced on the surface of the water twice before disappearing. Yuyue said his question had compromised her level of effectiveness. He then asked for examples of survivors. Having already chosen a better-shaped piece of ice, she faced the river and arced her arm overhead. The ice hit the water with a *dink dink dink dink*, creating a row of ripples. She gave herself a thumbs up, in celebration of the joy of victory. She criticized him for sticking his nose in other people's affairs, and asked what business it was of his whether other people's children survived. When she finished, she glanced at him contemptuously and said, "You don't have that kind of courage!"

He heard the provocation in her words, surrounded by the desolate, snow-covered landscape. If he were just to casually press her down to the snow-covered ground, he could change her perspective and convince her of his superiority. But he was in no hurry to prove anything. He locked eyes with her for a full minute, as if using infrared rays to make her transparent. A jackal would rather eat carrion than starve, but for a fresh piece of meat he was patient enough to play with his prey.

"Look at it from another perspective. Say you encounter the sort of thing Su Juli is facing . . . it would be hard enough to bear." His attitude was like that of an elder. "Of course I would be worried about you, too, and I would help you think of a way to abort the problem." As he spoke, another thought flashed into his mind. "Yuyue, you are very clever. Tell me honestly, if this were happening to you, what would you do?"

"Um, let me think . . . when the time came, I would make a civet cat take the place of the prince."

"No, that would be wicked. Moreover, every child is a national treasure. And where would you find a civet now that they've all been killed to save us from disease?"

"Well, you could consider hiding, or go into the mountains and give birth there." She was a little proud. "The law does not mention this, so there's a loophole."

He felt enlightened as he listened. You should engage in a game of hide-and-seek with the government. You should not have to witness them killing a child. When things had blown over, you could come back. It could be done, one step at a time.

Having such frequent contact with Yuyue, Mengliu's understanding of and trust in her had deepened. He felt she was the most clearheaded person in Swan Valley. She was calm, rebellious, and spoke clearly and logically. Occasionally she relied on the uniqueness of her genetic disposition to act without restraint. When she gave a backward kick like a mule, nobody could resist her power. Even Michael, the head of the hospital, seemed a little afraid of her, and was always careful not to provoke her.

Yuyue had both brains and beauty; she was a really stunning woman. Mengliu praised her. She was unceremonious in accepting his praise.

"Do you believe every child we would have together would be a genius?" she said, laughing. She put on her cashmere gloves. "But I don't want to have a child. I don't like children. You see the relationship between me and my mother is . . . so distant. Anyway, I don't want to be a reproductive machine."

"But, Yuyue, there are some things no one can defy. One day that official red letter will come to you, then you'll . . . "

"I'll jump off a ledge!" she unzipped her down coat. "I take it off and put it on . . . When it comes to my body, I am likewise master of myself."

Mengliu snorted with a laugh, obviously indicating that he thought she was terribly naive. She did not understand that the "self" was never free in Swan Valley. It didn't even exist.

She knew he didn't believe her. Raising her trouser leg, she knocked her right shin a couple of times. It sounded like hard rubber. "My jumping skills were not very good. I survived, but my leg did not. Damn . . . " She laughed cheerfully, into the wind, her face especially fair and clear. "I was only seventeen at the time, pure and noble . . . The next time they tried to force me into a marriage, I took poison . . . then I fell in love with a man, but he chose the fucking red letter, just like you. I understand you both. You see, I'm still intact, right? No one bothers me now. I used death to fight for my freedom. Don't say I don't understand it as well as you."

She spoke happily. He was shocked. When he came to himself, he found that she was already in his arms, and his arms and her body were welded fast together. He was not quite sure how they came to embrace one another. He touched her neck, which had the fragrance and light glow of fresh snow. For the first time, his hands discovered the real feeling of hair that was smooth as silk. She was a young girl, as dazzling as sunlight on the snow. He felt that if he whispered in her ear, she would blow away, like a petal carried off by a running stream. His kiss would defile her, like a dirty streak across the whiteness of the snow. So he just held her, frozen in stillness. He just held her, like the wind brushing a cloud, as if he were holding the hidden secret of spring, a sprouting seed, a river through the mountains, like holding time, like holding his past and present self. He felt the heat of his body warming the surrounding cold air, like an unsullied flower blooming in the middle of a pond.

After a while, as if she had been asleep on his bosom, Yuyue rubbed her eyes. Then she left him, as if she were getting up from a sofa, lifting her face slightly to see the river disappearing around a bend in the distance.

"Tell me, will I ever meet the person who is willing to die with me?" She turned to face him.

"Why do you want to die for love? You should think about how to live happily with the person you love." He was especially good at reasoning out such things; he didn't need to think about it at all. "Of course, it's more difficult to figure out how to live than how to die, and much more valuable."

"Really? I think it depends on the way you live and the way you die. I mean . . . " she paused and looked up at the snow on the tree, "death at the guillotine of freedom is valuable."

He very much agreed with what she said. But he had lost the ability to express such things, and he didn't know how to respond to her. She shook the branches of the tree, then quickly ran away, so that the snow dropped on him. She stood laughing on the side. This was how their serious conversation would end.

"Have any more people died at the hospital these past few days?" He changed the subject, suddenly recalling the matter of the infectious disease. "Was it 'just the flu'?"

"A dozen more have been admitted, one has died, and a couple are in a critical condition. Also, a nurse has been infected. She collapsed and died a few hours later. It's incurable. The hospital staff is running round in circles right now." Yuyue picked up a frozen leaf and stripped the ice from it, leaving the leaf imprint on the ice. She shut one eye and looked at him through the ice-leaf with the other. "We stopped short of wearing gas masks. Gowns, surgical masks, shoe covers, gloves . . . anyone who didn't know better would think we were a biochemical team. Michael reported the situation to the higher-ups in Swan Valley. I heard that they are sending out their top medical experts."

He had become a weird shadow through the ice, moving oddly. "The most critical thing right now is to inform the people, instruct them to stay at home and take preventive measures. As much as possible, they should not go out, so that we can reduce the spread of the infection and prevent an epidemic. Otherwise, the situation will be even more difficult to control in the future." He spoke flatly. His heart wasn't in what he said.

"The higher-ups have already enacted provisions stating that we cannot broadcast these things. In fact, we aren't allowed to say how many people have died, out of fear that this would cause a panic. To destroy the perfect image of the present, that will be hard to salvage." Yuyue threw the ice into the river. He noticed here was a flaw in the way her leg moved during the course of this activity. He felt guilty for noticing, as if he were responsible. "Michael, the deputy director, and the heads of the various departments were taken to a government building for a meeting. They came back and conveyed the spirit of the meeting to all of us 'grassroots comrades.' What a joke! They had learned the art of spinning and bluffing. Damn!" She looked as if she completely understood why things were this way. Her laughter flew to the sky like dandelion seeds, but the stem remained on the ground, standing gracefully.

Her laughter almost sent him to the sky as well. She was more to his liking all the time. "Conceal the epidemic? Paper can't contain a fire. This is probably the stupidest decision Swan Valley has ever made."

"Let them do what they want." She stepped on the snow, letting it crunch beneath her feet. "'The only regret I will have in dying is if it isn't for love'—that's from a novel, Gabriel García Márquez's *Love in the Time of Cholera*."

When he had read Márquez, those words hadn't made any emotional impact on him, but now he felt as if a knife had pierced his heart. It was on account of Qizi.

"Just don't die because of the plague." He did not want to get entangled in the question of love and death. "Do you dare to go with me to the nursing home? If there really is an outbreak of some plague, that might be the safest place. Let's at least go and familiarize ourselves with it." He was trying to rally her to his side.

"I'm not going. I'm staying at the hospital. If I can't die for love, I'll die for altruistic reasons," she replied perfunctorily.

Mengliu took the letter from his pocket. He had carried it with him constantly. "Do you want to read this?"

"A love letter?"

"Something like that," he joked.

Yuyue took it, making as if she were viewing a piece of art.

Mengliu had read it countless times. He even remembered the punctuation clearly, and could recite the whole thing by heart.

"I'm sorry, but I have to tell you a harsh reality. The truth is, you are living in a sheltered society where the truth is hidden. Our happiness is a lie. Our fermented tea contains chemical substances that will slowly wash your mind clean of the memory of your past, your motherland, and all your relatives. Then you will come to identify with everything here, and you will be at her mercy. The nursing home is an execution ground for the elderly. Living people are thrown into ovens, as if they were burning pieces of wood. Please break open the gate of the nursing home and have a look inside. You will find no one there, only ghosts."

"If this is true, I'm not the least bit surprised." Yuyue finished reading the letter very quickly, and her reaction was muted. "In Swan Valley, everything is possible. I have thought before that my mother must be dead. If not, she would have found a way to come out for a breath of air." He did not know whether this was what she really thought. Something in her tone made him think she didn't believe it, and he wondered whether he should continue discussing the matter with her.

"I'll go with you to see her now, then at least we'll know the situation clearly," he said.

"It's no use. I've been there many times. There's only a cable car to the nursing home."

"It sounds like a military base," Mengliu said. "Anyway, we have to find a way in . . . "

"Only if you turn into a bird."

"You said that all things are possible . . . and we are highly intelligent."

"The analytical data of those stupid machines makes everyone think they are special. Even you are confused."

"But you really are special."

"Oh, I've got it . . . " Yuyue suddenly grew excited. "Michael is retiring and next month he will go to the nursing home. On the eighth the cable car will come, and we . . . " She stared at his bloodshot, sluggish eyes, as if she were ready to hold his shoulders and shake him awake.

He marveled secretly at her imagination, how her thought and his had coincided so perfectly.

"But, what if we get in and then can't get back out? We need to let someone know . . . " As she went on, it was clear her mind was racing. "We need to find a couple more people." She was completely immersed in her own thoughts. He listened to her calm analysis, as if she were going through the stages of a game, overcoming difficulties along the way, and getting straight to the heart of the matter. In her narration, they were highly skilled martial arts warriors. They had become the Condor Heroes, and with the great rapport between them, they would settle every difficulty that lay before them.

She was, after all, an experienced young woman. When she started to depart from reality in her imagination, a light flooded from her face. He wanted to touch her satin black hair and porcelain skin, to put her into a love cradle, and to hum a lullaby to soothe her into a sweet, deep sleep. He reminded her that the adventure could endanger their lives, but she brushed this off contemptuously.

At that moment the sun extinguished itself like a burnt-out fire, and they grew a little colder.

19

The hospital now looked like an overinflated balloon that was about to explode. It was so overcrowded that the patients and non-patients mingled together. There were even people sleeping in the entrances to the washrooms. There weren't enough beds, the medication was stretched thin, and there was confusion everywhere. Some people resorted to unscrupulous methods to get a bed, pulling out the patients' tubes or blocking their noses, helping those who needed it to go on their way to a speedier death, and those who had the chance, to meet death immediately. Some tried their seductive charms on Michael, and even the general practitioners had to put on a stern front, so as to deter anyone from getting too close. Then visits were prohibited. People were quarantined without knowing why. Yuyue described it as like being in a silent war. The doctors would not say a word more than was necessary. Some doctors who had a more aggressive nature protested in secret, which resulted first in a yellow warning, then in a black threat, then a red education, and then, dejected finally, they would shut up. Before the arrival of the expert medical team, no one was qualified to diagnose the infectious disease definitively or announce the deaths, but rumors spread like wildfire. People hoarded food and medication in their panic, hoping they were just rumors as they awaited the official announcement.

Yuyue ridiculed the childish ways of the government, but she was only voicing her opinion on the matter. She wasn't hopeful. The situation was the government's baby, and she didn't care about its life or death. Drinking strong spirits was a sign of bad character, but this didn't affect her attempts to find pleasure. Whether there were problems or not, she always had a couple of drinks. When the day shift was over, she secretly procured wine prepared with dates and other ingredients. It would cause diarrhea and vomiting in those who were not accustomed to it, but once you got used to the strong drink, it kept you fit. Mengliu was completely adjusted to the habit, and they enjoyed peanuts, tofu slices, and dried beef as they drank and chatted in front of the fire until they were red in the face and lit up from within.

Yuyue constantly spoke of the deaths at the hospital, how the drugs were ineffective and the patients would die slowly and excruciatingly. One had stopped breathing under her care. She had not rested for three days and three nights, and she was weary to the bone. Just as she thought she would collapse, the medical experts arrived. There were eight of them in all, six men and two women, dressed like astronauts ready to visit the moon, each carrying a toolbox. They looked stern. Walking uniformly and resolutely across the lawn, they blew into the hospital entrance like a cold wind.

Yuyue enthusiastically described one of the women on the team, how young she was and how pretty. As Mengliu listened, his heart thumped. When Yuyue said Suitang's name, he stood up from his chair. He only feebly expressed his doubts, because he had known that eventually she would be brought here. He believed without reservation that she had come. He could not refute that reality. This was followed by a feeling of pleasant surprise, and an urgent need to see her, which sobered him up completely.

He tried to stay calm and downed another glass of wine. It had begun to snow again. The snowflakes floated lazily. He told Yuyue that the biggest benefit of snow was that it allowed one to stay indoors with old friends, chatting and drinking languorously before the fire, heedless of everything else. As she listened to his insincere talk, Yuyue smiled as brightly as a peach blossom, in a merciless accusation that his mind had already left the fireside. "If I were you, I would not be hiding here. I would have flown straight to the hospital."

Hearing this, Mengliu stood up and adjusted his clothes as if preparing himself to leave, but Yuyue mocked him again, saying that the hospital was completely off limits. Outsiders couldn't come and go as they pleased, unless they wanted to be quarantined for at least two weeks. Quarantine was not something amusing, sharing toilets and bathing facilities, crowded into a room with other people with only the roughest of provisions. More importantly, he would not be able to see Suitang. "But if you can tell me the most exciting thing that happened between you and her, I'll take you to see her."

Her teasing was all quite serious. Unembarrassed, Mengliu returned to his seat. In fact a number of times, as he sat in front of the fire and with the spirits working their way through his belly, he had wanted to talk about the women in his past, Suitang or Qizi, and those whose names he had forgotten, though they had each left an impression on him. He would gladly open the baggage of his past in this cold weather, sharing it with a beautiful girl, but really, what was the most exciting part? Did sex count? If he took the secrets between him and Suitang and told them to her, what would Yuyue think?

"Perhaps we will all die of the plague, even those who are sweetly in love. Why don't you discard your sense of shame and tell me all about it?" Yuyue seemed to have read his mind, for her words were hitting the mark. "Sometimes love can turn a devil into an angel."

Mengliu laughed. "You're amazing. I'm becoming more and more convinced that no one can compete with you, in science or the emotions." He was suddenly in no hurry to see Suitang.

Yuyue winked at him as she sipped her drink.

"If I tell you that I killed someone for Suitang, don't be surprised." He came straight to the point.

"The murderer was not you," she said dismissively. "It was love."

He ignored her irony, watching the flames dance in the fireplace as he slowly told her everything.

"I never thought I would speak of these things, but perhaps I really was a murderer. I may be a wanted criminal. Until this day, I don't know how Suitang feels about me. She looked like my first love Qizi. Deep down I took her as Qizi, not caring whether or not she loved me. I've told you about my affair with Qizi before. She disappeared, and might still be alive. Maybe she changed her name and got a fresh start. Suitang was my assistant. She had been swindled by a sick old poet called Jia Wan with whom she was deeply involved. One day Suitang told me her plan, and it frightened me. There was no way I could do what she had in mind, but when I saw her turn away in disappointment, I promised her. You know, for a surgeon it was really not that difficult. What Suitang wanted was quite easily accomplished during a heart bypass operation. She wanted me to destroy an artery near his heart while mending another, cutting it as if that were as common a thing as snipping a thread."

Yuyue refilled his glass and tossed another log on the fire.

"No one knows how Suitang got Jia Wan to change his will before the surgery, leaving her two million yuan whether she aborted his child or not. Suitang told me that she wasn't going to have Jia Wan's child. She was only twenty-three years old and there were things she wanted to do in life. She would use the money to start a foundation dedicated to poetry and poets. She said that if I didn't hold anything against her, and if I wasn't merely trying to get her into bed, we could officially date and be loyal to one another. She thought that with the two million, we could accomplish our ideals. If I could not accept her greedy and broken heart, then we should keep a distance like that between siblings, and she would deposit five hundred thousand in cash into my account. To tell you the truth, I calculated at the time that this dirty money, not being taxed and all, was equal to several years of salary for me. But even someone who is poor at math knows that two million plus Suitang was worth much more than five hundred thousand alone—moreover, I liked Suitang. She looked like Qizi. Of course, I also knew that even for women one did not like, one's feelings could change when two million yuan was involved. A man might easily feel he couldn't extricate himself from a situation like that, and the woman would think it was her charm that had captivated him. But there's nothing like cash to make a person understand himself less and less. You can always feel you are upright and aloof, then one day you find that isn't the case, and you're no better than a monkey rushing headlong for the prize, or a dog eager to grasp a bone. You take all the values you've built up over the years and smash them—though at least, for someone like me, those values had fallen to pieces long ago."

"That's true. A poet who doesn't write poems anymore can't do much, nor can he really talk about values." Yuyue's voice showed she was satisfied with his story. She was like a judge issuing expert opinions on the work of a performer. It was these words that pierced Mengliu's heart. When a person is as self-deprecating as he had just been, he is really after praise from others, but Yuyue had knocked him down a notch and made him feel lower than a dog. Still, he had to admit the truth of what she said. She was the only person he had ever met who was completely devoid of bullshit. Her comments were better than empty hypocritical words of comfort, and they brought a quick end to his self-pity, preserving the vital resources he needed to pull himself together. He knew what she meant—to act in the name of love was better than any of those things done by the authorities.

"After Jia Wan died, what happened to you and Suitang?" Yuyue wanted to know the outcome.

"She didn't get a thing. She was set up by Jia Wan and his wife."

"Poet, doctor, murderer. Yuan Mengliu, you *are* living in comfortable exile!" Yuyue laughed heartily again. Her nose was perspiring. She was like a spring. "Honestly. This place suits you. You are so free here. If only you were still writing, your status would be of the highest rank."

"That's a joke. Really—a big joke," he said, bored.

"Those who have suffered for a long time have even more right than others to express themselves. It's like the tortured having a need to cry out, so the argument that after this or that difficulty you cannot write anymore must be wrong."

He seemed to have drunk too much. He felt awful as he stood up again. "I have to go look for Suitang."

So he made his way through the wind and snow to the hospital. He accomplished nothing other than to get a whiff of the hospital's smell. It was a wasted errand. Yuyue brought news that Suitang would only get to have some rest after a few days. It was a ray of hope, but after a couple of days the ray of hope faded away. Suitang was infected and confined to a ward. She sprayed germs about when she talked, and was running a high fever. With life and death hanging in the balance, no one could see her.

20

Cold temperatures seemed to stop the spread of the infectious disease. Of course this was an illusion, but even more false was the impression that the whole thing had never happened. After a brief panic, people's emotions stabilized and they waited instead for some new, curious turn of events. The sun was still round, and it still came up in the east, and it still hung in the sky without falling. Those who craned their necks waiting grew tired after a while, and so withdrew their necks, and slowly themselves. Yuyue said that the hospital's morgues were full, and the incinerators were so overworked each day that the ashes of the dead were immediately flushed down the drain. When those in angelic white garments visited the families of the dead, fake ashes were handed over, along with false records and false compassion. But the flowers were genuine. The government was doing everything humanly possible.

Yuyue was the only one in the hospital not dressed in a hazmat suit. Unafraid of death, she spoke to the patients just like she always had. She patted Suitang's head, telling her not to worry, it was important to believe that she would not die. There was a man waiting for her.

This sort of talk did nothing for Suitang, who said with a hint of hatred in her words that she had not thought Yuan Mengliu was still alive. A week later she recovered miraculously and received a red pacesetter medal as a result. She was given two days' leave of absence from the hospital and, after promising not to disclose any information, was allowed to go outside.

Mengliu waited for her in the beech grove. He felt as if they knew each other from another life. She wore a black down jacket and her hair was pulled back in a very high bun, revealing her full forehead. Her brown plaid scarf covered her sexy white neck. She did not wear a hat, unwilling to hide her pretty hair. Her mouth chomped constantly on chewing gum.

When he asked her why she had come to Swan Valley, she said that her plane had been hijacked. The other hostages were dead. She was the only one who had been rescued, but she had been brought against her will to the hospital to help deal with the epidemic. She said the hostages could have all been rescued, but neither the police nor the hijackers had any intention of leaving witnesses behind. She did not consider herself rescued, since the police and hijackers were in it together, and she was the person they wanted.

"But you're just an anesthetist . . . Damn those human traffickers!" Mengliu, unable to explain the complex emotion he felt in a few words, swore bitterly. He had already reawakened to her unique charms and recovered his feelings from the past. It felt like he had been apart from Suitang for less than a year, but she seemed to stand decades away, blurring the concept of time for him. "Suitang, don't go back to the hospital. You'll die in vain . . . "

"I'm immune. I won't die. It seems you have been very happy here," she said, looking at him contemptuously. "It seems that what you are best at is playing hide-and-seek. Actually, you needn't hide. You know I won't cling to you. You know I don't like to beg."

"You . . . it's not that I wanted to stay here. I mean . . . I don't know how to explain it. I was knocked out by a huge wave while on a boat, then when I woke up I was in Swan Valley." Even as he said it, Mengliu found his own words unbelievable. He laughed ruefully. "I'm telling you the truth . . . What happened after the incident with Jia Wan? Did you get into any trouble?"

"Nothing happened. The insurance company investigated, and that was it. The funeral for that scumbag was very grand, with writers and poets coming from all over the country to attend the memorial service. There was an awards ceremony, and the deceased was granted the nation's highest poetry prize." She looked out at the sky above the woods, then spat silently. "No one was more qualified for this award than Hei Chun and Bai Qiu. And you—if you had continued to write poetry."

Mengliu thought that if the poetry prize was being devalued like this, poets didn't really matter. He wasn't concerned with poetry but with the Jia Wan affair. It had ended. He suddenly felt very light. He turned a gracious eye on the landscape around him.

The forest after a snowfall. A girl in black. A bough covered with ice on its north side. A pristine blue sky. A refreshing wind. Yes, he could remain calm. During his conversation with Suitang he kept recalling that the time he and Yuyue had decided on for their raid on the nursing home was only three days away, and he wasn't going to spend those days talking about poetry or the dead; he would have to focus on perfecting their plan. Of course, if he wanted to arrange a reliable network of agents, he would need to recruit Esteban, Juli, or Darae. There was no way to reveal all the ins and outs of it to Suitang now. He could only warn her that the place was not what it seemed.

"I know you have already obtained Swan Valley's certificate of citizenship." Suitang spat out her chewing gum and took a small bit of ice from the tree and sucked on it like it was candy. "How could you escape without letting me know? I want to ask you a question. If you don't want to answer, that's fine, but only tell the truth if you do. To you, am I really just a shadow of Qizi?"

"Of course not." Mengliu knew this was the moment for some hypocrisy, for sweet, kind words. Just like when a girl asked him in bed whether he would marry her, and he would always say that if he were not still waiting for his first love, he would marry. These sorts of words were useful for maintaining a girl's self-respect and confidence. "You are you. You are not like her," he said.

Suitang's mouth melted into a smile, and she quickly asked him about his relationship with Yuyue, and how many women he had been with in Swan Valley. Finally she asked whether he had written any poems for them.

"There were no women, and no poems."

He felt her voice piercing his defenses; every word was a confrontation. She thought that when she had failed to get the large amount of money from Jia Wan's will, he had abandoned her, and so she had every right to criticize him.

He kept an apologetic tone. "I often thought of you, but I could not get back. This damned place!"

It seemed that his story was full of holes. She wouldn't stop bickering with him, interrogating him. She didn't want anything from him, but she didn't want to be played for a fool either. She had felt like slapping him the moment she saw him, but instead she had acted indifferent. It was not because they were in the same boat again and she had to put away her personal grudges. It was more because when Yuyue had first told her he was here, she really was overjoyed, and when she saw him, her heart was filled with warmth and happiness. But she was afraid of losing face, so she had pretended to be cold, hoping to win back a little self-respect in his eyes.

It was as if she were reciting a tongue twister, drawing out the minute details of her rich emotions.

Of course, he understood, so he kept speaking in low tones, allowing her plenty of space to vent her feelings, wanting nothing more than to play his role once her performance was complete. At last, in good time, he caught hold of three fingers on one of her hands and pulled her to him saying, "If you keep crying out here, your face will turn to ice. If you want to come back to my fireside and continue crying, that would be fine."

So they returned to his house to continue their conversation.

She was surprised to find him living alone in such a large house. As she looked around, she said that only a wealthy man could live this way; a normal surgeon's salary wouldn't pay for more than the bathroom. If men did not sell their souls for their professions and women did not sell their bodies, what would become of the world? She rambled on. Who would dig out a three-room underground house, who would turn a scrapped vehicle into a mobile camper, who would fake a divorce for the sake of a house? She talked a lot, and energetically, and quickly forgot her tears. She said, "You must have had a windfall, or you're being kept by a rich woman. You're living in such luxury, no wonder you don't want to leave."

"My material comforts were not less there than here. At first, I didn't want to go back. I was attracted by the freedom they enjoyed here. In our art back home we wouldn't be allowed to paint a mustache on our leaders. Their art allowed them to strip their dead leader naked. But I know now that their freedom is only superficial."

The house was nice and warm. They sat cross-legged on the carpet. For a while, they almost forgot that they were living abroad. Her wounded feelings over Jia Wan had apparently healed, and her recent illness had had almost no effect on her. She was healthy and young, like fresh fruit on a tree. He could see that she was excited, that everything in Swan Valley seemed fresh and lovely, and that she did not intend to leave. He unceremoniously poured cold water on that prospect, telling her truthfully all that had happened to him, including Rania's death, the letter from the person in black, his conversation with the robot, and his doubts about the nursing home. He also summarized his own temptations when faced with beautiful women, but he didn't think that terribly important right now.

Artificial insemination and the prohibitions on sex surprised her, but hearing about the squid that nearly ate him and the waste disposal site turned her insides to ice. She moved closer to Mengliu and felt a little better. She asked him why he had not sneaked back to the site. He said he had tried many times. Once he became lost, and once he was nearly killed. He hid the additional factor of the woman, especially the more captivating moments with Juli. There was no need to complicate the issue.

Her chest heaved as she sat watching the flames. He looked at her silently, secretly surprised at his own cool head. The warm fire and the pretty young woman had failed to stir his body, or the appetites of the little beast within him.

Perhaps this was a good omen.

21

"What did you say? The nursing home is actually a crematorium?" Esteban's voice issued from the dark gray mattress, blurred and cold. "Oh . . . is that right? Then so be it. It's no big deal. When one is old one is useless, and fire has a purging power." He was a completely changed man.

There was no heating system in the mill, and it was filled with sacks of grain that lay everywhere, piled up to the windows. It wasn't too cold, but Esteban's words were frigid, his body like a toppled mountain. There was no energy in his voice. A half hour earlier, when Mengliu and Suitang had set out on their bikes to the mill, as if they were just out to enjoy the scenery, they hadn't expected to find Esteban in such a state. They had to put aside the matter of the nursing home and concentrate on the condemned man's health.

Mengliu knew what the punishment was for a man who had committed adultery. Those who kept repeating the crime would be put to death. First-time offenders might be condemned to five years of service as a coolie, living in exile with only vegetables to eat. The sick were not allowed to see a doctor. They labored during the day, while reading and making notes at night in order to keep their minds from degenerating to the point where they would be of no use after their release from imprisonment. In truth, some were ruined, but some were completely transformed, becoming thinkers and gaining a very different understanding of life. They buried themselves in books, gave lectures, engaged in theoretical discussions, became admired and celebrated gurus.

In Swan Valley, anything was possible.

Esteban wasn't concerned about his health. Mengliu, afraid he had contracted the plague, encouraged him to apply for permission to see a doctor. This was blasphemous to Esteban, who believed himself to be a sinner and fully intended to atone for his wrong-doing. There was nothing Mengliu could do about his pious, repentant attitude, and Esteban's stubbornness was driving him crazy.

Suitang looked on anxiously. Several times she started to speak, but Mengliu stopped her because he knew she had nothing positive to say. All the way there she had cursed Swan Valley, saying the people were deranged, lacked any discernment, were clearly a bunch of idiots. He replied that they enjoyed simplicity, the natural state of people living in abundance and reunified with their spirit. She included him in her ridicule, saying Swan Valley had made him short-sighted and weak-minded, as if he had been struck ill too.

"Dr. Yuan," she leaned the bike next to the trunk of a tree, speaking in a deliberately pinched tone, "if this continues, you will be just like them in time." She pretended her jacket needed a good beating to clean the spots on it, stomped the snow from her shoes, and looked up contemptuously at the snowcapped mountains.

All of this made Mengliu think of Qizi. But when Qizi was angry, her eyes welled up with tears and she would shout and yell.

He had not quarreled with Suitang before, and he secretly admired her energetic expression of discontent. He felt that a man should never engage in a war of words with a woman. A woman was like candy, and all you needed to do was keep her in your mouth and allow her to soften quietly until her hardness had completely disappeared.

So he smiled and said she was right. Swan Valley really was rotten and not worth bothering about, but for the sake of friendship he should try to help. He did not say that he was curious, or that uncovering Swan Valley's secrets was of great interest to him, for that was too much even for him to believe. Other than women, he wouldn't normally take the trouble to investigate into the truth of anything. The thought suddenly brought to mind his past silent self, like a pig eating, drinking, relieving itself, and sleeping, day after day.

This deeply engraved image of his past streamed through the empty spaces in his heart and quickly engulfed the last ray of light there.

"No matter what you believe, you must be treated, rather than insisting on your so-called . . . faith." Mengliu decided he would try one last time with Esteban. As he got up from the millstone and walked to the dim lamp, he smelled decay. "Sometimes faith is nothing but a guard who exists in name only at the gate of a village. If you are arrogant, you can walk through easily, but if you look left or right before you enter the gate, he will stop you and interrogate you."

Esteban did not move. He looked like a dead man.

"If you are stopped at the gate, what else can you do? There's nothing you can do but dream." Mengliu came at it from another angle. "And love . . . yes, you remember you are a father? Surely you don't want your child to be born fatherless? You have become enslaved because of him, but you have to grit your teeth and carry on living. Even if it is for your . . . so-called faith."

Suitang's expression said that she thought Esteban's faith was a load of bullshit. "For pilgrims, the temple is everything, all culture and happiness," she muttered. But she did not speak that softly.

She seemed impatient, so much so that she left the mill and went out to stand in the cold, looking up at the sky.

Mengliu was shocked. She said so bluntly exactly what he meant. He felt a little awkward but, even more, he was relieved, since to say anything else would be superfluous. He assumed Esteban had also heard Suitang. Seeing some movement, he thought the other man was trying to sit up, not imagining that he was simply changing his position so he could continue sleeping.

"A poet can do without poetry. Why can't a sinner who is sick go without a doctor?"

Mengliu was about to leave when he suddenly heard this barbaric logic coming from Esteban. He turned to see that Esteban was standing up and looked like an ancient warrior. His face was the canvas of a colorful oil painting, his hand clasped a spear, and he was pointing the end of it toward Mengliu's breast. He couldn't move, as if the lack of oxygen had made his brain sluggish.

Just then, Darae came in. Perhaps because of the cold, he looked bleak, dreary of spirit. That wise, handsome young man had become sluggish and dull. After pulling something from a box, he placed dishes on the millstone. There were four pieces of tofu, a wilted cabbage, and two slices of corn bread. It was standard criminal's fare, coldly waiting for a mouth to devour it.

"Darae, what has happened to your excellent skills?" Mengliu, very carefully moving his body away from where he thought the tip of the spear might go, tried to inject a bit of humor into his voice. He really didn't blame Darae, but the meal was too rustic to overlook. If he were still Head of a Thousand Households, he would have the best food served to Esteban.

"I gave him something good, but he won't eat it. What can I do?" Darae said.

"Are you also sick, Darae? I know the recent flu has been very powerful . . . No, I should say, since the epidemic began . . . " Mengliu tried to get a good look at Darae's face. "I'm worried that Esteban's illness . . . maybe you can persuade him . . . "

Darae just shook his head.

Mengliu suddenly felt discouraged. He saw Suitang pacing outside. Her image made him think of the situation with Juli. He engaged in some more useless talk, saying how a child couldn't possibly soak in alcohol, how they shouldn't be manipulated, how they should take Juli to the mountains to give birth, staying until things had blown over and she could come back.

Darae laughed, his laugh like a blast of cold wind piercing Mengliu's body, but he finally agreed to go with them to the nursing home. He agreed to help them, to serve as a lookout. He said he, too, wanted to know, once and for all, what was going on.

But Mengliu backed away from Darae in the end, feeling he could not be relied on. Suitang seemed to hate his half-dead attitude. She thought they didn't need to drag anyone else into it. Regardless of the outcome, it was a Swan Valley problem.

22

Accommodating two women at the same time always leads to trouble. Mengliu found that Yuyue had become difficult to get along with, never saying what she meant, remaining aloof, or merely answering any question with, "You should ask *her*." This "her" referred to Suitang. When she was with Suitang, Yuyue always seemed warm and friendly, as if they were sisters. They would even crowd him out of their private conversations, with one of them always ready to throw menacing glances at him. Mengliu knew that Yuyue intended him to feel in the wrong, and that they were the innocent ones, and women should always unite. Perhaps in their imagination he had already turned into something wicked, but he had no idea what he had done wrong. At first, neither of them cared for him, but now, probably because each had found a competitor, they were both inspired to possess him. He lamented at how diabolically clever the two goblins were. They never showed their true intent; they hid their dark hysteria behind happy faces. He once overheard them talking. They were quick to reach the consensus that he would write poetry one day, and that he would again "rise up." He didn't like this sort of prediction. It was like witches telling fortunes by casual divination. It was just superstition. Especially when it came to a matter as serious as poetry. They shouldn't make such irresponsible comments. No one had a right to tell him what he should do. His intentions were like his personal beliefs, and his privacy should be respected and protected. As usual, he didn't lose his temper but repeated his old line, "I am a surgeon, unable to do anything related to poetry. Please don't waste your fantasies on me."

The night before visiting the nursing home, they had dinner at Juli's house. The dishes were rich and the rice wine sweet. She was in good shape, not as worried as he thought she would be about

Suitang, and not in the least surprised by her arrival. Yuyue had already corrected Juli's view on the matter by declaring that Suitang was not Mengliu's girlfriend. They were simply colleagues who had sometimes worked very closely together in the past. The three of them had come to persuade Juli to try to escape Swan Valley, but in the end they didn't say anything. As soon as they entered her house, they knew that it would be a waste of breath to do so. Juli had more backbone than anyone. Dinner turned into a joyous affair. The rice wine made them tipsy and they lost all inhibition, laughing with abandon, and making Mengliu feel that he was a lascivious, fatuous, self-indulgent ruler in the midst of his wives and concubines. During the gathering, Juli, pregnant though she was, performed a dance. Her body moved sinuously as her hands held her belly. It was as if she were at the harvest, the light from the fire turned her face golden, and her shadow formed weird shapes on the wall. She was excited, quite different from her usual self. When they told her about Esteban's appearance at the mill, she was lukewarm, indifferent, as if the burden of his forced labor, the atonement, and the hanging between life and death were all normal aspects of love.

This beautiful life cannot be false. Even if it is, it is still beautiful. If it is not for the sake of rebuilding, why bother destroying it? The idea popped out of nowhere in Mengliu's head, throwing him into confusion. It is perverse to shake people out of their dreams. They don't need the truth. The truth is like a leftover scrap of bread; it's unnecessary.

At this point, their entertainments were turning ridiculous because they had become overly merry. It was as if they were all play-acting even though they were sincere. Under the influence of alcohol Suitang and Yuyue both urged Mengliu to recite poetry, booing and hissing when he refused to be drawn into their pranks. Suddenly he saw the balalaika on the wall and was grateful for the timely rescue. He took the instrument down. It had a solid body with an open-mouthed dragon carved at its head. The neck was made of rosewood and the drum covered with python skin. It looked very old. He plucked a few strings, and the sound was full-bodied, it lingered like smoke. He said he would perform a storytelling and ballad sequence in the Suzhou dialect, employing *chen diao*. When Yuyue asked what *chen diao* was, Suitang said, "I'm afraid it means clichéd tunes and phrases."

As Mengliu continued to pluck, testing the strings, he said that there were three genres of *pingtan*—chen diao, *ma diao*, and *yu diao*. They were skeptical at first, not believing a traditional surgeon could play pingtan. When he really did begin to play, they fell silent. He sang softly, and his face became strangely animated. No one understood the words, but they were mesmerized by the music. While they were indulging themselves, he ended the performance with a few violent chords.

"I have not seen anyone who could play that instrument," Juli said, holding her belly and wearing a look of perfect mental and physical well-being. "You play beautifully. I feel that tonight you are close to the heart of a poet, and your music reveals the secrets of that heart."

"You're wrong. I have no secrets. It's your own imagination." Mengliu smiled, stroking the head of the instrument. "On the contrary, what was on my mind just now was a surgical procedure," and he described the whole process, every bloody detail. They all listened quietly, none of them in the least horrified. He, on the other hand, was uncomfortable. He was remembering how he had caused Jia Wan's death with his own hand, and how he had harbored hatred toward him in his mind, a so-called poet who had sold out his friend for glory. A scumbag who had used poetry to cheat on a girl's affections, and in the year of the Round Square incident acted as a mole, betraying people in the Wisdom Bureau. But what was really dirty was the government who awarded Jia Wan the supreme poetry prize—that was equivalent to a public reward for a lackey, and a contemptuous insult to all poets. Thinking of this, Mengliu had become emotional. But he quickly recovered, fleeing behind the safety of the walls he'd erected around himself.

After their brief alliance, the three women went back to their own concerns. Only the crackle of the fire could be heard. There was a trace of hostility in the atmosphere, and the wind outside was whistling and sharp, distant and sorrowful like a wolf on the prowl. Inside it was like an oil painting in a warm hue; the nonliving and the living alike were quiet. Yuyue burped softly, then quickly covered her mouth. Juli stood up and began to clear the dishes. Suitang helped to empty the garbage into the bin. Suddenly, they all found something to busy themselves with.

Mengliu thought of the journey to the nursing home the following day. Would Suitang or Yuyue be the lookout? Yuyue's mother was inside, so it stood to reason that she should go in, but Suitang thought that Yuyue, being from Swan Valley, should be the lookout. If something happened, people would believe her. She and Mengliu were both outsiders—if they disappeared, so what? But Yuyue insisted she wanted to go in, saying that the plan had been hatched before Suitang had arrived. "It's my mother who is in there, not yours." They were like children bickering over a sweet.

But only two people could sit in the cable car.

In the end it was Juli who came up with a solution. When she had cleaned up, she cut two small pieces of paper, wrote on them, crumpled them up, and then like a general presiding over a meeting said, "You two draw lots to determine who will go and who will stay."

The scheme worked, leaving neither girl with anything to say. They reached out to draw lots, each took a small ball of paper. Just as they did so Shanlai came into the room, his body emitting a chill and his face blue.

"Señor Esteban has gone to the netherworld."

His weird expression made it appear that he was joking. Those in the room looked down at him in surprise.

"He was lying there, and no matter how I called, he wouldn't wake up." Shanlai looked at his feet. His pudgy shoes were embedded in circles of mud, making them look even clumsier. He raised his head and looked at them again and said boldly, "He's dead . . . really dead."

The house was like a grave. Then the commotion began.

Five minutes later, everyone left. The snow crunched under their feet as they ran toward the mill.

23

Mengliu didn't sleep a wink all night. Time flowed from the rising sun and stopped at eight o'clock. According to Yuyue's news, Michael would be leaving on the cable car at twelve, escorted by a male underling. Again and again, Mengliu imagined the scene. They would lurk around, waiting, their faces hidden behind black cloths, just like in a movie. If necessary, they would carry small arms, ready to stun or kill the underling, then rescue Michael and tell him that going to the nursing home was certain death. Michael would be so frightened by the sudden turn of events that he wouldn't resist. Completely misunderstanding Mengliu, he would stammer and say he could go back to the hospital and do whatever was required of him—he was not a man who liked leisure. He would slap his arms and legs and show how robust his body was. He would tremble and beg for mercy. Mengliu would have to knock him unconscious just to shut him up, and then drag him into the bushes. In his own imaginings Mengliu was a tall and powerful figure, cool in his fighting moves as he dealt with the monsters around him. But in reality, when he saw the sun rising over the windowsill, he grew nervous. He didn't want to resort to violence.

He preferred to settle it all with a civilized conversation. He had no confidence in a fight.

Today Esteban would be transported to the mountain. His attitude toward atoning for his sin and his bravery would earn him a high-level snow burial, and all charges of wrongdoing would be expunged at the funeral. He was an intellectual of Swan Valley and would be placed in a three-inch-thick ice coffin. A snow tomb would be erected, along with a giant ice sculpture for a tombstone. In good weather, everyone would be able to see the tombstone on the peak from the foot of the mountain, like a shining sword.

The previous night Shanlai had stayed at the mill while the others returned to Juli's house, where they alternated between sharing their memories of the deceased and moments of respectful silence. The glory of the dead had nothing to do with Juli's fate, and the law wouldn't spare the child in her belly. It would have to undergo the alcohol test as if nothing had happened. She was very confident and persuasion was useless. She was the only one who slept that night, and in the morning, full of energy, she made eggs and pancakes and porridge for breakfast, without any sign of grieving for her lost love. Mengliu, smelling the aromas from the kitchen as he went through his morning ablutions, thought of the war games that were soon to come. He was surprised at the murderous expression in the eyes of the man who looked back at him from the mirror, hovering above his overnight beard, below his shiny forehead. Maybe he should do as Suitang had said and carry a dagger and pepper spray with him, in case words didn't work. Yuyue said it was best to use an anesthetic, since it wasn't life-threatening. "If he says anything, just poke it up his ass, and he'll really sleep. Or use a brick and knock him out."

Before leaving, Mengliu embraced Juli. "Farewell," he said, hoping she would survive her plight.

When they departed, the funeral procession was crawling slowly across the side of the hill. If it hadn't been for the shadows it cast on the snow, it would not have been easy to see the pure white procession. They had no doubt that it included Shanlai and Darae. The sun-kissed snow was dazzling. Mengliu, Yuyue, and Suitang looked dignified in their sunglasses. Their consultations complete, they were ready to act according to plan and didn't speak as they traveled. Walking quickly, they reached their destination at ten o'clock. From far away, they saw the cable car on the peak opposite, like a bird cage hanging on a thin wire. It was skirted on both sides by cliffs. Below was a bottomless pit of silence. The dense virgin forest was still full of life in the piercing cold.

Mengliu's calves and stomach had turned to jelly, and Suitang was having doubts about the thin wires.

Yuyue said proudly, "If anyone wants out, it's not too late to go back. There is no way out once you're on the cable car." She underestimated Suitang, who was not the least bit intimidated.

They hid themselves in the bushes like cats.

"A fire in the snow would be good right now." They had already digested their breakfast and began to feel less and less able to fight the cold. Suitang was so cold she kept thinking of the hypothetical fire. "If we could roast some wild game . . . this would be a really nice trip."

"If you come back alive, I'll go with you on a camping trip in the snow." Yuyue pointed off into the distance, as if coaxing a child, then adjusted her artificial leg to a more comfortable position before continuing. "We'll have a huge camp fire, roast a wild rabbit, and a pheasant, grill mushrooms, barbecue pork . . . ah! Then we can drink some wine, you know, to warm ourselves up. We'll lie in the snow under the stars, tell ghost stories . . . " As she whetted Suitang's appetite, she was herself moved by her wonderful descriptions. Staring at the other two intently, she said with great seriousness, "I'll be here waiting for you. Don't you two run away. Be sure to come back!"

Mengliu smiled. "I can't say for sure."

The sun was directly overhead, pale and weak. He looked at his watch. Eleven forty-five. His heart banging, he clawed through the bushes and looked out. Each tree was like a human shadow, but there was nothing on the road. He felt frozen, barely able to control his fingers. Time seemed to have come to a standstill. The wind blew from time to time, raising a dust storm of snow. White clouds puffed from the three conspirators' nostrils. It seemed they could see each other's eyes through their sunglasses. Without knowing who reached out first, three pairs of thickly gloved hands were suddenly stacked one upon the other. With this action, their hearts were filled as with a divine mission.

There was a loud roar in the distance.

"Avalanche," Yuyue said, as if it were as common as rain.

"If you get caught, don't say anything. Don't mention anyone else's name," Mengliu instructed Suitang, as if he were a surgeon addressing his staff at the operating table. Then he stared at Yuyue and said solemnly, "Don't say anything to Michael until we come back." He released his hands from theirs, then took off his gloves and sunglasses and readied for action. "Wait for us."

Yuyue nodded and also removed her gloves, rubbing her hands and cracking her knuckles. "I've had practice in free combat." She had a lot of confidence.

"The cable car will only stop for five minutes. Attack furtively, don't confront anyone head-on," Suitang said. "Just one blow, then leave his life to fate."

"Shh!" Mengliu pointed to two figures in the distance. Suddenly, they could hear nothing but their own heartbeats. Perhaps he had been squatting too long. Mengliu's legs felt weak. He tried to stand but could not, as if branches had hooked onto his clothing, or plants had wrapped around his body. He heard the crunch of footsteps on the snow, getting closer and growing louder, until at last they were a mighty force thundering on his eardrums. His breathing became labored and he was dizzy. He forced himself to control his trembling. It was like a nightmare from which he could not wake.

"You wait here, I'll settle it." Perhaps perceiving Mengliu's fear, Yuyue deviated from the plan. She looked at her watch, then calmly went out and greeted those who approached. From a gap in the bushes Mengliu could see their lower bodies. Yuyue spoke the local dialect, occasionally mixing in an English word. She laughed heartily, as if meeting and chatting with old friends. As they joked, someone suddenly gasped, and Mengliu could just see Michael's escort clutching his hip, then staggering to the ground as if drunk.

She made easy work of the escort.

"Michael, they want to go over and have a look around for a while. You and I can wait here for them to come back. You don't mind, do you?" She pointed to the people who had just emerged from the bushes.

Michael looked bewildered. "Have I somehow offended you? When . . . ? Why should I be denied the chance to enjoy the benefits of the nursing home?" His face was still crimson, his cheeks trembled as he spoke. "Yuyue . . . don't be manipulated by these outsiders. Surely you've figured out that they don't have beliefs. They're just cowards, right to the core."

"Michael, attacking them will serve no purpose for you," Yuyue replied, laughing. She saw that Mengliu and Suitang had propped the collapsed escort against a tree trunk, so that he looked like he was having a nap. "I can't vouch for them to come back."

Michael moved close to her and said softly, "You heard the avalanche, right? I guess the funeral procession has been buried alive. A large-scale epidemic will soon break out. The medical team will retreat tomorrow. Swan Valley is doomed . . . I suggest you also go somewhere safe. It's better that you come to the nursing home with me and stay for a period of time . . . See, the cable car is coming."

The car had come to a stop just above the edge of the cliff, like a steel cage for a wild beast, with thick bars. The automatic doors propped open. A chill emanated from the empty cage.

Michael suddenly ran toward the car but tripped on a branch. By the time he recovered, his hands had been tied behind his back.

"Sorry to do this, Michael. If you're lucky, you won't have to suffer for long." Mengliu bound the director and the escort back to back, then gave the tape to Yuyue, in case she deemed it necessary to tape their mouths shut. He realized that the heroic self from his fantasies had emerged. His legs had stopped shaking. His mind was clear; he wasted no effort. He had dealt with the current scuffle with amazing efficiency and now caught Suitang's hand and headed toward the cable car.

As soon as they entered the car, the doors snapped shut. The floor beneath them was made of wooden planks, affording them a view of the misty abyss through the gaps when they looked down. Mengliu was frightened half to death. He had not heard Yuyue's final words clearly, though he had a faint notion it had been something about the avalanche. All of his energy went to quelling his fears. No matter how cold it was to the touch, he had to keep a firm grip on the iron railing. The cable car trembled violently, then started up, swinging slightly. It moved very slowly, but they could not overcome their fear to appreciate the grandeur around them. The strange rocks, towering trees, the cliff and its crevices covered with white flowers, and the gorgeous smoky clouds held nothing for them.

Suitang did not dare to look anywhere other than at Mengliu's chest, yet she seemed to see everything. "Put your gloves on," she said, shivering.

He opened his arms but kept one hand on a pole, afraid to let go. He didn't feel the cold. The truth was, he was afraid of heights. He was afraid to take an airplane. Even climbing a ladder set his legs trembling, and standing on the three-meter-high platform at readings had always made him dizzy. Now he was flying, and it was like suddenly reaching a climax. His spirit went back in time and the woman before him turned into Qizi. They were in the police bus going to their interrogation, their bodies close, but not looking at each other. She was gazing at the buttons on his chest in the same way as Suitang was now. He bent and looked at her eyes, and her lips, and thoughts of love surged through him, wishing the journey would go on forever, that the vehicle would never stop.

"Come, hold me. Close your eyes. Imagine we are on a boat . . . "

But before he had finished, the gliding cable car stopped convulsively. The entire cage vibrated.

Now the cable car was hanging above the abyss and shaking gently. If they so much as breathed, it rocked.

He had felt the urge to urinate when he first boarded the car. When Suitang screamed and grabbed hold of him, Mengliu nearly wet his pants in fear. His face was as pale as a zombie's, his mouth was tightly shut. Hoping to hide his complicated feelings, he squeezed out a smile, but it only made him look even more ghastly.

Suitang lay collapsed in his arms for several minutes before gathering her senses. Now she beheld an earthly paradise. Everything was bathed by the sun in a warm coating of yellow. They were above the clouds, close to the heavens.

"Ah . . . you see that cluster of clouds? Just like a castle." She tried to stand firm, without leaning on anything, as if she were on level ground.

He turned cautiously to see her castle, and it was indeed as magnificent as a heavenly palace, as if a beast guarded the gate and fairies floated around it. But then, in the blink of an eye, it looked more like a house on fire, with smoke billowing and wounded people falling to the ground.

He closed his eyes in an expression of torment.

"It's interesting how they change . . . Well, and then . . . " She continued to investigate the clouds, apparently grown completely accustomed to the dangerous environment. "It's like a big cruise ship cutting through a choppy sea. Look, there's a row of waves."

He, on the other hand, was thinking of the precariousness of their situation, that they might fall into the abyss at any moment.

"If the cable car has broken down and cannot move we will soon become mummies." He glanced at her full forehead with his half-closed eyes, wondering at her ability to enjoy the scenery. He didn't want to talk about the clouds. Inwardly, he cursed the damned cable car, though it wasn't so much out of hatred for the thing as an attempt to vent his fear. With one breath he damned the car's creators and a whole lot of other people and especially Swan Valley. Finally he calmed down.

"If we are going to die here . . . could you . . . compose a poem for me?" Suitang said. "I don't want to die silently . . . When people find us, they will have your poem, and people will remember my love."

"Women! Damn your vanity!" He liked her look of fearlessness before death. It was full of longing. But at the same time, he felt his heart jolt, and after the stabbing pain, a drop of blood dripped on Qizi's face. She had been pushed onto the stage by vanity, and now a greater desire was controlling her, making her sacrifice her life. If he were to replace vanity and desire with more edifying words, it would be idealism and faith. This was what had become clear to him, after much pondering. When he had devoted himself to working in the hospital in a desperate attempt to anesthetize himself against his memories of the past, people had taken it as an act of selflessness and applauded his exceptional conscience, praising him as a model of morality in the medical community.

"As long as I live, I will have my vanity." Suitang wore a look that suggested that she wanted to talk to Mengliu about love. "Will you write for me? Do it now. If we don't die it will still be a keepsake."

He was suddenly angry. "Do you know that I have a phobia of heights? I couldn't squeeze out a fucking fart right now, much less a poem."

"I'm afraid of heights too. But I'm not afraid when I'm with you. Do you know why?" Women are more able to maintain their composure at crucial moments than men. Suitang didn't get angry, even though she had every right to accuse him. "Because we are doing something meaningful."

Mengliu's face regained a little color, his shame doing much to dispel his fear of heights. He wondered why he had been losing to women so often recently, why they had continued to pamper him like a baby, tolerated and given way to him, overlooked all his flaws. He was like their dog. They had all been confused by his superficial heroism. He wasn't going into the nursing home because of Yuyue or for the truth, or at least, not completely. He lacked the quality of courage. He was naturally uninterested in truth, except for medical truth. But as for the question of how to go on surviving, he had his way . . . and his walks through the forest were proof of that. He would quietly take every opportunity he could to inspect the lay of the land. He drew a map of Swan Valley in his mind. It could not be completely isolated. There must be a way out. As for the river suddenly disappearing, he imagined that it must have continued flowing beneath the mountain, like a ghost. But now the river that flowed secretly beneath the mountains was filled with squid. Yes, that's definitely how it was. And this cable car was the instrument for crossing the river.

"Maybe we can get away from Swan Valley from here . . . if the cable pulls us over safely." He wanted to grab Suitang's hand, but his fingers were stiff. He felt excited by his ability to let go now and stand on his own. He was blowing on his hands and slowly rubbing them together to warm them. He tried several times to look down at his feet but failed. At last, gritting his teeth, he did look down, but all he could see was a river of rolling clouds.

Suitang said it would be horrible if they just ditched Juli and Yuyue. "Yuyue is waiting for you, you know. You must honor your word."

"They are on their own turf, with their own sense of law and order. We can't do anything about that." He found he was overcoming all of his mental obstacles. He looked out from their cage and was awed by the beauty around them. He was thinking, *Maybe the cable car stops here to let people feast their eyes on paradise before sending them to heaven. Such views only appear on a road close to heaven.*

A gust of wind ran across the valley, shaking the cage.

From afar, they must have looked like a fallen leaf hanging on a spider web.

Suitang whispered, clinging to Mengliu to balance herself, "Well, if you won't write, I can't force you. But I want to know why you are so hard-hearted. Even for a dying wish, you won't do this to satisfy me?"

" . . . If you want to think like that, I can't do anything about it. Qizi would understand. She knew what I thought. She chased me out of Round Square because she didn't want me to accompany her, to sacrifice myself fruitlessly. She was a true believer, but I wasn't. She thought of the public, but I only thought of her. I was just tagging along. To be honest, I did not want to share in the fruits of their victory—but even more, I did not want them to lose so tragically, blown away like ashes in the wind . . ." He was silent for a while, tears shining at the corners of his eyes. "So we need to think about how to get back . . . people cannot live without their motherland, even if it has no feeling for them, even if it takes everything from them, even if . . . ”

As he was speaking in this sombre fashion, in these parallel sentences, she interrupted him. “Here, chew this. I think we should make love now, right here.” She eyed him with a sort of apocalyptic indulgence.

He chewed the gum. He had thought of this possibility countless times, but today it didn't attract him at all.

The cage, seemingly startled by Suitang's words, began to twitch. With a burst, a bang, and a clicking sound, it started gliding toward the other side.

24

After entering a black hole, the cable car suddenly accelerated, whizzing along like a bullet. Mengliu felt like the top of his skull had been ripped off, and the skin on his face peeled back. Suitang's long hair whipped about him, burning his face like fire. Without thinking, he grabbed hold of the railing and pulled Suitang into a protective embrace. He heard her shout but couldn't make sense of the garble of words that came speeding out of her mouth. Then he couldn't hear anything, and after that he knew nothing.

When he awoke, they were lying on a wooden floor. The room was hot, and he was sweating. The beating of war drums slowly retreated from his ears, and he felt a kind of warmth, like sunshine after a storm. A ray of light struck his eyes, and he mistook it for the sun. When all the other lights came on one after another, he realized he was on a stage framed by a scarlet curtain, with a piano on one side, and various props on the other. The ceiling was dozens of meters high. He saw a circular painting on the ceiling and black velvet seats with yellow armrests filling three stories of the auditorium, all of which were empty. The white gauze curtains on the boxes were held back with gold herringbone hooks. He recognized Darae's work in the relief work covering the walls. At this point the familiar smell of the sea stimulated a memory. It seemed he had been here before— he remembered his conversation with the robot. Yes, that was here. Presumably the hall had been renovated extensively after the destruction he caused. He remembered it fully. It wasn't a dream. He pulled himself up and shook Suitang, who was like a sparrow hawk in full spin when she awoke, asking where they were as she looked around. When the light struck her body he saw fine traces of blood on her face.

"It doesn't matter where you are. It only matters that you have arrived safely," said a robotic voice, resonating around the whole space. "Now you both need to rest. In a moment, someone will come to show you to your rooms. I dare say that you will like the view, overlooking the sea on one side, the garden on the other, and with the stars overhead."

Mengliu ran to the front of the stage. He was enveloped by a strong golden light. "It's you again, the great spiritual leader." He enunciated his address carefully, leaning forward in an eloquent manner, with a fluid, natural dramatic flair. "An epidemic has broken out in Swan Valley. You shouldn't be hiding here. In fact . . . why don't you show your true face?"

"You really disappoint me, Mr. Yuan. You are still so long-winded. The punishment for trespassing on military land is to be thrown to the squid. But this depends on your luck. And my mood. Ha ha ha."

"Why don't you show yourself? Let me look at Swan Valley's spiritual leader, so I can see whether you are superhuman or not." Mengliu moved to a different spot, peering suspiciously into the dark. "Well, you're obviously just a machine. You aren't human. You have no heart, much less a sense of goodness."

There was another fit of soundtrack laughter. "Dr. Yuan, when you start using real language, like a poet, I will talk with you face to face. Farewell."

The light went out and the scarlet curtain closed from both sides.

A robot of indistinct gender appeared at the side of the stage, waiting for them. Following the robot, they walked through a dimly lit passage, accompanied by a sound like the sea crashing against rocks. After five minutes they entered a garden where snow covered the flowers, grass and trees, the pavilions, a stone bridge spanning an artificial lake, and, around the knot of the icy lake, a row of willows.

As Suitang walked, she repeatedly asked what military grounds had to do with the nursing home. The spiritual leader was full of hot air, just a pretentious fool. Suddenly remembering, she said, "Isn't he that robot person you mentioned?"

Mengliu nodded. He couldn't retell the whole of his conversation with the robot. Perhaps he wasn't a robot. The voice had been manipulated. Maybe he was a woman, but he had the cold processes of a machine. He remembered it had said it wanted to save him, to allow him a renaissance as a poet. That had developed into an argument about enslavement and freedom. A lot of information rushed into his head at the same time. To avoid watching eyes and listening ears, there were some things he could only discuss with Suitang in private. For now, he knew nothing about their situation, why they had been brought here, and what the military grounds had to do with the nursing home. Suitang's thoughts were even more bizarre. She said she feared that they had been put here for genetic testing, perhaps even to be disemboweled, their flesh flayed, tortured until they were neither humans nor ghosts, and then tossed into the incinerators like medical waste. When she said this, it made her own hair stand on end.

They crossed through a stand of low trees on a path with snow piled up on either side. Their sweat had not yet dried, making their icy clothes cling to their bodies, freezing them both through and through. After five minutes, they were separated, and another robot led Suitang away. In a building that looked like an ancient castle, the robot opened the door to a room, then stood at the door without moving, as if standing guard. Mengliu went into the room and, to his surprise, was greeted by dazzling luxury. There were rugs, crystal lamps, murals, large divans, bookcases, and a desk set before an expansive window, skirted by a tasselled curtain, through which he could see an azure sea. There was a card on the table, prompting him to ring the bell to call for assistance. He tried pressing the button, and someone answered him from outside the room. He knew what all this was about, but he was certainly not going to be taking this approach. He had no interest in pleasure. His spirit had died long ago. He could not be bought. He only wanted to go on living. He had to pretend he didn't know anything. *The less you know, the safer* was always an irrefutable truth.

"What is it they want?" It was hot in the room. He began to sweat again, so he removed his coat and spread himself out on the bed. The crystal lights in the ceiling were like ice, and looking at them gave him a chill. The ceiling panels were dark blue, filled with twinkling stars. He lay there thinking for a while, at a loss and feeling irritable. His stomach rumbled, so he rang the bell and asked for food, then went to the window and looked at the sea. Maybe he could find some inspiration there, but he found that the sea was actually airbrushed on the glass, and even the window was fake. Behind it was a blocked-up wall. He turned to the bookshelf and found Paul Celan and Walt Whitman among the books arranged there. He felt a surge of joy, which soon turned to horror. They even knew his favorite poets. He refused to touch them but quickly suppressed the disgust inside him, then reached out and fingered the spines of other books. He pulled out *The Golden Lotus*. There was no doubt in his mind the room had surveillance equipment and that spies somewhere were observing his every move. If they were really doing genetic experiments, then it would be necessary to observe him too. He stopped at the thought of genetic experiments, shuddering a little. He had done experiments on animals, and many of humanity's medical advancements had first been made on animals such as dogs, rabbits, rats . . . He personally had done experimental surgery on a dog, opening it up four times, the last of which was to remove the pancreas, draining the animal of life. The dog was continuously sick after surgery, lying down, or swaying as it walked. Up until it died it still wagged its tail each time it saw him. At the time he felt he had been cruel, and that sooner or later retribution would come. Perhaps this was his day of reckoning.

He put the book back, then pressed the bell again. He asked to talk to someone. While he was waiting for a response, he worried about Suitang, and at the same time thought of Qizi, of the time they had sat together in the interrogation room chatting, fearless. He remembered how she looked when she spoke, expressive and full of banter, her temper not as loud as her voice, stomping her feet in her tantrum, delicate and charming. How did a weak little girl suddenly become so big and independent? Her voice gathered strength. She used hand gestures to awaken her sleepy eyes, letting everyone know that the feces question was a human rights issue. At the time he thought it was funny, but he wasn't laughing now.

The door opened, and the person who entered carried a whole roasted rabbit, the flesh cut off and accompanied by the complete frame of its skeleton, brown and shiny with oil, with a special sauce and a plate of the local dough sticks. From the artful way it had been carved, he could tell this was Darae's work, and was even more certain of that fact after tasting it. From that moment he knew he was still a valued guest in Swan Valley. He ate and drank, leaving his utensils in a mess, and thinking all the while. This time he was determined to get to the bottom of things.

He heard a familiar voice coming from the corner.

"Mr. Yuan, now do you understand a little better? Our motive is simple. We just want you to write an ode for the increasingly large number of people in Swan Valley—you could call it 'Google's Swan Song'—to be sung at the five hundredth anniversary of our valley-building, which we will celebrate next month. You can use the opportunity to restore your identity and your glory as a poet. I can say for certain that your reappearance in the poetry world will be a fabulous event." The spiritual leader was uncharacteristically gentle, full of patience and amicability. "Your memory has been recorded. I have seen your whole history. Many years ago you wrote the poem *"For Whom the Bell Tolls,"* then when you left Round Square you also left poetry. But there is one minor issue—why were your actions and your poetry in such contradiction?"

He couldn't answer. He felt that his privacy had been invaded, and he had been stripped naked in public. Looking around for an excuse he glanced at the ceiling and saw that a certain star up there was emitting a weak red light. He knew there were eyes on him.

"Never mind if you don't answer, Mr. Yuan, there are pen and paper on the desk. You can start composing your Swan Song any time you like."

"Surely it's not just machines? Is anyone here?" he asked aloud. "I want to talk to someone. Where is Suitang? I need to see her."

"She is fine. After you have finished writing, you will meet."

"Goodness is the highest virtue in Swan Valley, but you illegally place a citizen under house arrest. It won't be good for you if this is made public."

"You don't need to worry about that. We're being very hospitable to you. We've given you the finest food Swan Valley has to offer, and the most comfortable lodgings," the spiritual leader said in a tepid tone. "Look how quiet it is here, much more conducive to writing than your West Wing. As long as you don't ring the bell, no one will disturb you."

A sudden apprehension rose in Mengliu. Testing just how much the spiritual leader actually knew, he said, "What West Wing?"

"You wouldn't have forgotten that. There was an acacia tree in the courtyard, and you kept a pot with a rose that refused to bloom."

"No! You're wrong. It did bloom! It bloomed!" Unable to bear the slanderous remarks against the rose, he interrupted without thinking. "It bloomed, and it was . . . "

"Bloomed?" The spiritual leader sounded surprised, as if it were hearing something impossible. "What color was it?"

Mengliu had retreated into his own memories and saw nothing but the rose before his eyes. "She said open, and it opened. She said it would be red, and it was red." His tone was almost that of a dream. "It bloomed six times in all, always with four blossoms, which remained open until the frost came. The scarlet petals would drop around the flower pot, then dry and harden. I collected them and laid them into a collage forming one word."

"Was it 'Qizi?'"

"No. It was 'Freedom!'" He was like an old friend pouring his heart out. "I was free. I got rid of her. No one would care about me anymore. Oh. I'm glad you know everything. I have nothing to hide, and nothing to talk about. I hope you understand my feelings. I have not told this to anyone before. Now I can really let go."

The spiritual leader was silent for quite a while, then said, "Too bad your fiancée did not see the flowers. That is to her credit."

"Later, I left the Wisdom Bureau and studied medicine for five years. As if to affirm my choice, my hands took naturally to the scalpel." He reached out his soft thin hand in a moment of appreciation. "The language of exile has no motherland. Writing poetry is just misguided."

"These excuses make it obvious that your problem is one of self-esteem, Mr. Yuan. Your talent is beyond doubt . . . but since the rose bloomed—and moreover, it was red—you should at least honor your promise—never to give up writing poetry."

"It's too late, useless. I have lost my imagination. Who can make a butterfly with broken wings fly? Poetry abandoned me, choosing of its own free will to fall short." Mengliu felt as if he had returned to himself after being put into a trance. He faced the red flashing star and said, "See, we can carry on an agreeable conversation. You might as well tell me about yourself now. Perhaps talking face to face. That would be better."

"As Swan Valley's spiritual leader I solemnly promise you, as soon as you finish your Swan Song, it will be your choice whether you stay or go."

"I recommend Darae. He's the most outstanding local poet. And he has a much better understanding of Swan Valley than I ca–"

"You have a month. I wish you well."

The red star suddenly went blank. The stars on the blue ceiling continued to glitter.

25

Over the next two days, Mengliu passed the time with *The Golden Lotus*, though secretly he was considering all sorts of counter-measures to employ against his captors. His days were not too difficult, spent idly reading the erotic passages. On the third morning, two robots entered uninvited, took down the paintings decorating the walls, and the crystal chandelier, leaving only a dim bulb for light, casting shadows on the four uneven concrete walls of the room. At four o'clock in the afternoon, they also took his bed and mattress, removed the carpet, and left him only a pile of tattered quilts. On the fourth day, the room was completely emptied, revealing a rugged cell with a cracked toilet and no water coming out of the faucet. His food, too, was stripped bare, to cabbage and tofu accompanied by a cup of cold water once a day. The bell was completely disregarded. He looked angrily at the pen and paper on the table, then threw them at the wall. Then the radiator was switched off, and even with all of his clothes on he was cold. He wrapped a quilt around him. On the seventh day he started counting the stars on the ceiling and used his footsteps to measure the room. He picked up the pen and paper, placed them on the small table, and stared at them for a long time. He had no water to wash himself with, nor clothes to change into, and the toilet smelled of urine and shit. He scratched his itchy body until the dry skin bled. He felt he had become an animal. Before long, he would grow fur all over his body and lose the ability to understand human speech. He would begin to howl.

On that seventh day someone new served his food, a young person. He was strong and good-looking, his skin and hair as black as a gorilla's, his waist flexible, his lips thin and wide. His eyes were those of an actor, his expression soft and tender, his face youthful and yet tainted with age. He was a quiet creature. He set the dishes down as if he were serving a meal to a king, with his eyes humbly lowered and his hands clasped. He bowed as if waiting for orders, and didn't seem to mind the pungent odor in the room. Mengliu tried to strike up a conversation with him. He didn't speak, just bowed at the waist in response. Mengliu thought perhaps he did not understand English. He scratched his head in distress. Not to speak with someone would surely drive the prisoner mad. Taking a few phrases of Swanese he had learned from Yuyue, he asked the simian fellow in tortured language if it understood English, suggesting that perhaps they could chat a while; he had a belly full of stories to share for free. He sincerely hoped the apelike creature would look up at him, even if it really was an ape. If all it did was watch him as he spoke, that would be enough.

Actually, his expectations had been too low. Using charming eyes to look askance at him a couple of times, the fellow began to speak. In an effeminate tone, he answered in perfect American English, looking on Mengliu with devotion the whole time. He said, "I'm your ardent fan. I know you're an awesome poet. I really admire you . . . you established your status in literary circles when you were only in your twenties. You're really amazing! The poems the Three Musketeers wrote, I read them all when I was ten, and yours are the ones I like the best. I always dreamed of getting a chance to meet and talk to you, but I never really believed this day would come. And . . . you're still so young! You have the grace of a poet, just like I imagined you would have."

As the monkey spoke, he shyly took out a little notebook and asked his idol for an autograph.

Perhaps because of his hunger, Mengliu felt slightly dizzy. Steadying himself, he took the notebook from the monkey's hand. The book contained autographs by many famous people. He leafed through it slowly, thinking how after so many years, in this strange place, a fan had emerged, and it made his heart churn a little. He thought of how fans had asked for the autographs of the Three Musketeers in just the same way years ago. The Three Musketeers would hide behind closed doors and practice their signatures in their free time. Hei Chun's autograph was very artistic, written with a flair that made it impossible to read. Bai Qiu's was clumsy and honest, belying his wisdom. But Mengliu had completely forgotten what his own signature looked like in those days. Certainly it was not the same as he had used to sign medical charts. He thought of finding a blank page to show off a little, just to satisfy the effeminate's request. Suddenly, a few words in Dayangese jumped out from the book, stinging his eyes and making his heart tingle. Yes! It was Qizi! He recognized it as soon as he saw it. It was Qizi's autograph! He grabbed the ape's hairy hand excitedly, barraging him with questions. The poor fellow, shaking like an electric shock had bolted through him, shot back, "It's not mine. I found it in a dead person's pocket."

"Where?" asked Mengliu.

"Underground. Probably only the bones are left now."

Mengliu said in an authoritative tone, "I don't mean the body. I mean, where did you pick up the book?"

The simian fellow looked frightened by his idol's expression. His thin lips were speechless for a while, then he said in a sorrowful tone, "It was in the woods. About five years ago."

Mengliu flipped through the pages of the autograph book once more and, holding it tightly to his chest, looked up and let out a long sigh. The clue's thread had been cut with a stroke, but the signature at least meant that Qizi might still be alive. The discovery made him shake uncontrollably. He seemed to smell her breath, to hear her voice on the wind, to see the shadow of her figure haunting the foliage.

The fellow placed his folded hands on his abdomen again and said shyly and cheerily, "If you want this book, it's all yours. I've always dreamt of giving my most treasured possession to my idol. Oh, God is good to me! I am so blessed! My name is Sama. If you can remember that—Sama—I will die happy."

Mengliu did not move, not even a twitch. Confronted with his fan's emotional expression of adoration, he offered no emotion of his own.

He ate nothing. Stimulated by the thought of Qizi, he suddenly felt it would be too shameful to eat in a stinking place like this, as if he were some barnyard animal. He had never been treated like this in his life, and he would hold his head up with dignity now. Changing tactics, he rang the bell and asked for someone to clean the toilet and allow him to shower and dress before writing his poem. A voice simply reminded him of the due date for the Swan Song, telling him to cherish his time and his life. If he failed to complete the task, he would be thrown in the river to feed the fish. He quietly cursed the ruthless robot. *It's unscrupulous to force a surgeon to write poetry. The arrogance of this authoritarian attitude! Well, let's just see how you'll make these hands write!*

As time went on, each day was harder than the one before. There was less food. Sometimes he didn't eat all day. The water was cut off again. His body was moldy and infested with bugs. Only the lice grew fat, and fleas, who leapt out from his quilt to attack what was left of him. He remembered how well he had dressed in the past, in shirts so fresh they always looked new, and clean underwear, always paying close attention to his sideburns . . . At that moment, if there had been a mirror in the room, he would not have been brave enough to look at his reflection. He was constipated and soon developed hemorrhoids. His breath was offensive, and his muscles atrophied. He knew they were trying to turn his dignity to dog shit. Then, when he had written a Valley ballad singing the praises of their goodness, they would elevate him on the poet's pedestal and restore the dignity he had lost.

He picked up the pen, looked at the paper, and struck the pose of one lost in thought.

Write, he said to himself, one poem, one ballad, ten lines, twenty . . . I just want to bathe and change clothes. It's very simple.

He started writing. The white paper was like a screen with a film flashing across it. Juli's gold-as-wheat body and coconut breasts, and a man's inward stirring and frustration. He kept writing. A red file, artificial insemination, Rania's blood flowing from the ward, through the forest, to the waste disposal site. He wrote faster and more wildly. His pen and the film were in a violent firefight, facing off in the chaos. Those sounds, those colors, the shouting, the distant snowcapped, wind-swept mountains, the sun like a sharp sword striking his eyes. His eyes were bleeding. He kept writing. Qizi's coquetry in the West Wing, the sadness on the radio, in Round Square. She turned into a phoenix and soared away from the smoke, speeding from the red earth, through the blue sky and into the pristine clouds. He wrote. He wrote! He wrote of Hei Chun and Bai Qiu. He wrote of sorrow and regret. He wrote of hunger . . . He and Qizi were together, fainting then transfused with energy, standing up together. They held their heads high and were inseparable. They pressed forward, speaking with one voice, moving toward the same goal. She leaned against him as if he were a great tree. Oh, and he wrote! Dazed with hunger, they entered a pretty restaurant and ordered Kobe beef, platters of sashimi, grilled saury, stir-fried seafood, gingko nuts, durian cakes, wine, spirits, sake, a table overflowing with fragrant food—so exquisitely fragrant. He poured the wine and gave it to her. Suddenly there was a gunshot. Blood splattered everywhere as Qizi's head flew off. As it flew away from her body, in her dilated pupils he saw himself. His face was dirty, unlike man or ghost.

He snapped out of his reverie. The mouthwatering cuisine disappeared. There was nothing in front of him but a stack of blank paper. Qizi was still in his mind, still her former pale, beautiful self, with sharp chin and dark almond eyes.

Barely able to suffer the horror of the dream, Mengliu was covered in sweat. His limbs were lifeless.

Though he wasn't hungry, and couldn't eat anything, the knowledge that she must still be alive strengthened him. Everything made sense again. She was watching him, listening to him. He had to respond to her, to make up for the past, to pay a belated tribute to all that their history represented after this long period of separation. He was pleased to see that his conscience was touched, that it had not been completely silenced.

At night he was hungry and cold. The wind moaned outside his cell. He couldn't sleep, so he sat beneath the light catching lice, listening to the crunch of their bodies as he burst them between his nails. Every time he thought of her he killed a louse. He wiped their blood on the walls and used it to draw Round Square, the people, the slogans, the feces, the vehicles, the police in their helmets . . . He looked for his place there but couldn't find it, and didn't know where he should draw himself. He faced the wall, deep in thought, until daybreak. He could only feel that night had turned to day. The room was always bathed in the same dim light. Just as he was thinking this, the light went off. The stars on the ceiling flickered out.

A bell burst into the depths of his mind with a sharp ring, shattering his sleep. It sounded for two full minutes, during which he felt the floorboards tremble and shake. Thousands of feet ran through his mind, along with the roar of waves, neighing horses, and the bursting permafrost. An amputee's shrill scream of misery. Suddenly the door opened. A light pierced the darkness and a chill wind entered in. He saw Qizi in the doorway—no, it was Suitang. She looked like she had just been to the beauty parlor. Her skin was pink and her long hair flowing. She said she had spent her days very well and that they had taken her to visit the nursing home. It was paradise. She loved it. She wanted to stay there. He was in a semiconscious state from hunger and sleep deprivation, but when he saw her he immediately grew clear-minded. He didn't bother at all about what she said; he just felt embarrassment at the filthy state of his own body. Trying to hide deep in his blanket he yelled, "Go away! Don't come in." He kept hollering until he couldn't hear any movement. He stuck his head out from under the quilt. Suitang stood above him, her hand outstretched.

"You should eat," she said softly, eyes full of sympathy and affection, "and then write some poetry, the Swan Song, or a love poem, or many, many poems, just like you used to do. You think you are sticking to your values, but it's all meaningless, it's all a cloud."

He ducked away from her pale hand and her red lips. Her eyes, too, were red, as if bloodshot.

"Suitang, I just want you to be happy. Whatever you choose to do is fine. That is your business," he said weakly. He was like someone about to die, filled to the brim with tolerance and peace. "I was in Beiping. I was in the crowd, yet I felt more lonely than I do in this room. I am with them every day now, we talk about women, we talk about poetry, we curse whomever we want to curse. I see Qizi every day, hear her speeches, chat with her about her dreams. If Swan Valley wants to destroy my flesh in the name of poetry, then that's just fulfilling my wish. Sometimes tainted things are good, though they make the heart uncomfortable—serious things, like ideals and beliefs, they make you ill at ease forever. Stifling the poetic impulse, it has been more painful than I imagined, like . . . don't think I'm vulgar, but it's like facing the woman you love and trying to control an erection, refusing to enter her body . . . I've written hundreds of poems in my mind . . . I don't want to publish them. I am ashamed. Poetry has become a whore's cry. Its dignity is in ruins. If the language of poets cannot furnish banners for the next generation . . . we haven't been taught yet how to use our language in the service of freedom . . . "

His logic had grown muddled and incoherent.

He cried softly, reaching out into the void, his head hanging down feebly. "I will stay with you to the end."

He spoke the last sentence as if from a dream, his voice so low even he could barely hear it, the rest of his words turning to wind between his teeth and lips.

"Who will write your names in the history books, martyrs? Those who write history aren't your people . . . You don't count as good citizens . . . Everything will be lost."

When Mengliu rose from his quilt, he found that the room had made a miraculous recovery. The crystal chandelier was lit, the floor was carpeted, the window opened onto the sea again, and the stars in the ceiling sparkled. A pleasant fragrance had returned to the room, the toilet had been cleaned, the books restored to the shelves. For a moment he was startled, thinking he had woken in a wedding chamber. He looked down and saw he was wearing a new robe, its belt tied with a slip knot. His red underwear was new, and just the right size. He couldn't help fumbling his hands over his face, finding it clean-shaven and his hair slightly damp, as if it had not yet dried after a recent shower. He panicked, wondering who had washed him clean. Who had undressed him without his permission? What had they done?

There were bottles on the nightstand, showing that he had been on a drip. The room temperature was just right. He wasn't hungry and his throat hurt, so he knew they had pumped food into his stomach. He angrily rang the bell. Suitang appeared in the doorway, her long hair flowing, with a cold look on her face. It extinguished his excitement. There was an invisible wall between them. A rush of emotion swirled in his heart and inflamed his face.

"You look good. Seems you've recovered well." She spoke casually, showing no signs that she had been under house arrest. Her eyes were like a rabbit's, as if blood might drop from them at any moment. "You're taking this too seriously. It's a poem for the occasion, easy enough to write. Do you really think it's worth your life? . . . We're down to the last three days. They will try physical torture. I suggest you eat and drink now. They will whip you, flog you. I hope you can survive the pain."

What did she say? Whip? Flog? They wanted to use torture on a surgeon, a common citizen? His expression was full of doubt. He didn't believe the spiritual leader of Swan Valley would be stupid enough to threaten torture. Brutal tactics should be used on important people, but he was just a powerless foreigner. He wondered whether it was really Suitang who had come. He couldn't tell what was illusion and what was real. "I hope you didn't betray yourself."

Suitang didn't answer but continued with her own train of conversation. "You think this pettiness can make you noble and great, cleansing you of your past cowardice and indifference . . . It's just wishful thinking. If you write your Swan Song poem, you can preserve yourself and leave Swan Valley. At least your poetry will save your life."

He thought Suitang must have been put under a magic spell to make her say those words. Once her sense of justice and art and order had disappeared, she grew dim, and her beauty turned tacky. She had already returned to the vanity of material things. The people of her generation simply didn't have ideals, and she was puzzled by his assertiveness and sense of mystery. Because she had never loved through troubled times, she would feel the deep love of an Akhmatova or a Pasternak to be ridiculous. He said goodbye to her, then calmly acknowledged that he was willing to die. He would leave no trace, nor would he need anyone to mourn for him.

26

At ten the next morning, the simian Sama visited. His appearance was startling. His hair was tied up with a black headband and his face painted with Chinese opera makeup. The hook-shaped eyebrows made him look quite handsome. He wore a blood-colored robe with a broad belt around the waist, and sleeves of the kind worn by actors in a martial role. His feet, clad in high boots, moved unsteadily. Mengliu had seen Chinese opera and thought his outfit an insult to it.

Sama pulled his expression into a smile and winked conspiratorially. Then he told Mengliu he first needed to complete a ritual, which was to recite poetry for his arms to hear, so that when they were filled with emotion they would not be too harsh. These words seemed as crazy to Mengliu as Sama's appearance, so he interrupted the recitation and asked Sama what was going on. Sama replied, "Today is the day you'll be whipped. For a professional thug, this would be nothing special, but for a poetry-lover like myself, it is a rare honor." He started reading again, and it was actually a verse from "For Whom the Bell Tolls." He finished with a flourish, then from behind his waistband he drew out a bamboo cane and flexed it until it formed a circle. As he released it, the cane made a whooshing sound and created a tremor in the room.

Mengliu was gripped with horror. He asked weakly, "Where will you strike?"

"The whole body."

"How many strokes?"

Sama, casting a charming glance his way, replied, "It depends on your endurance."

As he saw Mengliu's face slowly lengthening, like one who is making a vow to die without surrendering, Sama expressed the admiration he felt deep in his heart. He thought Mengliu possessed the appropriate attitude for a poet under the threat of flogging. He believed in a poet's moral courage, so he had decided to help the poor fellow. As if by magic, he pulled out a bottle of red pigment and whispered, "You've got to cooperate. Each time I whip you, you should scream, and you'll need to show agony on your face, too, if you're going to fool them." A look vaguely like love appeared on his face, and he used his shoulder to give Mengliu an intimate push as he quietly hid the paint.

"Now we go on stage."

"On stage?"

"Yes. Where I will whip you."

Woodenly, Mengliu followed Sama out of the room. The frozen lake was smooth as a mirror, with the light of the sun reflecting off it in a surreal glare. His dazzled eyes could barely adapt to the landscape around him. He hung his head as he walked. The cracks between the stones underfoot made him dizzy. Lashing? At first he thought this was a good word, that they wanted to encourage him. When he saw the bamboo cane, he understood it to be a whipping, like they might do to animals. But that wasn't anything very different. Once you've landed in the hands of people who'll use any means to control you, it doesn't really matter what they call it. "Yes, the place where you will be beaten." He thought the effeminate tone sounded like it was describing a place where peach blossoms were in bloom, a place full of beauty and longing. But that was true enough, too, since bruises would soon blossom across his back. If the cane was equipped with metal hooks, the blossoms would mature into rotted fruit. Perhaps his innards would gush out, flowing from his body. When this came to mind, he became unusually calm. He did not intend to accept Sama's kindness and to emit shrill screams to fake his pain. That sort of idea insulted a dignified man greatly. He hoped he would lose consciousness in a moving and tragic way with the first stroke, leaving his body to its fate. He really wished Qizi could see the scene, a poet enduring a beating without uttering the slightest groan.

They crossed a stone bridge. A lake. A forest. During the days of confinement Mengliu had grown accustomed to talking to himself, and now he was chattering all along the way.

"A lost decade. My fiancée. She's alive. I know she's been alive all this time . . . She couldn't come back, couldn't get in touch with me, couldn't find me. She knows I'm waiting for her. You don't think so?

Why would you say that? Do you know what love is? Everyone plays around a bit, but other than that? When disaster strikes . . . What Jia Wan said was right. He told me not to go out that night, that something big was going down . . . If I'd gone to warn her instead of collapsing into a deep sleep at home . . . The reason I didn't go with them to the court was not because of cowardice . . . it's because I really didn't know, and I really didn't believe that kind of thing would happen . . . no one believed it. They were innocent as doves . . . Now they're lost to the sky . . . "

He stopped Sama for a moment, wanting him to talk about the time he had found the notebook, who the dead person was, why he had died, and where he had lived, but Sama didn't know. Curious why a small book could be of such interest to his idol, Sama said, "We often find dead foreigners in the forest."

They soon reached their destination. The theater was completely empty.

The curtain opened. The backdrop on the stage was of a dark cell, its wall painted with angry script. A spotlight fell on it, illuminating a ladder, over which was draped a rope, the props for a flogging. The spotlight swept to stage left. There was an old narrow table, on which were a pen and paper, and a vase of unopened rosebuds.

Backstage, Mengliu was changed into a white frog suit, then moved toward the ladder, under the dim, sleepy dust swirling in the lighted air around him. He turned his back to the empty seats in the theater. There was a hole in his clothing, exposing his bare back, buttocks, and hips. He was like a wooden puppet going through an out-of-body experience. Under Sama's guidance he faced the ladder, arms straight and legs splayed, and allowed himself to be tied to the rungs. Sama patted his buttocks several times, then pinched, testing their elasticity and firmness to determine how much force to use as he swung his cane. Undoubtedly flogging was an art. The whip in hand and the interior of the mind had to work in unison to generate the right amount of pain without causing death. Sama understood what it took to create just such a masterpiece.

As he checked the bonds on his idol's hands, Sama asked softly, "Does it hurt? Is it too tight?"

Mengliu moved slightly, and Sama was almost in tears, thrilled at being in such close contact with his idol. Finally, he leaned into Mengliu's ear and said, "You look even more attractive than the crucified Christ. Remember to cooperate. You have to scream, okay?"

Everything was ready. Sama elegantly lashed the ground with his cane, and a resounding *thwack* stirred up the dust.

A band sounded from the back of the stage, an ensemble of erhu, *yueqin,* and a three-stringed lute.

After a moment the plaintive music stopped. Sama directed all his strength to his belly and squeezed out some lines from a play in a strange tone:

"My most loved and respected poet, before you endure the scourge of my rod would you like to change your mind?" The last word was uttered in a heavy tone, shrill and trembling. At this moment, the erhu grew articulate in its accusing tones. Sama ran his hand along the cane, applying red pigment to it. "Now I ask you in the name of the spiritual leader of Swan Valley, regarding your Swan Song—will you or will you not write it?" He pointed his finger with an actress's hand gesture, a classic pose made on stage to show delicacy and grace.

Mengliu's chin rested on the rung of the ladder. He was unable to move, and his eyes stared straight ahead. "I swear by my fiancée, you can give up . . . you're all crazy!" He matched Sama's tone.

Turning to face the audience, Sama laughed. Not without irony, he announced, "He says that for the sake of a woman he will . . . " He turned back again. "Oh? So this woman, what sort of extraordinary person is she?"

"She . . . she stared at the bleeding world without flinching, a thousand times greater than your spiritual leader!"

The ladder started to rotate, turning the front of Mengliu's body toward the audience. The light fell on him. His face was pale and sweating.

Slightly startled, Sama turned around and pulled out a thin booklet, flipping to his next lines. "You . . . you can't elevate your fiancée so as purposely to devalue our spiritual leader. This does not suit the spirit of debate, don't you understand?"

"Well, let your spiritual leader face me. Count it as my dying wish. I want to look on his ugly face so I can remember it and find him in hell."

"What do you want to find him for?" Suddenly, a small gong sounded twice. Sama turned to another page. "He selflessly serves the people, owing no one anything . . . "

"He deprived me of my freedom. He's deprived many people of their freedom, their rights, even their lives."

Sama put the booklet away and murmured, "My idol, pay attention to your lines. You're engaging in slander."

"What? I . . . I was tied to this ladder by you. What I am saying is true. I am the truth. You . . . don't even distinguish between right and wrong. You've reversed black and white, distorted the facts, smitten the innocent, made a lie of justice!" His words were as fierce as firecrackers. He paused, and the gong clattered three more times. "As a poet, I hate to use clichés. I hate it when language fails to express meaning, I fucking . . . "

"Wait a minute! You said . . . you are a poet?" Sama turned and faced the theater, breaking into a laugh. "Ha! Ha ha ha ha ha! . . . Did you hear that? He claims he is a poet!"

The idol's pale face had turned crimson. Now he was tongue-tied.

All six pieces of the ensemble sounded at once, hissing in disapproval.

Suddenly they broke off.

The idol seemed to awaken from a dream. "Yes . . . I am a poet . . . But now, as a poet, I solemnly tell you that I will never write poetry for Swan Valley!"

After he said this, the three-piece percussion group, the single drum, the large gong, and the small gong, struck up a manic military tone, a reckless, merciless racket.

Sama's whip cracked, and the first signs of redness appeared on Mengliu's white haunches. The accompanying music immediately turned joyous, and Sama began to appreciate his own value. Obviously a strict man, he completed each stroke with the same graceful posture. But his damned idol would not cooperate and remained mute. So Sama accompanied each stroke with a howl of his own. The whole scene had a tragic feel, which soon left him and his idol both covered in blood.

After ten minutes, Sama fell to the ground with a plop and declared the end of the flogging.

The soothing strains of the erhu were raised like a supplicant's hands toward the sky.

"When a poet no longer writes poetry, he acquires dignity, perhaps a far greater dignity than he ever had when he wrote." Sama slowly raised his head and stood up. Tossing the cane from his hand, he spread out his arms toward the auditorium. "Lying down or standing up—who can say which is more humble, and which more noble? Perhaps it requires more courage to stop writing, than to write."

The crimson curtain slowly closed on the stage.

The lights were extinguished.

27

In the past, during the dark nights of his soul, every day felt like three in the morning for Mengliu. Now there were no dark nights; the light in his cell blazed all the time, making red roses dance before his eyes. *Who was smoking and drinking in the room while I was asleep? What unpleasant smells, the whole place littered with cigarette butts, and could I still have slept like the dead?* Mengliu's throat was dry. On the nightstand were three cups, one with water, one with green tea, and one with rice wine. He drank them all and was still thirsty. The stars on the ceiling no longer sparkled. At the window the sea seemed to be moving, and there was a vague sound of waves. The door to the cell was unlatched, and the hint of a chill wind slipped in through the crack there. It wasn't cold, but it cleared his head. The unlatched door seemed to imply an opportunity for escape. He smiled contemptuously. How could he escape his own mind? He waited quietly for someone to come and take him to his suffering. He took this as a battle, a standoff; he would never flee.

A ray of sunshine squeezed in through the crack at the door, creating a bar on the ground that fell all the way to his feet. Extremely weak, he felt an unusual sense of fulfillment. His heart was like a radiator, throwing out heat. He opened the autograph book and stroked Qizi's signature, wondering whether she was dead. But he was numb inside and the concept of life and death no longer had meaning for him. He hid the book, then went to clean himself up. He washed his face and shaved. He could not see the person in the mirror clearly, and had no notion of his appearance. He did everything in very low spirits, stroking his face with his long fingers. When he came out, Suitang was in the room. There was a platter of sleek, sliced rabbit on the table, accompanied by a variety of spices.

"What's this? I'm a VIP again?" The tangy smell made his mouth water.

Suitang smiled. "This could be your last meal on Earth."

"If it's the first, that's good, and if it's the last, that's fine too. What's the point?" He ate greedily. "Tell me. There's no need to beat around the bush."

"Don't be so uncongenial. We are the only two of our kind in Swan Valley." Suitang's resentment had a hint of coquetry. "Sama has been sent to the mill for reeducation because of his dereliction of duty . . . Who knows, maybe it's all a sham. It's hard to believe your fan club could have penetrated to such a remote location."

"*So?*" he interrupted.

"You're angry? What are you angry with me for? I didn't betray my friend for glory . . . "

"This . . . is good. It tastes like Darae's work. Want to try it?"

Ignoring him, she walked straight to the window and pushed it open. The sudden gust that blew in struck him fiercely. Raising his head, he saw the golden shine of the sea outside and was astonished, as if he had seen a miracle. The genuine sea, boundless, waves crashing in the bay, seagulls soaring, and the sea breeze constantly blowing his way. His hand touched the ledge and on the wall a crack showed through. It was a sliding door. He opened it and found a balcony outside. It was connected to a long passage like a bridge standing above the sea. He could not help but grasp Suitang's hand, and she followed him obediently out the door. They reached the end of the bridge and turned to look back at the island far behind them. The sea and sky were both boundless; they couldn't believe they were on Earth.

"I've felt I was in a fog these past few days. Suitang, is this a dream?" A man may suffer from waking nightmares, especially when he has gone without sleep for nights. Standing in the dazzling sun, gazing at the vast world, his feelings might be even more overwhelming. Mengliu was on the bridge with the water rippling beneath him and a tempest stirring in his mind. He wanted to write a poem. The words were already on the tip of his tongue. No, on his lips, ready to fly out of his mouth at any moment, like a bird leaving its nest. No. It could not be. He looked into the distance and tried hard to swallow the verse. Apparently choking on it, his face reddened. Before long, he began to feel dizzy, nauseous, and bloated. He leaned his head over the sea and vomited. Pieces of rabbit that had turned to debris rained down on the water, then sank quietly.

Suitang said, "The sea breeze is not good for you."

"I must have been poisoned. If they want to kill me, it would not be difficult. Why bother poisoning me in secret?" he shouted as he turned back.

Suitang rushed after him, saying, "Are you crazy? I ate the other half of the rabbit. There's nothing wrong with me. Your empty stomach rejected the oily food. You should eat porridge first."

"Eat porridge? I would rather drink the west wind! Look at me. I could float away now."

He really did look like a sage. Stumbling like a kite that could not get liftoff, he almost fell into the sea several times more.

They returned by the same route. Strangely, the place they had come from was gone, and the entire topography seemed to have changed too. They had somehow ended up in a secluded courtyard halfway up the mountain. The wide doorway to the courtyard looked like the entrance to a square. There was a nude sculpture by the door and an abandoned armored vehicle topped with a long gun pointed off in the distance. There was nothing in the courtyard, only a large column shooting up to the sky in the center and below it, an area the size of a basketball court. Mengliu thought of the white chimney he and Juli had seen. He clearly recalled Juli's longing look. This should be it.

He walked around the base, but there was no entrance. He looked up but he could not see the top. He instinctively knew this wasn't a chimney. Perhaps it was a military watchtower. Its top would afford a panoramic view of Swan Valley, as well as the distant sea. Suitang agreed. As he checked the bricks, he asked where she had been in recent days and how she had been treated. Suitang prevaricated, saying, "I just can't describe the place. Don't think I'm making things up. It was like I was sleepwalking. I was in a different place every day. I had plenty to eat and drink, and I listened to a lot of lectures. They said you were writing a ballad."

"You really don't know me. I'm not like you, easily manipulated . . . even to the point of becoming their lobbyist."

"You try manipulating me. You're just pretending to be romantic," Suitang said.

"I couldn't bear to manipulate you. If I had wanted to I would've done so earlier." He knocked on a brick and listened to the sound.

"Well, why was I the fish that escaped the net? That Su Juli . . . "

He gestured for her to be quiet, as if he had made a major discovery. In truth, he only wanted to stop her line of questioning.

"Help me think. What would this building be used for? How can we get in?"

"Maybe it's a heating unit. It must be used to get rid of exhaust."

"Yeah, that's imaginative. Do you think we can get in?"

"I think . . . maybe the wall is a decoy. Somewhere there's a hidden switch or button."

"That's so old-fashioned. You might as well say, *Open sesame!* Or *pineapple!* Or whatever . . . "

As if this spell had had its effect, a door like that on an airplane suddenly slid open. He tripped on it and practically fell inside.

It was another hall of images, full of electronic screens flickering in silence.

On one screen, beasts beneath a canopy of trees. In a white robe, Esteban lies on a boulder covered with a white sheet. The mortician is shaving his head and beard. Four people, using only their hands, raise the sheet as if they are an honor guard handling the national flag. They solemnly place Esteban in the ice coffin, then cover it with a layer of white chrysanthemums.

The morning sun blazes on the ice. The vast sky is filled with puffy, unremarkable clouds.

A low-flying bird suddenly drops to the ground.

The band and the dozens of mourners are all in white robes, almost invisible in the snowy funereal world.

Shanlai and Darae are among them, wearing clumsy snow boots and sombre expressions. Their difficult journey through the deep snow creates an even deeper sense of ritual. The group of mourners is halfway up the hillside when the mountain bursts open. Blocks of snow tumble away, followed immediately by an influx of loose snow rolling down the hill. The snow swells and in an instant engulfs the group of dolllike mourners.

On a second screen, the hospital is empty. On the gate is an announcement saying that the plague had been brought by vultures. All birds and reptiles have been infected, and humans will inevitably be infected as well. The announcement makes no mention of the vultures' food source at the waste disposal site. Abandoned infants. The road with mobs of people fleeing the disaster, continually stumbling, no one bothering. Some are hastily buried or thrown haphazardly aside . . . They gather at the cliff edge because the cable car is the only way to the outside world. On the first trip, four squeeze into the trolley, but as it bumps and glides along, the rope suddenly snaps, and the cable car hurtles like a stone into the abyss.

On a third screen, a circle of people in white coats and learned faces stare at an aquarium. It is an academic discussion. There are observations and recordings . . . In the aquarium, a bloodied baby with its umbilical cord still attached is towed through a pool of alcohol, its hands and feet flailing like a dying fish . . . its mouth opens rapidly, then it no longer moves.

All of the screens told stories. Some were videos, some live feeds. Then all the smaller screens were turned off, leaving only a huge black-and-white screen still broadcasting. Its subject was familiar to Mengliu. It was the sit-in at Round Square . . . The crowd was in chaos. A large number of uniformed men entered the square . . . It was just like Shunyu's father described, a blood-filled night with half the sky scorched red . . .

A patch of bright light shot down from the top of the column through the darkness, but because it was so far away, it became dim by the time it reached the ground. Even so, everything inside the room could be seen clearly. There was an area like a disc jockey's podium, and in the middle of one of the walls hung a disorderly array of banners. They were flanked on both sides by several small machines. In the center was a leopard-skin chair, its back facing outward. Someone sat there, head only half exposed.

"I'm impressed. I didn't expect you to get here so quickly . . . Well, let's get to the end of the game." The voice from the leopard-skin chair was that of the spiritual leader Ah Lian Qiu, but still transmitted through a machine.

In such close proximity at last, Mengliu was very curious about Ah Lian Qiu's appearance, but he controlled his curiosity. "Ah Lian Qiu, spiritual leader, I do not know anything, nor do I want to know anything . . . I have no questions to ask you. I only request that you take care of the people trapped in Swan Valley, and tell us the way home." But as soon as he said "us," he realized that Suitang had not come in with him. She had stayed outside the door.

"The cable broke. There's nothing I can do about that. Surely you have discovered that they don't need me. Because they are self-aware and self-disciplined, they will govern one another . . . a good ruler's presence is not felt . . . a spiritual leader need only transmit a beneficial spirit, and there will be nothing to worry about . . . As for you, rest assured that you have earned your way back home. The road is open to both of you."

"Nothing to worry about?" Mengliu could not help but ask. "Don't you know the lives of all the people living here have been placed on the altar constructed by you, their spiritual leader?"

"When a person understands what he really wants, his nature as a human can be fully realized. Take Esteban, for example. He found his own worth, and in his death the noble dignity of the individual was restored to him." Ah Lian Qiu continued in a leisurely fashion. "A person should have a proper understanding of himself."

"I only have one more thing to say, spiritual leader." Mengliu controlled his voice and the rhythm of his speech. "Your spirit is nothing more than a lure. It just enables a system of annihilation. Some day . . . "

"If that's how you see it, that's your business." The leopard-skin chair began to turn around slowly, then stopped at one hundred eighty degrees. The spiritual leader Ah Lian Qiu sat in a wheelchair, head bowed, long hair covering his face. "So many years. Now you are finally free from the burden of history!" The leader ripped off the lapel microphone and raised her head, revealing the whole of her pale face.

All the horrifying things Mengliu had experienced in his life had not prepared him for this shock. He was stunned, and a doubt-filled scream escaped from his mouth:

"Qizi?"

"No. I am the spiritual leader of Swan Valley. I am Ah Lian Qiu!"

Hearing her real unaltered voice filled Mengliu with ecstasy. It was Qizi! He ran to her, but the podium on which she sat was encircled by a force field, and he was thrown back. It burned a hole in his clothes and nearly scorched another in his flesh.

She turned off the force field and rolled her battery-powered wheelchair down from the podium, coming slowly to a halt in front of him.

Ah, Qizi! She was as young and beautiful as the first time he saw her. He wanted to embrace her, to say, *I've never stopped looking for you. I knew you had to be alive.* But he stood there, rooted, his warm feelings curbed by something unseen. He faced Ah Lian Qiu. She looked at him with rational, calm, indifferent eyes.

"The Qizi of the past, like these two legs, was crushed by a tank." Ah Lian Qiu removed her two legs from her thighs. Her upper half sat in the chair on two stumps, like a bust.

Mengliu seemed to be welded to the ground. Feeling had left his own legs so that he remained stuck there, motionless.

"At the same time as I was crushed, so were truth and idealism . . . and beauty and goodness." She toyed with the prostheses. "Afterward, the people lived like fish returning to water, right? There was numbness, a philosophy of survival, but that doesn't mean their concept of the nation had changed."

"Qizi . . . " He wanted to wake her up, but he was actually the one who was confused.

"When he tried to save me, Hei Chun was badly burned . . . Shunyu's father hid us in a friend's hospital and, on the third day, secretly drove us to a place that was far away but safe. For a whole year we were constantly on the move, escaping from one place to another."

Mengliu was stunned. "I had no idea. I was looking for you . . . Hei Chun . . . where is he?"

"He was seriously injured. One eye was burned out. His fingers were damaged. He was unrecognizable . . . After we came to Swan Valley, he spent half a year writing *The Principles of Genetics*." Leisurely, she turned her wheelchair in a circle. "He said it was better than More's *Utopia*. The original manuscript is here."

"He wrote that book . . . I knew it was his writing style! But . . . does that mean that all along Swan Valley has been a product of your ideas?" Mengliu stammered. "Wh . . . where is Hei Chun? I want to talk to him."

"I'm afraid that will be a little difficult." She pointed to a table on the podium. "He is in the urn over there. For him, after finishing *The Principles of Genetics*, a life of the flesh was superfluous. It was his own choice."

"He . . . you . . . you two . . . " Mengliu feared his head would explode.

"How is Shunyu's father now? Does he still manage the Green Flower?" She chatted as she operated on her prostheses, calmly and skillfully.

"The tavern was seized. He was sent to prison . . . "

"Prison, huh? What crime did he commit?" She stopped the action of her hands. Her speech filled with emotion.

"There was a bunch of charges. Harboring known criminals, escorting insurgents, participating in subversion . . . He died during the second year of his imprisonment. I don't know how he died. No one could tell me . . . "

One of the artificial legs rattled and dropped to the ground.

She clicked a remote control and the electronic screens all flashed on again, creating a mess of fluorescence that flickered across her confused face, but the sadness in her eyes remained cold and bright.

"He is your biological father."

"Yes. When I found out, it was too late." He picked up the prosthesis and handed it back to her. "I didn't get a last chance to see him. And there were no ashes left . . . " His voice grew lower, finally sinking all the way to the ground.

She turned and reattached the artificial leg.

"Did you bring your xun?" she asked.

"No."

She looked at him, then moved the wheelchair beside him and reached out and took the xun from his pocket.

"Play a tune," she ordered, but it also sounded like a plea.

From the flawless accuracy of her action he knew she remembered their past, and it warmed his heart. It surged up in him. He could not refuse her order, or request. And right at this moment his confused heart also needed a release valve.

He kneaded the xun with both hands, then, without thinking, played "The Pain of Separation."

The cylindrical hall was like a giant speaker. The mysterious deep tune, fluctuating between regret and mourning, seemed to spread out and fill the universe. In every corner of the world, creatures listened to the music. They moaned, they howled, they lamented, they cried, and then they were silent.

Ah Lian Qiu slowly stood up from her chair. She struck the keys on her remote like a skilled typist, commanding the movement of her legs, the bending of her knees, her walk, and then her standing still, all in fluid motions. It was hard to tell they were prosthetics, but the mechanical rhythm of her legs could not be completely disguised, so that in the end she resembled a lifelike robot.

"There are two things that made your father proud," she said, as if preparing to see a visitor off. "One was your poetry, the other was the feeling in your playing of the *xun*. He planned to let the backlash from the demonstrations blow over, then sit down and have a good drink with you."

"Maybe he would be ashamed that I didn't stay by your side and protect you."

"No. The one you needed to protect was Shunyu, your half-sister. I had the whole square, the whole of Beiping—the whole crowd of people waiting for the truth—to protect me." Her voice grew rich with pride.

"Qizi?" He wanted desperately to do something to dissolve the distance between them, and thought that recalling the memory of the earliest stages of their acquaintance might be the best way. "I remember the interrogation room. You said you were developing a mysterious machine . . . At the time I laughed to myself, thinking it was impossible." He paused, suddenly alarmed. He looked at the lake and saw what looked like a tornado in the sky above it. "But you did it."

Ah Lian Qiu's nostrils flared as she sneered, "I am the spiritual leader of Swan Valley, Ah Lian Qiu."

"Qizi?"

"I am the spiritual leader of Swan Valley, Ah Lian Qiu."

"You've become a stranger . . . "

"Power, beauty, physical torture—you've withstood them all. You refused to write poetry. You have proved yourself a poet. You've got nothing to be ashamed of."

"I want to take you away. You can't stay here. Death is spreading through Swan Valley. It's over . . . "

"Leave? Where would I go? Back to your motherland? Ha!" Her wild laughter stopped suddenly. "Go back? Tell her, only when she chooses the most beautiful spring, when the red rose blooms, when she walks the truest path with the most sincere attitude, and admits her wrongs to me! Admits it to everyone! Admits it to the whole world!"

She left him angrily, walking to the podium with a mechanical but swift pace. She picked up a red cloth from the table and expertly wrapped it around her head. She took up the remote control in her hand, then as she walked, she recited the old poem "Hunger Strike," as if an audience of countless people were listening. "On sunny days, we are on a hunger strike . . . "

When her recitation reached its climax, she took a stack of paper from the drawer and tossed it skyward, as if scattering pamphlets. Her tone suddenly rose.

" . . . Democracy is life's highest form of existence. Freedom is an eternal, inherent right. Everyone has the right to know the truth . . . "

The leaves of paper fell. Mengliu picked one up. It was a page from the manuscript of Hei Chun's *Principles of Genetics*. It was exactly the section he was familiar with.

"To reconstruct the Roman Republic or the early emperor-governed Rome is possible. To achieve this goal, we must have people of courage and genius to constitute the ruling class . . . We do not need the common public to participate in politics . . . the contest between nations is only a contest between the quality of their people. It is a battle of knowledge. Therefore, to have a rich and powerful population one must begin with its genes . . . We will create a new society not because we are better than others, but because we are simple people with simple human needs—for air and light, health and honor, and for freedom and the highest spiritual pursuits. Our impartial behavior is innate . . . The excellent and new nation of Swan Valley, in a few years' time, we will demand the world's attention."

Qizi's voice rolled on, "Farewell, parents! Please forgive me. Your child cannot serve two masters. Farewell, citizens! Please allow us to serve you in this unusual manner . . . "

As quickly as he could, Mengliu scrambled to collect the scattered manuscript. He had caught a glimpse of the value and weight of the work. It was Hei Chun's vision. He had a responsibility to compile and publish it. And he had a great desire to read it.

Qizi finished her recitation with the shouting of a few slogans. Then, as if she had suddenly discovered Mengliu was there, she shouted at him, "You! How did you get here? Quickly, go back! Go back and wait for me!" She opened the door of the hall with her remote control.

Startled for a moment, he bent over and picked up more pages. He thought, I've agitated her with my appearance, and that's caused her to escape into the past, and now she is unable to return to the present.

"I'm not alone. I've got a lot of people here with me. Everyone is with me . . . You? You still haven't gone?"

Seeing that he did not move, she pulled out a gun. "Get out of here now!"

His heart pumped violently. "Qizi . . . calm down," he said.

She fired a shot, shattering the big electronic screen.

Like the barrel of the gun, her gaze was now pointed right at him.

He saw that she was trapped inside her fantasy.

He walked slowly out through the doorway.

In the icy air Mengliu realized that he had perspired a great deal in the room, though he was not sure whether it was because he was hot or because of fear. He was cold now, and his wet clothes clung to his skin. His heart tightened. He looked at the mess of papers clenched in his hand. For a moment he couldn't remember that this was Hei Chun's manuscript.

He hastily straightened the papers, rolled them up, and concealed them in his clothing. He found Suitang near the column. He suddenly heard a series of muffled explosions inside it, and felt the rumble under his feet. Looking up, he saw smoke billowing from the top, growing thicker by the moment.

In a confusion of anxiety he shouted out Qizi's name as he searched for the door. He banged on the wall as he ran around the column.

The flow of smoke from the chimney grew stronger. The wall was hot to the touch.

What was the password . . . *Open sesame* . . . *pineapples* . . . He shouted a confused flow of incantations, his feet and hands running rapidly around and across the wall. The bricks remained steadfast and unmoved.

Suitang seemed to come from nowhere; she grabbed Mengliu's hand and they bolted.

They had only run about ten paces when they heard a noise behind them so loud it threw their bodies to the ground. A wave of heat swept over their heads. Their hair felt like it had been singed. Sediment rained down on them until they were both buried in debris.

Mengliu slowly pulled himself up and looked back. The cylindrical building had collapsed and was burning in a chaos of smoke and fire.

A page of manuscript drifted down from the sky. Catching it, Mengliu read:

> *white doves have taken our eyes away*
> *and people are left with hungry tongues*
> *in a domain buried in silence*
> *where thornlike arms wave*
> *nothing in the world that exists*
> *is higher than you*
>
> *in this land, on this soil*
> *you are equal to the storm*
> *the sun itself may be imprisoned*
> *and the death bell will toll*
> *resistance will alter your face*

lightning will pierce the sealed horizon
silence is despicable
oh children! exalt your spirits
a mother has put on her dark shroud
and nobly welcomes a dawn
as bright as death

EPILOGUE

A banquet had been arranged on a cruise boat in Beiping. It had just gotten dark, and the boat was moored on the lake beside the moon. The lake's glittering surface extended to the barely distinguishable shore in the distance. The lights of houses could vaguely be seen. The cabin of the boat was like a small auditorium decked out for a celebrity performance seasoned with literature and art. Jazz and the smell of fruit juice mingled with the taste of champagne. The gathering swelled, evening gowns swished, voices bubbled, the sound of intimate conversation produced the inevitably dull buzz of a party.

Mengliu leaned against a window, looking apathetic, depressed, and weary. It seemed as if he had not quite awakened from sleep. His biological clock had been a mess. He had only just established his own pattern of day and night, operating according to his own laws. Over the years a quiet voice like a Jedi's constant meditations had run in the back of his mind, reciting Hei Chun's poetry and causing his mind to be in a constant state of tension.

"Lightning will pierce the sealed horizon . . . silence is despicable . . . "

He was wearing an archaic navy blue robe with flat black shoes. After returning from his years of travels, he had adopted this eccentric dress, and his speech had taken on a more discrete and elegant character, as he talked of Plato or Epicurus's garden city, playing the part of the poet on all occasions. Everyone has the right to self-correction. There is no shame in it. Theodor Adorno said that after Auschwitz poetry was impossible, but he later changed his views. If such a great philosopher could deny his earlier position, then Mengliu

SHENG KEYI

felt he had strong support. He continued to write poetry now, but for some reason he couldn't publish it. For a true poet, publication is not always the motive. He edited a national poetry journal, which collected a variety of voices, and he printed poetry in books to be read only by those who needed them. He knew what he was doing. He wasn't interested in happiness, or perhaps he thought this was happiness. His passion for women had not subsided, but he had renounced the world of frivolity and promiscuity, and now showed a heartfelt appreciation and respect for them instead.

It was an eclectic gathering of beauties clad in revealing evening dresses, elbows tucked to their sides to display their white necks and cleavage to the best advantage. The Mengliu from long ago would have already succeeded in his conquest and would be whispering to a girl in some private corner. But now he just stared over his wineglass, squeezed into a space in his own mind in a corner by the window, acting cool while appreciating the subtleties of his own heart.

He still remembered drinking the fisherwoman's leicha, sailing to the middle of the lake, suddenly being shaken by waves, then looking up over his arm where his sleeping head had lain at the fierce tornado and the black hole . . . After losing consciousness, he had found himself in a place called Swan Valley . . . He was sure he had lived there for a long time. It was a thrilling experience, full of wonderfully romantic times. He had finally found Qizi, and this time she had really gone. He missed the place, and Juli, and Yuyue . . .

Presently, the waiter came over and asked if he needed more wine. He nodded and handed over his glass.

Still, what was hard to understand was how he had woken to find himself again in the sailboat. The setting sun seemed to prove that he had just been in a deep sleep. The night was coming on. When he rowed the boat back to the village, the sky was dark and the fisherwoman and her husband were waiting for him by the lake with a lantern. They said they thought a monster from the lake had caught him and carried him away. He stayed the night, and while they ate, the couple told him of the monster's doings, how it hunted people during storms and carried them off . . .

Outside the window, the lake shimmered. Not far off, a small boat was moored. A red lantern hung from the front of its canopy. There were people in the boat chatting and playing the xun in soft tones.

At eight, Mengliu began to feel it was the middle of the night. The party had just begun. He knew nothing about the occasion, having been dragged along by his wife. Marrying Suitang had been the natural thing to do. He didn't need to think much about why he should marry her. He was in a sleepwalker's trance and felt that everything was an illusion. Known and unknown thinkers and professors, experts and scholars, black-, silver-, blonde-, or white-haired, they were all a blur before him. As they shimmered, he saw their mouths move in conversation, but he couldn't quite hear what they said.

This was the first time he'd met Qizi's legendary ex-boyfriend Dadong, the fellow who had blown himself up mixing chemicals when he was manufacturing fake antiques. His hair was already white. He had a puffy face and a singular ebony pipe dangling from his mouth. He was a real expert on antiques. He had established a name for himself in the field and earned a fortune, so now he wanted to "try his hand at running a film company."

Dadong had invited everyone to his party, mostly because preparations were complete for his company's debut film. It was called *Death Fugue*, and they were about to go to an island to begin shooting.

He presented a short teaser, indicating that the film was mainly a solemn commemoration of and reflection on the Tower Incident. It would not exclude his personal feelings toward Qizi. In fact, that could be said to be an important feature of the project.

"If our generation continues to remain silent, this whole incident will be erased."

Because of Yuan Mengliu's close relationship with the central figures in the Tower Incident, Qizi, Hei Chun, and the others, they had asked him to serve as the film's literary advisor and had confirmed this with a letter of appointment. Mogen was responsible for the screenplay—he no longer showed traces of the beaten-up, pained spirit Jia Wan's betrayal had occasioned in him. Dadong and Mogen shook hands with Mengliu and talked about the past with the enthusiasm of survivors.

Then everyone sat in their allocated seats as Suitang presided over a forum on "artistic freedom and urban violence." She had retired from her career as an anesthetist and, taking up the mantle of poetry, had become a leader in Dayang's "retro genre" movement.

"To free a person's thought from a benevolent authority isn't easy, because this sort of freedom requires one to walk away from the comfortable and alluring contexts bestowed by the authority, and to question the authority itself.

"The past should not be forgotten. Sometimes art is the only means by which we may find out the truth, and the only tool flexible enough for its communication. Some may think that freedom of expression depends upon one's environment, but I want to say to all poets and writers and artists that the environment shouldn't be the real issue. The real environment is in your mind. If you have a flame in your heart, then you can make any kind of water boil. If you have enough talent you can find the secret path to freedom."

Her voice, amplified to fill the room, was brimming with an embellished beauty.

SHENG KEYI was born in a small town in southern China and has lived in Shenzhen and Beijing. She is the author of ten novels, including *Northern Girls*, *Death Fugue*, *Wild Fruit*, *The Metaphor Detox Centre*, *The Womb*, and *Paradise*, as well as numerous short stories and novellas. Her work has been translated into a number of foreign languages and published all over the world. She has received several literary awards, including the Chinese People's Literature Prize, the Yu Dafu Prize for Fiction, and the Chinese Literature Media Award. Her debut novel in English translation, *Northern Girls*, was longlisted for the Man Asian Literary Prize in 2012.

SHELLY BRYANT divides her year between Shanghai and Singapore, working as a poet, writer, and translator. She has translated work from the Chinese for Penguin Books, Epigram Publishing, the National Library Board in Singapore, Giramondo Books, HSRC, Rinchen Books, and Maclehose Press and edited poetry anthologies for Alban Lake and Celestial Books. Her translation of Sheng Keyi's *Northern Girls* was longlisted for the Man Asian Literary Prize in 2012, and her translation of You Jin's *In Time, Out of Place* was shortlisted for the Singapore Literature Prize in 2016.

RESTLESS BOOKS is an independent, nonprofit publisher devoted to championing essential voices from around the world whose stories speak to us across linguistic and cultural borders. We seek extraordinary international literature for adults and young readers that feeds our restlessness: our hunger for new perspectives, passion for other cultures and languages, and eagerness to explore beyond the confines of the familiar.

Through cultural programming, we aim to celebrate immigrant writing and bring literature to underserved communities. We believe that immigrant stories are a vital component of our cultural consciousness; they help to ensure awareness of our communities, build empathy for our neighbors, and strengthen our democracy.

Visit us at restlessbooks.org